The Way You Say My Name

The Way You Say My Name

Sara Bell

P.D. Publishing, Inc.
Clayton, North Carolina

ISBN-13: 978-1-933720-57-9
ISBN-10: 1-933720-57-3

9 8 7 6 5 4 3 2 1

Cover design by Boulevard Photografica
Edited by: Day Petersen / Lara Zielinsky

Published by:

P.D. Publishing, Inc.
P.O. Box 70
Clayton, NC 27528

http://www.pdpublishing.com

Acknowledgements

Writers don't run on the same wavelengths as the rest of the known universe. We get caught up in listening to the characters in our heads and forget to return emails. We become lost in some new plot twist and burn dinner. We finally figure out why that dialogue on page thirty-five isn't working and before you know it we're an hour late for wherever we're supposed to be. It takes a special group of talented individuals to turn the average writer into a functioning human being.

My heartfelt thanks go out to Barb Coles and Linda Daniel for once again believing in my book enough to buy it. To Day and Lara — super editors — for knowing what I was trying to say even on days when I didn't. To Patty, a cover artist like no other, who took the sketchy ideas I gave her and churned out exactly the cover I wanted. The PD team has spoiled me beyond all reason. You all are stuck with me now.

I'd also like to say a big thanks to the Sara Bell Betas who never hesitate to proof-read for me (even if it's something they've already read fifty times) or give me feedback when it's so desperately needed. If a girl's only as good as her friends then I'm golden and it's all because of ya'll.

And last but never in anyone's wildest imaginings least, the most special of thanks to my family. The whole family, but I'm singling out David and our daughters. It takes special people to live with a writer: to put up with delayed dinners, the clacking keyboard at all hours of the night, the blank stares that come when Mama's dreaming up the next character to kill off. If I'm any sort of success at all, I have the three of you to thank.

Dedication

To George, the man who inspired the character of Pastor Oakley.
Thank you for teaching me we all have a place at His table.
And to David, because God sent you just for me.

Chapter One

Some things never changed: the smell of old socks coming from the boys' locker room; the long line of students blocking the halls while waiting to get on the bus. The way Dillon Carver's heart slammed against his chest every time he saw Jamie Walker.

James, he mentally corrected himself. He'd long ago given up the right to call him Jamie.

Dillon watched from his locker two rows down the hall as the object of his affection loaded books into his backpack. James's white-blond hair was in need of a good combing, as usual, but the messy style suited him. Dillon's heart pounded as he thought of all the times he'd run his fingers through that unruly mop. He grimaced. Jamie was with Ben now, and it was Dillon's own fault.

"You'll wear a hole in that boy with your eyes if you keep staring at him."

Dillon turned to see Megan Nash leaning against one of the lockers, her blue eyes sympathetic.

"I was just wondering where James's pet dickhead is. Hopefully he's slithered back under his rock."

"You mean Ben?"

Dillon snorted. "Who else?"

Megan pushed one long, red curl out of her eyes. "I know you're less than thrilled about James and Ben, but since James is out, if you keep making eyes at him, everyone will know how you really feel about him and they'll start to wonder about you."

Dillon shrugged. "They'll know soon enough, anyway."

"Maybe, but I think it would be better to stick to the plan. It'll be easier if you come out in your own time."

Dillon drew in a deep breath and then let it out slowly. "I hate the fact that you're always right."

"Hardly, but having three gay brothers does make me somewhat of an expert on the subject."

Dillon raised both eyebrows. "Three?"

"When Brandon married Nate, he became my brother, too."

"That's two." Dillon held up his index and middle fingers. "Who's the other one?"

"Randy." Megan smiled. "He came out just before the wedding."

"Only in your family could that ever happen." Dillon laughed, but he envied Megan her family, most especially her parents. They loved their children unconditionally, unlike his own mother and father.

He was so caught up in his thoughts, he didn't realize Megan was still speaking to him until she raised her voice to get his attention.

"So, are we still on for the dance tonight?"

Dillon groaned. "I don't know. I'd planned to ask Jim if I could squeeze in some extra hours at the pharmacy tonight. If and when my folks throw me out, I'll need all the money I can get."

"You work plenty. What you need is one night to take your mind off your worries." Megan flashed him a radiant smile. "What better way to do that than to spend the evening with yours truly dancing your cute little butt off?"

Dillon closed the locker door. "You're deranged, you know that?"

The last bell rang and Megan started for the door. "All part of my charm." She grinned at him over her shoulder but kept walking. "You know you love me."

Laughing as he followed her out, Dillon grumbled, "Yeah, yeah. I love you, though God only knows why."

Jamie watched from the corner of his eye as Dillon and Megan left, laughing and talking as if the rest of the world didn't exist. Knowing the two of them were together was bad enough, but to have it thrown in his face was almost more than he could stand. Before he had time to work up a decent depression, Jamie felt an arm glide around his shoulders. He knew who it was without even having to turn. "Are you pervin' on me in the middle of the hall?"

Ben laughed, moving away to lean against the wall. "Nah. I know a dead end when I see one. What can I say? You have an amazing ability to resist my considerable charms, not to mention an unholy attachment to that fuck-wad ex of yours." He let out a dramatic sigh. "I'd gladly exorcise the spirit of Dillon Carver from you if I could, but I'm fresh out of holy water."

"Keep it down." Jamie looked around to see if anyone was paying attention. "Someone might be listening."

Ben shook his head. "I don't know why you work so hard to front for that prick after what he did to you." Jamie started to speak but Ben cut him off. "Never mind. I've heard it all before, and we're never gonna agree." His expression softened. "You know your secrets are safe with me, J." He gave Jamie a sideways, cocky grin. "Since I can't seem to get into your pants, I guess I'll just have to settle for the thrill of being close to you."

"You are so full of shit."

"You didn't think my eyes were this brown naturally, did you?" Ben jerked his spiky, black-haired head in the direction Dillon and Megan had taken. "I see Mr. and Mrs. Plunkett High are still going strong."

Jamie shrugged, determined not to show how much he was hurting. "I guess they make each other happy. They've been together for almost four months now, so they must."

"If Dillon wants to play it straight, I say more power to him. If I was into chicks, I might even go after Megan Nash myself. As much trouble as I've been in lately, it sure wouldn't hurt to be banging the sheriff's sister." He heaved his tall, slender body away from the wall. "Since I haven't yet found a girl who can rev my engine, I guess I'll just stick with what I've got."

"There you go again, talking about your mystery man." Jamie closed his locker and clicked the lock into place. "Am I ever gonna meet this new guy of yours?"

Ben put his arm around Jamie's shoulders and led him toward the door. "Patience, young Walker. In time, all will be revealed."

"No more *Star Wars* flicks for you."

"Yeah, yeah." Ben squinted against the afternoon sun as they walked out to the parking lot. "I can't tell you anything about him just yet. He's still in the closet. Besides, he and I are keeping things cool for now. We're both free to date other people." He grinned. "Which reminds me, are you going to the Valentine mixer tonight?"

"I've got to," Jamie said. "The Gay-Straight Alliance is hosting it. I have to put in an appearance, being the G.S.A. president and all."

"How did the G.S.A. get stuck putting on a dance?"

"Principal Morgan insisted. He thought it would help boost Plunkett High's 'gay friendly' image. He wants the world to know that gay and lesbian students are free to express themselves at Plunkett, whatever the hell that means." Jamie shrugged. "At least ten same-sex couples have signed up to go, so Morgan's idea must be working."

Ignoring that last statement, Ben motioned Jamie toward his car. The 1985 Firebird was a sleek black beauty, into which Ben poured every dime he earned doing odd jobs for his foster mother.

Looking at the car almost made Jamie wish he knew how to drive.

"You waiting for an invitation?" Ben opened the driver's side door. "Get in so we can blow this place."

"I hear you." Jamie opened the car door and sank down into the bucket seat. He closed the door and waited until Ben was seated behind the wheel before saying, "Weren't you about to ask me something?"

"Yeah." Ben turned to better see him. "I was thinking...since you have to go to the dance tonight anyway, maybe you and I could go together."

"Like a date?"

"Not really. Just you and me hanging out, as usual." Ben whipped his sunglasses from the overhead visor and slipped them on. "If a guy can't go to a dance with his best friend, what's the world coming to?"

"What about the guy you're seeing? Won't he care?"

"Like I told you, him and me...we're casual." Ben's smile was arrogant. "Just think about the chance it'll give me and you to rub our illustrious presences in Dillon Carver's face."

"Ben—"

"The guy fucked you over six ways from Sunday. The least you can do is show him you aren't pining away while he's off playing the happy hetero."

Jamie laughed, won over as always by Ben's uncommon brand of charm. "All right then. If you really want to do this, you've got yourself a date."

Ben pumped his fist twice in victory, then started the car and peeled out of the parking lot.

Jamie's great-aunt Sadie was waiting in the kitchen when he got home. He dropped his backpack into a chair and bent to kiss her wrinkled cheek. Sadie smiled up at him, her green eyes crinkling at the corners. "How was school?"

Jamie went to the fridge and scrounged around until he found the package of cold cuts. Taking out the package, he snagged a loaf of bread from the counter and slapped together three ham sandwiches, grabbed a bottle of Coke from the door, and closed the refrigerator with his foot. Settling into a chair on the other side of the table, Jamie crammed his mouth full of sandwich. It wasn't until he was halfway through the first one that he registered he'd been asked a question.

"Same as always," he answered around a mouthful of ham and cheese on rye.

"You don't have to gobble your food." Aunt Sadie clucked her tongue. "No one is going to take it away from you." She watched him for a moment. "So...do you have plans for this evening?"

Knowing this was the tricky part, Jamie choked down a large chunk of bread and said, "Yes, ma'am. I'm going to the Valentine dance with Ben." Seeing the look of displeasure on Sadie's face, he placed the remainder of his sandwich on the table. "I know you don't like him, but—"

Holding up her hand in a signal Jamie took to mean "shut up", Aunt Sadie stood. Grumbling as she crossed the checkerboard tile floor, she stopped at the white double-sink and made a show of washing the dishes.

Jamie winced at the sound of banging pots and pans, but he was used to it. Over the years, the Queen Anne home Sadie inherited from her father had seen more than one of her hissy fits, and so had Jamie. For someone so short and slight, Sadie was a force to be reckoned with.

After a full two minutes of dish rattling and pan clanging, Sadie turned back to Jamie, a dish cloth clutched tightly in her hand. "I wish you could tell me what you see in that hooligan."

Jamie almost laughed at Sadie's old fashioned term. Her short, iron-gray curls had frizzed during her tirade, framing her rosy face. Even though he could tell she was fuming mad, Jamie marveled at how lucky he was to have ended up with her instead of in a foster home like Ben. No matter how fortunate he considered himself, though, Jamie knew his aunt well enough to know how stubborn she could be when she took a dislike to someone. He leaned back in his chair.

"Are you forbidding me to go out with him tonight?"

"You know better than that," Sadie said. "You're eighteen, old enough to pick your own friends. I just wish you had someone in your life other than Ben Lewis."

"Ben's a good guy." Jamie took a hefty swig of his Coke. "He just hasn't had the same advantages as the rest of us."

"That doesn't give him the right to do half the things he's done since Nora Slater took him in." Sadie shook her head. "You'd think he'd be grateful to have a home after living in foster care for most of his life. Why Nora didn't send that boy packing the day he turned eighteen is beyond me."

"I could ask you the same question." Jamie traced his finger along the edge of the scarred oak table. "Why didn't you throw me out when I turned eighteen?"

Aunt Sadie tossed the cloth into the sink and went back to the table. Using one short finger, she tilted Jamie's chin until he was looking directly at her. "How can you ask me that?"

"Why not?" Jamie shrugged. "Ben's only lived with Nora for three years; I've been sponging off you a heck of a lot longer than that." He turned out of her grip and looked away. "At least the state paid Nora to take care of Ben. What did you get when my mom dumped me here fourteen years ago?"

Sadie sat down in the chair next to his. "I got you, and I've never regretted it, not for an instant." She sighed. "By the time you came along, I was fifty years old and had given up hope of ever having children of my own. I assumed I'd spend the rest of my life alone." She gave him a sincere smile. "I've cursed my niece a thousand times for choosing drugs and that worthless boyfriend of hers over her own child, but not a day goes by that I don't thank her for bringing you to me."

"Then why doesn't Ben deserve the same chances I've been given?" Jamie asked. "Can't you even try to like him?"

Never one to concede defeat easily, Sadie stood and smoothed the wrinkles from her slacks. "I'll do my best to get along with him for your sake, but if he hurts you, he'll answer to me." She paused. "I wish you and Dillon could have patched up your friendship. He was a good influence on you. You were always so happy when the two of you were together."

Jamie held back a sigh. "It was Dillon's choice. There's nothing I can do about it."

"I still can't believe Dillon dropped you the way he did. So what if you're gay? You're still you."

She didn't know the half of it, and Jamie wasn't about to enlighten her. He couldn't resist ribbing her a little bit. "You didn't exactly jump for joy when I first told you I was gay."

"Nonsense. I admit, I was shocked at first, and I'm still not sure I understand it exactly." She gave him another of her warm smiles. "But I love you for who you are, not for whom you're attracted to."

Jamie nodded. Sadie's love was the one constant in his life. He only wished Dillon could have been as accepting. With a shake of his head, Jamie finished his sandwich, silently adding Dillon's abandonment to the long list of things he couldn't change.

Dillon stuffed the college acceptance papers into his desk drawer and locked it with relieved satisfaction. He'd done it. He'd been accepted to Garman College in upstate New York. It was prestigious, private, and known for its policies protecting gay and lesbian students. It was also James Walker's school of choice.

Once again, Dillon went over the plan in his head. Even if his parents cut him off, he'd still be able to swing tuition, and room and board, using student loans and the college fund his folks had made the mistake of putting solely in his name. It wasn't a lot of money, but once he got a part-time job to pay for books and living expenses, it would be enough. It would have to be. Living a lie was no longer an option.

He glanced at the clock. Five-thirty, time to get ready if he wanted to make it to Megan's by seven. He was heading for the shower when the phone rang. Grabbing the cordless from his desk, he pressed the talk button.

"Yeah?"

"Great phone manners, Carver."

Dillon grinned. "Since when do you give a rat's ass about manners, Barnes? Aren't you the same guy who can belch the Star Spangled Banner in three octaves?"

"A man's got to have a wide variety of skills to make it in this life, or so my dad always says. I'll have you know, there's more to Mr. Ashton Barnes the Third than the handsome, athletic specimen I present to the world. I believe in being well rounded."

"Uh huh. So, to what do I owe the pleasure of this phone call?" He and Ash were friends, but phone conversations between them were few and far between. Dillon knew something was up when Ash's voice dropped and all traces of the teasing tone he'd answered with disappeared.

"I stopped at Hailey's to get a bite to eat after school. Rooster and his boys were there, and I think they're planning something for tonight."

Dillon went rigid. "Rooster" was Roy Carmichael, the biggest homophobe on campus. If he was involved, it couldn't be good. "What kind of something?"

"I'm not sure. They shut their traps when they realized I was listening, but I'm pretty sure I heard the word 'fag' tossed out a couple of times. My guess is they're pissed about the G.S.A. hosting tonight's dance and they're looking to start trouble."

"Why did you call me?" Dillon tapped his fingers on the back of the receiver. "Why not Morgan or one of the teachers?"

"I know you and James Walker used to be tight, so I figured maybe you'd get in touch with him for me." Ash swallowed loud enough for Dillon to hear. "I would do it myself, but..."

"You're afraid everyone will think you're queer if you get caught sticking up for a bunch of gays. Is that it?"

Ash went on the defensive. "Look, I was just trying to help. I should have known better than to come to you with this. Everyone knows you ditched James the minute he came out."

Dillon felt like a total ass. He knew Ash was only trying to help, but there was no way Dillon could explain his overreaction without complicating things further. Instead, he said, "Wait..."

Ash didn't hang up, so Dillon took that as his cue to continue. "I'm sorry, man. You did the right thing by calling me. Thanks." When Ash didn't respond, Dillon figured there were only two things he could do: hang up or change the subject. He went for the subject change. "So, you got a date tonight?"

"Yeah. Chad and I are doubling with Blair Dees and Nina Ivan."

The two easiest girls in school. Given Ash's reputation with the ladies, Dillon should have known. "Who gets who?"

"Who cares?" Ash snorted. "We're only going to be at that lame-ass dance long enough to put in an appearance, then it's straight down to Pepper Road. You taking Megan?"

"To Pepper Road?" The thought of taking Megan to the number one make out spot in Reed didn't even bear repeating.

"To the dance, dumbass."

Dillon held back a sigh of relief. "Yeah. I was about to hit the shower when you called."

"Hey, don't let me keep you. I had P.E. with you three years running. I know how nasty those pits of yours get." Ash laughed. "I'll catch you tonight. And Carver?"

"Yeah?"

"Sorry for that crack about you dropping James."

"Hey, the truth hurts. You and me, we're good."

"Sweet. See you tonight."

Dillon disconnected as he debated his next move. He could call Principal Morgan or any one of a dozen teachers and let them handle it, but as president of the G.S.A., James had a right to know trouble was brewing. Dillon turned the phone back on and punched in the numbers. Even after two years, his fingers wove an automatic pattern over the keys. James answered on the second ring, his voice rich and smooth.

"Hello?"

The moment James spoke, Dillon's mind went blank. James said hello twice more before Dillon was able to say, "James?"

"Yeah, this is James." He hesitated. "Dillon? Is that you?"

"Uh...yeah. Have you got a minute?"

"Just one." The surprise Dillon had first heard in James's voice turned to wariness. "What do you need?"

Dillon needed a lot of things from James, but nothing he could say out loud. Not yet, anyway. Instead, he said, "I just got a call from one of the guys at school. He thinks the G.S.A. could have trouble from Rooster Carmichael and his crew at tonight's dance."

James was quiet for a minute. Finally he said, "Why did you call me?"

Dillon silently cursed his own stupidity. He should have known James would be suspicious of his motives. "I was just trying to give you a heads up."

"Not to seem ungrateful, but since when do you care what happens to a bunch of fags?"

"James, I—"

"I've got to go. Thanks for the warning." James hung up before Dillon could say another word.

Jamie couldn't help but laugh at Ben's choice of attire. Somehow he doubted Ben's ripped jeans, black leather jacket, and white tank were what the dance committee had in mind when they recommended casual wear. He glanced down at his own black pants and dark blue, button-front shirt. "Why is it I always feel overdressed when you're around?"

"Probably because you are. Looks good on you, though." Ben stood in the doorway giving Jamie a thorough inspection with his eyes. "Are you ready to go or do we need to say goodbye to your aunt first?"

"I'm ready."

"Good. You wanna tell me why we have to be there so damn early? You were a little hazy on the phone."

"I got a phone call warning me to expect trouble of the homophobe variety tonight. I called Principal Morgan and he suggested we hold an emergency meeting of the G.S.A. and the Student Council."

"A phone call, huh? Who from?"

"Dillon Carver."

"Carver?" Ben whistled. "Must have been some phone call. Wonder why he called you instead of Morgan?"

"Who knows? Dillon's on the Student Council. Maybe he'll enlighten us when we get there."

"Whatever." Ben pointed to the Firebird. "Your chariot awaits."

"You sure you don't mind going in early?" Jamie grabbed his coat from the hall tree and pulled it on, then closed the front door behind them. "I can get Aunt Sadie to drop me off if it's a problem."

"It's not like I have anything better to do." Ben kept walking. "When are you gonna let me teach you how to drive, anyway?"

"Ain't gonna happen, my friend." Jamie shuddered. "I told you about the time Aunt Sadie tried to teach me. I froze in the middle of oncoming traffic and nearly wrecked her car."

"Doesn't mean it'll happen the next time."

Jamie folded his arms over his chest. "There isn't going to be a next time."

Ben laughed at Jamie's surly frown. "Okay, chicken. Get in the car, but remember, this conversation is far from over."

The Student Council members sat on the left side of the rectangular table in the school's conference room while the G.S.A. officers took up the right. Dillon, as Student Council vice president, sat next to Megan, the president. The other members of both groups wandered in a few at a time and filled the empty seats. Principal Dan Morgan came in a few minutes later, waving to all assembled as he moved to the head of the table.

"I want to thank all of you for coming early. I promise we'll make this as brief as possible." Morgan's perfectly combed, wavy brown hair didn't move as he took his place behind the lectern.

Dillon fought down a wave of unease as the principal's brown eyes landed on him before scanning the rest of the room. It wasn't that Dillon found Principal Morgan unattractive. He filled out the black pants and gray turtleneck shirt he was wearing as well as any *GQ* cover model, but there was something about the man which struck Dillon as false, no matter how good the guy looked. Maybe it was the wooden smile he almost always wore, or that he tried just a little too hard to be the poster boy for gay and lesbian acceptance. Whatever it was, Principal Morgan gave Dillon a first class case of the creeps.

A noise at the door caught Dillon's attention. His gut clenched as James walked in with Ben Lewis at his heels.

Aiming an apologetic smile at Principal Morgan, James fell into a chair and then patted the chair next to him for Ben to sit. "Sorry we're late."

"No harm done. We were just getting started." Principal Morgan leaned into the podium. "Now that we're all here—" He broke off as Dillon raised his hand. "Yes, Dillon?"

"If this is supposed to be a meeting of the G.S.A. and the Student Council, then what's *he* doing here?" Dillon pointed one finger at Ben. "He's not a member of either one."

Before Principal Morgan could answer, James said, "Ben is my date, and he's here because I asked him to be."

Dillon felt the word "date" like a heart punch, but he tamped down the pain and persisted in his position. "He shouldn't be here."

"If you want me out, Carver," Ben said with a cocky smile, "you can always come over here and throw me out yourself."

Dillon started to rise but Megan grabbed his arm and pulled him back down. "No," she whispered. "Don't even think about it."

Principal Morgan cleared his throat. "I suggest we get back to the reason why we're here in the first place. Since these are special circumstances, Mr. Lewis can stay, but I'm warning you both," he looked from Dillon to Ben, "if I hear one more threat from either of you, the offender will be out of here and on his way to a three day, in-school suspension. Am I clear?"

Left little choice, Dillon nodded, his eyes going to Ben who nodded his agreement.

Satisfied, Principal Morgan returned to the business at hand. "There's a distinct possibility our gay and lesbian students will be targeted for violence tonight. To prevent this from happening, I've asked the sheriff and some of his men to patrol the dance." A murmur of complaints rose. Morgan threw up his hand for silence. "I'm sorry if this cramps your style, but we have to send a message that bigotry of any kind will not be tolerated here at Plunkett." He turned to James. "I want you to be especially careful. If these guys are upset because the dance is being hosted by the G.S.A., you will be the most likely target."

"Don't worry, Mr. Morgan. I've got Jamie's back. In fact, I'm gonna be all over him." There was such sexual innuendo in Ben's statement, several girls giggled, James blushed, and Dillon gnashed his teeth until his gums hurt.

Principal Morgan tugged at his collar. "Yes...well, I appreciate that, Ben." He looked down at his watch before readdressing the room. "If there's nothing further, you're free to go. I want you all to enjoy yourselves, but please be careful, and don't hesitate to report anything suspicious."

There was a rush as the room emptied. Dillon and Megan were on the side opposite the door, making them among the last to leave. Dillon watched with envy and anger as Ben took James's hand and led him out.

Megan rubbed Dillon's arm through the flannel shirt he had layered over his black t-shirt. He was sure she meant the gesture to be soothing, but he was beyond comfort. His own stupidity had cost him the only guy he'd ever loved, and he was beginning to believe he didn't have a chance in hell of making things right.

The darkened gym vibrated with one rock ballad after another. Not even the sight of no less than four deputies in full uniform had dampened the romantic mood, if the throng of couples making out all across the room were any indication. Ben pointed to a private spot on the edge of the dance floor before sweeping Jamie a mock bow. "May I have this dance?"

Jamie was shaking his head before Ben even finished. "No way."

"Why not?" Ben tilted his head to the side and waited.

"I've never danced before." Jamie flushed. "I'm not sure I know how."

Ben flashed him a killer smile. "Anybody can slow dance, J." He opened his arms. "Just lean into me and follow my lead."

Jamie's mind was a swirl of confusion as he worked to process the change in Ben. For two years, all Ben's advances had seemed half-serious, bordering on playful. Jamie wasn't sure how to explain it, but he could tell something was different tonight. Ben was treating him almost like private property.

"Come on, J. It's only a dance."

Ben's easy, open smile made it hard to resist, and after another minute's hesitation, Jamie accepted. Ben circled his arms around Jamie's waist and rocked his hips with the music, leaving Jamie to follow.

Ben laughed when Jamie finally started to relax. "See, this isn't so bad, is it?"

Jamie shook his head. It felt strange, being so close to Ben. Not bad, just different. The only other guy Jamie had been this close to was Dillon, and it was odd, sharing such a personal space with someone else. Jamie swallowed, thinking about the other things he and Dillon had shared.

Ben peered into Jamie's eyes. "What are you thinking about?"

"What a jerk I was two years ago."

"You mean with Carver?"

"Yeah, to let him use me like that." Jamie winced. "I should have known better."

Ben's hand sketched circles over the small of Jamie's back. "Carver was the jerk, J, not you. The guy didn't deserve you." His voice fell to a whisper, barely audible above the roar of the music. "I wish I'd met you first." Jamie started to speak, but Ben stopped him. "Shh. I know you don't feel the same way about me, and it's okay. At least let me show you what you've been missing." Before Jamie could protest, Ben lowered his head and covered Jamie's mouth with his own.

Dillon watched in horror as Ben rammed his tongue down James's throat. He and Megan were dancing not fifteen feet away from where the other couple stood, but when Ben started making out with James, Dillon stopped and stared at the two of them as his hopes crumbled.

Megan turned around to see what was going on, putting her hand over her mouth as she realized what she was seeing. "Oh, my God." She turned back to Dillon. "Are you okay?"

"Fucking peachy."

"Dillon—"

"Don't waste your breath." If he'd had any doubts about the relationship between those two before, Dillon sure as hell didn't now. Losing James to Ben Lewis might be no less than he deserved for being such a selfish bastard, but Dillon wasn't about to go down without a fight. "I can't stand here and do nothing while Lewis takes him away from me. I've waited for him too long to give up now." He watched as James pulled away from Ben and stepped off the dance floor, heading toward the bathroom.

Dillon started to follow and Megan put a hand on his arm. "Where are you going?"

He ran his fingers through his hair. "I have to talk to him, Meggie." He pulled away from her grasp and headed in the direction James had gone. When he opened the bathroom door and slipped inside James was bent over one of the sinks, splashing water on his face. Dillon moved as quietly as possible to where James stood. He pulled a paper towel off the roll, intending to hand it to James to dry his face when he was finished.

The clicking of the dispenser caused James to pop up in a sudden motion that sent water trailing down his neck. Dillon took advantage of James's surprise, using the paper towel to sponge the water from his cheeks. He followed one small bead down into the hollow of James's throat, causing James to blow out a strangled breath.

"What are you doing?"

"Your face was wet. I was wiping it off."

James snatched the paper towel out of Dillon's hand and backed away. "I can do it myself." He moved back even further. "Did you follow me in here?"

Dillon didn't want to make him any more uncomfortable, but his days of lying to James were over. "Yeah." James looked so alarmed, Dillon put up a placating hand. "I didn't come in here to cause trouble, Jamie. I just wanted to talk."

"James."

"Huh?"

"My name is James. Only my friends and family call me Jamie. As I remember, you chose not to be in either category."

Damn. Dillon had expected the rebuff, but it still hurt. "I just want to talk to you, James. Please."

"Why would you want to talk to me? We barely know each other now. Your choice."

"You're right." As openings went, it wasn't much, but it was a start. "I did make that choice, and it's one I regret. We used to be close. I was hoping we could be again."

"For weeks after you dumped me, I tried to talk to you, but you pretended like I didn't exist." James was shaking. "You got your mother to lie and say you weren't home when I called, and you ignored me in the halls like I was a freakin' stranger instead of the guy who—" He broke off, his chest heaving as he took one short, shallow breath after another. "I can't see any reason why you'd want to talk now."

"I can answer that one for you." The door swung open and Ben stepped in. "Ol' Dillon, here, is looking to get laid. He figures you were good for a quick fuck once, so why not give your ass another shot?"

Dillon's jaw went tight. "What were you doing, Lewis, listening at the door?"

"Actually, I came in here to take a leak. Imagine my surprise when I cracked the door open and heard you putting the moves on Jamie. Amazing how well the sound of bullshit carries."

"James and I are having a private conversation." Dillon's fingers knotted into fists. "There are at least two other bathrooms in this gym. Why don't you go find one?"

"I don't think so." Ben turned to James. "You okay?"

James nodded. "Yeah."

"Good." Ben held out his hand. "Come on. Let's get outta here."

James edged around Dillon and followed Ben out. Dillon was right behind them. "What are you, Lewis? His bodyguard?"

They'd reached the edge of the dance floor, and even with the music blaring, their raised voices were starting to attract attention. Dillon saw Megan coming over and cursed himself. He hadn't wanted to bring her into this, but it was too late to turn back now.

Ben whirled on Dillon, his face wreathed in anger. "Somebody's gotta watch Jamie's back. Haven't you hurt him enough?"

"I wasn't going to hurt him. All I wanted to do was talk."

James tugged on the sleeve of Ben's leather jacket. "It's okay. Let's just get out of here."

"But it's not okay. Not by a long shot." Ben didn't budge. "I'm sick of guys like Carver thinking they can walk all over us."

Megan came up behind Dillon, putting her hand in his. "Maybe we should go."

"Why don't you listen to your little girlfriend?" Ben gave Dillon an ugly sneer. "For a breeder, she makes good sense."

Dillon dropped Megan's hand and stepped in front of her, shielding her from Ben's view. "Leave her out of this. This is between me and you."

"That's funny. I could have sworn you were trying to make it between you and Jamie." Ben's expression went from go-to-hell smirk to evil grin in two seconds flat. "Then again, maybe 'making it' is your problem to begin with, Carver."

Dillon took a step forward, heedless of Megan's attempts to pull him back. "What's that supposed to mean?"

"Maybe the reason you're so hot to 'talk' to Jamie is because the little lady won't let you into her panties." Ben cast a sidelong glance at Megan. "Princess won't put out, so you're looking to get it somewhere else."

Dillon's face flamed. "Shut the fuck up."

"What's the matter?" Ben came a step closer. "Did you catch yourself a frigid bitch who ain't giving you any?"

Dillon had no memory of moving. All he knew was the satisfying feel of teeth hitting flesh as he belted Lewis in the mouth.

Lewis gave as good as he got. As soon as the shock wore off he pitched his body forward and sent them both tumbling to the ground. He and Dillon rolled, punches flying from both sides. Dillon wasn't sure who got in the most licks, but it felt damn good to give Lewis even half of the beating he deserved.

Dillon had just landed a solid smack to Lewis's jaw when he felt himself being hauled to his feet.

He looked across to see Nathan Nash holding Lewis with his arms pinned behind his back. Ben was putting up a good fight, but Nate was obviously a lot stronger than he looked. As he watched the struggle between Nate and Ben, Dillon began to wonder who it was holding him.

He tilted his head to the side and stared up into the flashing blue eyes of Sheriff Brandon Nash. Brandon's dark hair was standing on end from the struggle, and the look on his face was a mix of anger and pure annoyance. "Anybody care to tell me what the hell is going on here?"

Four voices started at once. Megan was yelling about Ben insulting her honor, while James was going on and on about being "ambushed" in the bathroom. Dillon did his best to stammer out a defense, but it was Ben who put the nail in all their coffins.

Still struggling to break free of Nate's hold, Ben said, "I know my rights. I don't have to tell you a damn thing without my lawyer present, but if your little wife here doesn't get the fuck off me, I'll file assault charges against both your asses."

Brandon might have been willing to let the incident go unpunished if Ben hadn't opened his mouth, but Dillon had no doubt the insult against Nate was the last straw.

With an audible sigh, Brandon said, "So much for the idea of sneaking in a few dances with my husband. Let's take this down to the station. I have a feeling we're in for a long night."

Chapter Two

Dillon hadn't realized he was drumming his fingers against the metal table in the dimly lit interrogation room until Megan reached across and put her hand over his. "Will you knock it off?"

"Sorry. Guess I'm not up on prison protocol." He put his hands in his lap. "It's not every day I get arrested."

"Brandon hasn't arrested you. Not yet, anyway." She looked down at her watch. "He's probably not going to, either."

Dillon wasn't quite so optimistic. "What makes you so sure?"

"We've been sitting in here by ourselves for almost an hour. If he were planning to charge you with something, he'd have done it by now."

Dillon snorted. "Yeah, right. I bet he's busy getting Lewis's side of the story, probably trying to figure out the best way to put us all behind bars." He covered his face with his hands. "God, I am so screwed."

"I'd say 'screwed' is an accurate description of the situation you're in right now."

The door was open and Dillon looked up to see Brandon lounging against the door frame. He came inside, pulling a discolored metal chair from against the wall and positioning it backward against the head of the table. Straddling it, Brandon added, "To just what degree you're screwed depends on your explanation of what happened tonight." He looked Dillon in the eye. "If dragging her into a brawl is your idea of taking care of my baby sister, you and I are going to have ourselves a talk."

Megan started to speak but Dillon stopped her. "He's right." He turned back to face Brandon. "I owe you both an apology." Dillon stood up and held out his wrists. "I'm ready to be cuffed and printed, or whatever it is you guys do."

"Sit down, kid." Brandon rolled his eyes. "You've seen way too many episodes of *Law and Order*." He sighed. "Next you'll be demanding your one phone call." He blew out another rush of breath. "I'm not going to arrest you, although I could book you for assault, easy." He pointed one long finger at Dillon's chest. "No less than six people saw you cram your fist down Ben Lewis's throat. Lucky for you, Lewis has declined to press charges."

"Really?"

"Yes, thanks to James Walker."

"James talked Ben out of pressing charges?" Megan sounded as surprised as Dillon felt.

Brandon nodded, directing his next remark to Dillon. "James told Lewis that both of you were acting like a couple of assholes — his words, not mine — and that Lewis should forget about the whole thing. At first I didn't think Lewis would go for it, but James seems to have a special hold over him and Lewis agreed to let it slide." Brandon narrowed his eyes. "Lewis isn't pressing charges, but that doesn't mean you're off the hook. I want to know what's going on, and I want to know now."

Megan looked up at her brother. "Ben insulted me. Dillon was only trying to defend me."

"I know all about wanting to protect the people you care about." Brandon's eyes slid down to his wedding band, then looked up at Dillon. "If you tell me right now this grand passion you feel for my sister motivated you to rush to her defense, we'll chalk this one up to young love and call it a night."

Dillon knew he was being offered an easy out, and part of him was dying to agree with everything Brandon said and be done with it, but a larger part of Dillon — the part that was tired of lying and hiding — wouldn't stand for it.

He was surprised at how calm his voice sounded when he said, "I am in love, Sheriff, but not with Megan." When Brandon's expression started to change, Dillon rushed out, "Don't get me wrong. I love Megan." He turned and gave her a weak smile. "She's the best friend a guy could ask for, but loving her and being in love with her are two different things." He cleared his throat. "I can't be in love with Megan because that spot belongs to someone else." Taking a deep breath, he jumped head first out of the closet. "I'm in love with James Walker."

To Brandon's credit, he didn't so much as flinch. Turning to his sister, he said, "Go down to my office and tell Nate to come here, please."

"Bran—"

"Just do it, Meggie." Brandon rubbed his hand over his face and rose to his feet. "I think I should put on a fresh pot of coffee while we wait, the stronger, the better."

Ben and Jamie sat side by side on a bench outside Deputy Sam Whit's office. Whit gave them both a long, hard look. "Do both you boys have someone coming to pick you up and sign you out?"

"Yes, sir," Jamie said. "My aunt's on her way to get me, and Ben's foster mom said she'd be here in a sec."

Sam nodded. "I'll be in my office when they get here. Have both ladies see me before you leave." He went inside and shut the door, leaving them alone.

Ben waited until he was sure Sam was gone before turning to Jamie. "I'm sorry about this, J. I hope I didn't get you into trouble with your aunt."

"She didn't exactly sound thrilled about it when I called her, but I don't think she'll stay mad for long. For an old lady, she's cool." Jamie paused. "Ben?"

Ben sighed. "You're gonna ask me about that kiss I gave you, right?"

Jamie nodded. "I figure you did it to piss off Dillon."

"That's part of it. I've seen the way he watches you. The guy's still got a thing for you, but he doesn't have the balls to do anything about it." Ben shrugged. "I guess I wanted him to see what he was missing."

Jamie rested his head back against the wall and closed his eyes. "He's with Megan, now. I highly doubt he's missing anything I could give him." He opened his eyes and turned his head to the side so he was looking at Ben. "You said part of the reason you kissed me was to get back at Dillon. What's the other part?"

Ben took a deep breath. "I did it because I love you." He must have seen the alarm on Jamie's face because he said, "Not like that." He moved his fingers down his leg and tugged at the rip in his jeans. "I know you'll always have a thing for Carver." His lowered his voice so that Jamie had to strain to hear him. "I love you, J. Like a friend." He shook his head. "Make that a brother." Another sigh. "I'm no damn good with this sentimental shit, but I need you to know that you mean more to me than anyone else ever has or ever could."

"What about the guy you're seeing?"

"We give each other a good time, but he'll never mean as much to me as you do. Besides," Ben made a face, "any guy I get involved with will be history once he finds out the truth about me."

"The right guy won't care about the trouble you've been in."

"I'm not talking about that." Ben's eyes focused on Jamie's face. "You have no idea what I'm capable of, J. I've seen things, done things, that would make you vomit."

"Ben—"

Ben held up his hand. "What I'm trying to say is, thanks for sticking with me the way you have. You've stood by me through two shoplifting arrests and a bust for that joint I had in my pocket during shop class. You even took up for me when I got suspended for chucking those smoke bombs in the girls' john a couple of weeks ago."

"That one was a stroke of genius on your part." Jamie snickered. "I don't think I've ever seen anything funnier than Tina Marks running down the hall with her panties around her ankles screaming 'Fire' at the top of her lungs."

Ben laughed too, but his amusement was short lived. "That's my point. No matter what I do, you're always there for me. You've never once let me down."

He got quiet for a minute and Jamie saw a fine sheen of moisture in Ben's eyes. Before Jamie had a chance to say anything about it, Ben straightened and shook it off. "I hope Nora gets here soon. I told my boy I'd meet him before midnight."

"You're meeting him tonight?"

"Yep."

"Where?"

"You know the old Tanner textile mill?"

"You mean that rundown ol' factory? It's been closed for what, ten years?" Jamie shuddered. "Place is bound to be crawling with rats."

"Not the factory itself." Ben laughed. "There's an old foreman's house on the backside of the property where we meet. Not a rat in sight."

"Aren't you worried about getting caught?"

"Nah. His family owns the place. They bought it for a tax write off; they never go down there." Ben might have said more, but the clatter of heels approaching sounded against the tile floor.

Jamie looked up and saw his Aunt Sadie barreling toward them. She wore the same sour look on her face as she'd worn the day she caught Millicent Edwards pulling an ace out of her stocking during their weekly stud poker game.

Sparing Ben not a glance, Sadie said, "I can't believe you, Jamie, getting hauled down to the police station like some common criminal. What's next? Shall I get you a set of lockpicks and the number of a good bail bondsman for graduation?"

"It was my fault, Miss Banks." Ben's tone was even and polite. "Jamie didn't do anything wrong."

Aunt Sadie looked down her nose at him, no small feat considering they were already nose to nose, even with Ben sitting and Sadie standing. "My mother used to say, 'Wrestle with dogs and you'll get up with fleas.' You're a mangy cur if ever I saw one, Benjamin Lewis."

Jamie started to interrupt her but Ben stopped him with a subtle shake of his head.

If Aunt Sadie noticed the gesture, she didn't let on. "Do I need to speak with anyone before we can leave, Jamie?"

"Yes, ma'am." Jamie pointed to Sam's office. "Deputy Whit has some papers for you to sign."

"Fine. Let's get it done so we can go home."

Jamie got up, but then glanced back down at Ben. "What about Ben?"

Sadie turned with a sniff. "What about him?"

"Nora isn't here yet." Jamie swallowed. "Couldn't we wait until—"

The look Aunt Sadie gave him was answer enough. She stomped into Sam's office after issuing Jamie a terse command to follow her.

As Jamie moved to comply, Ben reached up and grabbed his hand. "Hey, Jamie?"

"Yeah?"

"Thanks again. For everything."

Jamie nodded, struck by the feeling that nothing else needed to be said.

Dillon took a long, bracing sip of the scalding coffee Brandon had passed across the table to him. He'd hoped the tar-like mixture would clear his head, but all it really did was make him itch to brush his teeth.

Megan came back a few minutes later, with Nate right behind her. He took one look at their faces and said, "What's going on?"

Brandon pulled another chair away from the wall and dragged it over to the table for Nate. The look of trust and devotion on Nate's face as he seated himself and waited for his husband to do the same filled Dillon with both awe and despair. He was stunned by the realization that such a love between too guys was possible, but he ached with the fear that he'd blown his only chance at ever having it for himself.

Brandon reached over and took Nate's hand. "Dillon has something he needs to tell us. I wanted you to be here to listen in."

Nate raised an eyebrow. "I thought this was an interrogation."

Brandon sighed. "I could've sworn it started out that way, but it looks like I was wrong about a lot of things." He trained his eyes on Dillon. "You ready?"

Dillon started to speak, then stopped and turned to Megan as she reseated herself by his side. "I think it might be easier if I did this one on my own."

"You sure?"

Dillon nodded and Megan stood, grabbing her coat from the back of the chair before glancing over at Brandon. "Do you think one of your men could give me a ride home?" She reached out and squeezed Dillon's shoulder. "Unless you want me to wait outside for you."

Dillon shook his head. "I'll be okay. You've already done more for me than I can ever thank you for."

"Not true. I just did what any friend would have done."

Brandon pointed to the door. "Ask Dewey to take you home. He's on tonight." Megan nodded and, with one last squeeze for Dillon, she left. Once the door closed behind her, Brandon said, "Tell him."

Dillon cleared his throat. "I'm gay."

Nate's eyes went wide. "I think I'm speechless."

Brandon certainly wasn't. "I'm willing to give you the benefit of the doubt here, but before you tell us your story, I need to make one thing perfectly clear. If I find out you've led my sister on while you were out screwing guys behind her back, you'll wish to God you hadn't."

"Nice one, Mr. Sensitive." Nate popped Brandon on the shoulder. "I think what Brandon is trying to ask in his own, ever so subtle way is, how long has Megan known that you're gay?"

"Almost from the first." Dillon traced the rim of his coffee cup with one finger. "Megan and I have been friends for years, and since we're both on the student council, we shared chairmanship of the homecoming dance together. She didn't have a date and neither did I, so she suggested we go together." He grinned. "I told her I didn't really want to, but you know how she is. She's pretty darn persistent when she wants something. For some reason, she wanted me to take her to that dance."

"If persistent is a nice way of saying 'pest', then yes, she is." Brandon's voice was laced with affection. "When Megan gets an idea in her head, it's damn near impossible to change her mind."

Nate smiled. "Wonder who she gets that from." He ignored Brandon's playful slap on the arm and turned his attention back to Dillon. "So, what happened? How did Megan find out the truth?"

"Well, and I sincerely hope you don't kick my ass for saying this, Sheriff, but after the dance, Megan asked me to take her down to Pepper Road."

Brandon's mouth fell into a frown and Dillon held up his hand. "She didn't really want me to take her there. It was all part of her plan to shake me up bad enough to admit the truth. When she asked me to take her down there, I freaked out and told her I couldn't do it. That's when she asked me — point blank — if I was gay. She said she'd seen the way I watched James and figured it out for herself." He couldn't stop his smile. "Megan couldn't have planned it any better. I was so tired of keeping it a secret that I broke down and told her everything."

"I'm not surprised Megan figured you out," Brandon said. "She's a pretty sharp kid. I'm still not thrilled that you used her for cover, whether she was a willing participant or not. And I'm still waiting to hear about James's place in all this."

Dillon scrubbed his hand across his face. "I've known James since kindergarten but we didn't start hanging out until we were in second grade, playing on the same Little League team." He smiled. "I wasn't the greatest player in the world, but James totally reeked. His aunt signed him up thinking that playing on a baseball team would help him make new friends, but he was so scared of the ball, he ducked every time it came to him. His aunt asked the coach to pick someone on the team to help him get over his fear, and the coach picked me. My dad was none too happy about that." He bit the inside of his cheek. "He didn't like James because his mom was a druggie who'd dropped him on his aunt, but I didn't care. James and I spent a whole summer working on his swing." He laughed again. "He never did get any better at baseball, but from that time on, we were together almost every day — riding bikes, fishing down at Patterson Creek. We did everything together." Dillon stared down at his hands. "At least we did until I fucked everything up."

Nate reached out and put a hand over Dillon's clasped ones. "You mean when you realized you were gay?"

Dillon nodded. "I think I always sort of knew, if that makes any sense, but as I got older, the feelings got harder to control." He blushed. "I, uh, started having these dreams."

Nate patted his hands again before leaning back in his chair. "Dreams about James, I'm guessing."

"Yeah. I knew I wasn't attracted to girls, but that was the first time it really hit me that I might be gay. And it scared the shit out of me."

"I can imagine it did."

"You don't know the half of it, Dr. Nash." Dillon took another sip of his coffee but didn't actually taste it. "My parents raised me to believe being gay is a sin. According to them, everyone who engages in 'deviant behavior' like homosexuality is headed straight to hell."

"First of all, I'm Nate and this is Brandon. No more of this 'Dr. Nash' and 'Sheriff' stuff. Secondly, I hope you know that what your folks think about gays is a load of homophobic crap."

"I know that now. Megan started dragging me to church with her as soon as I told her the truth about myself, and the pastor there has opened my eyes to a whole new way of thinking. I'm beginning to see that my parents and the church they belong to are full of it, but back then I thought there must really be something wrong with me. And I had no idea how James would react if I told him I was gay, let alone that I was having fantasies and dreams about him. Rather than risk it, I decided to play it straight."

Brandon stretched his long legs out to the side. "The truth finally came out, I take it."

"Yes. James and I were up in his room playing video games one day after school." As bittersweet as the experience had been, the memory made Dillon smile. "I'll spare you the details, but we ended up fooling around, and not long after that, James told me he was in love with me."

Nate studied Dillon's face. "Is that how your relationship started?"

"Calling it a relationship is way too generous." The bitterness and self-mockery in Dillon's voice were impossible to miss. "James gave me everything he had, but calling it a relationship implies I gave something back, and nothing could be further from the truth. I took and I took, but I never once gave him anything." A wave of self-loathing hit him hard. "Not a damn thing."

"What do you mean?"

"I'm not sure I'm comfortable spelling it out for you." Dillon gripped his cup with both hands. "To put it the nicest way I know how, I thought as long as I let James do all the work, I wasn't really gay. In my mind, kissing him was gay and touching him was gay, but letting him touch me was okay."

"In other words," Brandon said, "you believed as long as you never reciprocated, you and James were just a couple of buddies playing around."

Dillon nodded miserably, his face in his hands, unwilling to look at the revulsion he was certain he'd see on both men's faces. "God, I was such an asshole."

To his surprise, Dillon felt two large hands gently tugging his own away from his face. He looked up and saw Brandon standing over him.

"I'm not saying what you did was right, but you're taking responsibility for your actions now and that says a lot about how far you've come." Brandon sat down next to Nate. "Go ahead and tell us the rest of it, kid. You'll feel better once it's all out in the open."

Brandon's nonjudgmental tone gave Dillon the strength he needed to continue. "Even though I didn't give him anything in return, James stuck with me. We dated in secret for months, spending all our spare time together. I knew almost from the first that I was in love with James, but I was too much of a coward to tell him the truth." A harsh laugh escaped his lips. "Hell, I couldn't even admit it to myself. I guess I thought we'd drift along forever like we had been."

"When did things change?" Nate sounded no more condemning than Brandon. "Something must have happened, or you wouldn't be in the mess you're in now."

Dillon nodded. "Not long after we hooked up, James told me he wanted to come out."

Brandon whistled. "Bet that scared you shitless."

"God, yes. I couldn't even admit to myself that I was gay, and my boyfriend was ready to tell the whole world. Oh, he promised not to out me — only himself — but in the back of my mind, I was sure everyone would figure out I was gay, too. I mean, James and I spent all of our time together, and neither of us had ever dated girls. It wouldn't take a genius to fill in the blanks."

"So you dropped him." Brandon made it a statement, not a question.

"Not right away. I worked on him for a while — begged him not to come out — but he wouldn't wait. James said he was tired of lying about who he really was, and even though I admired him for having the balls to out himself, I was too scared to stick around." Dillon's teeth pressed into his lip as he remembered those first, dark days. "I cut off all ties with him, wouldn't answer his calls or talk to him at school. And when James finally did come out, I pretended I didn't even know him anymore." He felt sick as it all came rushing back, but he forced himself to continue the story. "My parents found out right away, what with my mom being a freshman English teacher at the high school and all. She didn't say much, but my dad went ballistic." He cringed at the memory. "Dad came into my room, ranting and raving about how that little 'homo' wasn't welcome in our house. When I told him James and I weren't friends anymore, he seemed satisfied. As far as my parents were concerned, that was the end of it."

"Obviously," Brandon said, "that wasn't the end of it for you."

"Not even close. I tried to fool myself into thinking I hadn't really loved James, but cutting him out of my life was like hacking off my own arm. I did my best to forget him and move on, but I couldn't. About a year ago, I gave up and accepted the fact that I would never be happy until I had James back in my life. I knew I couldn't begin to make up for the hell I'd put him through until I took care of a few things first, including my own coming out. There isn't a doubt in my mind my folks will pitch me out on my ass the minute they find out I'm gay, so I've been working and saving as much money as I can. I just turned eighteen last month, and I have enough put away to make it on my own for the rest of the school year and the summer."

"What about college?" Nate folded his hands in his lap. "I hope you're planning on going."

"As a matter of fact, I got my acceptance papers today." Despite the situation, Dillon experienced a small swell of pride. "I'll be starting Garman College in the fall."

Brandon raised a brow. "In New York?"

"Yeah. That's where James is going." Dillon blushed. "I know because Megan works as a student aide in the office and I bribed her to take a look at his files." He took another drink of his tepid coffee. "I have a college fund in my name and I bought and paid for my own car, so my parents can't touch either of those things. If I'm careful, I should be able to make it until school starts."

"Brandon and I could help you," Nate said. "We have more than enough—"

Dillon stopped him. "I appreciate that, but this is my problem and I have to work it out on my own."

"I admire that," Brandon said, "and I can see you've put a lot of thought into your plan, but what will you do if James refuses to take you back? I believe you when you tell me how sorry you are, but you delivered one hell of a blow to the guy. What if getting him back is a no-go?"

Dillon had considered that possibility a thousand times, and he was ready for it. "Even if James tells me to go straight to hell, it won't affect my coming out. I'm tired of hiding all the time."

Brandon nodded and then looked down at his watch. "It's almost one o'clock in the morning. I hate to do this, but you'll have to call your folks to come and get you. Even though you're eighteen, you still live at home, which means I have to have a parent's signature before I can let you go."

Dillon's stomach knotted. "My folks are out of town for the weekend, celebrating their twenty-fifth wedding anniversary. They won't be back until Sunday night."

"Damn. Is there anyone else you can call? A grandparent or an aunt or uncle, maybe?"

"No." Dillon thought for a minute. "I do have an older brother. Heath. Could he sign for me?"

"How old is he?"

"Twenty-three."

"I'd rather he was older, but I can't have you staying here for two days until your folks get back." Brandon pulled his cell phone out of his pocket and passed it across the table to Dillon. "Call your brother."

Dillon nodded, but before he had a chance to dial, Brandon pulled a card from his shirt pocket and handed it over. "This has my work, home, and cell numbers on it. If you need us, call." Brandon got up then, pulled Nate to his feet and led him toward the door. "Nate and I will be waiting in my office. Have your brother come in and sign you out when he gets here." He paused with his hand on the doorknob. "You know your mother will find out about the fight, don't you? News of your little heavyweight match with Lewis will be all over the school come Monday."

"I know. I'll tell my parents about it when they get home."

Brandon nodded. "Good luck, kid. God knows you're gonna need it."

Dillon watched with both relief and dread as his brother wove his way through the rows of desks. Heath had sounded none too happy on the phone, probably because he had a hot date and being called down to the police station in the middle of the night was screwing with his plans.

At six-two, Heath was just a couple of inches taller than Dillon, with the same brownish hair and same light green eyes. Physically, the two were a close match, but that's where all similarity ceased. Whereas Dillon had done his best to please his parents over the years, Heath couldn't have cared less what anyone thought of him, his folks included.

Spotting Dillon almost immediately, Heath reached him in three long strides. "You want to tell me why you had to call me down here? Where are Mom and Dad?"

Dillon stood and stretched his cramped muscles. "They went to the Poconos for their anniversary."

"Oh, yeah. Twenty-five years of wedded bliss." Heath snorted. "Never mind the fact that they've only stuck together that long because no one else would put up with either one of them." He put his hand on Dillon's shoulder and steered him toward the door. "You said on the phone you needed someone to come down here and sign you out, right?"

"Yeah. Sheriff Nash is waiting in his office for us."

Heath nodded. "Let's get to it."

Brandon had the papers waiting for them. The signing out process took no time at all, a fact that Dillon actually found himself regretting. It wasn't that he enjoyed spending the night at the police station, but Dillon knew his brother. As soon as the two of them were alone, Heath would demand to know the truth about his fight with Lewis.

Heath's truck was parked just outside the main door of the sheriff station, right in front of a fire hydrant. Dillon pointed to Heath's back tire.

"You'd think a firefighter would know better than to block a fire plug."

"Yeah, well, most firefighters don't have to bail their kid brothers out of jail after pulling a double shift."

Dillon gritted his teeth. "You didn't have to bail me out; I was never charged. All you had to do was come down here and pick me up. It's not like I asked you to give me a kidney or something."

"Maybe not, but it's still an inconvenience." Heath stopped beside his truck and crossed his arms over his chest. "I think it's time you told me what happened."

Heath didn't seem to mind that they were standing on the sidewalk within hearing distance of anyone who cared to listen, but Dillon did. "Why don't we get in the truck, and I'll tell you about it on the way home?"

"Not happening, little brother. Knowing our parents, they'll find a way to blame this on me like they do everything else. We're not stepping foot off this sidewalk until you tell me what's going on."

Dillon could tell by the set of Heath's shoulders that he was serious. *Might as well get it over with.* "I took Megan to the dance tonight."

"Megan Nash?"

"Yeah."

"Are you saying the sheriff busted you for taking his little sister to a dance?" Heath's eyes narrowed. "You didn't do anything stupid like take her parking, did you? So help me, Dillon—"

"It wasn't anything like that." Dillon faced Heath down. "I got hauled in here for fighting."

"With who?"

"Ben Lewis."

"James Walker's boyfriend?"

Dillon winced. "Yeah. That's him. Ben and I got into it, he insulted Megan, and I decked him."

Heath tensed. "He insulted Megan?"

"Yeah, but that's not what started the fight. He was pissed because I was trying to talk to James."

"What, he thought you were trying to put the make on his guy or something?"

Dillon nodded. "That's exactly what he thought."

"And why would he think that?" The suspicion in Heath's voice was impossible to miss.

Dillon took a deep breath. "Because I was. I'm in love with James, Heath. I have been for years."

Dillon hadn't expected Heath to be thrilled with the news, but he was unprepared for the raw loathing he saw on his brother's face. "You're gay? You rotten bastard." Heath's anger caught Dillon so off guard he didn't see his brother's raised fist, but he sure as hell felt the punch.

Chapter Three

Dillon had no time to brace himself for the right hook Heath delivered to his jaw. Dillon staggered backward, anger and pain radiating off him in waves as he clutched his aching jaw and glared at Heath. "You wanna kick my ass because I'm gay? Is that it? Go ahead and try."

"You think I hit you because you're gay? I don't give a flying fuck about that. You can screw the whole male contingent of the Plunkett High Young Republicans League for all I care." Heath shook his head in disgust. "Homophobic is the one thing I'm not."

Dillon rubbed his sore jaw. "Then what the hell did you hit me for?"

Heath's eyes flashed in the dim glow of the street lights. "Being gay isn't something you can help, but toying with a girl's affections is a definite choice."

"Toying with *whose* affections? Are you talking about Megan?"

"Yes, Megan. Who else have you been leading around by a string for the past five months?"

"Whoa. Heath, you've got it all wrong. The thing about Megan—"

Heath balled up his fists again. "You're the one who's got it all wrong if you think a sweet girl like Megan deserves to be used as cover while you chase cock behind her back."

Dillon rested one hip against the side of Heath's truck as he began to get an idea of where Heath's anger was coming from. "How would you know how sweet Megan is? As far as I know, you've only met her once, and that was at Mom and Dad's Christmas party. You wouldn't even have been there if Mom hadn't called and guilted you into it."

Heath shifted uncomfortably. "Megan volunteers with the Reed Boys and Girls Club after school. They taught a week long course on fire safety and I was one of the guys who got roped into helping out." His expression of fury returned. "Anyone who gives up her free time to help out underprivileged kids deserves a lot better than to be treated like your token girlfriend."

"For your information, Megan knows I'm gay. She has from the start. You're right about what kind of person she is, though. She's sweet and generous. That's why she volunteered to help me get James back. Megan and I are friends, Heath; that's all we've ever been. If you don't believe me, call her and ask her." Watching the wind go out of Heath's sails would have made Dillon smile if his jaw hadn't been hurting so bad.

"She knows?"

"Uh huh."

"Oh." Heath stared down at his shoes for a full minute and a half before his head snapped back up. "You should have told me that before I tried to dislocate your jaw."

"How was I supposed to know you've got a raging hard-on for my quasi-girlfriend?"

Heath shook his head. "It's not like that. Megan is...she's special. I'd hate to see her get hurt is all."

On that, the two of them were in perfect agreement. "I've made a lot of mistakes," Dillon said, "but screwing Megan over isn't one of them."

"Fair enough." Heath went to the driver's side of his truck. "Why don't you tell me the rest of it on the way home?"

"Drop me off at my car, will you? It's still parked in the senior lot at school."

"Works for me. Get in."

The ride back to school took just long enough for Dillon to give Heath a repeat of the story he'd told Brandon and Nate. To Heath's credit, he listened without interrupting, and when Dillon was through, Heath didn't seem inclined to pass judgment.

He pulled his truck in behind Dillon's Lumina. "For what it's worth, I hope this thing with James works out the way you want it to." Heath paused. "You know Mom and Dad won't stand for having a gay son, right?"

"I know." Dillon grabbed the door handle. "Thanks for the ride, and for signing me out with the sheriff."

"No problem. Hey, sorry about your jaw."

Dillon shrugged. "No big deal. I'll just tell Mom and Dad I got clipped in the fight with Lewis. They'll never know the difference."

"When are you planning on telling them the rest of it?"

Dillon climbed out of the truck and gave his brother a long, searching look. "When I have to, I guess."

"Fair enough. Good luck, little brother."

Sunday afternoon, Jamie stretched out on his bed, thankful the morning's sermon hadn't lasted long. It was bad enough that he'd had to spend an entire Saturday cleaning the basement to assuage Aunt Sadie's wrath, but trying to concentrate on the preacher's words had proved impossible; his mind was still reeling from Friday night.

Jamie flipped through the channels but couldn't find anything he wanted to watch. He'd just decided to surf the 'net when the phone rang. Since Aunt Sadie wasn't home, Jamie grabbed the extension in his room.

"Hello?"

"So, did old lady Banks ground your ass, or what?"

Jamie laughed. "I told you she wouldn't. I had to clean the basement, but I would have had to do that sooner or later, anyway."

"Cool."

"What about Nora? How bad did she bust you?"

"She was fairly pissed," Ben said, "but she got over it quick. She wouldn't let me go back out to see my guy, though, so I waited until she went to sleep and climbed out my bedroom window."

"Didn't she hear your car?"

Jamie could almost hear Ben smiling. "Nope. My boy picked me up two blocks from the house. He dropped me off at the same place about an hour later."

Jamie couldn't pass up the opportunity to tease him. "An hour? Is that all it takes for you guys?"

Ben's voice lost all sense of levity. "We didn't even go there, J. He was too pissed over that kiss I gave you."

"Wait a minute. Your mystery man was at the dance?"

"'Fraid so."

Jamie let out a low whistle. "Dude, I'm so sorry."

"Don't be. I'm the one who kissed you, remember? Besides, I was about ready to break it off with him anyway." Ben made a clicking sound with his tongue. "The guy was getting way too serious for my taste."

"What are you gonna do now?"

"What I always do — the best I can, which right now includes washing my car."

Jamie shuddered. "It's twenty-three degrees outside. You'll freeze your nuts off."

"A small price to pay for giving my car that special glow." Ben laughed. "Quit worrying, J. I'll bundle up. Catch you in the morning." He hesitated. "If your aunt will still let you ride to school with me."

"She will."

"Cool. Catch you later."

"Later."

Jamie placed the phone back in its cradle and was just about to log on to the 'net when he heard the doorbell. He made it to the door as the bell sounded again. Flinging it open, Jamie came face to face with Dillon Carver.

Seeing James standing in the doorway almost caused Dillon to lose his nerve. That James looked less than happy to see him didn't help, and neither did the half-spoken, half-barked, "What do you want?" that came out of James's mouth. Forcing a smile, Dillon pulled the package from behind his back. "I brought you these."

James took the bag of chocolate chunk cookies that Dillon had bought from Morton's Bakery just that afternoon and held it away from himself like it was poisonous. "Why would you bring me cookies?"

Dillon cleared his throat. "I remembered that you liked these. And," he braced himself, "I was hoping maybe we could talk."

James looked down at the box in his hand for a long, tense minute. Finally he said, "Come on into the kitchen and I'll pour us some milk to go with these."

Relieved, Dillon nodded and followed James down the narrow hall of Sadie's old Victorian home. He found it comforting to note that nothing much had changed. Same bold floral wallpaper, same elegantly outdated furniture. Though he knew he no longer belonged there, Dillon felt an unexpected sense of homecoming as James led him through the house.

When they reached the kitchen, James pointed to the table. "Sit down."

Dillon did as he was told and watched as James pulled glasses and plates out of the cabinet. He put two cookies on each plate, poured milk into both glasses, and then juggled everything to the table. Dillon met him halfway and took the plates from James's arm where they were balanced, his fingers brushing James's elbow in the process.

James shivered at the contact but quickly backed away. Hiding his hurt over the slight as best he could, Dillon returned to the table with James, staying a safe distance behind him. After they were both seated, James said, "Not to be rude, but what do you want?"

Dillon took a deep breath. "I want to apologize for what happened with Lewis. I'm not sorry for hitting him, especially not after what he said about Megan, but I *am* sorry for getting you caught in the middle of it."

"It's over with." James stared at Dillon over the rim of his glass. "You could have told me that over the phone. What gives?"

Dillon set his glass on the table and gathered his courage. "I want you in my life."

James leaned back in his chair and crossed his arms over his chest. "After the hell you put me through?" He shook his head. "Sorry, but I'm not into masochism."

Dillon took a deep breath. "You have no idea how sorry I am for the way I treated you." He locked eyes with James. "All I'm asking is a chance to prove it."

"What will your parents say? Or those dumbass jocks you hang around with?" James looked away. "How will they feel about you hanging out with the school fag?"

"Please don't call yourself that." Dillon sighed. "I couldn't care less what anyone else thinks. I want to be with you. As far as I'm concerned, that's all that matters."

"Look," James's eyes narrowed, "if you think we can pick up where we left off before you dumped my ass, you're out of your freakin' mind."

"I know that isn't possible, but..." Dillon hesitated. "You and I were friends once. I'd like to see if we could be again."

"Just friends?" James studied Dillon's face with open skepticism. "That's all you're asking for?"

"I won't lie to you," Dillon said. "I'd like to be more to you than just someone to hang out with, but I'll settle for whatever you can give me." He stared down at his plate. "Unless you think Ben will mind."

"Why would he?"

Dillon brought his eyes back up to James's face. "If you were my boyfriend, I wouldn't want to share you with anybody."

"Not that it's any of your business," James shifted in his seat, "but Ben isn't my boyfriend. He and I are just friends, but that doesn't mean I'm ready to pick up where you and I left off." He uncrossed his arms and folded his hands on the table. "Besides, what will Megan say about you spending time with your ex? Oh, that's right." His tone turned sarcastic. "Megan doesn't know about us. Nobody does."

"Yeah, she does. Like you and Ben, Megan and I are nothing more than friends. She's not my girlfriend and she never has been." Dillon paused only a second before telling him the rest of it. "Megan isn't the only one who knows about me and you. I also told Brandon and Nathan Nash. Hell, I even told Heath."

"You really expect me to believe that bullshit?" James curled his lip. "Next you'll be telling me you're ready to come out to the whole world."

Dillon kept his tone steady. "I am." James started to say something but Dillon held up a hand to cut him off. "I don't expect you to believe me, but I intend to prove it to you if you'll give me the chance."

James chewed a bite of cookie in silence. Finally he said, "If you're serious about coming out, I can't stop you, but don't do it on my account."

Dillon's heart plummeted. "Are you saying you want me to leave you alone?"

"That's not what I meant." James's voice dropped an octave. "Coming out is something you have to do for yourself. I shouldn't figure into the decision."

"I know that. When I come out, it'll be because I'm ready." Dillon looked into James's eyes, again. "That doesn't mean I'm not hoping the two of us can be together again."

"Why now?"

"It's taken me a long time to summon up the courage to be honest about myself, including the feelings I have for you." Dillon wasn't sure how much James was ready to hear, but he'd been asked a question and he was going to answer it. "I never stopped wanting you; I just didn't have the guts to do anything about it."

"I'm not sure—"

"Please, don't decide anything right now. I only want you to take some time and think about what I said." Nervous now that his feelings were all out in the open, Dillon rose to his feet. "I've got to go. My folks will be back any minute and I've got to tell them about that fight with Lewis before Mom hears it at school." James started to rise, but Dillon stopped him. "I know my way to the door. See you at school tomorrow." He was halfway to the hall before he turned around and said, "Thanks. For talking to me, I mean."

James shrugged, as if it were no big deal, but as Dillon left, he found himself hoping against hope it had meant something to James, if only just a little.

By the time Dillon got back to his house, his parents were already home. He pulled the Lumina in beside his father's Buick and got out, all the while praying things weren't going to get ugly. He entered the house through the back door, nearly knocking his mother over in the process.

Angela Carver pressed her hand over her heart. "Dillon, you scared me to death." She stood on her tiptoes and kissed his cheek, then went back over to the table and resumed unpacking a grocery sack. "Did you have a good time while we were gone? I understood you to say you were taking that Nash girl to the school dance."

Dillon gritted his teeth, hating the way his folks always referred to Megan as "that Nash girl". Forcing himself to remain calm, he said, "Yeah. Uh...about that. I have something I need to tell you guys."

His mother raised her frosted blond head, her hazel eyes boring into him. "I take it this is something we aren't going to like."

"Probably."

Angela sighed. "Your father's out in the garage, unloading the car. Wait for us in the dining room while I go and get him. Sounds like we need to have a family meeting."

Dillon bit back a sigh. A "family meeting" consisted of either or both of the Carver boys sitting on one side of the table and their parents on the other, staring them down. Normally, just the mention of a family meeting was enough to make Dillon queasy, but he wasn't worried this time. Sooner or later, he knew his parents would be throwing him out. He found the thought strangely liberating. For the first time in his life, Dillon felt as if he no longer needed his parents' permission to live his life. Even so, he felt he owed his mother and father a certain amount of respect. He sat down at the dining room table and waited as ordered.

His father came in a few minutes later, stooping his tall body to keep from hitting his head on the door frame. Douglas Carver's graying hair was mussed and the green eyes behind the round glasses — eyes so like Dillon and Heath's — flashed with irritation. "Your mother tells me you have something you want to talk to us about."

"Yes, sir." Dillon waited until his mother came into the room and both his parents were seated. Clearing his throat, he said, "There was a fight at the dance Friday night and I got hauled in to the sheriff station."

Angela's mouth opened in a horrified circle. "You were arrested?"

"No, ma'am. No charges were filed, that is." Dillon swallowed. "Like I said, I was hauled in for fighting, but the sheriff was already at the dance because of a threat made against some of the gay students."

"I blame Dan Morgan for that." Angela's lips formed a tight frown. "What did he think would happen when he trotted out all those homosexuals and rubbed them in the faces of God-fearing children?" She made a disgusted sound in the back of her throat. "Was anyone hurt?"

"No, ma'am."

Douglas peered at his son over the top of his wire frames. "If no one was hurt, how'd you come across that bruised jaw?"

"Ben Lewis insulted Megan, and I ended up punching him. Sheriff Nash and his husband broke up the fight and took us down to his office."

"Nathan Morris and Brandon Nash are not married." The expression on Doug Carver's face was chilling. "Marriage is intended for a man and women, and only a man and woman."

"Nathan Nash."

"I beg your pardon?"

"Nate legally changed his name when he and Brandon got *married*." Dillon put a little extra emphasis on the last word.

Doug waved that away. "I couldn't care less what he calls himself. Those two are not now, nor will they ever be, married. That aside, Ben Lewis is a hoodlum. Nash has some nerve taking you in for questioning when everyone knows it was probably Lewis's fault. You'd think Nash would be glad to have someone taking up for that sister of his."

"What's that supposed to mean?"

Dillon's voice held a rising anger that caused his father to push his chair away from the table in preparation for standing. "Don't take that tone with me, young man. Because of her brother's lifestyle, Megan is bound to be the object of ridicule, and you know it. Nash should be glad to have someone sticking up for her."

Dillon set his jaw. "The only people who would give Megan a hard time because of her brother are small minded bigots whose opinions don't matter, anyway."

"Now, see here—"

"Dillon, how did you get out of jail?" Angela cut her husband off with practiced ease. "Did the sheriff release you?"

"James Walker talked Lewis into dropping the charges against me."

"Charges against you?" Dillon's father was a study in righteous indignation. "Weren't you the one who should have been pressing charges against him? You didn't put that bruise on your own jaw, did you?"

"I threw the first punch, Dad. James talked Ben into dropping the charges and I was free to go. But since I still live under your roof, I needed a parent to sign me out. You guys were out of town, so Brandon let me call Heath to come down and fill out the paperwork."

Douglas folded his arms over his chest. "I might have known Heath was involved in this. He doesn't have time to come and see his parents, but he's conveniently on call to pick his brother up from jail."

Angela put her hand on her husband's shoulder. "Well, I for one am glad Heath was home. I hate the thought of Dillon having to spend all weekend down at the sheriff station." She looked at her son. "That doesn't mean you're getting off free on this one, young man. Go upstairs while your father and I discuss a suitable punishment."

Dillon stood, but Douglas stopped him. "There'll be no punishment."

Angela looked as shocked as Dillon felt. "Douglas, we have to do something. This type of behavior is intolerable."

"Boys fight. And given the nature of the fight, I think it's safe to say it won't happen again. I'm just thankful Dillon no longer associates with that Walker boy. I have no doubt he was a large contributor to this whole fracas."

"James didn't do one thing wrong, not a single thing." Dillon ground his teeth. "And as far as breaking off my friendship with him goes, that's the worst mistake I ever made."

Doug laughed, the mockery so thick in his voice Dillon felt ill. "Why? What did he ever do for you?"

Dillon was tempted almost beyond resistance to tell him, but he forced himself to wait. For his plan to work, his timing had to be just right. Ignoring his father, he said, "If that's all, I'd like to be excused."

"No, that's not all. I believe I asked you a question."

"Let him go," Angela said. "I think we've done enough talking for one night, and I'm sure Dillon has homework."

He didn't, but that didn't stop Dillon from nodding his head and escaping the room. He had to get out of there before his father said another word.

Jamie cursed under his breath and pulled his coat tight against his neck. No matter how many layers he wore, there was nothing he could do to combat the cold as he started the long walk to school. He could have called Aunt Sadie to pick him up, but he hated to bother her. Since she'd retired from her nursing job two years earlier, she did her best to stay busy. Today was her day to volunteer at the public library, and she'd already left by the time Jamie realized Ben wasn't coming.

Snuggling into his clothing, he set off at a fast pace. He'd almost made it to the end of the first block when a car pulled up beside him and a familiar voice said, "Get in."

Jamie peered through the Lumina's rolled-down passenger window and gave Dillon the most nonchalant look he could manage with his teeth chattering. "No, thanks. It's not that far, and I don't mind walking. Ben's probably just running late. I'm sure he'll stop and pick me up any minute now."

Dillon blew out a harsh breath, sending little clouds of smoke swirling through the frigid air. "Christ, James, you're gonna freeze out there. Just get in the car. You can meet up with Lewis at school."

Dillon must have seen the indecision on Jamie's face, because he said, "All I'm offering you is a ride. I meant what I said yesterday — no pressure."

Jamie stood for a full minute, caught somewhere between indecision and the desperate need to believe Dillon had really changed. While Jamie was trying to make up his mind, he failed to notice that Dillon put the car in park and got out.

Dillon walked around to where Jamie was standing and opened the passenger door. Ever so gently, he tugged on Jamie's arm, urging him toward the car. "Come on. Please get in the car." When Jamie still hesitated, Dillon, without ever letting go of Jamie's arm, stuck the glove of his right hand in his mouth and tugged it free with his teeth, then took it and stuffed it into his coat pocket. With his warm fingertips, Dillon traced small circles on Jamie's wind-reddened cheeks. "You're almost frozen through. Let me see if I can help." Before Jamie could protest, Dillon leaned forward so that they were almost touching. As Jamie stood before him in frozen silence, Dillon opened his mouth and huffed warm air onto Jamie's frosty skin.

Jamie was too stunned to say a word as Dillon persisted in his task. When he seemed satisfied that Jamie's skin was warmer, Dillon again nudged him toward the car. This time, Jamie went without protest.

The ride to school was quiet, but to Jamie's surprise, it wasn't an uncomfortable silence. He could still feel Dillon's warm breath on his cheeks, still feel the moist heat from his body. And the fact that Dillon had done all that on a busy street didn't escape him, either. Anyone could have seen them, and Dillon hadn't seemed to care. Before Jamie had time to reason it all through, Dillon pulled the car into the senior parking lot.

Jamie stopped just short of opening the door. Turning to Dillon, he said, "Thanks for the ride. And thanks for, um, warming me up." He was mortified to feel himself blush.

Dillon's grin caused the blush to darken. "You're more than welcome for both." He laughed. "I always loved the way your cheeks get all hot and red when you're embarrassed. God, you're cute."

Jamie didn't know what to say, but he couldn't stop the smile that lit his face. Giving Dillon one last muttered thanks, he started to get out. Dillon reached out his hand and stopped him. "James?"

"Yeah?"

"I was hoping you might eat lunch with me at Hailey's today. We both have fourth period lunch and a free period afterwards. We'd have over an hour and a half before we actually had to be back in class."

Jamie raised his eyebrows. "How did you know I have a free period after lunch?"

It was Dillon's turn to blush. "I had Megan check your schedule."

That little bit of knowledge did more to warm Jamie than any amount of heat ever could, but he decided to play it cool. "Just lunch? That's all you're asking for?"

"Just lunch."

Jamie's head told him to say no, but his heart answered before his brain could shut it up. "Okay. Where do you want to meet?"

"How about meeting me at my car after third period?"

Jamie nodded. "I'll be here." He got out, carrying the image of Dillon's grateful smile with him.

His first three classes seemed to drag on forever. Though he tried to fight it, Jamie found himself getting excited about the prospect of spending an hour and a half with Dillon. It was amazing that after all the heartache, Jamie still felt an electric shock zing up his spine every time he saw Dillon's face.

When the bell rang ending third period, Jamie flew out of class. He'd almost made it to the double doors when a tug on his coat sleeve stopped him. He turned and found the soft blue eyes of Megan Nash staring up at him.

His first reaction was panic. Dillon had lied to him. Megan was there to warn him off. All those things Ben had said at the dance were true. Dillon just wanted Jamie for a side dish while waiting for Megan to become the main course. God, how could he have been stupid enough to trust Dillon again? Jamie was just about to go from panic to anger when Megan spoke.

"Dillon sent me to keep you company until he gets here. His mother caught him after class and asked him to move some boxes from the teachers' supply closet to her classroom. It'll only take a second, but he didn't want you to think he was standing you up for your lunch date."

"Date?" Jamie cleared his throat. "He called it a date?"

Megan smiled. "Of course that's what he called it." When Jamie made no response, her face fell. "Was I not supposed to say that? He told me you guys were taking it slow, but I just thought... I didn't mean to screw this up. Damn, damn, damn."

All the relief Jamie felt knowing that Megan knew — that Dillon hadn't lied — bubbled up. He started laughing and couldn't stop.

Megan watched him for a full minute before she started laughing too. When they'd both subsided, she said, "Does that mean you're not mad?"

Though Jamie had known Megan for years, he couldn't recall ever actually having a conversation with her. It wasn't that he didn't like her, but they moved in different circles. He should've found it harder to open up to her, but for some reason, he spilled his guts.

"I'm not mad, just relieved. When I saw you standing there, I thought maybe..."

Megan was nothing if not quick. "Oh no. You thought I was coming to tell you to back off. No wonder you had that look on your face. I'm so sorry."

"No, don't apologize. You didn't do anything. It's just something I have to deal with."

"Does that mean you're giving Dillon another chance?"

"I honestly don't know."

Megan nodded. "Perfectly understandable. For what it's worth, I'm rooting for you guys."

Her sincerity put Jamie at ease. "Thanks. That means a lot to me."

Dillon came up from the back hallway. "What means a lot to you?"

"Lunch," Megan said. She gave Jamie a wink that only he could see. "Lunch means the world to him, Dillon. The boy is skin and bones. Go. Feed him." She gave Dillon a peck on the cheek, then stunned Jamie by doing the same to him. Before either could say anything to her, she was gone.

Jamie shook his head. "She's a firecracker."

"That she is." Dillon pointed to the door. "You ready to go?"

Jamie nodded. The ride to Hailey's was much like the ride to school, silent but comfortable. Jamie played with the radio while Dillon sang along in that off-key squeak of his. Dillon pulled up to the curb and threw the car into park.

They got out and made for the restaurant, but Jamie stopped just short of opening the door. "Are you sure you want to do this?"

"Sure. I'm starving."

"That's not what I meant."

Dillon sighed. "I know what you meant, and the answer is yes. Like I told you before, I couldn't care less what anyone else thinks. Now, can we please go in and eat? I wasn't kidding about the starving part."

Jamie followed Dillon inside. Hailey's Café was the epitome of a small town restaurant, from the white vinyl covered booths to the blue checkered tablecloths. The enticing smells coming from the kitchen were enough to drive a hungry man insane, as evidenced by the nearly packed house. Hailey Johnson, the owner, met them at the door. The blue-eyed blonde gave them a thousand-watt smile as they entered.

"Hi, guys. Would you like a table, or are you going to sit at the counter?"

Dillon leaned forward and whispered in Hailey's ear, at which she smiled again and nodded. When Dillon stepped back to Jamie's side, Hailey said, "Follow me, boys. I thought you might like to eat in the party room. No one's back there right now, so you'll have some privacy while you eat."

The party room was just that, primarily reserved for the large luncheons and dinners Hailey catered. It was separated from the rest of the café by a thick blue curtain.

Hailey seated them at a booth on the far wall. Jamie tossed his coat on an empty table before sitting down. After Dillon shed his own coat, Jamie expected him to take the seat across from him. Dillon surprised him by sliding in on the same side.

Hailey offered menus, but neither needed them. After ordering two plates of spicy chicken fingers and fries with Cokes to wash them down, Dillon and Jamie settled in to wait.

Dillon pulled a napkin from the old-fashioned chrome holder and twisted it into a ball. "I hope eating back here was okay with you."

"Why wouldn't it be?" Jamie looked around at the familiar knotty pine paneling and the Norman Rockwell reproductions on the walls. "I love this place."

Dillon turned to face him, so close they were practically nose to nose. "I didn't mean the café. I meant eating back here. Alone."

"I think it's nice." Jamie was surprised by how husky his own voice sounded.

"That's why I asked Hailey to put us back here. I didn't want you to think I was ashamed to be seen with you." Dillon leaned in even closer. "That's not it. I just wanted you all to myself." His sweet, hot breath fanned Jamie's face.

Jamie stared at Dillon's mouth, wondering how his lips would taste. In the past, Dillon had resisted all of Jamie's efforts to kiss him. Would this new Dillon — the one who always seemed to know exactly the right thing to say — push him away if he leaned forward just a quarter of an inch? As afraid as he was to know the answer, Jamie had just decided to test the theory when Hailey came back with their Cokes. They broke apart in an instant.

If she noticed, Hailey didn't let on. "Your food should be out in two shakes. Can I get you anything while you wait?"

His eyes fastened on Jamie, Dillon said, "Nothing for me. I have everything I need, thanks."

Hailey laughed. "I can see that. I'll leave you alone then." She left unnoticed.

Jamie swallowed. "I'm not sure what to say."

"You don't have to say it; I already know. I'm pushing too hard." Dillon drew in a ragged breath. "I swear to God I'm trying not to, but being this close to you again is making me crazy."

In a bold move that surprised them both, Jamie picked up Dillon's hand and squeezed it. "You're not pushing. This new you is just taking me a while to get used to." When Dillon looked uncertain, Jamie turned his hand over and made circles on Dillon's palm with his fingers. He delighted in the shudders he felt running through Dillon's body. "Give me time to adjust."

Dillon laced his fingers through Jamie's. "Okay." He was about to say more but the food arrived, cutting off further conversation. The obvious reluctance with which Dillon released his hand made Jamie's heart beat a little faster. *Damn.* If lunch with Dillon was this good, Jamie couldn't wait for dinner.

The ride back to school was more like a walk down memory lane. Dillon couldn't ever remember feeling closer to James than he did at that moment. They talked about everything and nothing, just as they'd done so many times in the past. Two years melted away and Dillon began hoping that, in time, all the pain he had caused would dissolve as well. He studied James from the corner of his eye as he drove, following the elegant curve of James's chin, the slight tilt of his ski jump nose. His body responded as James laughed at something he'd said, the rich, gravelly sound vibrating deep within him. He willed himself to relax as he whipped into the parking lot.

James slipped on his gloves. "I really enjoyed lunch. I wish you'd at least let me pay for my half."

"No way. You were my..." He trailed off, afraid to say the "D" word.

James grinned. "All right, but I get to pay next time. I just hope you're a cheap date."

Did he hear him right? "Next time?"

"Well, yeah. That is, if you want to."

Dillon lifted James's chin with one finger. "All right. You can pay next time."

James smiled, then looked down at his watch. "We'd better go. We've only got ten minutes until the fifth period bell and I still have to run down to my locker."

Dillon nodded. "Can I give you a ride home this afternoon? I don't have to be at the drugstore until four, so I'll have plenty of time."

This time there was no hesitation from James. "I'd like that. Meet you at the lockers?"

"You know it."

Dillon was so high on thoughts of seeing James after school he barely remembered walking back into the building. Nor could he recall a single thing Mrs. Murdock, his geometry teacher, said during the fifth period class. When the bell rang, he practically raced out of the room, anxious to finish the day. He ducked into the bathroom, took care of business, and then headed to class.

His last class, Government, was usually a snooze fest. Mr. Whitewood, the teacher, was a nice enough guy, but he spoke in a sleep-inducing monotone. Dillon hurried in, expecting to find the rest of the students in their seats. Instead, he saw chaos.

Weeping girls, whispering and dabbing at their eyes, stood huddled in clusters throughout the room. He saw a group of jocks in the corner, Rooster Carmichael among them, his meaty face as red as his scrubby hair. He was laughing and saying something, but Dillon couldn't tell what. The rest of the students were in scattered groups, chatting in corners or sitting on desks and speaking in hushed tones. He waited for Mr. Whitewood to call them to order, but a quick visual search of the room showed no sign of the teacher.

The door swung open and a breathless Megan rushed in, heading straight for Dillon. "Oh, thank God! I came in here a minute ago and couldn't find you. Where have you been?"

"I stopped by the bathroom. What's up? Why is it like a funeral home in here?"

Megan froze. "You haven't heard?"

"Heard what?"

"About five minutes ago, Principal Morgan made an announcement over the intercom—"

"The one in the bathroom's busted. What happened?"

"Dillon..." Megan put her hands to her chest, trying to catch her breath. "Ben Lewis is dead. Principal Morgan didn't give any details, just said we need to keep his friends and family in our prayers."

Friends and family? James. "I've got to get to James." Dillon was already on his way to the door. "Can you remember what his last class is? I think it's English Lit."

"No, it's Art, but that's not the problem. I went down to the art room as soon as I heard what happened — you know, to check on him — but he wasn't there."

Dillon froze. "What do you mean, he wasn't there?"

Megan's eyes were bright and worried. "James is gone."

Chapter Four

All the euphoria from lunch evaporated in the split second it took Dillon to get to his car. He peeled out of the parking lot, squealing the tires. He had to get to James. He was out there, alone in the cold and grieving for his best friend.

Dillon drove like a maniac, taking the most direct route to James's house, finding him a half-block from school. Dillon pulled alongside him and rolled down the window. "James?"

James turned to look at him, his eyes glassy and dazed. "Dillon?"

"Are you okay?"

James shook his head. "You heard about Ben?"

For the second time that day, Dillon put his car in park and got out to go to James, this time approaching him with care. The blank look on James's face scared the daylights out of him, but he did his best to keep the worry from showing.

"I heard." He took James's hand and led him, unresisting, to the car. "Let me take you home." Closing the door after James climbed in, Dillon whipped out his cell phone and removed Brandon Nash's card from his pocket. Trying the home number first, he prayed to God someone was there who could help. When Nate picked up on the second ring, Dillon wanted to weep with relief.

"Hello?"

"Dr. Nash, it's Dillon Carver. I need your help."

"What's the matter?"

The concern in Nate's voice was almost Dillon's undoing, but he knew he had to stay strong for James. "It's James."

"James Walker?" The light must have dawned, because Nate said, "Oh my God! He was dating Ben Lewis, wasn't he? Then he knows?"

Dillon bit his lip, a brief moment of jealousy rearing its head before he got it under control. "About Ben's death? Yes, sir. They weren't dating, but they were close. And the whole school knows. Principal Morgan announced it right before sixth period."

Nate swore. "How did Morgan find out? Brandon's still at the scene, and I know for a fact he hasn't spoken to the press yet."

"I don't know. I missed the announcement, but according to Megan, he didn't give any details."

Nate swore again, this time using a word that seemed out of place coming from the staid doctor. "What's done is done, but I feel damn sorry for Morgan when Brandon finds out. He'll kill him for interfering with his investigation." He blew out a deep breath. "So, what's going on with James?"

"I'm not sure. I found him on Harp Street, not far from school. His eyes are glassy and he seems really stunned."

"It sounds like he's in shock. Where are you now?"

"Still on Harp Street. I called you as soon as I got him in the car. Should I take him to the hospital?"

"If the shock is fairly mild, the patient usually does better in his own home. Where does James live?"

"With his aunt at 2238 Lambert Lane. She's probably not home, though. She usually keeps busy during the day." A thought occurred to him. "Should I try to get in touch with her?"

"Go ahead and get James home," Nate said. "I'll meet you there, and then I'll call her myself after I've examined him. That way I can explain what's going on without scaring her to death."

"Okay, Doc. I'm headed there, now. And, Doc? Thanks."

"Glad to help. I'll see you in a few minutes."

Even when Dillon got in the car and closed the door behind him, James didn't stir. With one eye on James and the other on the road, Dillon drove the short distance to Sadie's house. He pulled into the driveway. "James? We're at your house. Do you have your keys?"

James reached into his pocket and handed over the keys, but made no move to get out of the car. Dillon led him into the house. Once inside, James stumbled up the stairs. Dillon started to follow, but thought better of it. If James needed to be alone, so be it. With nothing else to do, Dillon sat down on the bottom step to wait for Nate.

He didn't have to wait long. About five minutes after he sat down the doorbell rang. Without even checking to see who it was, he turned the knob, letting Nate in with a weary sigh.

"You have no idea how glad I am to see you."

Nate placed his medical bag on the floor and closed the door behind him, then did something that surprised the heck out of Dillon. He wrapped both arms around him and pulled him into a crushing hug. What surprised Dillon even more was how good it felt. Neither of his parents were touchy-feely folks. His mother was moderately affectionate, but his father rarely did more than pat him on the back, and the older he got, the less often that happened. Dillon found himself returning the hug tenfold.

"Everything will be okay. I promise." Pulling back, Nate said, "Where's James now?"

"Upstairs, in his room. It's the last one at the back of the upstairs hall, to the right. At least, it used to be."

Nate nodded. "I'll go up and check on him." He reached down and picked up his bag. "While I check him over, why don't you see if you can find a phone number for his aunt?"

"I will." *Phone number? Shit.* Dillon smacked his forehead. "I need to call my boss."

"Go ahead. I'll come back downstairs as soon I'm done."

Dillon waited until Nate was on his way upstairs before pulling out his cell phone. Keying in the number, Dillon waited for someone to pick up.

"Savings Central Drugs. How may I help you today?"

"Carl? It's Dillon. Is the boss around?"

"Hey, Dillon. Did you hear about Ben Lewis?"

Dillon wasn't surprised by the question, considering Carl also went to Plunkett. "Yeah."

"I bet it was a drug deal gone bad. Everyone knew Lewis was a user. Either that or a gay love triangle." Carl sounded like he was giving a lurid recap of a *C.S.I.* episode. "Bet James Walker found him with another guy and offed his ass."

Dillon fought the urge to start pulling out his own hair. "Could I please speak to Mr. Pembroke?"

"What? Oh, sure. Just a sec while I get him."

Dillon endured a lame rendition of a Garth Brooks song while he waited for what seemed like an eternity. He'd just decided to hang up and try again when Jim Pembroke picked up.

"Dillon? Carl said you needed to speak with me. Sorry it took so long, son. I was in the back taking inventory."

"No problem. I'm calling to tell you I probably won't make it in tonight. I know it's short notice, but I swear I'll make up the time."

"Don't worry about it. Your work record here is darn near perfect. In fact, I think this is the first time you've ever called to tell me you weren't coming in." Pembroke paused. "I don't mean to pry, but is everything all right?"

"I just need time to get a couple of things sorted out."

"Take all the time you need, son." The warmth in Mr. Pembroke's voice was reassuring. "I'll see you as soon as you can make it back in."

"Thanks, Mr. P. See you soon."

After hanging up, Dillon searched around for some hint of where Sadie might be. He'd just abandoned his efforts when the front door opened and Sadie came barreling inside. She spotted Dillon immediately and came to a screeching halt.

"What are you doing in my house? And whose Buick is that in the driveway?" She glanced around the living room, then marched down the hall to the kitchen. Coming back to the living room, she said, "Where is Jamie, and what in the blue blazes is going on?"

Dillon was saved from having to answer by Nate coming back downstairs at exactly that moment. "I think maybe I can clear that up, ma'am." Nate walked into the living room and motioned to one of the richly upholstered sofas. "Do you mind if we sit down to discuss this, Miss Banks?"

Sadie put her hand to her chest. "Dr. Nash, what are you doing here? Is it Jamie? Is he all right?"

Nate took her elbow and led her to the sofa, joining her there and gesturing for Dillon to take one of the wingback chairs. When all were seated, Nate said, "Miss Banks, James suffered a mild shock. Dillon found him wandering out on Harp Street, dazed and confused."

Sadie gasped. Nate put a hand on top of her smaller, shaking one. "James is going to be all right. Dillon called me as soon as he found him. I gave him a brief examination, and it's my feeling the shock is only temporary. I can write him a prescription for a mild sedative if you'd like, but I prefer to let these things run their course, especially given the nature of the situation. If you want a second opinion, I'll understand completely."

Sadie shook her head. "That won't be necessary. I know your reputation and I feel comfortable enough to go with you on this. But, Dr. Nash—"

"Please, call me Nate."

"Only if you'll call me Sadie. Now, as I was saying, I appreciate you coming and looking Jamie over, but if someone doesn't tell me just what in the bloody hell is going on here, I swear before the Lord Jesus Almighty I will pull out my Grandmother Banks's cast-iron skillet and lay open both of your thick heads."

Dillon didn't smile over the threat. The situation was too damned serious. "Ben Lewis was killed this morning."

Sadie pressed her knuckles to her breastbone. "No wonder Jamie's in shock." She looked to Nate. "Are you sure he's going to be all right?"

"I believe he'll be fine once he has a chance to absorb what's happened. He was resting when I left him; that's what he needs most right now." He stood. "If you'll excuse me, I'd better call Brandon and let him know what's going on. Once James's initial shock wears off, I'd like to have Brandon talk to him directly and explain exactly what happened to Ben."

Sadie nodded. "That sounds reasonable. I'll let him rest until the sheriff gets here. Oh, did you need to use the phone in the kitchen?"

"No, ma'am. I have my cell." Nate pulled it out of his pocket. "I'll just take my bag back out to the car and place that call."

The minute Nate was gone, Sadie did her version of a verbal pounce. "Thank you for bringing Jamie home, but given the way you and your parents feel about my nephew, I think it would be best if you left."

The metallic taste of raw panic rose into Dillon's throat. He'd just re-established a slight connection with James, tenuous at best, but enough to have him hoping. He couldn't lose it now. Clearing his throat, he said, "Miss Banks, please don't send me away. I need to be here."

Sadie's hawk eyes narrowed on Dillon's face. "And why is that?"

Dillon's voice was choked with emotion but he kept his eyes locked with Sadie's. "Because I'm in love with him."

Instead of the stunned silence Dillon expected, Sadie nodded. "I thought so."

Dillon felt like he'd been whapped with a brick. "You knew?"

Sadie shrugged. "Just because I never married doesn't mean I don't know what love looks like. I saw the way you and Jamie used to smile at each other when you thought I wasn't looking. From there it didn't take an act of genius to realize why the two of you spent so much time together. Didn't take me long to put together the reasons why you broke off all ties with him when he came out either. You were afraid your parents would find out you were gay."

"Yes, ma'am." He stood and paced the length of the room. "I got scared and ruined everything."

Sadie leaned back into the soft cushions of the sofa and smoothed her fingers over the skirt of her dress. "What about now?"

Dillon came back to sit beside her on the couch. "I'm still scared. I know my folks will toss me out once I tell them the truth, but I'm going through with it just the same."

Sadie reached out and ruffled his hair the way she had when he and James were kids. "For what it's worth, you have my support."

Before Dillon had a chance to tell her how much that meant to him, the front door opened and Nate came back in. The look on Nate's face was grim as he removed his coat.

"Brandon's on his way." He hung his coat on the hall tree and tucked his gloves into the pocket. "I'm not sure how much of what he has to say will help James, but we can always hope. I'm going to go up and check on him again."

Sadie and Dillon both nodded. Dillon longed to go upstairs with Nate, but forced himself to wait instead. He prayed whatever the sheriff had to say would give James some peace, but the gnawing in his gut told him otherwise.

Jamie wrapped himself in a fog. He kept the truth about Ben at bay by pushing at it with a blank wall, a wall of carefully crafted ignorance. He could hear someone talking to him, but in the fuzzy blankness, it didn't matter. Here, in this place, Ben was still alive because Jamie said it was so.

Gradually, though, the fuzzy comfort began to ebb. The reality of someone in his room, prodding at him, urging him back, proved to be too much. He fought and struggled, but in the end, he was no match for the persistent pull of consciousness. He opened his eyes to see Nate Nash standing over him.

"How are you feeling?"

Good question. He gave Nate a feeble shrug. He hoped his non-response would prompt the doctor to leave.

Nate showed no signs of giving up or going away. He sat down on the side of the bed. "Are you in any pain? Have any nausea or dizziness?"

"No." Jamie's reply was little more than a soft grumble. "I just wanna go back to sleep."

Nate's eyes were filled with sympathy. "Try to stay awake for a few minutes more. Brandon will be here soon to talk to you."

"About Ben?"

"Yes."

Jamie burrowed further under the layer of covers, but Nate didn't move from his post on the edge of the bed. "I understand how you feel. I promise, it does get better."

Anger slowly replaced Jamie's initial shock. "You can't possibly know how I feel."

If Nate was surprised by the venom in Jamie's voice, he hid the reaction well. "I know it seems that way right now, but I swear, I do know what you're going through."

That did it. "Oh yeah? Did you lose your best friend?"

Nate's reply was a matter-of-fact. "Yes."

Being proved wrong smack in the middle of a boiling rage stopped Jamie short. He looked down at the covers. "Oh. Sorry."

Nate actually smiled. "It's okay, James. I was angry when I lost Amy, too."

Amy? That name sounded familiar. Then it hit him. "Wasn't she the lady doctor who was killed in an explosion?"

Nate's eyes took on a far-away gleam. "That was her. Amy Vaughn. She and I came here together from Georgia to open a medical practice. The explosion that cost Amy her life was actually meant for me." He swiped a hand over his face. "I was a complete basket case after she died. It took me nearly a month to function like a normal human being again."

"How long were you friends?"

"Almost twenty years."

Shame overtook him. "Damn. You lost your best friend of twenty years, and here I am making you relive it when I barely knew Ben a tenth of that time."

"Two years or twenty, it doesn't matter; it hurts to lose someone you care about. Everything you're feeling right now is perfectly natural. Don't be surprised if you have a wide range of emotions to deal with over the coming days and weeks."

Jamie sighed. "Does it ever stop hurting so bad?"

"I don't think the sense of loss ever completely goes away, but it does get easier to handle. I wish I could give you a timetable, but it's different for everybody." A knock sounded on the door. "I imagine that's Brandon," Nate said. "Are you ready for this?"

He wasn't, but that didn't stop him from nodding. Nate called out, "Come in," and Brandon Nash entered the room.

Nate stood and greeted Brandon with a hug and a peck on the cheek. "How'd it go?"

Brandon draped his arm around Nate's waist. "We won't know anything until the coroner's report comes in." He glanced toward the bed. "Is he ready for this?"

Jamie sat up. "Don't talk about me like I'm not here."

Brandon grimaced. "Sorry. According to Nate, that's a bad habit of mine. So, are you ready to hear what happened to Ben?"

"No, but tell me anyway."

Brandon dragged one of the chairs closer. Straddling it backwards, he waited for Nate to resume his seat on the edge of the bed, then said, "Because this is an ongoing investigation, I can't give you all the details, but I can tell you the bare facts."

"Okay."

"Just after breakfast this morning, I got a call about an accident out on Tully Road. The body of a young man was found lying on the side of the road, not far from a black Firebird. I didn't know it was Ben Lewis until I got to the scene. We'll have to wait for the autopsy before we determine an exact cause of death, but all preliminary reports indicate Ben was the victim of a hit-and-run."

Jamie clutched the blankets tighter. Even though he was still dressed in his sweater and jeans — not to mention being under a mound of covers — he felt chilled to the marrow. "He was murdered?"

Brandon shook his head. "It's a crime to hit someone and leave the scene of an accident, but that doesn't mean it was a homicide."

Jamie hoped his blank look conveyed his lack of understanding.

Nate stepped in. "What he means, James, is that Ben's death was probably unintentional. There are at least four bars out on Tully Road. More than likely, the person responsible was drunk, didn't see Ben standing there, and then panicked when he hit him."

"Why would Ben be out of his car in the first place?"

"The front tire on the driver's side of Ben's car was flat. Since his car was pointing back in the direction of the Reed City limits, he'd have been facing traffic while trying to change it." Brandon leaned his arms on the back of his chair, resting his chin on his forearm. "We found a disassembled jack and a tire iron not far from the body. Most likely, he'd just gotten them out of the trunk and was headed to the front of the car when he was hit."

Jamie wasn't sure what to say. He appreciated the sheriff's honesty and was glad to know what had happened, but that didn't do anything to ease the feeling of loss. If anything, knowing Ben's death was probably the act of some drunken asshole made it worse. His death was meaningless, just one more statistic in an endless tally.

Nate cleared his throat. "Do you have any questions, James?"

"Just one. Did he..." His voice cracked. "Did he suffer?"

Brandon shook his head. "I can't say for sure, not until the report comes back, but I honestly don't think so. Judging by his injuries, I'd say death came quick, if not instantly."

Jamie went back to picking fuzz balls from the blankets. "Thanks." He took a deep breath. "If you don't mind, I think I'd like to be alone now."

Nate stood, and Brandon did too. "We understand. I'll make sure your aunt has all our numbers, just in case you need us. You can call anytime, for any reason."

Jamie nodded and lay back down, burrowing beneath the covers again, his eyes already closing. Brandon gave him an awkward pat on the shoulder before leaving; Jamie barely felt it. Sinking back into the merciful darkness, he was asleep before they even left the room.

How long he slept, Jamie had no idea, but the first face he saw when he woke up was Dillon's. He was sitting in the bedside chair, doing his homework. The minute Jamie stirred, Dillon was at his side, his books and papers scattering across the floor in his haste.

His green eyes sparkled in the dim light of Jamie's bedside lamp. "Hey, you're awake."

"Yeah. What time is it?"

Dillon checked his watch. "Eight thirty."

Jamie sat up, wiping the sleep from his eyes. "I thought you had to work tonight."

Dillon eased down on the bed beside him, tucking one leg up under himself. "I told my boss I wouldn't be in."

"Why?"

Dillon shrugged "I thought you might need me, and I wanted to be here in case you did."

For the first time since waking, Jamie got a good look at Dillon. His hair was mussed and his eyes were bleary. He looked tired and worried. For some reason that angered Jamie.

So Dillon was worried. So what? Jamie had just lost his best friend, the one person who was there for him when his life fell apart. No, when Dillon *ripped* it apart. Two years of pain and an afternoon's worth of grief mingled and came spewing to the surface.

"You thought I might need you?" Jamie's sudden outburst startled Dillon so much he jumped off the bed as if he'd been stung, but Jamie didn't care. "I needed you two years ago. Where were you then?" He whipped off the covers and stood, thankful he had gone to bed fully clothed instead of stripping to his boxers as usual. "When you fucked

me over and tossed me away, Ben was there for me. You think now that
he's gone you can just slide in and take his place?"

"No, that's not what I think." Dillon took a step back. "I told you, I
want us to be friends again."

"Uh huh." Jamie kept advancing. "Like we were friends two years
ago? What's the saying? Friends with benefits?"

Dillon swallowed. "I've lived with the guilt and shame of what I
did to you until it feels like I've never been without it. There's nothing
you can say to me or about me that I haven't said to myself."

"Oh, yeah?" Jamie was practically in Dillon's face. "Well, here's
something you've never heard me say before. Get out. Get out of my
house and out of my life."

Dillon spoke softly but his voice was strong. "You don't mean
that."

"The hell I don't." By now, Jamie was yelling. "You threw me away
two years ago and now it's my turn. My turn to make you feel like
you're bleeding inside, deep down where nobody can fix it." The tears
came, damn them, but he blinked them away. He had to finish it, had
to wound Dillon the way he'd been wounded. "I hate you, more than
I've ever hated anybody. Ben was my best friend. You can never take
his place." As soon as the words were out of his mouth, the tears began
to fall in earnest and Jamie's knees gave way beneath him.

Two strong arms caught him before he hit the floor. Dillon cradled
him to his chest as Jamie sobbed through the pain and misery. It
seemed like hours before Jamie was cried out and Dillon helped him
back to bed. Covering him up, Dillon sat down beside him and pushed
the hair back from Jamie's forehead.

Jamie shuddered and Dillon adjusted the covers. "You warm
enough?"

"Yeah."

Using one corner of the blanket, Dillon wiped Jamie's eyes and
cheeks. Jamie felt like he should say something, but he wasn't sure
what. "Dillon—"

"Don't try to talk right now. Just rest."

He shouldn't have been tired, but he was. Still, as crazy as it
seemed after the way he ordered Dillon out of his house a few minutes
earlier, there was one fear Jamie had to put to rest before he could go
to sleep again. "You won't leave, will you?"

"I think it's a safe bet you aren't gonna get rid of me anytime
soon."

Jamie closed his eyes. "Dillon?"

"Yeah?"

"I don't hate you."

Dillon ran his fingers through Jamie's hair, brushing against his
scalp and making Jamie tingle down to his toes. "I'm glad. Now rest. I

promise I'm not going anywhere. I'll be right over there in the chair when you wake up."

Jamie nodded, exhaustion and the warm comfort of Dillon's presence lulling him to sleep.

Dillon woke with a start. It took him a minute to remember where he was. *James's house. I must've fallen asleep in the chair.* He glanced down at his watch. *Eleven o'clock. Damn. I am so dead.*

James was still sleeping, the rise and fall of his chest visible even through the bulky blankets. Dillon allowed himself only a minute to enjoy the sight before reaching into his pocket and retrieving his cell phone. Dillon punched in the number, watching the whole time to make certain he wasn't disturbing James. Other than the occasional muffled snore, James didn't make a sound.

His mother picked up on the first ring. "Hello?"

"Hey, Mom. It's me."

"Where in God's name are you? Do you have any idea what time it is? You were supposed to be home two hours ago."

"Yes, ma'am. I know that, but something came up."

"You'd better have a life or death reason for staying out this late on a school night, young man."

"Ben Lewis's body was found today. I'm sure you heard about it at school."

"Yes, I did. Most unfortunate but not surprising, considering the lifestyle he chose. Those people usually come to a bad end."

Dillon was a heartbeat away from telling her that he was one of *those people*, but he stopped short. Tonight was about James. There'd be time enough for true confessions later. "Regardless of whether or not he was gay, the guy's dead, Mom."

"As I said, it's unfortunate, but I don't see what Ben's death has to do with you. You hated each other. I talked to Principal Morgan today. He said the only reason he didn't expel the both of you for that fight Friday night is because Sheriff Nash hauled you downtown. He assumed that was punishment enough. You're both lucky."

Dillon loved his mother — he really did — but sometimes she could be so dense it set his teeth on edge. "I'm sure Ben will really appreciate not being expelled now that he's dead, Mom. Must be a huge load off his mind."

"Your sarcasm is not appreciated." Angela's voice took on the acid tone that Dillon so hated. "You have yet to tell me what Ben Lewis's death has to do with the reason you didn't come home."

Dillon knew his next words would be the beginning of the end, but he wasn't backing down. "James Walker was Ben's best friend. He was devastated by what happened. I brought him home, and that's where I am now."

"I thought your father and I made it clear we don't approve of your association with that boy."

"*That boy* was the best friend I ever had. If I'm lucky, he will be again." *That and a thousand things more.*

"I'm not sure what's gotten into you tonight but we'll discuss this when you get home. I expect you here in the next fifteen minutes."

"No."

"I beg your pardon?"

Dillon was shaking but he kept his voice steady. "I'm not coming home tonight, Mom. I promised James I wouldn't leave him, and I'm not going to."

"I don't recall giving you a choice."

The ice in his mother's voice made Dillon feel ill. He was already in it up to his eyeballs. *Might as well finish myself off.* "You may not have given me a choice, Mom, but I made one just the same."

"So I see. Your father and I are going to discuss this, Dillon. I expect you home tomorrow when I get in. Principal Morgan has called a teachers meeting after school, but it shouldn't take more than an hour. I'll ask your father to come home early so the three of us can have a long talk about your attitude."

"Yes, ma'am."

His mother hung up without saying goodbye but Dillon didn't care. It wasn't like she was going to be talking to him for much longer anyway.

A soft voice broke him out of his revere. "I got you into a world of shit with your folks, huh?"

Dillon looked down into James's face. In the muted light of the lamp, James looked so achingly perfect that Dillon had to fight with himself not to lean down and kiss him. Instead he said, "You big faker. How long have you been awake?"

"Long enough to know your mother is mad as hell."

"What else is new?"

James sat up. "I hate being the one to cause problems between you and your family."

"It's not your fault they're bigots. I think it's poetic justice that two of the biggest homophobes in Reed got stuck with a gay son. Talk about a karmic bite in the ass."

James laughed, the first time Dillon had heard that sound since lunch. "I never thought about it like that."

Dillon slouched down so he could see James's face. "How are you feeling?"

"I'm not sure how to feel right now."

"I guess that's normal. Probably take a few days to sink in."

"Yeah." He lowered his eyes. "I'm sorry for all that stuff I said to you. I didn't mean it."

Dillon tugged at the hair at the nape of James's neck, gently urging his head up. "I had it coming, but I'm glad to know you don't hate me."

Before James could reply, the door opened. Sadie stood in the doorway, wearing pink pajamas and a long, fuzzy white robe. She hid a grin as the two of them scrambled to opposite sides of the bed. "You're awake. Thank heavens. I came in here earlier to check on you, but you were both sound asleep. Are you feeling better, Jamie?"

"A little. Dr. Nash said grieving is a process." He looked at Dillon from the corner of his eye. "Dillon helped me through the worst of it, I think."

"I'm glad to hear that." She gave Dillon a knowing smile. "I assume you're spending the night?"

It was Dillon's turn to blush. "Yes, ma'am. That is, if it's all right."

"Of course. I've got the guest room all ready for you."

"Thank you."

Sadie left and Dillon was about to follow her out when James said, "Dillon?"

"Yeah?"

"Sleep well."

Dillon smiled down at him. "You, too. See you in the morning."

James nodded. "See you then."

As Dillon made his way to the guest room, he thought about the looming confrontation with his parents. He was surprised to realize not even his own impending doom could quash the joy he felt knowing he would see James first thing in the morning. He only hoped James would be as glad to see him.

Dillon parked his car in the usual space. Killing the engine, he turned to James. "You sure you want to do this? Your aunt said she'd write you an excuse so you could stay home today."

James zipped his coat and donned his gloves. "So I can sit at home all day and think about Ben? I'm better off here. At least I'll have something to take my mind off it."

Dillon reached over and squeezed his hand. "Okay, then. Meet me back here for lunch?"

"How about meeting me at the lockers, instead? It's too damn cold out here."

Dillon laughed as he got out of the car. "I'll see you then."

If days went any slower, Dillon had never seen one. The school day started with a thirty minute period of mourning for Ben Lewis led by none other than Dan Morgan himself. The auditorium was filled to capacity with crying girls — most of whom had no idea who Ben Lewis even was — and a passel of laughing jocks who saw this as a prime opportunity to perfect the fine art of the spitball. Dillon did his best to catch a glimpse of James, but the throng of pseudo-grievers made it impossible. Megan sat beside him through most of the assembly, rolling her eyes every time Morgan started in about the "brevity of life" and the "utmost importance of living each day to its fullest". At least Dillon managed to avoid his mother. Time enough for his execution after school.

The classes after the assembly were filled with talk about Ben from people who wouldn't have spit on him had his guts been on fire. Not while he was alive, anyway. Seemed that sudden death made a guy popular.

When the fourth period bell rang, Dillon was ready. He had vivid fantasies of kidnapping James and keeping him for the rest of the day, the two of them shutting out the whole world. Unfortunately, Ashton Barnes and Chad Minton got in the way.

They were waiting for Dillon at his locker. Ash and Chad made quite a contrast. Ash was tall and slender, whereas Chad was short and stocky. Ash's hair was a rich black, cut short and shot through with auburn lights that made his brown eyes seem even darker. Chad was a blue-eyed blond with a buzz cut. Ash was old money, and Chad was no money. Even so, Dillon could count on three fingers the times he'd seen one without the other.

Dillon eyed them both as he opened his locker. "What's up?" It wasn't until after he said it that Dillon noticed how angry Ash looked.

He stood with his fists balled, his feet braced, and his spine rigid. "I heard some rumors about you, Carver. I was hoping you might clear them up for me."

Dillon threw his books inside and slammed the locker door. From the corner of his eye, he saw Megan and several others gathering in the hall. *Oh great. An audience.* He rested one shoulder against the metal door, keeping his voice calm and his posture relaxed. "Rumors, huh?"

"That's right. Word has it you spent the night at James Walker's house last night. Since those are the same clothes you had on yesterday, I'm guessing it's true."

Ash was doing all the talking but Chad stood beside him, bobbing his head in agreement. He reminded Dillon of those flocked plastic dogs people put on the dashes of their cars.

As calmly as if he were discussing the cafeteria's mystery meat special, Dillon said, "I'd be glad to clear that little rumor up for you, Barnes, but seeing as how it's none of your business, I don't think I will."

Ash stepped closer. "I'm making it my business. Word's out you and Ben Lewis were fighting over James at the dance. I also heard you had lunch with James yesterday."

Dillon crossed his arms over his chest. "I wasn't aware having lunch with a friend is a crime."

Ash wasn't giving up. "The way I hear it, you and Walker are a lot more than friends. What's up, Carver? You fagging out on us?"

Ash was the one who'd called him about a possible gay bashing at the dance. What was with the homophobic jock routine? *To hell with him. I'm not going to play his little games.* In as clear a voice as he could muster, he said, "No, Barnes, I'm not fagging out on you."

He heard a noise behind him and turned to see James, his face pale and stricken. Dillon had been about to clarify his last statement, but James didn't know that. He thought Dillon was going to deny him again. The spark of anger Dillon had seen in James's eyes last night was now a blazing inferno.

James threw his books on the floor and faced Dillon, not caring that half the school was watching him.

"So much for coming out, huh, Dillon? Tell me something. Exactly when weren't you 'fagging out'? Were you just a straight boy in disguise all those times you fucked me?"

This is it. The whole city of Reed could watch for all he cared, but Dillon was going to show James how he felt about him once and for all. "I never fucked you." James started to argue, but Dillon put up his hand. "You've had your say; it's my turn now." He turned his back on Barnes and all the rest, using his body to urge James backwards until he was up against the lockers. Putting one hand on each side of James's head so he couldn't get away, Dillon spoke, his voice loud enough for everyone within twenty feet to hear.

"What I was about to say when you walked up was that I wasn't 'fagging out' because that implies I just woke up one morning and became gay. How can I 'fag out' when I've known I was gay for over six years?"

The gasps and whispers following his announcement reminded Dillon of something out of a cheesy movie. If they thought that was a shocker, the student body of Plunkett High hadn't seen anything yet.

"I stand by what I said — I never fucked you." James opened his mouth to protest, but again Dillon cut him off. "I was a selfish bastard. I used you without ever giving you anything back, and for that I'm more sorry than you'll ever know. Even as lowdown and rotten as I was, though, I never once fucked you. Every time I took you, it was making love." Without giving James a chance to respond, Dillon lowered his head and covered James's mouth with his own.

Chapter Five

At first, Jamie was too startled to respond as Dillon's mouth came down on his, but it wasn't long before Jamie was kissing him back, audience be damned. Just when he thought he'd go mad from the pleasure of it, Dillon pulled away.

Straightening, Dillon turned back to Ash. "Does that answer your question, Barnes, or do you have some more for me?"

Ash was shocked, but quick recovery was one of the things that made him such a hot commodity on the football field. He redirected his anger at Jamie. "God, Walker, Ben's body isn't even cold yet and you've already moved on. So much for true love, I guess."

"What would you know about it? You barely even knew Ben. If you and those dickwads you call friends ever spoke to him it was to tell him to fuck off or to call him a queer or a fag. Where do you get off telling me what I'm supposed to feel?"

Chad stepped up. "Who you calling a dickwad, Walker?"

He wasn't any taller than Jamie, but he outweighed him by a good sixty pounds. Not that Jamie cared. He could take him. "You, no-neck. I've seen you and Rooster Carmichael hassling Ben more than once."

Chad took a step forward but Dillon's next words stopped him cold. "Touch him and you're a dead man."

Ash was on that in a second. "Did you make the same kind of threats to Ben? What did you do, warn him off Walker and then run him down with your car when he refused to back away?"

He knows how Ben died? Sheriff Nash said that information hadn't been released to the public yet. Jamie stared him down. "How did you know Ben was hit by a car?"

Ash shrugged. "Everybody knows. It's all over town."

Chad came to stand behind Ash. "You trying to say Ash had something to do with Lewis's death? You're the one who's cheating on his dead boyfriend."

"Not that it's any of your damned business, but Ben wasn't my boyfriend."

Ash snorted. "Yeah, right. That's why he was licking your tonsils Friday night."

He might have said more, but the sharp sounding of footsteps coming down the hall cut him off. Principal Morgan took one look at the four of them, squared off in the center of a mass of onlookers, and said, "What's going on here?"

Ash spoke first. "Nothing, sir. We were just...talking."

Principal Morgan lifted one perfectly shaped eyebrow and put his hand on his Armani clad hip. "Looks more like you were setting up for a sparring match to me. James, were these boys bothering you?"

"No, sir. Like he said, we were just talking."

Principal Morgan made no secret of his disbelief, but he must have decided to let it slide, because he said, "Fine." He addressed the group as a whole. "All of you, show's over. Get to class." He waited until all of the onlookers — including Chad and Ash — left before turning back to Dillon and Jamie. "You want to tell me what really happened? Off the record, I swear."

Jamie shook his head. "It was nothing, Mr. Morgan, I promise."

"If that's what you tell me, than that's what I'll go with, but just remember, if you ever need to talk, you know where to find me." He waited until Jamie nodded and then made his exit.

As soon as Principal Morgan left, Megan came charging back from her hiding place on the opposite side of the double doors leading to the main hall. She was out of breath and her face was flushed.

"I thought Ash's eyes were gonna pop out of his skull over that kiss."

"Barnes isn't usually such an ass, but I'm glad he at least knows know where I stand." Dillon reopened his locker and took out his coat while Jamie picked his books off the floor. "Listen, James...I know I promised you lunch, but I've got something I need to take care of."

Megan spoke before Jamie had a chance. Her tone was light, but he could hear a slight quivering in her voice. "Don't worry about James. I'll take him home this afternoon."

Home. That's when it hit Jamie. When Dillon's mother heard about that kiss — and she would, probably any minute now — Dillon would be thrown out of his own home. Dillon hadn't just proved his feelings to Ash and Chad; he'd outed himself to the whole world.

Jamie wasn't sure what to say. "Dillon, I...I'm so, so sorry."

Dillon came to stand in front of him. "None of this is your fault. I'm just going home to pack up so I'll be ready to leave by the time they get there. My dad will bitch and moan, but that's about it. I'll be fine. You'll see."

"Where will you go. What—"

"Shh. I told you I'll be fine."

"At least let me go with you. I can help."

Dillon shook his head. "I appreciate the offer, more than you know, but this is something I have to do by myself." He gave Jamie another quick kiss and then took off.

Jamie was devastated. He sank back against the lockers and was doing a slow slide to the floor when Megan grabbed his arm and hauled him back up.

"Oh no, you don't. First rule of a crisis is 'deal with it, now, fall apart later'. And this is a crisis if ever I saw one."

Jamie nodded. Dillon needed him too much for him to wuss out now. "I'm hoping you have a plan."

Megan patted his cheek. "One thing you'll learn, James — I always have a plan."

Dillon pulled into the driveway. It was amazing the things he noticed now that he was going home for the last time: the missing slat in the swing hanging from the porch; the tree he'd planted for Arbor Day when he was in the fifth grade. As he unlocked the front door and went inside, the creaking of the hinges his father was always after him to oil, coupled with the smell — that smell that was unique to every home — hit him hard. He was about to lose the only home he'd ever known.

It hurt, but he honestly believed living his life out in the open — free to be the man he was supposed to be — would be compensation enough. Pastor Oakley once preached about that verse from the Bible, *What does it profit a man to gain the whole world and lose his own soul?* At the time, Dillon hadn't understood, but now he thought he did, only in reverse. He was about to lose everything — the whole world as he knew it — but it didn't matter. He was getting his soul back. As long as he could finally live life on his terms, Dillon could do this.

The actual packing didn't take long. He'd stopped at a fast food place on the way home and gotten some boxes. He emptied drawers, closets, and shelves, not lost to the irony that all his worldly possessions fit into six large boxes labeled *Happy Time Burger Palace. The Place Where Happy Smiles Stretch A Mile.*

When he was sure he had everything he wanted to keep, Dillon loaded up his car. It took some doing, but he was able to cram it all in there. Thank goodness he wasn't a packrat like his brother. It had taken a rented van to get Heath moved out. Funny, all it took to get Dillon out of the house was one kiss and six boxes.

When he was finished, Dillon moved his car from the driveway to the street and locked it, just in case his dad tried to block him in or stop him from leaving. Not that he would. Dillon was pretty sure Doug Carver would be all too happy to shed himself of his "deviant" son. That done, Dillon went back in and sat down on the couch to wait.

At four thirty, he heard his mother's car come tearing into the drive. She must have phoned his father from school, because Dillon heard his dad's Jeep pull in right behind her. *Time to face the firing squad.*

Angela came in first. Her hair was a mess and Dillon could tell she'd been crying. He might have felt guilty, if not for the first words out of her mouth. "Thank God you're here. I heard how that Walker boy attacked you in the hallway. We'll see him prosecuted for molesting you like that."

Doug slammed the door behind himself and motioned for Dillon to stand. "Get your coat. We're going down to the police station right now and press charges. We're talking to the city cops, too. No use in trying to get help from that pansy sheriff. Nash won't be willing to bust Walker for forcing himself on you, but I intend to find someone who will."

Dillon stood. "You've got it backwards. I'm the one who kissed James, not the other way around."

"Nonsense. Get your coat right this minute, and your mother and I may be willing to forgive you for your insolence last night."

"It's not a lie. I kissed James. I can get any number of people to back up my story. How do you think Mom heard about it? Dozens of witnesses saw me back him up against the lockers and stick my tongue down his throat."

"Stop it." His father's face turned a mottled red as he tugged at his shirt and tie. "I will not have you talking that kind of filth in my house."

His mother grabbed the phone book from a side table drawer. Flipping through, she said, "James Walker is to blame for this. We need to cancel out his influence. A friend of mine told me about a doctor whose specialty is deprogramming kids who've been brainwashed."

Brainwashed? Good God. "I don't need to be deprogrammed. I'm gay, not a cult member."

His father snorted. "Same difference."

Dillon could feel himself starting to lose control. "I kissed James because I wanted to. I've been wanting to for years."

His father took his coat off, slapping it down on the coffee table. "I'm not about to stand here and listen to my son talk about being a no good...a worthless..."

"What's the matter, Dad? Can't find the word? Just pick something from your regular list. What'll it be? Poof? Queer? Sodomite? I don't think there's a slur I haven't heard you use."

His father was so angry his eyes were bulging, but his mother wasn't ready to give up her theory that her son had been coerced. "Dillon...these feelings you're having aren't real. This is James Walker's fault, all of it. He has you in thrall, darling."

Listening to his parents talk about James like some evil guru was taking its toll. Dillon shoved his fingers through his hair. "You insist James turned me gay. What would you call that? Metamorphosis? Nah, too much like a butterfly, and those are too beautiful to be compared to us ugly ol' sinners. How about 'the change'?"

His father's voice cut in like solid steel. "Stop it."

Dillon was beyond listening. "You're right. The change sounds too much like a female thing. We homos may be girlie boys, but not quite that girlie, huh, Dad? I've got it. How about *gayification?* As in, 'James is responsible for my *gayification.*' Wonder if they make an antidote for that? You know, a spray that kills all those gay germs. Something like *Gay be Gone* or *Gay Away.*"

His father took a menacing step toward him. "I won't tell you again. Shut up."

"You shut up. Shut up with all the excuses you keep throwing out so you won't have to face the truth. I'm gay, Dad. I'm a fag. A great big one. God willing, I'll marry James and we'll settle down to raise lots of little faglets together."

"Dammit, I said that's enough." His father raised his hand and was about to strike when a voice at the door said, "Go ahead, Carver. I'd love a chance to lock your ass up for assault."

All heads turned to see Brandon Nash standing in the doorway, Megan and James behind him. Brandon unclipped a pair of cuffs from his belt. "Go ahead, Dougie. We're waiting."

If there was one thing Dillon's father hated more than gays, it was being called "Dougie". But even as filled with rage as he was, he wasn't stupid enough to go after Brandon. Instead, he looked down at Dillon. "Get out of my house. You're not welcome here anymore."

Dillon ignored his mother's crying. Grabbing his jacket, he started for the door. He'd almost made it when his father's voice called out, "Dillon?"

"Yes, sir?" He almost choked on the ingrained bit of respect.

If his father felt anything for Dillon besides disgust, he didn't show it. "Give me back your house key. If and when you come to your senses and ask for forgiveness for this path to Hell you've chosen, you can come back. Until then, if you step one foot onto this property, I'll have you arrested for trespassing." He turned back to Brandon. "Did you get that?"

Brandon gave him a two fingered salute. "I hear you loud and clear, Dougie, and I'm sure Dillon did, too. The braying of a jackass is hard to miss."

Dillon's father was apoplectic, but Dillon refused to look at him. He pulled the house key from his key ring and placed it on the coffee table. Without a second glance toward either of the two people who'd brought him into the world, Dillon left.

Outside, the frigid evening air helped clear his head. As soon as they were off the driveway and onto the public street, James hugged Dillon tight. "Thank God, you're okay. I was worried sick."

Dillon relaxed into the embrace for a full minute before pulling away. "I'm fine. I told you I would be." He glanced over at Brandon. "I owe you, man. Thanks." He grinned next at Megan. "I have a feeling you're behind all this."

"Yeah, she is," Brandon said, "and that's a bone I've got to pick with you, kid. I told you to call me anytime you needed me. Why, then, do I have to hear that you're in a boat load of trouble from my baby sister and not from you?"

"Sorry. I thought I could handle it."

"Well, next time, you call. That's what family is for."

Dillon raised one eyebrow. "Family?"

Brandon shrugged. "If being the fake boyfriend of my baby sister for almost five months doesn't make us related, what does? From now on, you need me, you call."

"Yes, sir."

"Good. Now, did you get all your stuff from the house?"

Dillon nodded. "It's all in my car."

"I want you to stay with Nate and me over at our place." Dillon started to speak, but Brandon said, "No arguments, either. I called Nate at the hospital and he's all for it. You can—"

The sound of a truck coming up the street stopped the conversation. Dillon almost did a double take when he recognized the vehicle.

Heath parked behind Dillon's Lumina and got out. "Nice night for a family reunion, huh?"

Dillon could almost feel his parents peering out through the picture window in the living room, trying to see into the rapidly falling dusk. He ignored the prickling of the hairs on the back of his neck and gave his full attention to his brother. "Heath, what are you doing here?"

"Someone," Heath flashed Megan a brief grin, "called to tell me that you might be in some kind of trouble. Why didn't you call me?"

"The kid seems to have a problem with the whole asking for help thing." Brandon shook Heath's hand. "If Megan hadn't called me when she did, your dad would probably be kicking your brother's ass right about now."

Heath winced. "Guess the kiss that rocked Plunkett High didn't go over too well with Ma and Pa Carver, huh?"

Dillon sighed. "Let's just say Mom and Dad now have one son, and it ain't me."

Heath's grin was pure mischief. "In that case, they won't have any offspring left when they find out you're living with me."

Dillon thought maybe his ears needed cleaning. "With you?"

"Yep." Heath glanced back at Brandon. "Megan told me you were going to ask squirt, here, to come stay with you and the doc, but you guys are still newlyweds. The last thing you need is some snot-nosed kid hanging around." When Brandon started to protest, Heath said,

"Besides, I moved out because I couldn't stand living under ol' Adolf Carver's roof." His eyes softened as they focused on his little brother. "The only thing I regret about breaking free is the time I missed out on with Dillon." The lightness came back into his voice. "This'll give us a chance to catch up."

Brandon nodded. "I can understand that, but do you have enough room at your place?"

"It's a one-bedroom apartment, but I have a fold-out couch."

Brandon started to speak again but Dillon stepped in. "It's just until I find my own place. Like I told you before, I've been expecting this to happen and I'm prepared."

"Look, Dillon, there's no need to find a place of your own. Nate and I would be glad to have you for as long as you want to stay. Besides, you'll need all the money you can save up for when you start Garman in the fall." Brandon seemed to realize almost as soon as he'd said it what a slip-up he'd made. "Damn. I didn't mean to say that."

James gave Dillon a long, searching look. Dillon could feel all the color draining from his face. James must think he was some kind of stalker or something.

"You're going to Garman? In New York?"

"Uh...yeah. I got my letter the other day."

"Either you already knew that I'm going to Garman, or this is one heck of a coincidence."

Dillon felt more in knots now than he had fifteen minutes ago when his dad almost hit him. He cleared his throat. "I knew." When James didn't say anything, Dillon rushed out, "I knew, and I put in for Garman so the two of us could be in the same place, but I swear I'm not stalking you or anything."

If James was upset, he didn't show it. "Pity. I was looking forward to an obscene phone call every now and then. How are you at heavy breathing?"

Dillon's breath rushed out of his lungs in a gust of relief. "You're not mad?"

James took his hand. "I'm not mad."

Brandon sighed. "Thank God. I thought sure I'd screwed things up with my big mouth." He smiled. "I understand why you want to move in with your brother, but I want you know the offer to stay with us is always open." His smile widened. "Nate will be so disappointed. He was looking forward to the pitter patter of little feet."

It was just after nine by the time Jamie made it home. Moving Dillon into the pigsty Heath called an apartment had been an experience. Megan's comment that she knew self-respecting gutter rats who wouldn't live in that place had been dead on. Jamie hoped Dillon was up to date on all his shots.

He found Aunt Sadie in the kitchen, still dressed in her day clothes and nursing a cup of hot chocolate. She motioned for him to sit down.

"I have to hand it to you, Jamie. When you decide to cause a scene, you certainly do it up right."

Jamie sank into the chair. "What happened?"

Sadie took a long sip of her drink. "The phone has been ringing nonstop since I got home. Must have been some kiss."

Damn. "Aunt Sadie...I can explain."

Sadie placed her cup back on its china saucer. "There's no need. What you and Dillon do is your own business. I told Douglas Carver as much when he called, raving about how you'd corrupted his son. Don't worry. I set him straight."

Don't doubt that a bit. "What did you say to him?"

Sadie did her best to look the perfect picture of old fashioned gentility, but Jamie wasn't buying it for a second. She shrugged. "Nothing much. I mentioned I'd read somewhere that homosexual tendencies are usually passed down from father to son."

God, I love this woman. "You heard no such thing."

"No, but Douglas Carver doesn't know that. I wouldn't be surprised if he's going through his family tree even as we speak, trying to find the gay branches. Knowing I got his goat made all the other phone calls bearable."

Jamie sighed. "Who else called?"

"Nathan Nash phoned to tell me Douglas threw Dillon out of the house. If I were a man — and about twenty years younger — I'd give Dillon's father the worst beating of his miserable life."

"If you were twenty years younger, you'd do it man or not."

"Good point. Where's Dillon staying, by the way?"

"With his brother."

"Good. Let Douglas and Angela choke on that for a while." She got up to take her empty cup to the sink. "Did you want some cocoa, dear?"

"No, ma'am. Were those all the phone calls?"

Sadie drizzled dish soap into her cup and swished it around while she thought. "Someone called and left his number for you. I believe his name was Anton or Alton. Something like that."

"Ashton?"

Sadie twisted the knob and opened the faucet. "That's it. Ashton."

Jamie wasn't ready to deal with Ash. Not again. "I'll talk to him later." Much later, if he had his way.

"Well, his number's on the notebook by the den phone if you change your mind. Oh, and before I forget, Nora Slater called."

Jamie's heart sank. *Poor Nora.* She must be devastated, and he hadn't even thought to call her. He didn't realize he'd said it out loud until Aunt Sadie came back to the table and squeezed his shoulder.

"Nora has buried two husbands. She, of all people, understands about grief. She called to see how you were, and she also said she'd like to talk to you as soon as possible."

"Should I call her tonight?"

"No. She sounded worn through. It might be best to wait until after the arrangements are made. Hopefully, the inquest will be completed soon." She was about to say more when the phone rang. Sadie snorted. "I should have taken that blasted thing off the hook and been done with it."

"I'll get it. You've fielded enough calls today." He crossed the room and lifted the receiver. "Hello?"

"James? It's Nate."

"Hey, Doc? What's up?"

Nate hesitated. "First, tell me how you're feeling."

"Still hurts like hell, but I guess that's normal."

"It is. Just let me know if it gets to be more than you can handle."

"I will. Is that why you called, to check on me? Not that I don't appreciate it, because I do."

"I know. I'm glad you're out of the worst of it, but I'd be lying if I said that's the only reason I called."

Jamie was afraid to ask but the words came out anyway. "What is it?"

"Brandon wanted me to call you and let you know what's going on with the investigation. He'd have called himself but he's down at the station, wrapping up some loose ends. He's made an arrest, James. He's found the man who hit Ben."

Chapter Six

Jamie sat in the sheriff's office with Dillon, waiting as patiently as he could manage while Brandon chugged down his coffee. When he realized they were both watching him, Brandon looked up with an apologetic grin.

"Sorry about that. I was up all night trying to wrap up this case." He took another sip. "I'm sorry to call you both down here so damned early, but I wanted you to hear this from me before I make a statement to the press. Hell, for all I know, Dan Morgan will beat me to the punch and make another one of his infamous announcements."

Jamie cringed, remembering all too well Morgan's last nasty surprise. "Did you ever figure out how he knew about Ben?"

Brandon made a face. "Claims he heard it through the student grapevine. After ever so politely telling him I think he's full of shit, I had a nice long chat with Morgan about what will happen the next time he leaks information about an ongoing investigation."

Dillon grinned. "Translated: you ripped him a new one."

"Let's just say I'll take great joy in locking his ass up for obstruction if he does it again." Brandon sighed. "Guys like Morgan think they know everything and can't wait to share said knowledge with the rest of the world. That's why I wanted you to hear this from me first."

Jamie's body went rigid. He felt Dillon take his hand, but as comforting as that was, Jamie didn't even look at him. All his attention was focused on the sheriff and what he was about to say.

Brandon got straight to the point. "As soon as we found Ben's body, I contacted every auto repair shop within a three hundred mile radius, asking them to get in touch with me if anyone came in with extensive front-end damage. Yesterday evening, I got a call from a shop over in Naperville, a place called Clyde's Customs. Clyde Shire, the owner, said a guy popped in first thing Monday morning with a story that didn't quite add up. The man was driving a Ford Taurus, and claimed he'd hit a dog. The minute Clyde saw the amount of damage to the guy's grill, bumper, and undercarriage, he felt sure the man was hiding something, but he had no idea what. Clyde might have dismissed his suspicions altogether if it hadn't been for the man's behavior. He was nervous, kept insisting the work be started that day. When Clyde told him it would be a week before he could even get the parts, the guy freaked out and took off. That's when Clyde called me and gave me the Taurus's tag number." He paused long enough to take another swig of his coffee before looking to Jamie again. "Before I tell you the rest of it, you need to know that this investigation is far from closed, so I can only give you the details we'll be releasing to the press this afternoon. The D.A. has given me permission to give Ben's friends and family an advance warning. I've spoken with Nora already, so now it's your turn, as unpleasant as this is."

Jamie swallowed. "I understand, and I'm grateful for the heads up."

"Some of this will be hard to take, so if at any time you want me to stop, just say so." Brandon killed the rest of the coffee and set his cup aside. "My men traced the tag number to a woman named Marcy Sledge."

Jamie wondered if he looked as confused as he felt. "I thought you said a man brought the car into Mr. Shire's shop?"

"I did. Marcy Sledge is the registered owner of the car, but there's no way she was driving it."

"How do you know?"

"Mainly because she's been dead for seven months. We at the Reed County Sheriff's Department frown on deceased persons operating motor vehicles. They tend to veer to the left." Brandon reached for the top file on a stack of about twenty situated on the right side of his desk. "Marcy Sledge is resting in peace, but her son happens to be alive and well." He removed a picture from the file and handed it to Jamie. "Meet Barry Sledge, age forty seven."

Jamie's hand shook as he took the picture. "He's the one who—"

Brandon's eyes filled with sympathy. "Yes. There's not a doubt in my mind he's the one who hit Ben."

Jamie searched every inch of the ordinary face in the mugshot: the slightly crooked nose, the brown eyes, the graying hair. It was plain from his deep wrinkles and scars that Barry Sledge was no stranger to hard living, but nothing in the photo indicated the man was a killer. There was nothing sinister about him. That angered Jamie. This guy was responsible for taking Ben's life. How dare he look so normal?

Brandon leaned over and took the picture from Jamie's hand. "I know that look, James, and I know what you're feeling."

Jamie doubted it. "You think so?"

"Yeah, I do. You were expecting the man to be some kind of monster, maybe have red eyes or a set of horns. How could a normal, average Joe like Barry be responsible for taking Ben's life? You're thinking there must have been some kind of mistake."

Okay, so he does know. "Yeah. It doesn't fit."

Brandon put the picture back in the file. "Let me tell you something, kid: between my time with the F.B.I. and my stint here, I've been a cop for almost nine years. I've arrested more people than I can count, and I haven't seen a perp yet who fits the monster description.

Oh, I've arrested some truly evil bastards, but not a one of them looked the part." He set the file back on top of the stack and leaned forward, his hands clasped in front of him. "Barry Sledge is your classic town drunk: three D.U.I. convictions, six arrests for public intoxication, two mandatory commitments to a state funded rehabilitation center, and a five-year suspension of his driver's license. The guy's a walking statistic."

And now Ben is a statistic, too. A dead one. Jamie shook himself, trying to free his mind of the grief and anguish, but it didn't help. Ben's death was meaningless, and there was nothing he could do about it.

Brandon spoke again. "If you're not ready to hear the rest, it can wait."

"I need to get it over with." Jamie felt Dillon squeeze his hand.

"As soon as I ran the plates and found out Marcy Sledge was dead, I looked to her next of kin. That's how I found out about Barry. I showed his mugshot to Clyde Shire, who made a positive I.D. The actual arrest was textbook. Sledge was still living in his mother's house, so we didn't even have to hunt him down. We found the Ford behind an old shed in the back yard. Good old Barry was in the house, drunk off his ass. We impounded the car, hauled Sledge down to the station, and waited for him to sober up. The minute his head cleared, he was ready to cut a deal. He gave a full confession, and we have several witnesses who saw him tossing back tequila shots in a bar not far from the accident scene. With any luck, his guilty plea is a done deal. We won't have to take it to trial."

Jamie's head shot up. "What do you mean it won't go to trial?"

"I figured that would be a sticking point for you." Brandon sighed. "The court system is so flooded these days — even in a small town like Reed — the District Attorney will do anything he can to lighten the case load. A jury trial could take weeks and cost thousands of dollars. With Sledge pleading guilty, the D.A. will set up a quick allocution hearing where Sledge will admit to his crimes and the judge will pass sentence."

Jamie's eyes flashed, his anger so potent he crushed his fingers around Dillon's hand without realizing it. Dillon grunted and Jamie let go altogether. He mumbled a quick, "Sorry," to Dillon before turning back to Brandon. "A sentence that will be less than what he would get from a jury. Because he's pleading guilty, he gets to cut a cushy deal."

"I wouldn't exactly call it cushy, kid. The charge is vehicular manslaughter. With his previous convictions, Sledge is looking at a twenty year sentence before he'll even be eligible for parole."

Jamie stood, his body lance-straight. "So he gets twenty years, so what? At least he's got twenty years left. That's more than Ben has, thanks to him."

Dillon reached out for him, his voice soothing. "I know you're upset, but Brandon's doing his best for us, and for Ben."

Jamie knew Dillon was right but it didn't help. He ignored Dillon's outstretched hand, but did offer a weak apology. "Sorry, Sheriff."

"At least knowing what happened will give you some closure." He stood. "Speaking of closure, Nora wanted me to let you know that Ben's body has been released for burial. She's having him cremated, so there won't be an actual funeral. A memorial service is being held Saturday night at the First Christian Church."

That was where Brandon and Nate went. Jamie knew because Megan and Dillon had both mentioned it. Since Ben and Nora didn't go to church at all, Jamie knew without having to ask the service was Brandon's doing. "Dillon, could I have a second alone with the sheriff, please?"

"Sure." If Dillon was bothered by the request, he didn't show it. "I'll be waiting in the car." He gave Jamie a smile and walked out.

As soon as Dillon left, Jamie walked over to where Brandon stood and held out his hand. "I just wanted to say thanks. I'm guessing you were the one who set up the memorial service."

Brandon shook Jamie's hand. "No big deal."

"Yes, it is. Ben wasn't the easiest guy to get along with, but the only reason people didn't warm up to him is because they couldn't see how special he was." *Damn.* His eyes were getting watery again. "Anyway, thanks."

Brandon shrugged. "All I did was make a couple of phone calls. Nothing major. I was glad to help, James."

"Call me Jamie, and please tell Nate and Megan to do the same."

Brandon smiled. "Will do. Now, get out of here before school starts. And, Jamie?"

"Yes?"

"I know you're upset about Sledge cutting a deal, but Ben's killer will get what he deserves. I'm sure of it."

Jamie nodded to be polite, but something deep inside told him that Brandon was wrong. Dead wrong.

Dillon's first day back at school since coming out wasn't at all what he expected. He dropped an unusually quiet James off at the door to his homeroom and then headed to his own class. Except for a couple of whispered comments and one *faggot* thrown at him by Rooster Carmichael, most everyone who spoke to him was positive — even downright friendly — about his newly established orientation. One kid asked him to join the G.S.A., and another patted him on the back and said, "Way to go."

He and James took Megan to Hailey's for lunch, and even there the climate was nothing but pleasant among adults and students alike. He also managed to avoid even a glimpse of his mother, something he was in no way ready for. Now he sat in his last class of the day, almost convinced he was home free, when Dan Morgan's voice came over the intercom. "Mr. Matthews?"

Dillon's English teacher said, "Yes, sir?"

"Send Dillon Carver to my office, please."

Dillon's heart sank as he gathered up his books. *And here I thought I'd made it. I should have known better.*

The principal's office was one hall down from the English department. Dillon knocked on the door and then pushed it open when Morgan called out, "Come in."

Morgan stood when he saw Dillon. "Please close the door and have a seat."

Dillon took the visitor's chair in front of Morgan's desk and dropped his books to the floor. While Morgan seated himself, Dillon took the opportunity to look around.

The cinder block walls had been painted a rich brown to match the stylish mahogany desk. Framed art prints hung around the room and an oriental rug covered the vinyl floor. The office looked like it belonged to a young executive rather than a high school principal.

Principal Morgan sat back in his chair and laced his hands together, his index fingers forming a steeple that he pressed to his lips. "I imagine you're wondering why I called you down here."

"I have a pretty good idea."

"I'm sure you do. That kiss you gave James Walker yesterday kicked up quite a stir."

"Yes, sir. I know it's against school policy, but before you suspend me, I want to make it clear James had nothing to do with it. I kissed him, and if anyone is punished, it should be me."

Morgan shook his head. "You misunderstand me, Dillon. Neither of you is going to be punished. Yes, kissing on school property is frowned on, but under the circumstances we'll overlook it." Morgan paused, more for effect, Dillon thought, than anything else. Finally he continued, "I called you in here to talk about your mother."

"What's she got to do with this?"

"I understand this is a sticky situation, but I'm going to be as candid as I can. Your mother called me last night, ranting and raving about you and James. She wanted me to expel James for corrupting you, and she wanted me to have the school counselor refer you to a psychiatrist. She also hinted that since you're eighteen and out of her reach, I should tell the psychiatrist I feel you're a danger to yourself and need to be admitted to a state hospital for observation."

Dillon felt like he was going to throw up. "That's a lie!"

"Calm down." Morgan held up his hand. "That isn't going to happen. Not only is it illegal, it violates your rights and goes against everything I believe in. Angela Carver may be a gifted teacher, but I refuse to let her use Plunkett as a forum to further her own personal prejudices. I told her as much last night."

Dillon snorted. "Bet she liked that."

"She told me she won't come back to work as long as you and James are still students here. I reminded her that a refusal to come in violates her contract. She refused to budge on her position, leaving me no choice but to suspend her without pay pending a school board hearing. In all likelihood, your mother is going to be fired."

Dillon hated what his mother was trying to do, but he still loved her. It hurt to know he was the reason she was losing her job. He sighed. "Is there anything you can do? She has tenure here at Plunkett, and James and I will be graduating in less than four months. Couldn't she just take a leave of absence until then?"

Morgan shook his head. "Angela has a reputation for taking her agenda against homosexuals into the classroom with her. I've had several complaints from the parents of gay and lesbian students, all claiming she singled out their children for persecution. So far, I haven't had any solid proof of wrongdoing, so she's kept a clean record. Now, having seen the extent of her bigotry firsthand, I can say with all honesty that I no longer want her working in this school."

Dillon slumped in his chair. He hated this. So what if he was in love with another guy? Why did his parents have to go nuts over it? Dejected, he gathered his books and stood. "Was that the only reason you wanted to see me?"

Principal Morgan rose from his chair and came around the desk. He put his hand on Dillon's arm. "That, and to tell you I admire you for being brave enough to be honest about your sexuality." The hand on Dillon's arm started moving in slow strokes that made Dillon uncomfortable. "I know it couldn't have been easy, and if there's anything I can do for you — anything at all — just let me know. I'm a good man to have on your side. I've got connections."

Dillon stepped away. "Uh...thanks, Mr. Morgan. If there's nothing else, I'd better go before the last bell rings."

Principal Morgan nodded and smiled his ultra slick grin. "Of course. Just remember what I said." Then the bastard winked.

Dillon couldn't have moved any faster had his feet been on fire. He tore out of the office and made straight for the bathroom. He splashed water on his face, hoping to calm himself. *Did Morgan just hit on me?* He could still feel the touch of the man's fingers as they'd slid over the fabric of his shirt.

I have to be wrong. No way would a principal hit on one of his students. I'm definitely losing it. He took a deep, calming breath and dried his face, telling himself he'd imagined the whole thing. Even so, Dillon made a mental note to avoid Dan Morgan as much as possible in the future.

For the next two days, Dillon and James did a polite dance around each other. Their conversations were comfortable enough, but there was no hint of the romance Dillon was aching for. Megan kept telling him to give James time and not to push. Dillon knew she was right, but that didn't make it any easier.

Dillon groaned as a ridge of the lumpy sofa bed frame pressed into his back. He really needed to go apartment hunting. Not only was he working on a serious case of bed back, but he couldn't stand to keep living in Heath's nasty apartment, not without a tetanus shot. He'd cleaned where he could, but his efforts were futile in the face of all of the filth. Dillon was no neat freak, but he drew the line at three week old pizza lying out on the table and a thin black layer of grease surrounding the tub.

He rolled over with a sigh. Saturday morning. He wasn't scheduled to work again until Monday night. He tried going back to sleep, but he couldn't. Tonight was the memorial service for Ben, and Dillon was worried. Not about the service itself, but about James's reaction to it. Brandon had said something about closure, but Dillon had serious doubts as to whether or not James would find it.

Stretching to rid himself of the last vestiges of sleep, Dillon untangled from the covers and stood. He located a pair of clean jeans buried underneath a pile of plastic grocery sacks Heath had unloaded last night and then thrown on the floor. Dillon couldn't even gripe at his brother about it because Heath had already left for work. He shook his head and reached for his shirt. He'd just finished dressing when someone knocked.

Dillon opened the door to find Megan and her mother standing on the stoop, an arsenal of cleaning supplies piled behind them. He didn't realize he was staring until Megan said, "Aren't you gonna let us in?"

"What? Oh, yeah. Sorry." He reached for the caddy full of cleaners Megan's mom was holding. "Here, Mrs. Nash, let me take that for you."

Every time he saw her, Dillon marveled at the resemblance between Megan and her mother. Gale Nash was an older version of her daughter, all fiery red hair and big blue eyes. She shook her head. "I've got this, sweetie. And if I've told you once, I've told you a thousand times, call me Gale."

"Yes, ma'am." He grabbed the rest of the cleaning supplies from the stoop and carried them into the house. Closing the door behind him he said, "Not to sound like I'm unhappy to see you, but what are you guys doing here?"

Gale held up the caddy. "We're here to clean this pigsty." She looked around and shook her head. "From the looks of it, we got here not a moment too soon. Meggie, you start in the bathroom. Dillon, you take your brother's room. Heath might not like a couple of females rooting through his things." She stepped over a pair of Heath's well worn jockey shorts and wrinkled her nose. "Though from the looks of it, he's not overly picky about his possessions. Meanwhile, I'll start in the kitchen."

"You don't have to do this," Dillon said. "I know you have better things to do than clean up after us."

Gale patted his cheek. "You're a sweet kid, and I love you. Now hush up and get to work."

Dillon knew an order when he heard one. Without another word, he did as he was told.

Six hours later, there wasn't a surface in the apartment that didn't shine. The fresh smells of pine cleaner and disinfectant filled the apartment, and Dillon could actually see the carpet for the first time since moving in. He stood in the middle of the living room, grinning at Megan and Gale. "I can't thank you enough for doing this."

"You worked just as hard as we did. Thanks aren't necessary." Gale tilted her head and studied him for a minute. "It's hard for you to accept help, isn't it?" Dillon nodded and Gale said, "There's a big difference between being responsible and being trapped by stubborn pride." She walked over to Dillon and wrapped him in a tight hug.

Dillon hugged her back, grateful for the comfort. Before he could say anything, Gale backed away. "Now, do you have a suit to wear to Ben's memorial?"

"Yes, ma'am. I hung it up in Heath's closet when I moved in."

"Megan, run out to the van and grab my steam iron. Dillon, get your suit. We should have just enough time to get your clothes pressed before Megan and I have to run home and get ready for the service ourselves."

"You're coming tonight?"

"Of course. We consider you family. Don't you know that's what family is for?"

Dillon didn't know that. He'd never been around a family like the Nashes before. He wasn't sure just why they considered him one of their own, but he was damned glad they did.

Dillon pulled his Lumina into the parking lot of the First Christian Church of Reed and parked two spaces away from Sadie's car. He'd attended this church with Megan more times than he could count. He liked the open atmosphere, the lack of condemnation. The preacher at his mother and father's church was an expert on hellfire and brimstone. Nothing like two hours of sin and conviction to make a guy want to throw himself out a third story window.

Walter Oakley, the preacher at First Christian, was different. He spoke of love and forgiveness. Dillon knew that James went to the Methodist Church with Sadie. He wondered if James's pastor preached about love and forgiveness, too. Dillon certainly hoped so. From James, Dillon needed both.

The first person Dillon saw when he entered the church foyer was Brandon, deep in conversation with James's aunt. Dillon shook Brandon's hand and then kissed Sadie's cheek.

Sadie patted Dillon's shoulder. "It was good of you to come. I know you and Ben Lewis weren't exactly friends."

"That's an understatement," Dillon said. "From what I hear, the two of you weren't on the best of terms, either."

"Too true. I thought — and still do — that Ben Lewis was a hoodlum of the first order. I'm sorry to see any young man end up the way Ben did, but I can't say I'm surprised." She gave Dillon a warm smile. "Since neither of us were members of the Ben Lewis fan club, I can only assume we're here for the same reason — to support Jamie."

"Yes, ma'am." Dillon looked around. "Speaking of James, where is he?"

Brandon pointed to the right side hallway. "I saw him go into the prayer room about ten minutes ago. He looked kind of pale."

Dillon was down the hall like a shot. He'd never been in the prayer room before, but he'd seen it on his way to the church kitchen, two doors down. Even if he hadn't known where to find it, the raised voices coming from within would have served as his guide. He recognized James's voice and he heard the word, "No." That was all he needed to hear.

Dillon flung the door open. James was backed into a corner, his hands held out in front of his chest. Ash Barnes stood about a foot from James, his face flushed with agitation. Dillon slipped inside and before the door even closed behind him, he heard Ash say, "What's the matter? I'm not good enough for you?"

"I told you, it wasn't like that with Ben and me."

"And I told you, I'm not buying it. I saw that kiss Ben planted on you at the dance. I want the same thing you gave him." Before Dillon or James could stop him, Ash made his move.

Chapter Seven

"What the hell are you doing, Barnes?" Dillon's voice cut through the stillness of the room, distracting Ash and giving Jamie the momentary advantage he needed. Jamie raised his knee and planted it right where Ash least wanted to be hit. He clutched his nuts and down he went.

Ash collapsed onto the floor and lay there, unmoving. Jamie made a face. "He's drunk." The stale smell of whiskey filled the room.

Dillon nodded and wrinkled his nose. "Shit. What are we supposed to do with him now?"

"I don't think you're allowed to say 'shit' in church."

"I think even God would agree that 'shit' is the right word to use in this case. The service is supposed to start in fifteen minutes. We can't just leave him here like this."

Dillon was right. As much as Jamie would have liked to leave Ash in a miserable pile, he couldn't. He wasn't even sure what Ash was doing there. He'd barely known Ben.

Jamie was just about to try his luck at getting an answer from Ash, who'd started moaning, when the door swung open and Chad Minton came into the room. He took one look at Ash and whirled on Dillon. "What did you faggots do to him?"

Dillon's face turned red and Jamie could tell that he was just about to blast Chad when Ash spoke up, his voice thick and slurred. "It was my own fault. If my damned father hadn't made me pay my 'respects to a fallen classmate', I wouldn't even be here. Help me up."

Chad came to Ash's aid. "What will your dad say if the two of us ditch before the service starts?"

"Like he'll even know. He and stepmother number five left for Europe about two hours ago. Second honeymoon, they called it. Funny, seeing as how they've only been married for three months." With Chad's help, he stumbled to his feet. They were almost to the door when Ash turned back. "James?"

"Yeah?"

Ash opened his mouth, then closed it again before any sound came out. Jamie figured he was about to apologize but the words must have stuck in his throat, because all he got out was a squeaky, "Never mind," before Chad helped him out the door.

Once they were gone, Dillon put his hands on Jamie's shoulders and looked into his eyes. "Are you okay?"

"Yeah. He didn't hurt me."

"Not for lack of trying. What happened?"

"Pretty much what it looked like. I came in here to pray for Ben, and the next thing I knew Ash was in my face."

Dillon took a deep breath. "The guy's a prick. Try to put him out of your mind." He looked down at his watch. "We should go. It's almost time for the service to start."

Jamie and Dillon headed for the sanctuary, choosing a seat next to Megan, three rows from the stage. Aunt Sadie was sitting with the Nash family, one row back. The place was packed, from the first pew down front to the balcony above. Jamie was willing to bet half the people there hadn't even known Ben. *Hearse chasers, looking for a good show.*

Jamie noticed a blown up picture of Ben — grainy and having been lifted from the yearbook — placed near the altar and cloistered by floral arrangements. Since Ben had been cremated, there was no casket, and Nora had wisely chosen not to showcase his urn. Jamie thanked heaven for small favors. He looked around for Nora, but couldn't see her in the throng of designer-clad spectators.

Walter Oakley approached the pulpit, a pleasant looking man, with thinning gray hair and round, wire-framed glasses. He'd seemed nice enough when he'd greeted Jamie in the hallway, but even so, Jamie dreaded what he was about to hear. He expected some long winded diatribe about how everything happened for a reason and how they shouldn't grieve for Ben because he was in a better place.

Oakley adjusted his glasses and looked out at the crowd. "I usually begin each funeral or memorial service with a prayer, and then I deliver a heartfelt sermon about celebrating a life well lived and rejoicing because a soul has been reunited with his Lord. Then again, most funerals I preside over are those of older folks — such as myself — who've had a chance to sample the world and all its wonders. There is no way I can celebrate the passing of an eighteen-year-old boy whose life hadn't even started.

"Benjamin Lewis left this earth a babe, another victim of a senseless tragedy that defies all logic and reason. Though Ben was not a personal friend of mine, time and again I've seen young ones like him fall, cast down before ever really having had a chance to rise. At times like these, I wish I had a direct line to God. I'd ask Him why Ben Lewis was taken, why he experienced so little joy in his young life only to have what little happiness he'd managed to find so cruelly snatched away." Oakley removed his glasses and pinched the bridge of his nose. "Since we can't do that, we're asked to trust God and to believe the answers will someday be made clear to us. No matter how strong their faith, this offers little solace for those left behind." He replaced the wire frames on his nose and scanned the crowd. "There is a certain peace to be found in our Creator, but it is often hard won in the face of such tragedy. As He prepared His disciples for the Crucifixion and the trials to follow afterward, Jesus spoke of such a peace — as we are told in the thirty-third verse of the sixteenth chapter of John — when He said, "'These things I have spoken to you, that in Me you may have peace. In the world you have tribulation, but take courage; I have overcome the world.'"

Oakley closed the prayer book he'd earlier placed upon the lectern. "Jesus overcame the world, and through Him, so may we. That is not to suggest the road between the here and the hereafter will be a smooth one. We are assured of just the opposite. My prayer now is not for Ben, who's reached the end of his journey among us, but for his family and friends, those left behind and trying to find order in chaos. Would you bow your heads?"

Jamie closed his eyes, and though he heard the words of Oakley's prayer, he couldn't wrap his mind around them. He liked the fact that Pastor Oakley hadn't tried to explain away Ben's death with some tired old speech, but he still wasn't sure how he was supposed to feel or what he was supposed to do to obtain the closure everyone kept going on about. Jamie didn't even realize the prayer was finished until he saw movement from the corner of his eye and noticed other people raising their heads.

"I think now would be a good time to hear from those who knew and loved Ben," Oakley said. "If any of you would like to say a few words of remembrance, please step forward at this time."

Nora Slater went first. Jamie always marveled at what a striking figure Ben's foster mother made, with her long brown hair and olive complexion. At five-eleven, she reminded Jamie of a willow tree, slender and elegant. Nora was the only stable adult influence Ben had ever known. Too bad she hadn't gotten him sixteen years sooner.

As Nora approached the lectern, her hazel eyes scanned the crowd, finding Jamie almost immediately. They exchanged looks before Nora said, "I'd like to thank all of you for coming. I'm overwhelmed by the turnout." Her voice became thick but she held it together. "Those who didn't know him probably thought Ben was a tough guy, a kid who gave a lot more crap than he took." She managed a weak smile. "There was another side to Ben, a softer side. To those lucky few he loved—" Again she looked at Jamie. "Ben gave everything he had. It's that Ben whom I say goodbye to today." Tears began to roll down her cheeks. "That's the boy I grieve, the boy I was proud to call my son." Nora said another quick thank-you, nodded to Walter Oakley, and returned to her seat.

There was an awkward pause while Oakley waited for the next speaker to come forward. Dillon leaned close to Jamie and whispered, "You going up there?"

Jamie shook his head. He'd never make it through without losing it. Dillon seemed to understand. He gave Jamie's knee a light squeeze before pulling back his hand.

Oakley was just about to reclaim the pulpit when Dan Morgan stepped on the stage. "If you don't mind, Pastor, I have a few words I want to say."

Pastor Oakley moved back to his chair as Morgan took his place at the podium. His suit looked to be hand tailored, and as usual, his hair was perfectly styled. He stood before the memorial crowd like a politician addressing potential voters.

"We're here today to mourn the passing of one of our own, a young man cut down in the prime of his life. Ben Lewis was perched on the cusp of manhood, only to be plucked from our midst by an almost unfathomable tragedy. We come here today to make sense of the senseless, to infuse logic into the illogical. As Mr. Oakley so deftly pointed out, such a happening is difficult to understand, but I think I may be able to put Ben's death into a perspective you can all relate to."

Morgan smiled again, but this time Jamie could have sworn he saw something behind Morgan's grin, some malicious intent buried beneath the flashing white teeth and the prep school charm.

Morgan placed both hands on the lectern. "Like Mr. Oakley, I put great store in the principles laid out for us in the Bible. Now, I'm not up on chapter and verse, but I think I can make my point just the same. To paraphrase, whatever a man sows, that's what he'll reap. You ask why Ben Lewis had to die. I'll tell you why. The evil that Ben did in life finally caught up to him. Ben Lewis sowed seeds of sin and strife. How ironic, then, that Ben's life should be taken by a drunkard, a man whose own life has been just as fruitless and violent as Ben's."

Jamie heard Walter Oakley clear his throat as Nora gasped and someone else cursed, but Morgan was far from finished. He pulled a folded piece of paper from his breast pocket and then continued.

"Lest you take my word for it," he shook out the paper, "I have here a list of Ben Lewis's indiscretions. And these are just the ones we know about." Holding the document in front of himself like a banner, Morgan said, "Benjamin Lewis was a rapsheet with legs. Between the ages of eleven and fifteen alone, Ben was arrested four times for solicitation, had five petty theft charges, got sent to juvenile hall three times for misdemeanor assault, and was implicated in two separate drug busts. Ben lived in twelve different foster homes and did over six months in two juvenile detention facilities. Perhaps if those 'kiddie jails' had kept him until he turned eighteen, he'd still be alive. For some reason, he always seemed to get out early for good behavior." Morgan snorted. "Good behavior was something Ben Lewis knew nothing about. Even after he ran away from his last foster home and Nora Slater so graciously took him in, Ben couldn't seem to get his act together." Morgan paused. "The question is, should we really be grieving for Ben Lewis? I say he got what he deserved."

"And I say you're full of shit, Morgan." Brandon Nash stepped up on stage and gave Oakley an apologetic glance. "Sorry about that, Pastor, but only a craven coward talks trash about a dead man in front of his loved ones." Morgan opened his mouth to speak but Brandon beat him to the punch. "Sit down, Morgan. You've had your turn. You're lucky as hell I can't think of anything to charge you with for exposing Ben Lewis's juvenile record."

That shut Morgan up and propelled him back to his seat. Brandon took the pulpit, his eyes flashing. Brandon's anger soothed Jamie. At least someone besides Nora and himself was outraged over Morgan's comments.

"I'm not much of a public speaker." Brandon spoke with obvious reluctance. "I leave all the diplomacy crap to my better half. I certainly wasn't elected sheriff because of my people skills. But the fact is, I did get elected, and that put me in a unique position where Ben Lewis was concerned." He shifted so that his hip was propped against the podium in typical Brandon Nash style. "There are two kinds of arrestees: the kind that clam up on you and go all quiet, and the kind who get mad as He— um, heck, and raise the roof. Ben was in the second category. I got to see the worst of him, the angry, belligerent side. He was brought in on a variety of charges — all misdemeanors, I might add — and never once did he come in without setting the whole station on its ear. Even so, I can honestly say I admired Ben Lewis. I may not have agreed with everything he did, but I admired the person he was underneath the tough guy exterior."

Brandon's blue eyes scanned the room. "Ben Lewis was a survivor. He didn't just give up because life dealt him a lousy hand. Was he bitter? Yeah, a little bit. But he didn't let that bitterness keep him from living a full life. Ben Lewis lived his life like there was no tomorrow." Brandon's eyes settled on Jamie. "I can't say for sure, but I believe if Ben Lewis were here with us right now, he'd tell those he cared about to do the same thing." With that last bit of advice, Brandon nodded to Pastor Oakley and exited the stage.

Pastor Oakley wasn't about to give Morgan a chance to say anything further. The minute Brandon relinquished the pulpit, Oakley reclaimed it, thanked everyone for coming, and ended the service.

Dillon stood. "You ready to go, James?"

"Jamie."

"Huh?"

"My friends and family call me Jamie." He lowered his voice for Dillon's ears only. "I always loved the way you say my name."

Dillon's smile was the best thing Jamie had seen in a long time. "Jamie, are you ready?"

Jamie stood up and slipped his hand into Dillon's. "I'm ready." And he was. Ready to start living again.

Dillon and Jamie wound their way through the sanctuary, stopping just long enough to say goodbye to Megan and to tell Jamie's Aunt Sadie they were leaving. They'd almost made it to the door when they ran into Nora.

Her eyes were red and her face was pinched, but Dillon could tell the smile she gave Jamie was genuine. She took Jamie's hand and pulled him in for a tight hug. "Thanks for everything." Her eyes were filled with tears when she pulled back. "I can never repay you for making the last two years of Ben's life so special."

"He did the same for me. He was a friend when I needed one the most."

Nora patted his shoulder, then said, "I hate to do this now, but I'm not sure when I'll get another chance." She looked around. "Is there somewhere private we can talk? This shouldn't take long."

Dillon spoke up. "You could use the prayer room, if it's empty."

"That should do. I have all the documents right here."

Jamie looked as confused as Dillon felt. "Documents?"

Nora nodded. "Ben's will."

Jamie's eyes went wide. "Ben had a will."

"He sure did. I know it's odd, given his age, but one thing about Ben most people didn't know, he was a meticulous record keeper. You'd never have known it to look at him, but he saved everything. He also had a near photographic memory. That kid never forgot anything."

"Ben?" Dillon didn't mean to say it, but it slipped out, anyway.

"I know." Nora didn't sound offended. "It doesn't fit his personality, not the one he showed to the world, anyway. I think Ben saw being smart as a hindrance. Let's face it, in the life he had before he came to Reed, intelligence wasn't what people wanted from him." Her jaw tightened. "Dan Morgan was only too happy to point that out, the bastard."

Dillon put his hand on Nora's arm. "Why don't the two of you go ahead and get this part of it over with? You'll feel better once you do."

"I'd like for Dillon to hear this, too," Jamie said. "If you don't mind, that is."

"Of course." She hesitated. "I know some would consider reading a will at a memorial service to be in poor taste, but I just felt like I had to do this. You understand, don't you?"

"Yes, I do." Jamie pointed down the long hall. "The prayer room is right down here."

The three of them descended the hallway and entered the prayer room. Dillon hung the "occupied" sign on the outer knob and closed the door. Nora took one of the high-backed leather chairs, leaving Jamie and Dillon to share the couch.

She removed a manila envelope from her purse. Placing a pair of reading glasses on her slightly sloped nose, she opened the envelope and shuffled through the papers until she found the one she was looking for. She scanned it for a second, then looked to Jamie. "Are you ready for this? Ben wrote it out himself, but he had it notarized and then filed by a lawyer, so it's all aboveboard."

"I'm ready."

"Good. I'll just read this as it's written, and then if you have any questions, I'll answer them after we're finished. It's pretty straightforward, so I doubt you will." She cleared her throat. "*If you're reading this, then it means I've bitten it. I hope being dead doesn't suck. My lawyer said I have to at least take a stab at making this official, so here goes. I, Benjamin Neil Lewis, being of sound mind and body, do hereby leave the balance of my savings account, which at present comes to three-hundred, sixty-five dollars and fourteen cents, to my foster mother, Nora Slater. It could be less than that by the time I actually kick the bucket, but hey, a guy's got expenses. I also leave to Nora my arrowhead collection. Nora, I know you've always liked Indian stuff, and I want you to have it.*" Nora stopped, and Dillon could see that her hands were shaking.

"If you need to do this later..." Jamie said.

"I appreciate the thought, but I need to get this done if I'm to find my own peace over losing Ben." She smoothed out the paper and began again to read. "*With the exception of those two things, all my worldly goods I leave to my friend James Walker. I'm also leaving him my most prized possession, my nineteen-eighty-five Pontiac Firebird, title of which can be found in my safe deposit box at the Reed Savings and Loan. Nora has the key, J. There are a couple of other things in the box I need you to take care of for me, buddy, seeing as how I'm dead and all. I trust you, J, and I know you'll do the right thing. Oh, and if you scratch my car while you're learning how to drive it, I'll come back and haunt your ass.*"

Nora stopped to gauge Jamie's reaction. "How are you holding up? Are you ready to hear the last of it?"

Dillon was proud of the strength in Jamie's voice when he said, "I'm good. Let's finish it."

Nora nodded and then continued. "*Now, about my body. I'm not much for pushing up daisies, and the whole worms-feasting-on-my-dead-flesh thing creeps me out, so I want to be cremated. As the song goes, 'It's better to burn out than fade away.' So set me on fire and be done with it. And Nora? Stuff a few firecrackers in my pockets first, will you? Give those morticians a little excitement in their lives. Wait. My lawyer just told me that they cremate you naked. Damn. In that case, Nora, there are several holes on my person where you could shove those babies. I'll leave the choice of orifices up to you. Having said that, there's only one question left. What to do with my ashes. I've never cared much for the thought of spending all eternity sitting in a glorified flower pot on someone's mantle, so I'm asking you, Nora, to give my ashes to Jamie. J, this next part is for you. You've had almost as much unhappiness in your life as I've had in mine, and that's saying something. I have a feeling things are gonna change for you, and soon. If I'm right, the next time you feel happy — and I mean truly, deeply, completely happy — I want you to find the most beautiful spot you can think of, and spread my ashes out. I like the thought of seeping back into the dirt. Dust to dust and all that jazz. Anyway, I've said pretty much all I need to. Just be happy, J and Nora. I love you guys."*

Jamie sat in silence while Nora refolded the paper and put it back into the envelope. Dillon wished there was something he could say, but he found himself at a loss.

Nora pulled one more envelope from her purse, this one larger. She walked over to where Jamie sat, handing it to him. "This is your copy of the will, along with the keys to Ben's car, and also the key to the safe deposit box. You can pick up the rest of Ben's things anytime you like."

Jamie stood and took the envelope from her. Dillon stood as well, just as Jamie said, "Nora...I can't drive. I don't even know what I'm gonna do with that car. If you want it—"

"No, honey. Ben wanted you to have it and so do I. Besides," she gave Dillon a warm smile, "I don't think you'll have any trouble finding an instructor." She pulled Jamie close and gave him a rocking hug, then surprised Dillon by doing the same to him. A minute later she pulled back. "Okay, guys, I'm going home now. Just come by whenever. There's no rush." She left without waiting for a reply.

Jamie drew in a deep breath and then let it out slowly, like he was having trouble gathering his thoughts. Finally he said, "Wow."

"'Wow' is right. How do you feel about all this?"

Jamie shook his head. "I'm not sure. I still can't believe Ben had a will or that he hired a lawyer. Where would he get the money? Attorneys don't come cheap."

Dillon had wondered the same thing. "Maybe when you open the safe deposit box, you'll find some answers."

"I hope so, but something tells me it isn't going to be that easy."

Dillon didn't argue. He had the same sinking feeling.

Monday after school, Dillon drove Jamie to the Reed Savings and Loan. Mr. Lee, the bank manager, greeted them in the lobby. "Good afternoon, boys. Can I be of some assistance to you?"

"If you aren't busy," Jamie said, "we could use your help."

Lee smiled. "What do you need?"

Jamie fished his key out of his pocket. "My friend had a safe deposit box. When he d—" He took a deep breath. "When he died, he left the contents to me. I have the will, if you need to see it."

"That won't be necessary. The key is enough." Mr. Lee motioned for them to follow him to his office. Once there, he opened a strongbox located on top of his filing cabinet and searched for the matching key. "Found it. If the two of you will follow me, I'll fit my key in first, then leave you to open the box in private."

The vault was little more than a metal room with a table and a couple of chairs. Mr. Lee pulled box number five-sixty-seven from its cubicle and placed it on the table. After unlocking his side, Mr. Lee waited until Jamie popped the latch and then slipped out to give them privacy.

Dillon sat across from Jamie, watching for any sign of distress as Jamie removed the lid and rifled through the contents. Dillon could see two envelopes, one manila, the other a white, legal sized paper with the D.M.V. seal on it. The car title, he guessed. He could also see a brown paper sack — filled and folded — taking up the other end of the box.

Setting the envelopes aside, Jamie reached for the sack. He upended it, spilling the contents onto the table. Dillon stared in blank-faced astonishment as bundle after bundle of banded, hundred dollar bills spilled out. Jamie's hands were shaking. "Good God."

Well put. Dillon had never seen so much cash in his life.

Jamie said, "Would you count it please? I can't think."

Dillon went through each stack of bills, putting them back in the sack as he went. When he was done, he placed the bag back on the table. "Finished."

"What's the verdict?"

"You aren't gonna believe it. Hell, I counted it, and I don't believe it."

"How much?"

Dillon folded his now shaking hands in front of himself on the table. "Give or take a couple of hundred, I'd say you've got about forty-two thousand dollars on your hands."

Chapter Eight

Jamie clutched both envelopes to his chest, afraid to open them. For now, those letters were a silent link to Ben. If he opened either one and found proof the money was dirty — as Dillon seemed sure it was — Jamie knew that link would be shattered.

The Lumina pulled into Jamie's drive. "We're here."

"Thanks."

Dillon hesitated, then finally said, "What will you do about the money?"

"I'm not sure. That's why I put it back in the safety deposit box. Until I decide how to handle this thing, it's safer there."

"I still say you need to talk to Brandon about it."

Jamie sighed. He'd known Dillon was right the first time he suggested talking to the sheriff back at the bank. But Jamie's reasons for waiting still stood. "I can't. Not until I find out where the money came from."

"Jamie—"

"I don't want to drag Ben's name through the mud if I don't have to. If I find out the money was a result of something illegal, I promise I'll talk to Brandon."

Dillon put his hand on the back of Jamie's neck, stroking the short hairs there with the edge of his thumb. "I know you will, but I worry about you. Who knows where that money came from? You have no idea what sort of shit Lewis was into."

"I'll be careful."

"I know you'll try, but you aren't like Ben. You don't have any idea what the guy was capable of. You always see the good in people."

"You say that like it's a bad thing."

Dillon used the hand on Jamie's neck to pull him forward until their foreheads were touching. "No way. I thank God you're so trusting and forgiving. You never would have given me another chance otherwise." Without changing positions, Dillon glanced down at his watch. "Damn. I've got to get to work." He gave Jamie a quick peck on the lips. "Call me if you need me. And don't do anything about that money without telling somebody first. Promise?"

Jamie kissed him and said, "Promise," as he reached for the door handle. He watched Dillon back his Lumina down the driveway, waved, and let himself into the house. He was thankful to find Aunt Sadie gone. He needed privacy.

Jamie went to his room and locked the door. Bouncing onto the bed, he opened the D.M.V. envelope first. The title to the car. Nothing unusual about that. Next he opened the manila envelope. Inside were two smaller envelopes, one thin, the other overstuffed. The thin one was labeled *J: Open First*. The other was labeled, *To Be Revealed Later*. Jamie sighed. Ben had been nothing if not dramatic.

Jamie tore into the first envelope. The shock of seeing Ben's handwriting hit him full force, but he made himself read it.

> *Dear J, If you're reading this, you've obviously opened the box and seen the money. I know what you're thinking, and the answer is no. I didn't knock over a liquor store or rob a bank. I earned that money and I want you to have it. And before you ask, no, I didn't earn it doing odd jobs for Nora. I can't tell you where it came from, J. That's a part of my life I don't want you to be touched by. Knowing you, you'll be afraid to take it, but please, do it anyway. I probably shouldn't say what I'm about to, but you need to know how I feel. I'm sorry in advance for the guilt trip.*

The paragraph ended and Jamie took a deep breath before continuing to read.

> *I'd always intended that money to be for us, a nest egg for the day you finally realized I was the guy for you. Crazy, I know, but from the first day I saw you, I loved you. You made me a better person, made me want to put someone else before myself for the first time in my life. Unless I miss my guess, Carver's starting to come around. I've seen the way he looks at you, and I know you'll forgive him eventually. This money is my gift to you, Jamie. Use it to start a life with the guy. The life you and I could never have.*

Jamie's hands shook, rattling the paper as he set the letter aside. He'd known somewhere inside Ben had been in love with him, even though Ben had denied it that night at the sheriff's office. Even so, to see it stated so baldly was a shock. Several aching minutes passed before Jamie was able to pick the letter up again.

> *I have no right to ask this next part, but when has that ever stopped me? The second envelope goes to the guy I was seeing. I swore I'd never tell anyone who he was, and I have to keep my word on this one. I know, I know — I'm dead, and honesty was never one of my strong points, so why the burst of conscience now? The thing is, J, I took something from the guy I had no right to take. I'm not proud of it, but I used him. For that reason, I ask that you not open the other envelope. I*

hate involving you in any of this, but you're the only one I can really trust. Knowing you, you'll figure out who he is. When you do, please, give him the letter. And tell him I said I was sorry. No, scratch that. When he sees what's inside, he won't believe you, anyway. Okay, enough of this. I've got a date with a cloud. I love you, J. Be happy. Ben.

Jamie refolded the letter and stared down at the fat, still-sealed envelope with disbelief. *What the hell am I supposed to do now?*

Dillon, Megan, and Jamie sat hunched in a corner booth at Hailey's the next day, trying to decide exactly that. Dillon reacted just as Jamie thought he would.

"I say you open the envelope, find out who the guy is, and be done with it."

Megan, who was sitting across from Dillon and Jamie, shook her head. "Jamie's already explained why he can't open it. It's a matter of ethics."

"What about Lewis's ethics? God knows what he got Jamie mixed up in by leaving him that money. Now he wants to send him on a scavenger hunt? Find the missing boyfriend and you win a prize? Ethics, my ass."

A shadow fell across the table. "From what I hear, your ass has seen a shitload of action lately, Carver."

Jamie felt Dillon tense beside him and turned to see Roy Carmichael standing over them, a couple of his thug boys at his side.

They didn't call him Rooster for nothing. His round face was always beet red and his dark brown hair stuck straight up on top of his head like a rooster's comb. Jamie heard a rumor that Rooster's eyes were brown, too, but they were small and beady enough to look black. He was medium height but thick and well muscled from years of training with the football team. Jamie knew there were reams of athletes out there with near genius I.Q.s — guys totally undeserving of the dumb jock label. Rooster was not one of those guys. In fact, calling him dumb was giving him way too much credit.

"I didn't realize you'd taken an interest in my ass, Rooster." Dillon appeared calm, but Jamie could see the tick in his jaw. "Like what you see?"

Rooster's face grew even redder, though Jamie would have sworn that wasn't possible. "I hear you switched teams."

Dillon shifted in his seat. "What's the matter? You afraid I'm gonna hit on you? Trust me, buddy, you ain't got that to worry about."

"You think you got all the answers, don't you?" Rooster flexed his fists. "In that case, why don't you tell me what makes a normal guy like you go from banging a choice piece like Megan, here, to shoving it up Walker's nasty ass."

Dillon started to stand, but Megan and Jamie reached for him at the same time. Megan put her hand on Dillon's arm. "He's not worth it."

Jamie slid his arm around Dillon's waist and whispered, "She's right. Let it go." Jamie felt Dillon relax a little just before he turned back to Rooster.

"If you think this is some kind of battle of wits we've got going here, I hate to burst your bubble, but you came to this fight unarmed. Now, I believe you asked me a question."

"You're damned right I did. What turned you queer?"

"Damn, Rooster, you mean you don't know what makes a man gay?" Dillon paused, and Jamie could tell he was building up to something. Finally Dillon said, "Okay, I'll tell you, but this has to stay between us. I was bitten."

Rooster scratched his head. "What the hell are you talking about?"

"Just what I said. You asked me what turned me queer and now I'm telling you. I was walking home alone late one night, when out of nowhere, this rabid homosexual jumped me and bit me right on the ass. I tried to fight him off, but you know those homos have superhuman strength. Anyway, he bit me on my left cheek, then took off. The whole thing shook me up, but I thought I would be okay once it was over. It took me a few weeks to notice the changes. At first the signs were subtle: the sudden urge to redecorate my room, the uncontrollable desire to do Megan's hair. Then, as the phases of the moon progressed, I noticed other things: the need to wear lace panties, the insane hope of one day owning my own flower shop. Before I knew it, I was jacking off six times a day to pictures of Brad Pitt and Russell Crowe. Of course, I won't be a full fledged gay boy until I bite someone else and pass on the *dark gift*." Dillon stood. "Hey, Rooster, you wanna be my first convert? If I turn just four people, I win like a toaster oven or something."

The entire café burst into laughter, including Hailey, who was standing a few feet away, watching the whole show. Jamie and Megan were both rolling, shaking so hard the booth moved a couple of inches. Even Rooster's buddies were cracking up. The only one not amused was Rooster.

"You are so full of shit, Carver."

Dillon looked hurt. "I am not. Here, I'll prove it to you." He reached for his belt and began to undo the buckle. "Let me show you my scar. That guy took a plug out of my ass."

Rooster backed up. "I'm out of here." He turned to his cronies. "Let's jet." He threw one last look at Dillon and Jamie. "This ain't over.

You and your little boyfriend are gonna pay. With Lewis dead, the count is one fag down. I say we make it three for three."

Rooster left and Dillon fell back into his seat. Megan wiped her eyes. "That was the funniest thing I think I've ever seen."

Jamie leaned against Dillon's shoulder, doing his best to stop laughing. "I had no idea I'd hooked myself to a comedy genius."

Dillon waggled his eyebrows. "There are a lot of things you don't know about me, but I'll be glad to show you all of them later on."

Hailey walked up to the table, her face flushed, fanning herself with a menu. "I've been thinking of hiring live entertainment for the Friday and Saturday night crowds. Do you do stand up?"

Dillon blushed. "Sorry, Hailey. I didn't mean to cause a scene."

"Don't you dare apologize. I thought you handled yourself with untold restraint. I kept expecting you to knock him on his rear. I like your method much better. You put him in his place without ever lifting a finger."

"Thanks. Um...if you have our check ready, I think we'll go." Dillon looked to Jamie and Megan, who nodded in agreement. "I believe I've had enough excitement for one day."

Hailey shook her head. "Lunch is on the house for all of you."

"You don't have to do that."

"Of course I do. That's the best laugh I've had in weeks. I'll be telling that story for years to come."

Jamie and Megan thanked her. Dillon added, "Thanks, Hailey. And thanks for not getting mad."

Hailey patted his arm and walked back toward the kitchen. As the crowd in the café resumed eating, Dillon said, "If you're ready, we'll head back to school."

As if they shared a brain, Jamie and Megan said in unison, "As long as you promise not to bite us."

The debate about what to do with the second letter continued through the rest of the week. Jamie did his best to recall something — anything — Ben might have said that gave away the identity of his mystery boy, but nothing came to mind. He fastened a cuff on his dark green button-up shirt and grabbed his jacket. There'd be plenty of time to stew over the mystery later. Dillon was taking him out on their first official date and Jamie refused to spend the whole evening worrying. He headed down the stairs just as Dillon's car pulled into the drive.

After taking in dinner and a movie, Jamie and Dillon sat inside the Lumina, holding hands and sharing an occasional kiss, but mostly just talking. How long they'd been parked in Aunt Sadie's driveway, Jamie couldn't say. This was one of the things he'd missed the most with Dillon, the quiet times, the conversation. Dillon got him on a level no one else — not even Ben — ever had. He still couldn't believe the two of them were together starting fresh. It seemed like a dream he hoped he'd never wake up from.

A flicker caught Jamie's eye and he laughed as he saw the porch light switch on and off for the fourth time. "That one was only two minutes behind the last." He sighed. "I guess that's Aunt Sadie's signal for me to come inside."

Dillon picked up Jamie's hand and kissed it. "I like your aunt's style. My father would've marched out here and yanked me out of the car."

Jamie studied him for a minute. "Do you miss your folks?"

"A little bit, I guess. I mean, there are things I miss about them, certain qualities, but I know they can never accept me the way I am. Deep down I know I'm better off."

Jamie's fingertips brushed the hair back from Dillon's brow. "I understand." He leaned forward and kissed Dillon, a light brush of lip against lip, but enough to send sparks flying. "As much as I hate to, I'd better go. Aunt Sadie does so much for me, the least I can do is respect her wishes."

"That's one of the things I admire about her. She does what she does because she loves you, not so she can hold it over your head. Douglas Carver doesn't do anything for anybody unless he can get something out of the deal. My father thinks he owns the world."

It was like someone flipped a switch. The nagging memory that had plagued Jamie since the minute he read Ben's letter finally popped to the surface. That night at the sheriff station, Ben had told Jamie about meeting his boyfriend at the old Tanner textile mill. Ben's exact words were, *His family owns the place.* Jamie pulled Dillon into a bone-jarring hug.

"Not that I'm complaining, but what was that for?" Dillon stroked Jamie's hair.

Jamie pulled back and kissed him again. "For making me remember something I've been trying to think of for days. I know who he is, Dillon."

"He who?" It took Dillon a minute before realization dawned. "You mean—"

"Yeah. I know how to find Ben's boyfriend."

Knowing how to find somebody and actually finding them were two different things. After a week of searching, Jamie and Megan were no closer to the answer. She'd been pulled into the project almost immediately, but the two of them were having little luck. They scoured the records at the courthouse and city hall, but the red tape and nonsensical filing system made digging up any sort of useful information impossible. Dillon helped as much as he could, but between work and school, he had little time to spare. Jamie sat in the basement of the courthouse, pouring through deeds. After an hour of searching through file after dusty file and finding nothing, he looked across the table.

"I don't think it's in here. Maybe we should ask somebody."

Megan brushed a speck of dust from the end of her nose. "I'm all for that, but who?"

"How about your brother?"

"Brandon would want to know why we wanted the owner's name."

And then I would have to tell him about the money. Damn. Megan was right. There was no way he could go to Brandon. At least, not yet. He was fresh out of options when Megan said, "What about Heath?"

"What about him?"

"He works for the fire department. I bet they keep records of all the inspections done on factories and businesses in the area."

"Yeah, but Tanner Textiles has been closed down for years. The owners would have no need for fire inspection reports."

Megan shook her head. "If the new owners are using the property as a tax write off, they probably have insurance. And if they have insurance, they had to have it inspected. I bet Heath could get a copy of the report, which would have the property owner's name on it."

"You make a good point, but you're forgetting one thing."

"What?"

"Just like Brandon, Heath would want to know why we're looking."

Megan shrugged. "So we tell him."

"Huh?"

"Well, unlike Brandon, Heath isn't duty-bound to report the money. Besides, he loves Dillon. I know he'll want to help."

Jamie hoped she was right, but he wasn't betting on it.

"You found forty-two-thousand dollars *where?*"

Jamie did his best to dissolve into the couch cushions but Dillon had learned long ago the best way to handle Heath was not to back down. "You heard us the first four times we said it."

Heath got up from his perch on the chair and paced back and forth across the apartment's small living room. "Let me get this straight. Ben Lewis left Jamie a wad of cash and some hokey deathbed confession letter, but instead of going to the cops like normal people, the two of you have decided to break out your junior detective kits?"

Dillon hated to do it, but Heath left him no choice. He would have to play the M card. Winking at Jamie, Dillon said, "I told Megan you wouldn't help us, but she swore up and down you would." Heath's head spun around so fast, Dillon was surprised he didn't get whiplash.

"You dragged Megan into this. Damn it, Dillon—"

"Think about it, Heath. Do you really think I could force Megan to do anything she didn't want to do?"

Heath sank down into his chair wearing that same defeated look that most of the men in Megan's life wore. "No, Megan knows her own mind. Was it really her idea for me to help?"

"Yep."

"You know it could take me a while to access the records, don't you?"

Jamie spoke up. "We understand. We're just grateful for the help. Me most of all, since Ben was my friend in the first place."

Heath leaned his head back and closed his eyes. "I'm not gonna get out of this, am I?"

Dillon hid his smile. "Not unless you want to disappoint Megan."

Heath's sigh was pure resignation. "That's what I was afraid of."

Heath had warned that it would take a while to find the owner of Tanner Textiles. A "while" turned out to be three days. Friday afternoon, Dillon, Megan, and Jamie sat waiting in Heath's living room for a full report.

"Are you sure Heath said to meet him here?"

Dillon glared over at Megan from where he sat on the couch with Jamie. "No less sure than I was the first three times you asked me."

Megan sat in Heath's favorite chair, her legs curled beneath her. "I know, I know. I'm a gnat buzzing around and bugging the crap out of you both, but I can't help it. I want this thing resolved so you and Jamie won't have to worry about it anymore."

Dillon was immediately contrite. "I didn't mean to snap. Ever since Heath called this afternoon and asked us to meet him here, I've been on edge."

Jamie squeezed Dillon's hand and gave Megan one of his killer smiles. "At the risk of sounding like a puss, I just want to thank both of you for helping me."

Heath came in before they had a chance to answer. The anticipation in the room was so thick, Dillon swore he could taste it. Jamie stood, keeping a death grip on Dillon's hand. Dillon and Megan rose as well, but it was Jamie who said, "Did you find the owner of the property?"

"Yep. It wasn't easy, either, let me tell you. I spent my day off combing through old inspection reports, code violation tickets, rewiring permits—"

Dillon scowled at his brother. "Would you tell us already?"

Heath had the good grace to look apologetic. "Sorry about that. Anyway, the property owner is listed as a Mr. A. F. Barnes, Junior."

Megan gasped, and Jamie said, "You mean—"

"A. F. Barnes, Junior, otherwise known as Ashton Franklin Barnes the Second, only has one son." Dillon swore. "Ben's boyfriend was Ash."

Chapter Nine

"Maybe I'd better do this alone."

Dillon hesitated, key poised in the Lumina's ignition. "No way. Not after Ash tried to attack you at the memorial."

"He was drunk."

"Who's to say he won't be drinking this time?"

Dillon had a point but Jamie wasn't about to tell him so. "You won't jump down the guy's throat, will you?"

Dillon gave Jamie his most angelic smile. "Me? Never." When Jamie made the "Yeah, right" face, Dillon said, "I promise I'll be the soul of understanding and compassion."

By the time they pulled up at Ash's house, it was pushing seven o'clock. "He may not even be home. It is Friday night."

"Then we track him down." Dillon parked at one end of the circular drive and shut off the engine. "I want you to give him that damn envelope and be done with it. There's no way you can start putting Ben's death behind you when you're constantly getting dragged back in."

On that, they were in perfect agreement. Jamie wanted to end this once and for all. He had a bad feeling about what was in that letter to Ash. He figured Ben had some fuzzy concepts about right and wrong, but he chose to remember Ben as the loving, devoted friend he'd been, not the desperate kid who often did whatever struck his fancy to earn a quick buck. Jamie didn't want to know any more than necessary.

Ash's house smacked of wealth, from the cobblestone paths leading to the house from all directions to the mansion itself. Jamie was certain Ash's father must be having some sort of party. Every one of the more than twenty windows at the front of the house was brightly lit, giving the red brick, colonial façade an eerie orange glow. Jamie stopped short of the double front doors. "It looks like they've got company. Maybe we should go."

Dillon shook his head. "I don't think so. Remember what Ash said at Ben's memorial service? His father and his new wife have gone on a second honeymoon. It's only been two weeks. I doubt seriously if they'd be back yet."

"Maybe Ash is having a bunch of his football cronies over."

Dillon looked around. "Then where are all the cars? Or the loud music? Knowing the crowd Ash hangs around with, if he were having a party, someone would be shit-faced and standing in the front yard crushing beer cans between his naked ass cheeks."

With that unpleasant visual in his head, Jamie rang the doorbell. He and Dillon waited, listening while the chimes echoed throughout the home. Jamie half expected one of those old English butlers to answer the door, but it was a red-eyed Ash answered the summons.

Ash took one look at Jamie and Dillon and turned white as death. "What are you doing here?"

"We came to talk to you. You gonna let us in, or what?"

"Look, Carver, if this is about what happened at that memorial—"

Jamie stepped in. "It's not, Ash. We know you were drinking that night or none of that stuff would have happened."

Jamie thought he saw Ash relax a little, but not much. "If you're not here to kick my ass, then what are you doing here?"

God, this is hard. Jamie cleared his throat. "I, um...I have a letter for you."

Ash narrowed his eyes. "A letter? From who?" His eyes went wide. "You're not suing me for assault, are you? Look, I know I was out of line, but I never really touched you. If you think you're gonna make me pay just because I made a play for you, you can forget it."

"We're not here to sue you, dumbass." Dillon glared at him. "We're here to deliver a letter from Ben."

"Ben who?"

Jamie knew what was coming. He tried to signal for Dillon to stop, but it was too late.

"Ben Lewis," Dillon said. "You know, the guy you were screwing?"

Ash looked first at Dillon, then at Jamie. After giving them his best impression of a deer caught in the headlights, he threw up.

Dillon cleaned up the mess in the entryway while Jamie got Ash calmed down enough to clean himself up. Sitting in the family room while Ash finished showering, Dillon took a good look around the room. He'd been there a couple of times before for some of those raucous parties he'd mentioned to Jamie. One thing always struck him: no matter how many people were there — be it ten or a hundred — the house always seemed empty. The furnishings were top of the line and Ash's father had obviously spared no expense with the decorating, but the place had a museum-like quality, as if no one actually lived there.

Ash came back in a few minutes later. His hair was still wet and he was wearing fresh clothes. The thing that got to Dillon, though, was the lost look in Ash's eyes. Dillon's heart immediately started to soften toward the guy as he recognized the look. Ash had been in love with Ben.

Ash took the chair directly across from the sofa Jamie and Dillon shared. He was quiet for several minutes before saying, "How much do you know?"

"Not much," Jamie said. "Ben told me that his boyfriend used to meet him at the old Tanner mill, said his boyfriend's family owned the place. We used that information to track you down."

"Why? Are you going to out me because of the way I've treated you?" Defiance sparkled in his eyes. "Go ahead. At this point, I don't care."

"We aren't here to out you." Jamie pulled the thick envelope out of his coat pocket. "Ben left me the key to a safe deposit box. There were two letters inside, one for me, and the other labeled, 'To be revealed'. In his letter to me, Ben's last request was that I find out who his boyfriend was and give this to him. I've done that." Jamie held out the envelope.

Ash looked at it long and hard before reaching out to take it. Even then, he held it between two fingers, as if it were a poisonous snake about to strike. "What's in here?"

Jamie shrugged. "I couldn't say. Ben asked me not to open it, so I didn't. My job was to find out who you were and to deliver it." He stood up, prompting Dillon to do the same. "I've kept my word. Now maybe Ben can rest in peace."

Jamie turned to leave and Dillon followed. They'd almost made it to the door when Ash said, "Wait." Then a little quieter, added, "Please?"

Jamie turned. "What is it?"

Ash lowered his head. "Could you stay with me while I open it? I...I'm all alone here. My dad won't be home for another week, and—" He broke off, but not before Dillon heard the trembling in his voice.

Jamie returned to the couch. "Is that why all the lights are on? Because you feel a little less lonely that way?"

Ash looked up. "How did you know?"

"I used to turn all the lights on at Aunt Sadie's, right after my mom left." Jamie smiled. "Used to drive my aunt crazy, but I think she understood."

Ash sighed. "My mom is busy with her new husband and their kids, and my dad...well, I know he loves me, but he's got his own thing going. Know what I mean?"

Jamie nodded and reclaimed his seat on the couch. Dillon joined him. "Where's Chad? I thought you two spent the weekends hanging out."

"He wanted to, but I didn't feel like it. I haven't felt much like partying since...well, you know."

"Since Ben died?"

The look Ash gave Jamie was heartbreaking, even to Dillon. "Yeah. Not since then."

Dillon couldn't stand it. "Look, Ash. You and I have been friends most of our lives."

"So?"

Dillon leaned forward. "So, friends confide in each other. Talk to us, man. Tell us what happened."

Still holding the letter, Ash leaned back in the chair and closed his eyes. "There's not a whole heck of a lot to tell. I've known I was into guys for a while now, but except for the occasional encounter at the rest stop out on the interstate, I haven't done anything about it. When the urge got too bad, I'd go out there, take care of business, and be done until the next time. That's where I met Ben. Well, not met him, exactly. I mean, I knew him from school, but the rest stop is the first place we ever hooked up."

When Ash paused, Dillon said, "Not to be an ass, but what about all those girls you've slept with?"

Ash opened his eyes. "I wasn't using them as a cover. I like girls — even like the sex — just not as much as I do with guys."

Jamie nodded. "You're probably bisexual, then."

Ash closed his eyes and leaned back again. "Probably, not that it matters anymore. I don't want to be with anybody, male or female. All I wanted was Ben. Then he dumped me, and before I could make it right, he died."

"What happened?"

"Ben and I met after the dance. I got so pissed over that kiss he gave you, I told him to make a choice: me or you." Ash glanced at Jamie. "I know I was wrong, especially since I'd been with Blair Dees that night, but Ben was the one who wanted to keep things light. He insisted I keep dating girls so no one would get suspicious. Hell, maybe I was using girls as a cover, after all." Ash laughed, the sound about as joyful as a public execution. "Ben told me it was no contest, that he'd choose you every time. I begged him to stay with me, to make some kind of commitment. I even told him I was ready to tell everyone about us, my father included. He freaked out, said he didn't want that with me. He left, but not before telling me he never wanted to see me again." He took a quivering breath. "It's not every day a man loses the only person he's ever really loved. I spent the next twelve hours calling him every thirty minutes, begging him to meet me at the foreman's house so we could talk. He finally gave in somewhere around call number twenty-three. I guess he was on his way to meet me when he was hit by that car."

Jamie looked like he wanted to say something but Ash must not have noticed. Dillon saw it, though. It took him a minute, but the pieces eventually clicked. If Ben was on his way to meet Ash, what was he doing out on Tully Road, in the opposite direction from Tanner Textiles?

Ash picked up the envelope, holding it with a firmer grip this time. "You really don't know what's in here?" When Jamie shook his head, Ash said, "Might as well find out," and tore into it.

Dillon watched as Ash pulled a folded piece of white paper and a packet from one of those twenty-four hour photo places out of the larger envelope. Ash went for the letter first.

He started to read it, then stopped. Holding the paper out, he said, "Would you read it? I don't think I can."

Dillon wasn't sure if Ash was talking to him or Jamie, but judging from the look on Jamie's face, he was in no better shape to read it than Ash. Swallowing hard, Dillon leaned over and took the letter from Ash's hand. Clearing his throat, Dillon began to read.

"Dear Ash, I've done a lot of really bad shit in my life, but I can honestly say I've never felt guilty about any of it. Not until now, that is. Most of the guys I screwed over had it coming. The way I see it, they got what they deserved. But not you. The only real crime you committed was getting mixed up with a hustler. Yeah, that's me. I was a hustler, Ash. A whore. I was pretty damn good at it, if I do say so myself. Where do you think I learned all those little tricks I used on you?"

Dillon winced. *Way too much information.* He sighed and continued reading.

"I can't take all the credit. I learned from the best, a guy named Birch Carpenter. Birch was my foster father. He was also my pimp. He started me early, and by the time I was fifteen, I was pulling in the cash. Not that I ever saw any of it. Birch gave his boys just enough for clothes and food. At first, it seemed like an okay deal, but the older I got, the more sick of it I became. That's why I finally ran away. I was picked up and sent to Nora's, and from there, you know the rest. Just thinking about how much money I made for that guy pisses me off, so I'd better shut up about him. Before I do, though, there's one more thing I have to tell you about good ol' Birch.

"Birch was a sleaze, but he was damned smart for a piece of slime. Birch always said, 'Diversify your interests.' I had no idea what that meant when I was fifteen, but now I know it's the same thing Nora means when she says, 'Never put all your eggs in one basket.' Anyway, Birch's idea of diversifying his interests was to tape his boys having sex with their clients. We aren't talking your average clients here, either. Some of the guys were city leaders, police officers, trust fund babies. Birch had a stable of wealthy regulars. Why do you think no one's ever been able to shut him down? He has too many satisfied customers in high places for that to happen. Like I said, Birch is smart. He'd tape these guys having sex with us, and then use the tapes for leverage. Not only would he get the fee they paid him to do us, but he'd have something he could use against them later on.

Sometimes he'd ask for more money, but most of the time it was favors he was after. I hated the guy, but he was a good teacher and I'm a quick study. I decided to diversify my own interests. That's where you came in."

Dillon felt ill. He knew what was coming. Apparently Ash did too. Across the coffee table, Ash was a sickly shade of white, but it was his expression that chilled Dillon to the bone. Rather, his lack of expression. Not a single one of the thousand emotions Ash had to be feeling was written on his face. In a dry monotone, he said, "Finish it."

Dillon looked to Jamie. The pain on his face was evident, but Jamie only nodded, signaling Dillon to do as Ash ordered. With little choice, Dillon picked up where he'd left off.

"Our meeting at the rest stop was no accident. Oh, the first time I saw you there, I had no idea you were gay, but I soon found out. I watched you and another guy going at it in one of the bathroom stalls. I knew you were rich, so I staked you out. Took me about two months of groundwork, but I finally engineered a run in with you. I built our relationship slowly, and the minute I had your trust, I knew I was ready for phase two. You helped by choosing the mill as our meeting spot. Lots of places to hide a camera in that old foreman's house. I'm not as high tech as Birch was. I used a time lapse thirty-five millimeter camera instead of a video feed, but it worked the same way. I'd set the timer before you got there, get you all hot and bothered, and by the time we were both naked — slide show city.

I took the pics to a one-hour photo place before heading down to your dad's office. I told him unless he wanted to see the photos plastered all over the Net and beyond, he'd pay up. Since I didn't need any favors, I asked for cold, hard cash. Your dad forked it over without even putting up a fight. My plan worked better than I'd ever dreamed. The only problem was, I grew to like you too much.

I'm what Nora always called a one-man man. She claimed that no matter how much I screwed around, there would always be one special guy who would hold my heart. She was right about that. I wish that guy could have been you, but the truth is James Walker had me wrapped around his finger from day one. Just because I couldn't love you, though, doesn't mean I didn't care. Okay, I didn't at first. To me you were just a red hot meal ticket. But after I got to know you — as a person, not just as a wallet — I realized what I was doing was seriously fucked up. When you started telling me you loved me and begging me not to break up with you, I lost it. That's why I broke things off. Don't get me wrong. I didn't feel bad enough to give back the money, but I couldn't keep doing what I was doing. Who knows? Maybe doing that one decent thing will get me into Heaven. I used to believe if there was a God, he wouldn't waste his time on me, but meeting J changed all that. Only God could send someone like him into my life. Anyway, in the inner envelope you'll find the negatives and the only copies of the pictures I took. Well, besides the ones I gave to your dad, but I'm sure he destroyed those the first chance he got. Just so you know, your father didn't seem to be upset by the fact that you were gay, Ash. He was mad as hell that I was using you, but the gay thing didn't seem to enter into it. He may have a hard time showing it, but the guy does love you. He said he'd do anything to protect his son. When you read this letter, try to remember that someone really cares about you, even if I was never able to. I'd say I'm sorry, but you'd never believe it after all this — Ben."

Dillon refolded the letter, at a total loss for what to say next. Dillon looked to Jamie, who seemed every bit as lost as he did. Ash was the only one of them who looked like he was still in control. He stood and started toward the door without even looking at the pictures.

Jamie stood too. "Where are you going?"

"To take a whiz. Why, you wanna come hold it for me?"

Normally Dillon would have laughed at such a smart-ass comment, but there was nothing funny about the flat, even tone Ash used when he said it. Dillon said, "You okay, man?"

Ash shrugged. "Sure. Why wouldn't I be? So I got fucked over. So what? Won't be the last time."

Jamie reached out to him. "We want to help you. I mean—"

"Look, Walker, can this wait until I get back. Unless you want to come in there with me while I piss, it'll have to." He left before either one of them could say anything more.

Jamie collapsed back into the couch.

"Are you all right?"

"Sick to my stomach." Jamie put his head in his hands. "How about you?"

"The same."

Jamie leaned back and closed his eyes. "I hope Ash is able to move past all this. The way he looked just then scared the hell out of me." Jamie opened his eyes again and sat up. "Speaking of Ash, he's been gone a little too long to suit me. I think I'll go check on him."

"Want me to come with you?"

"No, he'll feel like we're ganging up on him. Where's the closest bathroom in this place?"

"Down the hall and to the left, if I'm remembering right."

"Gotcha."

Jamie had been gone for less than a minute when Dillon heard him screaming. "Dillon, help me!"

Dillon was down the hall in two seconds. Jamie was holding on to Ash's legs as Ash sagged like a rag doll from what looked like a belt lashed to the railing for the glass shower doors. Unfortunately, in keeping with the scale of the house, whoever designed the bathroom had oversized the shower stall, making the top of the thick brass railing only about two feet lower than the bathroom's nine foot ceiling. Jamie was doing his best to hold Ash up so he could breathe, but he was staggering under Ash's weight. Dillon ran to help, taking Ash's body on himself.

The stool Ash had stood on while he tethered the belt was still within reach. Jamie picked it up and stood on his tiptoes to unbuckle and undo the thick leather. The minute Ash was loose, Dillon lowered him to the floor and pulled the belt free of his neck. Ash was breathing, but barely. His pulse was thready as Dillon whipped his cell phone out of his pocket and called nine-one-one, praying to God help would get there in time.

Brandon handed Jamie and Dillon each a cup of steaming coffee. They were the only three people in the waiting room of Chicago General's I.C.U., and Jamie was grateful. He couldn't shake the picture of Ash's limp body from his mind. He felt sick and responsible. If he hadn't given Ash that letter, none of it would have happened. His only consolation was that Ash was still alive, albeit barely.

Brandon sat down across from Dillon and stretched his long legs in front of himself. "Let's go through this one more time, just so I'll have it all straight in my head when I go back to the station to file my report. You say you went to see Ash because you had some papers that belonged to him."

Jamie said, "Yes, sir," and then felt the slight nudge from Dillon's knee. Brandon didn't seem to notice it, but Jamie got the message, loud and clear. Dillon wanted him to tell Brandon everything, but Jamie couldn't do it. Not yet.

Brandon took a sip of his coffee. "When you got there, did he seem anxious or depressed at all?"

Jamie played it off. "I don't know Ash well enough to judge his mood."

"Uh huh. And these papers you say you had of his, what were they and how did you come to have them in your possession?"

"I didn't read them, Sheriff." True enough. Dillon had read the letter out loud at Ash's request. "I'm not really sure why I ended up with them, but when I realized the papers belonged to Ash, Dillon and I took them over there."

Brandon narrowed his eyes. "So the fact that you were at Ashton Barnes's house the night he tried to off himself was just a stellar coincidence?"

"Yes, sir."

Brandon crossed his legs, ankle over knee. "Whatever the circumstances, he's damned lucky you showed up when you did. What made you decide to go back to the bathroom and check on him? Did you have a reason to be worried?"

Jamie was *this* close to coming apart under the questioning. He was grateful when Dillon stepped in. "Actually, Jamie had to pee, and he figured Ash would be finished. Speaking of Ash, how is he?"

"I'm not sure. My brother Keith is a neurologist on staff here. He's handling the case. If anyone can put Ash back to rights, it's him." Brandon paused. "If Ash does pull through, it will be a while before he can go back home. He'll need to see a team of psychiatrists and counselors, and those guys will have to be satisfied that Ash won't try to kill himself again before they let him leave. Even then, he'll need therapy, maybe even medication."

God, what a mess. Jamie rubbed his hands over his face.

Dillon leaned forward. "Here comes Keith." He watched the eldest Nash brother coming down the hall. Keith looked a lot like Brandon, dark haired and blue eyed, but there was no doubt which one was the doctor and which one was the sheriff. Keith just screamed bedside manner, while Brandon was the picture of a no-nonsense cop.

Brandon, Jamie, and Dillon all stood as Keith held out his hand to Jamie. "Keith Nash, brother to Megan and this lug right here, as well five assorted others."

Jamie shook his hand. "James Walker. Megan talks about you a lot."

Keith beamed. "Of course she does. I'm her favorite brother."

Brandon elbowed him in the ribs. "Quit clowning and tell us about Ash."

Keith eyed Jamie and Dillon. "Normally I'd only give this information to Ashton's next of kin." He looked to Brandon. "Any luck getting in touch with his dad?"

"Not yet. I got through to the secretary at Barnes Securities, his dad's company. She said she'd try to reach him, but I have no idea when that will be."

Keith nodded. "Since these two saved Ashton's life, I don't think his father will mind if I bend the rules for them. If he does, he can take it up with you." He grinned at Brandon.

"Gee, thanks," Brandon said.

Keith launched into his report. "The M.R.I. shows no obvious signs of brain or spinal cord trauma, no small miracle. His vital signs were faint and iffy when he came in here, but now they're steady and improving. Those are encouraging signs, but we aren't out of the woods yet. Ash hasn't regained consciousness, and we can't find an obvious cause. I'm guessing shock, but that's just speculation on my part. He's got a two-inch-wide contusion encompassing the circumference of his neck, most noticeable in the front where the bulk of the force was exerted against his skin. A good plastic surgeon could probably decrease the appearance of the scar, but Ash will always carry a reminder of what he tried to do. And that's not the only thing. Ashton's vocal cords were damaged. He'll be able to talk, but his voice will never sound the same. Even so, I count him as one very lucky young man. Our goal now is to keep him from ever trying this again."

"I already explained to them about the observation and the counseling." Brandon looked down at his watch. "I'd better get back to the station and fill out my report." Brandon clapped his brother on the back. "Keep me posted." He squeezed first Dillon and then Jamie on the shoulder. "You two call me if you need me, or if you think of anything else that might help Ash." The look he gave them let Jamie know Brandon knew they were hiding something, he just wasn't pressing it. With one last goodbye to all three of them, Brandon left.

"I've got rounds to make before I'm off for the night," Keith said. "Why don't the two of you go on home? I'm guessing it'll be hours before Ash wakes up, and even then you'll have to wait until he's moved out of I.C.U. before you can see him."

That sounded like a plan to Jamie. He was tired, tired of all the sickness and death, and tired of trying to reconcile his memories of Ben the Friend with his knowledge of Ben the Blackmailer. He felt Dillon take his hand and lead him toward the exit. Jamie was more than happy to let Dillon take charge.

The elevator ride down to the parking garage was largely silent. It wasn't until they were halfway between floors nine and ten that Dillon said, "Are you worried about Ash, or are you thinking about Ben and what he did?"

Jamie grimaced. "A little of both, I guess. That, and I'm still trying to figure out what Ben was doing on Tully Road when he'd promised to meet Ash at Tanner Textiles."

Dillon leaned against the south wall of the elevator. "Maybe Ben never intended to meet with Ash that night. Standing a guy up is a sure way to get that 'fuck off' vibe across to him."

Jamie shook his head. "I don't think so. Ben was way too direct for that. If he'd wanted to tell Ash to fuck off, he'd have done it."

"Maybe," Dillon said, but Jamie could tell he had his doubts. After a few minutes of silence, Dillon added, "Since you didn't tell Brandon about the money, I'm guessing you're nowhere near ready to let this thing drop."

The elevator doors opened to their floor and Jamie stepped out, leaving Dillon to follow. "No, I'm not."

"You're planning something, aren't you?" Dillon sighed.

"Yes, and you won't like it."

Dillon made a face. "Somehow that doesn't surprise me."

Just as Jamie predicted, Dillon didn't like what he was planning. Even so, Dillon was supportive and offered only minimal protest when they pulled up in front of the Reed County Jail the following Monday after school.

"You sure you want to do this?"

"I'm sure. The only person who might know what happened that night is Barry Sledge. He's the last person to see Ben alive."

"The guy's in jail for vehicular homicide. He hasn't even been sentenced yet. What makes you think he'll tell you anything?"

Jamie reached for the door handle. "I don't have anything to lose by trying. I'm hoping if I approach him the right way and show him I'm not a threat, he'll open up to me."

"Just be careful. And hurry. Keith sent word through Megan we can see Ash this afternoon."

"He's awake?"

"Awake and in his own room." Dillon left the car running and leaned back in the seat. "I'll wait here for you." Jamie reached for the door handle just as Dillon said, "Hey, Jamie?"

"Yeah?"

"I..." He trailed off and Jamie could tell he was measuring his words. Finally, he said, "I'm here if you need me."

Jamie leaned over and gave Dillon's lips a soft brush with his own, then got out of the car.

Unlike the small cluster of holding cells attached to the sheriff's office, the county jail had the look of a prison, from the gray, peeling paint on the walls to the stands of metal detectors anchored in the lobby. After signing in, Jamie was led to the visitor area, a row of glassed-in booths with a phone on either side of the glass. The officer in charge instructed Jamie to have a seat at booth seven and wait. Jamie swallowed against the butterflies in his stomach and did as he was told.

Barry Sledge was led in a few minutes later. Even with the orange jumpsuit and the cuffs encircling his wrists, Sledge didn't look like a killer. Jamie did his best to remember this man was responsible for Ben's death, but one look at Sledge's pitted face and brown, sorrow-filled eyes had Jamie pitying the man.

Sledge sat down and picked up the phone, motioning for Jamie to do the same. Jamie picked up in time to hear Sledge say, "There must be some mistake. I was told I had a visitor, but I don't know you." His voice was scratchy and strained, years of alcohol abuse having made its mark.

"My name is James Walker, and I need to talk to you. I promise I'll make it quick." Jamie hesitated. "I'm a friend of Ben Lewis."

All the color drained from Sledge's normally ruddy face. He started to hang up the phone, but Jamie stopped him. "Don't hang up. Please. This is important and you're the only one I can ask."

Sledge hesitated but put the phone back to his ear. Jamie started over. "I have reason to believe Ben was supposed to have been somewhere besides Tully Road that night. Since you were the last person to, uh...see him, I was hoping maybe you saw something — anything — that might help me understand what he was doing out there."

Sledge looked around, making sure no one was standing behind him. Finally, he said, "Look, kid, all I can tell you is what I told the cops when they picked me up. I was driving home from Philly's Tavern when I saw this kid laying in the middle of the road. I didn't see him until it was too late. There wasn't anything I could do for him, so I split. I didn't see nothing or no one besides that."

Jamie's mind was reeling. "What do you mean Ben was 'laying in the middle of the road'?"

Sledge screwed up his face. "What are you, deaf? I meant just what I said. I was moving along Tully Road at a fair clip and all of a sudden, there was this kid, just laying there." Sledge snorted. "Not that the cops believed me. Thought I was lying to save my own skin. That court appointed asswipe lawyer they assigned me swore up and down all the tests confirmed that kid very well could have died from the impact of my car. That's when I knew I couldn't get out of it, so I took the deal the D.A. offered and told 'em what they wanted to hear. I may have hit that boy, but let me tell you something, Mr. James Walker, I didn't kill him. You want my opinion? Ben Lewis was dead before I ever came along."

Chapter Ten

"The guy's a drunk on his way to the pen for God knows how long. He's lying to save his own ass."

"Why now, though? He's already taken the deal. What could he possibly have to gain by making up this story?"

Dillon waited until the doors closed and then pressed the button for the sixth floor. He did his best to rein in his temper, but he was mad as hell at Sledge for stringing Jamie along. "Who knows why people lie? Maybe he's one of those sick fucks who enjoys playing games with people's heads. Or maybe he feels so guilty about offing Ben that he's made up this story to make himself feel better. Who knows? I'll tell you one thing. Brandon will be pissed when he finds out you went to see the guy."

The elevator doors opened onto the sixth floor of Chicago General. Just before they got off, Dillon brushed his fingers across Jamie's cheek. "You mad at me?"

Jamie leaned into Dillon's hand. "No, I'm not mad at you. I know you're only trying to help."

That's something, anyway. They walked off the elevator and searched for room 618, the number the volunteer at the visitor's desk had given them. They found it without trouble and were just about to go inside when someone said, "Hang on a second, boys."

Dillon and Jamie turned, and came face to face with Ash's father.

Ashton Barnes the Second looked nothing like his son. Ash was tall and dark-haired, while Mr. Barnes was of medium height and blond. He wore a white silk shirt and black tailored slacks, whereas Ash was a jeans and t-shirt guy. The only similarity at all was in the eyes, and, even there, Ash's eyes were a darker shade of brown than his father's.

After shaking hands with them both, Barnes said, "There's a private waiting area down the hall. Do you think we could go down there and talk?"

Dillon wanted to say no. He'd had enough of waiting rooms and private chats. He took one look at Mr. Barnes's pleading face and heard himself saying yes just as Jamie agreed also.

Once they were seated in the waiting room, Mr. Barnes said, "I don't know how to thank the two of you for what you did." He looked down at his hands where they lay trembling in his lap. "I know I wouldn't win any Father of the Year awards, but I love my son. I'd be lost if anything ever happened to him. When I think about what could have—" He broke off, his voice strained with the effort of holding back his tears. Once composed, Barnes said, "I just thank God you were there."

Jamie shook his head. "You don't understand. This whole thing was my fault to begin with."

Dillon was about to protest when Barnes beat him to it. "I saw the letter and the pictures. When he woke up, Ash told me everything. My son told me you had no idea what was in that envelope when you took it to him."

"If I'd known, I never would have taken it over there."

"At least Ash knows the truth about Ben. Maybe now he can get on with his life."

Jamie cleared his throat. "There's something else you need to know. It's about the money."

"You mean the blackmail money?" Jamie nodded and Barnes sighed. "I'm sorry Ash had to find out about that. I knew he'd would be crushed when he found out Lewis was using him to milk me for cash. I hoped if I paid Lewis off, Ben would go away and Ash would be none the wiser."

Jamie took a deep breath. "The thing is, Ben left the money to me when he died."

It was Mr. Barnes turn to look shocked. "You're kidding."

"No, sir. Believe me, I wish I was." Jamie rubbed his hand across his face. "That money belongs to you. I want you to have it back."

"I don't know what to say. That's very generous of you, James, but you don't have to do that. I owe you for saving my son's life."

"No, you don't. To be honest, I wouldn't feel right about keeping it now, no matter what. Knowing what Ben did changes everything. The money is in a safe deposit box. If you'd like to meet me at the bank tomorrow after school, I'll give it to you then. I'm not sure how much of it Ben spent, but I do know there's about forty-two-thousand dollars left."

"Forty-two-thousand? You must have miscounted."

"Like I said, Ben may have spent some of it—"

Mr. Barnes shook his head. "I wasn't trying to say that any money was missing. In fact, just the opposite. I paid Ben one lump sum of twenty thousand dollars. That means there's twenty-two thousand extra in that box."

Jamie and Dillon stood outside the door to Ash's room. Jamie hoped he'd wiped the confusion off his face so Ash couldn't see it. The last thing Ash needed right now was to be dragged back into a mess.

Dillon knocked on the door. They heard a weak, gravelly "Come in," and entered the room.

Ash was lying in bed wearing a hospital gown and a manufactured smile. He looked like pure hell, but he was alive, and that's all Jamie cared about. Ash had been victimized by Ben, and for some reason, Jamie felt responsible. If he'd been able to love Ben back, maybe Ash never would have been involved.

Ash broke him out of his morbid thoughts. "Sit down." He motioned to a couple of bedside chairs.

Dillon took the chair closest to the wall, leaving Jamie to sit directly facing Ash. Jamie had a feeling Dillon had done that on purpose, and Jamie couldn't fault him. He and Ash needed to talk.

Ash apparently had the same idea. "Dillon, could I talk to James alone for a sec?"

Dillon nodded. "I'll run down and get something to drink. You guys want anything?"

Ash managed a laugh. The sound coming through his injured throat reminded Jamie of the scrape of metal against concrete. "No, thanks. They're pumping me so full of fluids now I feel like I'm gonna pop."

"Nothing for me, either, thanks."

"I'll be back in a few, then." Dillon pulled the door closed as he left.

There was an awkward moment of silence while Ash searched for what he wanted to say and Jamie waited. After staring down at his hands for a full three minutes, Ash looked up and said, "I'm sorry."

"You don't have to—"

"Please. It hurts to talk, so just let me get it out." Jamie nodded and Ash continued, "I have a whole lot to apologize to you for, from that stupid showdown in the hall and the way I acted at the church, to trying to kill myself while you and Dillon were in the next room. For what it's worth, I only did that at the church because I wanted to know what it was Ben saw in you. I wondered what you had that I didn't. I guess I thought if I could try you out for myself, I might see it and then, it wouldn't hurt so bad. Pretty stupid, considering the only thing Ben ever saw in me was a pay-off."

"Yeah, well...I loved Ben, but in this case, he was an idiot. He could have had something real with you. It's not your fault he didn't seize the opportunity."

Ash settled himself against the pillows. "Maybe one day that will matter to me, but right now I can't really see it that way, you know?"

Jamie leaned forward and put one cautious hand on Ash's arm. "Just because Ben wasn't it for you, doesn't mean there isn't a guy out there waiting for you. If you keep trying to hurt yourself, you'll never find him."

Ash closed his eyes. "I know. It just hurts so bad. I felt so alone. Dr. Nash recommended a shrink here at the hospital who's helping me work through it all. Dr. Carson said as long as I keep all my therapy appointments and submit to an evaluation every month, I can probably go home in three or four weeks."

"Cool." Jamie hesitated. "What about school?"

Ash closed his eyes. "You know, huh?"

"Yeah. I'm sorry, man. You may not believe this, but Dillon and I didn't tell anybody."

Ash opened his eyes and the look he gave Jamie was pure sincerity. "I never thought that."

"So, how—"

"How do I think the fact that I had a flaming affair with Ben got plastered all over the school?" Ash shrugged. "Who knows? Chad came rushing in here this morning, yelling at me, wanting to know when I turned 'fag' on him." Ash snorted. "Like this is something I did to him. I tried to explain, but he wouldn't listen. He left without telling me where he'd heard it, but to be honest, I don't really care. So, I'm out. So what? What am I gonna do, kill myself over it? You see how well that worked out the last time." He pointed to the bandage encircling his throat. "Believe me when I say I won't be trying that again."

Jamie gave Ash's arm a squeeze before withdrawing his hand. "When can you go back to class?"

"I won't have to. Morgan came to see my dad this morning, not long after Chad left. Told him I have enough credits to graduate. My college acceptance is already in, so all I have to do now is wait it out until fall." He lowered his eyes. "I'm glad I won't have to go back. I hate the way people look at you when they know you've tried to commit suicide. It's like they're just waiting for you to crack and try it again. I've seen enough of that from the few people who've visited me. You and Dillon are the first visitors I've had who haven't made me feel like a charity case."

Jamie nodded. "A person can only stomach so much pity before he feels like he's gonna hurl. When my mom ran off, people looked at me the same way, like I was some kind of freak. Believe me, I understand exactly how you feel."

Ash smiled, a real smile this time. "I believe you do, James. I really believe you do."

Jamie had only been home for twenty minutes when the phone rang. It wouldn't be Dillon; he'd just dropped Jamie off on his way in to work. Jamie was tired and nursing a headache. He hoped the caller would just go away, but after the sixth ring, he gave in.

"Hello?"

"Wanna tell me what in the hell you were doing down at the county jail talking to Barry Sledge?"

"Well, hello to you, too, Sheriff. Great to hear from you."

"Don't dick around with me, kid. You have no business rubbing elbows with people like Sledge. Haven't you been hurt enough?"

"I know you're not happy about me meeting with Sledge, but he said some stuff I think you need to hear." Jamie took a deep breath. "He said he was pretty sure Ben was already dead when he hit him."

"Uh huh. And did he also tell you that Santa Claus, the Easter Bunny, and the Tooth Fairy were all planning a coup to break him out of jail? Because that scenario is just as likely as the one Sledge is trying to sell you."

"So you won't even look into it?" Jamie could feel himself getting angry. "Ben's death doesn't mean enough to you?"

Brandon's sign reverberated through the phone. "I understand how much you want Ben's death to mean something, but the truth is, it was just another meaningless tragedy. Sledge left out a few details when he told you his story."

"Such as?"

"Did he tell you the autopsy results indicate that Ben died from injuries sustained in a high velocity impact?"

Jamie could feel the wind draining out of his sails. "No, he didn't."

"Big shocker there. I guess he also forgot to mention my men investigated his claim and found no evidence to back up his story. Oh, and I suppose he neglected to mention that at least seven people at Philly's Tavern saw him down enough tequila to intoxicate a third world country."

Brandon might be right about Sledge, but he didn't know about the blackmail. Jamie intended to keep it that way, at least until he found out about the origin of the other half of the money. If Ben had another innocent victim out there, the last thing Jamie wanted to do was put that poor man through the hell Ash had suffered. Forcing out the words, Jamie said, "I'm sorry, Sheriff. I guess I wasn't thinking."

Brandon's voice softened. "The only thing you have to apologize for is calling me sheriff. We're friends, so it's Brandon or Bran to you. As for you wanting to believe Sledge... I understand. Just talk to me first next time, okay?"

Jamie felt guilty as hell for hiding the truth from Brandon, but he managed to tamp it down. "I will."

"Good. Stay out of trouble, kid."

The minute Jamie heard the click, he disconnected and began to massage his throbbing temples. He had to identify Ben's second victim. He fell asleep at the kitchen table with his head propped on his arms, still wondering how in the hell he was going to pull that one off.

At four o'clock on Friday afternoon, not long after Dillon dropped Jamie off and headed to work, Megan showed up on Jamie's doorstep with her calculus book in hand. "Have mercy on me, dear sir."

Jamie laughed. "Sorry, I suck at calculus."

Megan gave a dramatic sigh. "I'm doomed."

"Come in and have some of Aunt Sadie's left over lasagna. It's a cure-all for just about anything."

"Now you're speaking my language. Lead the way, most kind and gracious host."

Jamie led Megan into the kitchen and instructed her to sit down while he pulled the lasagna out of the fridge. Putting a huge pile of the stuff onto a plate, Jamie slid it into the microwave. Before long, the heavenly smell of pasta, marinara sauce, and melted cheese filled the kitchen.

Megan sighed in rapture. "There ought to be a law against anything smelling so good. I feel sorry for Dillon and Heath, eating out of cans and boxes all the time."

"Can I ask you a personal question?"

Megan propped her feet on an empty chair. "You can ask me anything you want. Doesn't mean I'll answer it, but you can always ask."

"You know Heath's got a thing for you, right?"

Megan snorted. "Sure he does. That's why he avoids me like the Black Plague."

Jamie was shocked. "Heath does that?"

"Yep. When he did Fireman's Week at the Boys and Girls Club, I thought Heath and I were actually working toward a friendship. Even when Dillon moved in with him, he and I were able to talk. You know, kid around. We got along great. Then I kissed him and all that went up in flames."

The microwave dinged, but Jamie couldn't tear his eyes away from Megan long enough to take the lasagna out. "You kissed him? When?"

Megan actually blushed. "The day after Ben's memorial service. Heath came over to thank Mom and me for cleaning his apartment. As he was leaving, I walked him out to his truck and he gave me a hug. I looked up, he looked down, and before I knew it, total lip-lock."

"So, how was it?"

The dreamy look on her face would have been sappy on anyone else, but on Megan it was cute. "It was perfect. Talk about fireworks. That boy has the softest lips. Incredible doesn't even cover it." She scrunched her eyebrows together. "At least it was until he freaked out on me. One minute he was kissing me back and the next minute he was hollering about how I'm too young for him and how he's not ready to make a commitment. It was one kiss, for heaven's sake. It's not like I asked him to elope with me."

Jamie nodded in sympathy as he took the plate out of the microwave and brought it to the table. Ignoring Megan's offer of help, he went back to fetch a couple of forks and two Cokes from the fridge.

She waited until Jamie was seated, then stuck her fork into the warm, gooey pasta and brought it to her lips, savoring it like a last meal. Washing her food down with a healthy swig of Coke, Megan said, "I heard you and Dillon went to see Ash at the hospital."

"Yeah. Thanks to Keith's handiwork, I think he'll be okay."

"Poor guy. He's lucky you and Dillon found him when you did." Megan scooped up another forkful of pasta. "I gather the rumors are true, then. He really did try to kill himself because he was having an affair with Ben Lewis. I'm assuming you guys went over there to give him Ben's letter?"

Uh oh. "Yep."

"What did it say?"

Jamie adored Megan and he hated keeping secrets from her, but this was Ash's secret, not his. Keeping his voice neutral, Jamie shrugged. "You know. The usual stuff." *Usual when your boyfriend was blackmailing your father, that is.*

Megan swallowed another mouthful of food. "Ash must have really been in love with Ben to want to kill himself over the guy. Especially with Ben's past."

Ben's past. That was it. For the second time in as many weeks, Jamie had one of those instant bursts of understanding. If Birch Carpenter taught Ben everything he knew, Birch might be able to tell him something — anything — that would help Jamie ferret out the identity of Ben's second victim. Not that he probably would. Birch was just as likely to tell Jamie to go to hell, but as with Sledge, Jamie figured he had nothing to lose by trying. He got up from the table so fast he nearly knocked his chair over. "Megan, I have to go."

"Now?" Megan pointed to the half-full plate. "You're not even done eating."

"I...uh, something's come up. I have to catch a cab to Chicago."

Megan narrowed her eyes. "This has something to do with that Sledge guy saying Ben was already dead, doesn't it?"

"Dillon told you about that?" Jamie smacked his forehead. "Of course he did. Yes, it does, but I can't tell you what it is."

Thinking the conversation over, Jamie grabbed the phone book from the counter and flipped through the pages, looking for the number to Reed's only cab company. Striding across the room with all the grace of a queen, Megan laid her hand across the top of the phone book. "Tell me who it is you have to see in Chicago."

At least in this Jamie could be honest. "Ben was a hustler before he came to Reed."

"A prostitute?"

"'Fraid so. I need to talk to some of the people from Ben's past. I can't tell you why exactly, but I need some information from someone who knew Ben before he came to Reed."

Megan took the phone book out of Jamie's hands, closed it and placed it back on the counter. "There's no way you're taking a cab to Chicago." Megan pulled her keys out of the front pocket of her jeans. "I'll drive you."

Who'd have thought a pimp would be listed with directory assistance? Jamie had been afraid that finding Birch would be a hassle, but all it took was a quick call to four-one-one. Megan wanted to call the number listed, but Jamie refused. Better not to warn Birch they were coming. With any luck, they'd zip through the drive to Chicago, have a quick word with "good ol' Birch" as Ben had called him, and be back in Reed before anyone noticed they were gone.

It all sounded so easy when he and Megan planned it out. Jamie should have known better. The minute he saw the yellow crime scene tape wrapped around the brick pillars on either side of the driveway, Jamie knew they were in trouble.

Megan double checked the driving directions from the Internet. "Maybe this is the wrong house."

Jamie shook his head. "I don't think so. Pull over there, by the curb."

"Why? There's tape all over the place. We're not supposed to go in there."

Jamie did his best not to give her one of those "duh" looks. "We're not supposed to be in Chicago hunting down a kiddie pimp, either."

Megan pulled her car to the nearest curb. "I'm going with you."

"Meggie—"

"Look, Jamie, we're not supposed to be here. We've already established that. Do you really want to waste time on an argument you know you aren't gonna win?"

The woman knew how to make a point. Jamie got out and walked around to Megan's side of the car, opening the door for her with a resigned sigh. As they approached, he took a second to study the house. It was an old Victorian design in a luxurious, well-maintained neighborhood. Not exactly what he'd expected. A cold shiver went down his spine as the two of them made their way around the pillars and tape. Even in the dying light of late afternoon, Jamie could see well manicured grass. He could easily imagine Ben or one of Birch's other boys coming home after a hard day of whoring to mow the lawn. He thanked God he'd had Aunt Sadie to take him in when his mom ditched him. If not, he could have just as easily become prey to Birch or someone like him.

The main house was dark, and the deep porch's arched openings were cordoned off with more of the bright yellow tape. Even in the shadows, Jamie could see deep red stains on the concrete floor. *Blood.*

He turned to face Megan, and seeing his own fear reflected on her face, said, "I don't see any sign of Birch Carpenter. Maybe we should go."

Megan raised her hand to point at something behind Jamie's back just as a massive hand clamped down on his shoulder. A deep, scratchy voice said, "Birch Carpenter is dead, and you aren't going anywhere."

Chapter Eleven

Dillon looked at the storeroom clock for the second time in as many minutes. Eight o'clock; it would be at least another hour before he could see Jamie. It wasn't that Dillon minded working until closing. He'd done it more times than he could count. Still, he couldn't remember ever before being this anxious to leave. He wanted to be with Jamie so bad he could taste it. It was a raging need, a burning he couldn't explain. Like if he didn't see Jamie soon, he wasn't gonna make it. *God, I've got it bad.*

Jim Pembroke stuck his head through the stockroom door.

"Dillon, you've got a phone call on line four."

"Thanks, Mr. P. I'll pick up back here."

As soon as Mr. Pembroke left, Dillon grabbed the receiver of the employee extension located directly underneath the time clock. "Hello?"

"You know, kid, I'm not sure which one has less sense: your boyfriend or my sister. If you ask me, neither one of 'em could find their way out of a round room with no damn corners."

The minute he heard Brandon's voice, Dillon's heart settled somewhere in the vicinity of his stomach. "What happened?"

"Oh, not much. Well, not unless you count Jamie and Megan being picked up by the Chicago P.D. in front of a dead man's house. A dead man, I might add, who was the prime suspect in an ongoing investigation into a child pornography and prostitution ring. A dead man who was murdered in cold blood not three feet from his own front door."

Brandon had to be talking about Birch. Jamie and Megan had gone to see Ben's pimp. *Birch is dead?* Dillon couldn't even think about that right now. First he had to know Jamie and Megan were okay. Dillon sank down onto a nearby stack of plastic packing crates. "They were arrested?" Dillon could hear Brandon drawing in a deep breath.

"They weren't arrested, though not for lack of trying. They were caught snooping around the deceased's residence. That was after they crossed enough crime scene tape and no trespassing signs to wallpaper an entire house. A cop spotted them hanging around the place and called the lead detective working the investigation. It just so happens I know the guy who's handling the case. He used to work for the force here in Reed, a man by the name of Hank Kilgore. Since the killer's still at large, Detective Kilgore thought a couple of kids snooping around the guy's house was more than a little bit suspicious. That's why he hauled them in. Kilgore's a good guy, and he recognized the Nash name the minute he ran Megan's I.D. He called me and asked me to vouch for them both." He sighed. "I managed to convince him Jamie and Megan had nothing to do with the murder, but I couldn't very well tell Kilgore what they were really doing at the house because I don't have a freakin' clue. By the way, you knew that Jamie doesn't have a driver's license, right?"

Dillon nodded, then realized Brandon couldn't see him over the phone. God, he was rattled, and not just from Brandon's sudden shift in topic. "I know he doesn't."

"You need to work on that. Not only does a boy his age need to know how to drive, but he doesn't have any picture I.D. All he had on him was his social security card and a credit card his aunt had given him. Since Sadie Banks was listed as the co-holder of the card, Kilgore very well could have called her. They're lucky he called me first."

That was the God's honest truth. "Sadie will kill him."

"I talked Kilgore out of calling her by telling him I would handle it myself," Brandon said. "The point is, Jamie needs I.D. I guess he could get one of those non-driver cards with just his picture and personal information on it, but he really does need to know how to drive." He paused. "I suppose I could teach him if he wanted me to."

Dillon was stunned. "You aren't mad at him?"

"I'm not gonna lie and say I'm happy about whatever it is Jamie's got going on. Hell, I know he's hiding something, and this latest caper of his just proves it. I'm also more than a little ticked that Megan got involved in this mess, but I also know my sister, and I know there was no way Jamie could talk her out of sticking her pug nose into his business." He paused. "The Chicago force has been trying for years to shut Birch Carpenter down for suspected sex trafficking involving teenage boys, but no one's been able to prove anything. Apparently Carpenter was well connected enough to keep his fostering program going with only token protest from a handful of concerned citizens. I know Birch was Ben Lewis's last foster father."

Dillon cleared his throat. "I'm guessing you read Ben's juvenile file."

"Read it from cover to cover when the poor kid was killed. I combed through every word of that report, Dillon. That's why there isn't a doubt in my mind that Ben's death was an accident." Brandon snorted. "Fat chance of me ever convincing Jamie of that. He's on some bizarre crusade about Ben. Going to visit Barry Sledge in jail was bad enough, but when Jamie starts seeking out professional scumbags like Carpenter, he's screwing around with things he doesn't understand. Carpenter was shot six times at point blank range with a three-fifty-seven magnum revolver. The perp used hollowpoint bullets that ripped the hell out of the body."

"What does that have to do with Jamie?"

"Nothing, directly. But here's the thing. I was a profiler with the F.B.I. before I came back to Reed and ran for sheriff. One of the first things I was taught was to guess a killer's motivation. The police took thirty thousand in cash out of Carpenter's house at the same time as they took the body. That rules out robbery. Given Carpenter's character, you'd think self-defense could have been a factor, but considering Carpenter was killed on his own front porch with his keys in one hand and a bag of groceries in the other, it looks like the shooter lay in wait for him and caught him by surprise on his way home from the store. Not exactly the act of someone fighting for his life. A hired killer would have fired one bullet — two at the most — straight to the head or the heart, just enough to get the job done without the added risk of extra shots to draw attention. That takes care of the professional hit theory and leaves only one motive."

"What's that?"

"Revenge. The person who killed Carpenter was mad as hell. There's no way he'd have emptied that gun into Carpenter's body otherwise. Hell, the first shot probably killed the guy. No, that was rage taking over. And a guy who has enough hatred inside himself to lay in wait for a man and turn him into hamburger on his own doorstep wouldn't hesitate to take out Jamie and my sister if he thought the two of them were getting even remotely close to finding out who he is." Brandon's voice lost all traces of rancor. "I'm telling you all this because I care about you and Jamie. I wouldn't waste my breath explaining if I didn't believe there was a real risk involved. I care too much to stand back and let you guys get hurt. I'll do whatever it takes to protect the two of you, same as I would with Megan. I want you and Jamie to have a long and happy life together." Another pause. "That's assuming you want to spend the rest of your life with Jamie."

Dillon had spent the last two years dreaming about nothing else. There wasn't a doubt in his mind he wanted Jamie — and nobody but Jamie — from now on. He'd heard more than one person say eighteen was too young to make that kind of commitment, but Dillon couldn't care less. He knew his own mind and heart better than anyone else ever could. The only feelings he was unsure about were Jamie's. Did Jamie want him, and nothing but him, till death did them part? After all they'd been through, he was half afraid to know the answer.

He couldn't bring himself to voice those concerns to Brandon, so all he said was, "Yes, I do."

Dillon didn't see the trap coming until it was sprung. Brandon's voice was laced with smug satisfaction. "Good. Then you can drive over to Chicago and pick him up. Grab my sister, too, while you're at it. Kilgore's done with them, at least for now. Seems Jamie and Megan fed him some cock-and-bull story about wanting to know more about

Ben's life before he came to Reed. Whatever it was they told him, Kilgore bought it. He's agreed to let this little incident go as long as Jamie and Megan stay away from his investigation." He snorted. "Yeah, right. Just swing by the station and I'll give you directions on how to get to the precinct where they're being held."

Damn. "You set me up."

Brandon snickered. "You can blame Nate. It was his idea for you to pick them up."

Dillon rubbed his forehead. "I'm confused. Why can't Megan just drive them both back to Reed herself?"

"Because, even though they weren't officially arrested, Megan's car was impounded for being illegally parked in front of Carpenter's house. She doesn't have the cash on her to bail it out, so I'll give you the money when you come by to get the directions and we'll kill two birds with one stone. I was all set to go over there and get them myself, but Nate felt sure I'd cause a scene. I swear, my own husband has no faith in me."

"I'll be at your office as soon as I square things with my boss." Dillon hesitated. "Hey, Brandon?"

"If you're gonna thank me, kid, you might want to save it. Just because I'm not going to pick them up tonight doesn't mean I don't have a thing or two to say to Jamie and Megan about this little misadventure of theirs. This isn't the amateur detective hour, and I'll be damned if Jamie isn't going to get that through his thick skull even if I have to pound it in there."

Dillon actually smiled. "That, I don't doubt. But I do want to thank you. For everything."

"Yeah, yeah. You're welcome. Now go get your guy before some sex starved jailbird decides to make Jamie his bitch. Knowing my sister, she'd want to watch."

With that rather disturbing picture in his head, Dillon disconnected. The first thing he did was seek out Jim Pembroke. He found him up front, talking to one of the pharmacists. "Hey, Mr. P., can I talk to you for a sec?"

"Sure." Jim nodded to the pharmacist and motioned Dillon toward his office. "We can talk in here, if that's okay with you."

"That'd be great." Dillon followed Jim into his office. Once seated, Dillon said, "I hate to do this, Mr. P., but something's come up. I need to leave."

Jim leaned across his desk, his dark gray hair ruffled from a night at work and hazel eyes boring into Dillon's skin. "Is everything all right with you, son?" Before Dillon could speak, Jim held up a hand. "I don't mean to pry, but you went from never missing a night of work to having to take leave at a moment's notice. The change in you has me worried."

The skin on the back of Dillon's neck began to prickle. He needed his job too badly to lose it. "Mr. P., are you gonna fire me? I know I've taken some extra time off lately, but—"

Jim shook his head. "Calm down. I have no intention of firing you. Like I've told you before, you're the best employee I've got. I just want you to know, no matter what's going on in your life, you can talk to me about it." He paused. "I heard a rumor you're no longer living with your folks."

Dillon swallowed hard. "No, sir. I'm living with my older brother, Heath."

Jim nodded. "I understand young men your age sometimes have problems relating to their folks. Heck, I may be three times older than you are, but I haven't forgotten what it feels like to be eighteen. The point is, my door is always open for you, Dillon. I'm more than willing to help in any way I can."

"Thanks. I'll make up tonight's time, I swear it."

"Not necessary. Now go on. Take care of your business. I'll see you on Monday night."

Dillon almost screamed his relief as he left Jim's office. He'd cleared the first hurdle. Now all he had to do was get to Jamie and Megan. Dillon clocked out and had almost made it to the front door of the shop when he ran headfirst into Heath. *Oh great.* That was all he needed. Heath's face was flushed and Dillon was pretty sure it had nothing to do with the cold outside. "What are you doing down here?"

"Did the sheriff get in touch with you?" Heath growled.

Oh, crap. "Yeah, he did."

"Good. He called the apartment first, looking for you. Thought maybe you had the night off, he said. What's this about Megan and Jamie being arrested in Chicago?"

"They weren't arrested, just picked up by the police." *Oh, yeah. Like that is so much better.*

"Picked up?" Heath's panic was near painful to watch. "Is Megan okay?"

Dillon started walking toward the door. "She's fine, at least as far as I know. I don't know why you won't just tell her you're crazy in love with her and be done with it."

Heath followed. "Never mind about that. Tell me what in the hell Megan is doing in jail."

"It'll have to wait. I'm on my way to pick her and Jamie up now."

Heath was hot on his heels. "You can tell me on the way there. I'm going with you."

Well, fuck a duck on Sunday morning. If Dillon's night got any worse, he didn't think he'd survive it. He forced himself to stop the pity party before it reached full swing. Time to fetch his boyfriend out of the slammer. Dillon slipped into the driver's seat of his Lumina and waited for Heath to climb in on the other side. It was gonna be a long night.

Carrying a thick manila file Jamie assumed must be Birch Carpenter's, Detective Kilgore came back into the stale office, his coffee colored skin dripping with sweat despite the frigid air outside. Flipping his waist length braids over his shoulder, Kilgore slapped the file down and took a seat on his side of the rickety wooden desk, putting himself directly across from Jamie.

Kilgore had the dark, exotic looks of a swimsuit model, but the expression on his face was harsh and unyielding. His amber eyes probed first Jamie, then Megan, who was seated just to Jamie's right. Finally Kilgore said. "Damn, it's hot in here. Stupid furnace malfunctioned again. You sure I can't get you kids anything to drink? A soda, maybe?"

Jamie shook his head just as Megan did the same. He wished he'd said yes about the drink when Kilgore went on with, "All right, then. Let's go over this thing one more time. What were the two of you doing at Birch Carpenter's house?"

The guy had to be related to Brandon in some way. They asked the same kinds of questions and gave the same damning looks. Jamie sighed. "I only wanted to talk to him."

"What about?"

Jamie froze, not sure how to answer. Megan stepped in. "As I said before, Detective Kilgore, Jamie lost his best friend recently. It just so happens Jamie's friend Ben Lewis lived with Birch for a while. We were hoping Mr. Carpenter could tell us something about Ben's life before he and Jamie met. You know — childhood stories, funny memories, anything that might help Jamie find a little bit of peace and comfort after losing Ben the way he did."

Damn, she's good. Jamie could actually see Hank Kilgore's eyes softening.

"I can understand why you'd want to find out all you can about your friend, especially after Sheriff Nash explained to me what happened to the boy, but hunting down guys like Carpenter isn't the answer. He wasn't the kind of guy who'd keep a scrapbook of happy memories involving his foster kids."

"I understand, Detective. I made a mistake by snooping around in Ben's past. It won't happen again." Jamie had his fingers crossed under the table. If he told one more lie, he just knew his nose was gonna start growing.

"I'm not saying you aren't entitled to find out all you can about Ben. All I'm saying is you're going about it the wrong way." Kilgore made a face. "Birch Carpenter used anyone and everyone he came in contact with, his foster children especially. I can't say any more than that without jeopardizing the case, but I can say you want to talk to someone who actually knew Ben, and Birch wouldn't have fit into that category. You want someone who knew Ben the person. Old schoolmates, fellow foster brothers, former teachers: anyone who might have taken the time to get to know the real Ben Lewis."

Out of that whole speech, Jamie heard only one phrase: former foster brothers. He hadn't even thought of that. Jamie gave himself a mental slap on the forehead. Birch was bound to have had a stable full of boys, especially if he'd been raking in as much money as Ben claimed. One of the other guys was almost sure to know something that might tip Jamie off as to who Ben's second blackmail victim had been.

Forcing a cough, Jamie said, "Detective Kilgore, my mouth is kinda dry. Do you think maybe I could have a soda, after all?" Jamie broke into another fit of coughing. Megan reached over and patted him on the back.

Kilgore stood up. "I'll be back in just a sec."

The minute the detective left the office, Jamie stopped coughing and turned to Megan. "If you're done beating the daylights out of me, go stand at the door and keep a lookout."

"A lookout for what?" But even as she asked, Megan moved to the door.

Jamie flipped open the file, relieved to see it was, indeed, Carpenter's. He winced at the crime scene photos laying on top. *Fuck.* The guy who took Carpenter out meant business. Jamie forced his eyes away from the bloody pictures and flipped through the file. He passed over a picture of Birch before he'd been shot. Nice enough looking guy: mid-forties, fake tan, big smile.

As with Barry Sledge, there was nothing in Birch's picture to indicate the monster within. After giving the picture a brief once over, Jamie started his search again, going through the folder until he came to a page marked *Household Occupants*. He gave the document a quick scan, making certain it was what he was looking for. Without giving himself time to think about what he was doing, Jamie ripped the paper out of the file, folded it into a sloppy square, and slipped it into his front pocket. He closed the file just as Megan came back to her chair.

"What did you take out of that report?"

Even whispering as she was, Megan sounded scared to death. Jamie felt sick with guilt for putting her in that position. "The less you know right now the better. I swear I'll tell you all of it as soon as I get it straightened out." Jamie reached over and squeezed her hand. "I know I've said it before, but I'm sorry for getting you into this."

Megan managed a weak smile. "It was my idea to come with you, remember? No apologies necessary."

Jamie was about to say something else when Kilgore came back in. He handed a soft drink can to Jamie and said, "All right, you two, since Sheriff Nash vouched for you, you're free to go. Your ride is here, and it seems he brought the money to free Miss Nash's car from impound. They're waiting for you up front."

They? Jamie's heart sank. He knew without asking who'd come for them. If it had been Brandon and Nate, Brandon would have been in the office and in his face already.

Jamie and Megan left Kilgore's office and came face to face with a wounded Dillon and a furious Heath.

Megan tried to speak, but Heath held up his hand. "No way, lady. You and I are gonna pick up your stuff and get your car out of impound while Dillon and Jamie talk. I think the two of us are overdue for a little discussion of our own."

Megan's eyes crackled. "You and I don't have a darn thing to say to each other, Heath Carver. You're not my keeper."

Heath took her arm, gentle in spite of his anger. "Somebody damn sure needs to be. Honest to God, Megan, what were you thinking?" Before she could answer, Heath placed one finger over her lips. "Unless you want this to escalate into an all out screaming match in the middle of the police station, I think we should go get your car now."

Megan nodded her head mutely and followed Heath toward the clerk's desk. Dillon waited until they were gone and then pointed to a row of plastic chairs just outside the booking area. He sat down and, as soon as Jamie took the chair next to his, he said, "Would you please tell me what's going on here?"

Jamie took a deep breath and spilled out the entire story, from sitting in Aunt Sadie's kitchen eating lasagna to getting picked up by the cops at Birch's place. When he was done, Jamie glanced Dillon's way. "I guess you're pretty mad, huh?"

Dillon ran his fingers through his hair, causing it to stand — literally — on end. "Mad, no. But I am confused about a couple of things."

"Like what?"

Dillon rested his elbows on his knees and turned his head to look at Jamie. "Why would you come all the way to Chicago to talk to Birch?"

"I was hoping he could lead me to Ben's second blackmail victim."

Dillon clenched his fists in exasperation. "If there is a second victim. For all we know, Ben stole that money. Either that or he fucked some guy who was stupid enough to pay big bucks for a cheap piece of tail."

Jamie winced. He was pretty sure Dillon's crude speculation came more from irritation and worry than anything else. For that reason he did his best to ignore it.

"I believe Ben got that extra twenty-thousand the same way he got the first twenty. Blackmail, right down the line." Jamie gave Dillon a pleading look. "If you're being honest with yourself, I think you believe it too."

Jamie could tell Dillon was doing his best to be patient. It wasn't working, but at least he was trying. "For the sake of argument, let's say I do believe Ben had another sucker on the hook. That still doesn't explain why you came all the way to Chicago to talk to a kiddie pimp. What makes you think the other blackmail victim isn't someone Ben met in Reed? How could Birch have possibly helped you find out who the guy is?"

"It's just a gut feeling. If it was someone from Reed, someone like Ash, then why didn't Ben feel guilty about it? He felt bad enough about Ash to leave that letter and give back the photos. Why wouldn't Ben feel bad enough to do the same for the other guy? Also, if this new guy was someone Ben met while in Reed, how come I never knew about the relationship? Ben told me about Ash. Even though he never mentioned him by name, I knew he was seeing someone. If Ben had something similar going on with another guy, I think I would have known about it."

"Yeah, sure. Just like you knew that your best friend turned Ash into his own personal cash cow?"

Unable to bear the sarcasm and disdain, Jamie turned his head.

Dillon sighed and, tucking one finger under Jamie's chin, turned his head so the two of them were facing again. "So, what, you think this guy is someone from Ben's past?" The look on Dillon's face said he wasn't sure he was buying into that theory.

That bothered Jamie. He wanted Dillon to believe in him, to see things his way. "I think it's a definite possibility. Ben said in his letter to Ash that Birch took pictures and made videos of his boys with their clients. He also said Birch used that stuff to blackmail some pretty powerful men. What if Ben kept his own records from those days?"

Dillon sat up straight. "You think Ben had his own set of blackmail pics from when he was a prostitute?"

"I think it's a definite possibility. And I also think there's only one way to find out. I have to talk to some of the guys who lived with Birch during the time Ben was there."

Dillon narrowed his eyes. "And just how are you planning to find them?"

Jamie flushed. "I sorta swiped a list of names from Birch Carpenter's police file."

"You did *what*?"

"Shh! Somebody's gonna hear you." In a calmer tone, Jamie said, "In the file, there was a list of guys who were living in the house at the time of Birch's death. Beside each name is a phone number where the guy can be reached. Some of them may have come in after Ben left, but a couple are bound to know who he was."

Dillon stifled a snort. "Let me guess, you're gonna go home and contact each one."

Jamie sat up straight and stiffened his spine. "No, I'm gonna check into a hotel here in Chicago, spend the night, and contact each and every one of them tomorrow morning." He looked Dillon right in the eye. "I'm not coming home until I find someone who can tell me what I need to know."

"Seems like you've got it all figured out." Dillon stood and walked over to one of the narrow windows overlooking the front parking lot. Jamie knew as dark as it was, Dillon probably couldn't see a thing, but that didn't stop him from standing there for a full minute, just staring. Finally he turned back to Jamie. "There's only one part of this equation I'm unsure of." Dillon leaned against the wall, his arms crossed over his chest. "You keep saying *you're* gonna hunt down information about Ben. *You're* gonna spend the night in Chicago. There's a whole lot of 'you' in what you just said, and not a single 'us'. Where do I fit in, Jamie? You have all these plans and it seems like I'm not in a single damn one of them."

Jamie could see the pain in Dillon's eyes and he hated himself for causing it. "I didn't leave you out of my plans to stay in Chicago because I wanted to hurt you. You just seemed so mad at me when you came in here, I didn't think you'd want to be included."

"Of course, I was mad." Dillon threw up his hands. "Did you even stop and think about what could have happened to you? It's bad enough you got hauled in here, but God Almighty, Jamie, what would you have done if you'd run into the guy who offed Birch? You could have been killed."

Jamie didn't know what to say. Dillon was shaking, and Jamie realized it was more fear than anger talking. He stretched out his hand. "Dillon—"

"No." Dillon pressed himself further against the wall. "You can't talk this away. I'm not gonna stand by and watch you put yourself at risk time and time again. I can't lose you again. I love you, damn it."

Dillon and Jamie grabbed Jamie's coat and wallet from the desk clerk and caught up with Megan and Heath out in the impound yard. Neither Megan nor his brother looked too happy, and Dillon could certainly sympathize.

Megan stood beside her car. "Who's gonna ride with who?"

Dillon cleared his throat. "You and Heath head on back to Reed in your car. Jamie and I are gonna stay the night at a hotel here in Chicago."

Jamie gaped at Dillon, seemingly shocked by Dillon's decision to stay in Chicago with him. Dillon wasn't sure if Jamie was happy about it or not. *Well, that is just too damned bad.* There was no way Dillon was going to leave him in Chicago alone. It was bad enough he'd confessed his love in the middle of a Chicago police station only to have Jamie stand in mute silence and stare at him, but Dillon would be damned before he let Jamie put himself at risk again. Jamie would just have to deal with it.

Heath raised his eyebrows but just said, "Fine, but I'm driving." He glared at Megan, daring her to argue.

To Dillon's surprise, she didn't. Instead, at the word *hotel*, Megan's eyes began to sparkle. "Okay by me, but I have something in my trunk I need to give Jamie first." She grabbed Jamie by the wrist and started pulling him toward the vehicle.

Once Megan and Jamie were out of earshot, Heath said, "A hotel room?"

"Don't ask."

Heath nodded, pulling his coat tighter against himself to keep out the chill March wind. "You need any money?"

Dillon shook his head. "I'm good." He stared down at his shoe for a second. "Can I ask you something?"

"I think you just did."

Dillon looked back up at his brother. "This is serious."

"Sorry, squirt. Go ahead."

"How, um...how do you know when your partner is ready to move the relationship to the next level?"

"You mean sex?"

Dillon's face was on fire. "I was thinking more along the lines of a serious commitment, but I guess sex sorta goes with that."

Heath clamped his hand on Dillon's shoulder. "I've never made a commitment to anyone, but I do know a thing or two about sex. The thing is...the only experience I have is with girls. I'm not sure if it's different with guys, but I'd say the best way to tell if a guy is ready is to look for signals. That's what girls usually do. Give you a sign, I mean."

Dillon's curiosity overcame his embarrassment. "What kind of signals?"

Heath shrugged. "It differs from girl to girl. Sometimes it's a look they give you, a certain word they say. Others are pretty damn bold about it. I had this one girl tell me she wanted me to fuck her unconscious, but I ended up turning her down. Girls like that really aren't my style." His eyes drifted to Megan as she and Jamie walked back towards them. "I like my women softer, more feminine." He shook himself and turned back to Dillon, squeezing his shoulder again. "I think you'll know. 'Til then, try not to stress over it."

Jamie and Megan came back up just as Heath finished. Jamie carried a small duffle bag. Megan asked, "You wouldn't stress over what?"

Heath crossed his arms, towering over her. "Just never you mind." He held out his hand. "Keys."

Megan screwed up her face. "God, you're bossy. What did I do, grow another father when I wasn't looking or something?" Still, she handed the keys over and said goodbye to Jamie and Dillon.

Heath took her arm and led her to the car. Turning back, he said, "Be careful. Both of you. And call if you need me."

Dillon nodded. "We will."

Dillon and Jamie walked back across the impound yard to the visitor's parking lot in silence. The anger and fear Dillon had felt when Brandon called him had been replaced by a new worry. He was about to check into a hotel room with the only man he'd ever loved. He was scared of making the wrong move, but more scared of making no move at all. Not only had Jamie given him no indication of how he was feeling, he hadn't returned Dillon's declaration of love. Dillon had never felt so much turmoil — so much confusion — not even when he came out to his folks. He prayed Jamie would give him some signal to show him what he should do. God knew he needed it.

If Jamie was planning on giving Dillon any hints, he was taking his own sweet time about it. The only discussion once they were in the Lumina and on their way out of the parking lot was which of the hundreds of hotels in Chicago they should check into. There was also an argument about who should pay for it. Dillon wanted to pay for it himself, but Jamie insisted on using the credit card his aunt had given him for emergencies. Dillon was pretty sure Sadie wouldn't consider hunting down the foster children of a murdered scum-sucker like Carpenter an emergency.

The hotel debate was settled when Dillon had to stop for gas not far from the police station. When he stepped inside to pay, he asked the clerk, a guy not much older than himself, if he knew of any decent places in the area.

The clerk peered through the Plexiglass shield to the window beyond. As dark as it was outside, Jamie was plainly visible sitting in the car under the bright lights of the convenience store parking lot. Dillon saw the look the clerk gave Jamie and was fully prepared for some smart remark. Instead, the guy gave him a genuine smile. "There's a place not too far down the road here, a hotel called the Preston Inn. It's a nice place, clean and all, but since the new owners just re-opened after a complete remodel, it's reasonably priced, and they don't ask too many questions, if you know what I mean."

Dillon got it. He thanked the clerk and waited while the guy wrote out directions. Once done, he headed back to his car. After a quick replay of the conversation — most of it — Dillon got the go ahead from Jamie and they headed to the Preston Inn.

It was a relief for Dillon to see the hotel was in a nicer part of town. Street lamps lined the sidewalk in front of the building, and a parking garage just behind the freshly painted, white-brick structure provided ample safe parking. He pulled into a spot across the street from the hotel.

As soon as the car stopped, Jamie turned to him, a look of surprise visible on his face even in the dim glow of the streetlights. "Why didn't you pull into the parking garage?"

Time to put his cards on the table. "I'm not pulling into the garage until you and I get a few things settled."

Jamie pulled in a deep breath. "What things?"

"Things like, what is it you want from this relationship?"

"I'm not following you."

Dillon could tell. *Time to spell it out.* "Are we an 'us' — a real couple — or are we just two guys playing around. I know I'm serious, but I'm not sure about you. The more of these plans you make without me, the more I feel you pulling away."

"I swear to God it isn't like that." Jamie reached for his hand. "I want us to be partners." He let go of Dillon's fingers long enough to wipe his face with his palm. "I know I shouldn't have run off like that without talking to you first. I just didn't want you to be mad at me."

Dillon picked Jamie's hand back up. "People in relationships get mad at each other. It's part of the deal. That's where trust comes in."

Jamie nodded. "I want that, too." He paused. "You said you had 'things' you needed to know, as in more than one. What else?"

Dillon cleared his throat. He was going to do it. He was going to offer up his heart on a silver platter. "I need to know what you want to happen tonight. I told you I loved you and you didn't say a word. God, you don't know what that did to me — to tell you how I felt and have you just stand there."

Jamie went totally still. "You're wrong. I know exactly how it feels."

Christ. He'd said the wrong damn thing again. How many times had Jamie told Dillon he loved him, only to have Dillon brush it off? Maybe this was payback, an eye for an eye. "Is that why you didn't say anything? Are you giving me a taste of my own medicine, or is it that you really don't love me and don't have the heart to tell me?"

Jamie shook his head with violent intensity. "No. God no!" He let go of Dillon's hand and laid his own hand on Dillon's chest, just over his heart. "I didn't say anything because I was in shock. That's the first time you've ever said you loved me. I wasn't sure if you even meant it or not."

Dillon put his hand over Jamie's and looked into his eyes. "I meant it, every word. I love you."

Jamie's voice was soft, but his words were sparkling with clarity. "I love you, too."

To hear those incredible words spill from Jamie's soft lips again — to be able to say them back — took Dillon's breath away. "What is it you want from me? Tell me and it's yours."

Jamie leaned forward until his mouth was almost touching Dillon's. "I want everything you have to give." His voice turned husky. "And right now, more than anything, I want you to make love to me."

Chapter Twelve

Dillon had asked for a sign and he'd sure as hell gotten one. But there were several ways for two guys to make love, and as he stood waiting in the spacious lobby of the Preston Inn while Jamie checked them into a room, Dillon couldn't help but wonder which way Jamie wanted things to go. Dillon was so nervous, he didn't even realize Jamie was standing in front of him, talking.

"I said, are you ready to go up?"

"You got the room already?"

Jamie held up an old fashioned brass key. "Yep. Room four-sixteen is now officially ours."

Dillon glanced over at the blond-haired, uniform-clad desk clerk who was doing his best to watch them without looking like he was. "Did he give you any trouble?"

Jamie shook his head. "Just took my card, scanned it, and gave me the receipt. After I signed it, he told me to ring down if we needed anything." Jamie hesitated, the duffle bag Megan had given him rattling slightly as his hands trembled. "Are you ready to go up?"

Dillon was pretty sure his palms were gonna start dripping sweat any minute. He'd never been so nervous, not even the first time he and Jamie had made love. Back then he'd convinced himself it was nothing more than two buddies playing around. This time Dillon knew exactly what it meant. Clearing his throat, he managed to say, "Yeah," before following Jamie to the elevators at the other end of the lobby.

Dillon barely remembered the ride up or the walk to the room. He waited in a trance while Jamie unlocked the door and led him inside. Jamie flipped a switch by the door, causing lamps on either side of the bed to come on, bathing the room in soft, romantic light.

The room itself was nice enough. The walls were painted a warm beige color with little red roses stenciled on top. Three floor-to-ceiling windows took up the east wall. Dillon wouldn't have cared if the room had been painted green with purple polka-dots and had no windows whatsoever. All his attention was focused on the massive, king-sized oak bed filling the middle of the room. Jamie's eyes seemed glued to it, as well. So much so that Dillon was the one who had to shut and lock the door.

When he was done, the two of them suffered an awkward moment of silence, both of them just standing there, looking at the bed. Finally Dillon said, "Did you call your aunt to let her know where you are?"

That snapped Jamie out of it. "I forgot all about that. God, she's gonna be so pissed." Jamie grabbed for the phone on the bedside table. "How do you dial out on this thing?"

Dillon pulled his cell out of his pocket. "Here. You can use mine."

Jamie took Dillon's phone, but hesitated before dialing the number. "I'm not sure what I'm gonna tell her."

Dillon sat down in one of the overstuffed arm chairs located in a small sitting area not far from the bed. "Tell her the truth. As much of it as you can, anyway." Dillon could actually hear Jamie gulp for air.

"You mean—"

"Tell her that the two of us are here in a hotel room in Chicago. Tell her we're spending the night together."

Sadie took it better than Jamie thought she would. "Am I to assume from this announcement you and Dillon are about to begin a new phase of your relationship?"

Jamie sat on the edge of the bed, dying from the embarrassment of discussing this with his aunt. She'd asked him a question and he was going to answer it. "Yes, ma'am. That's the plan."

"And is this something you're ready for?"

He'd been asking himself the same question. Before, he'd been nothing more than a quick fuck for Dillon, a toy to be played with and then put away when Dillon was done. But that was a different time, a different Dillon. They were both different people. Jamie might be nervous, but there wasn't a doubt in his mind Dillon was who he wanted.

Jamie looked over at his guy, relieved to see Dillon looked just as nervous as he did. That one thing, seeing the ever confident Dillon come undone, helped Jamie give his answer. "Yes, ma'am. I'm ready."

"All right, then. Put Dillon on the phone, please."

Oh, no. "Aunt Sadie—"

"Jamie, do as I say." Her voice softened, laced with love and affection. "Put him on the phone, son. I have a couple of things I want to say to him, and then I'll let the two of you get on with your night. And, Jamie?"

"Yes, ma'am?"

"Remember that I love you and I support you, no matter what. Now, give the boy the phone."

Jamie walked over to where Dillon sat and handed him the phone. Dillon straightened from his slouch and said, "Hello?"

Jamie couldn't hear what Sadie was saying, but he found the play of emotions moving across Dillon's face fascinating. Dillon's cheeks went from white, to red, and then paled again. More than once, he said, "Yes, ma'am," and toward the end he answered something she'd said with, "No, ma'am. Never, I swear it." To Jamie's amazement by the time he disconnected, Dillon looked far more relaxed than he had when they'd first entered the room. He stood up, shed his heavy jacket and tossed it to the floor, then helped Jamie pull his own coat off and pitched it in the same general direction. Once that was done, Dillon put his arms around Jamie's waist and pulled him close.

Jamie's head came to rest on Dillon's chest, the steady thump of his heartbeat the most reassuring sound Jamie had ever heard. He lifted his head only long enough to say, "What did Aunt Sadie want to talk to you about?"

The rumbling sound of Dillon's soft laughter tickled Jamie's cheek. "She wanted me to know where she stood on the whole 'me-and-you-having-sex' thing."

Jamie moved back within the circle of Dillon's arms so he could see Dillon's face. "And where exactly does she stand?"

Dillon grinned. "She's cool with it, I guess, but she said if I hurt you again, she's gonna come after me with her grandfather's deer rifle. I believe she said something about using my balls for target practice."

Jamie shuddered. "If that's what she said, then how come you seem calmer now than you did a few minutes ago?"

Dillon trailed the fingers of his right hand up and down Jamie's spine. Jamie felt the tingle, even through his shirt. "Because when Sadie warned me what would happen if I hurt you again, I realized something."

Jamie could feel himself dissolving under the gentle pressure of Dillon's hands. "What's that?"

Dillon pulled him in even closer. "I realized I could never hurt you like that again, because this time I'm going to put you first. This relationship isn't about me, it's about us. I only want to make you happy."

"You do."

Dillon shook his head, still holding Jamie tight. "That's not what I meant." He moved back, catching Jamie's hands in both of his and stepping away so that only their fingertips were touching. "The times before...when we were together, I was always in charge, always on top. Tonight I want it to be different." His voice dropped to a husky rasp that Jamie felt all the way to his bones. "Tonight, you tell me what you want and we'll go from there."

Jamie lifted Dillon's left hand up to his lips and kissed each finger. "Tonight I want you to top me."

"You sure?"

"Yeah. I want to replace all the bad memories with new ones. Happy ones."

Those words had an immediate effect on Dillon, but not the one Jamie expected. Dillon turned away from him, grabbed his coat, and started for the door.

"Where are you going?"

Dillon paused at the threshold of the open door, turned and gave Jamie a sheepish grin. "Sorry. I got a little ahead of myself. It's just that, if you really want me to do this, I'm gonna need to get some supplies. There's an all-night drugstore not far from here. I saw it on the way in."

"That isn't necessary."

"Yes, it is. We didn't use anything before. No lube, I mean. I could have really hurt you, and I'm not gonna take that chance again."

Jamie pointed to the small duffle bag he'd placed on the floor near the bed when they'd first walked in. "Megan gave us everything we need."

Dillon closed the door. Tossing his coat onto a nearby dresser, he came back into the room proper. "I beg your pardon?"

"That's what's in the bag Megan gave me. See, she was counting on me having to make the first move, and she thought maybe she could help."

Dillon groaned. "I'm afraid to ask, but do you have any idea what's in that thing, exactly?"

"Megan called it a do-it-yourself gay sex kit."

Dillon's eyes looked like they were in danger of jumping out of his skull. "Please tell me you're joking."

"'Fraid not."

Dillon picked up the bag and set it on the bed. Sitting beside it, he began to remove the contents. Jamie sat down beside him and watched in amazement as Dillon pulled out three videotapes, two pairs of matching silk boxer shorts, a book titled *The Joys of Gay Sex,* a bottle of lubricant which neither of them paid much attention to, and a package of condoms. A *large* package of condoms. A package of forty-eight, to be exact.

"Jesus Christ, what was she thinking?"

Jamie couldn't help but laugh. "Maybe she was just being optimistic."

"If Megan thinks we're gonna use forty-eight condoms in one night she isn't being optimistic, she's just plain delusional."

Jamie laughed. "Did you read the titles on those tapes?"

"Uh huh. Somehow I don't think *Ride 'Em Cowboy, Hung,* and *Pounding the Ranger* are classic westerns."

"Wonder where she got gay porn?"

Dillon shook his head. "I'm afraid to ask." He picked up one pair of the boxers. "These are nice." He reached for the second pair. "Look, she even got us the right sizes."

"It was sweet of her to go to all this trouble, but I don't think we're gonna need most of this stuff." Jamie put everything back in the bag except the condoms and the bottle of lubricant. He placed the lube on the nightstand and studied the package of condoms for a second. "What about these? Are we gonna need them?"

Dillon seemed surprised. "Why would we?"

This was the part Jamie dreaded. Dillon knew about Jamie's sexual history, because Dillon *was* Jamie's sexual history. On the other hand Jamie had never had the courage to ask if Dillon had been with anyone else in the time they were apart. He was about to find out.

"Just in case you've been with anyone that might, you know..."

Dillon took the condoms out of Jamie's hand and tossed them in the direction of the bedside table, near the lubricant. "There hasn't been anyone else. There never could have been. You're it for me."

"Really?"

"You're the only one." Dillon slipped both his arms behind Jamie's back and, using the weight of his body, eased Jamie down onto the bed and came to rest on top of him. "If you want me to use a condom though, I will."

Jamie shook his head, his body already heating at the thought of Dillon being inside him, encased in latex or otherwise. "No. I want to feel you, just you."

Dillon's breathing increased. "I want that, too, but first I want to do something we've never done before."

"And what would that be?"

Dillon grinned. "I want us to get undressed, slide under the covers, and just make out."

"Make out?"

"Yep." Dillon wiggled his hips, causing Jamie to squirm underneath him. "Make out. You know, kissing and stuff."

Jamie popped him on the shoulder. "I know what making out is, you jerk. I just never thought you'd wanna do it."

Dillon's eyes glittered as he braced himself on his elbows and ran the fingers of his right hand through Jamie's hair. "We missed out on a lot of the good stuff because of my stupidity. I want a chance to do it right this time." He pulled himself off Jamie and stood, holding out his hand. "What do you say? Wanna climb under the covers with me and suck face?"

Jamie took Dillon's hand. He toed off his shoes and socks as Dillon did the same. Instead of undressing himself, though, Jamie reached for the buttons on Dillon's shirt. Dillon hissed in a breath as Jamie slid first one button then the next through the holes until the button-up shirt Dillon was wearing over his t-shirt was undone. Jamie freed Dillon's arms from the fabric and allowed the shirt to fall to the floor. Slipping his hands under the hem of the t-shirt, Jamie pulled it up and over Dillon's head, sending it to join the other shirt on the floor.

Dillon moaned and bit his lip as Jamie smoothed his hands over Dillon's chest. But when Jamie's fingers dipped lower to the waistband of his jeans, Dillon stopped him. "Better let me do that or this is gonna be over before it starts."

That was the last thing Jamie wanted. He stepped back just enough to allow Dillon room to pull off his jeans.

He looked incredible, standing there nearly naked. His body was perfect, but it was the man himself — the man Dillon had become — that took Jamie's breath away. Clad in only a pair of gray boxer-briefs, he moved in toward Jamie and returned the favor of undressing him.

Jamie stood stock still, enjoying the sensations as Dillon's hands roamed over his body, freeing him of first his pullover shirt, then his jeans. Just as he'd done with himself, Dillon left Jamie's cotton boxers in place. Giving Jamie a smile that made his knees feel like Jell-O, Dillon said, "God, you're beautiful. You ready?"

Jamie nodded. Dillon went to the bed and pulled back the covers, waiting for Jamie to slide under before doing the same thing himself. The minute they were both in bed, Dillon reached for Jamie, taking him into his arms and pulling Jamie underneath his hard body. Without saying a word, Dillon lowered his head and covered Jamie's mouth, using his teeth and his tongue to tease Jamie's lips apart.

Jamie allowed him entrance as Dillon tasted him, kissing him with an intensity that left Jamie weak. He wasn't sure whether minutes passed or hours. Dillon's mouth made the journey from Jamie's lips, to his chin, to the tender skin of his throat, time and again, teasing Jamie, making him ache deep inside. The heat and feel of Dillon on top of him was almost more than Jamie could stand, and at the same time, it wasn't quite enough. Jamie was so hard he hurt, and judging from the velvet weight Jamie felt on his leg, Dillon was too. It was time to do something about it.

"Dillon?"

He paused, his teeth tugging on Jamie's tender earlobe. "Don't you like that?"

"God, yes."

Dillon released Jamie's ear long enough to smile down at him. He leaned forward and kissed Jamie's nose. "Then what is it?"

"The kissing is nice, but I want more."

Dillon pressed his lips against Jamie's cheek. "But I'm not done kissing you yet."

"Dillon—"

"Shh. I just said I wasn't done kissing you yet. I didn't say where I was gonna kiss you." And before Jamie could reply, Dillon began a slow journey down Jamie's body with his tongue.

Jamie writhed in agony as Dillon circled first his left nipple and then his right one with the tip of his tongue. Dillon was thorough and showed Jamie no mercy. Using his front teeth, Dillon tugged and pulled, causing Jamie's hips to come up off the bed. *Who knew his nipples were so damn sensitive?*

Dillon didn't stop there. He licked a hot trail down Jamie's chest, into the sensitive hollow of his stomach, which sucked in a breath as Dillon tickled his belly button. When he felt Dillon reach the waistband of his boxers, Jamie was certain Dillon was going to stop.

Dillon was under the covers now, his head hidden from view. Jamie couldn't see what he was doing. Then he felt a firm tug and the soft whisper of cotton as it slid free of his legs. Dillon pulled down the covers and rose up on his knees, tossing Jamie's boxers to the floor. The cool air hit Jamie's heated skin, but it did nothing to cool the fire inside him. Especially not when Dillon lowered his head.

Again Dillon settled himself over Jamie, only this time Dillon's arms wrapped around Jamie's hips, trapping him in a tender embrace. Using the softest of caresses, Dillon flicked across Jamie's most intimate skin with the tip of his tongue.

Jamie was going to die; he just knew he was. Dillon took his time, working across Jamie's flesh with his tongue. God, Jamie wanted so badly for Dillon to do more, but he couldn't get the words past his throat. That's when Dillon read his mind. Just when Jamie thought he couldn't take it anymore, Dillon opened his mouth and took Jamie's cock inside.

Jamie's head thrashed from side to side against the pillows as Dillon increased the wet suction. He was too large for Dillon to take all of him, but it didn't matter. The moist heat, combined with the loving way Dillon's hands cupped Jamie's hips and butt, brought him to the brink in seconds.

He issued a garbled warning, but Dillon refused to back off. Jamie could feel the rising contractions racing through his stomach — could feel the release coursing through him and flowing into Dillon. He half expected Dillon to pull away in disgust, but instead Dillon stayed with him, taking all he had to offer until Jamie sagged against the mattress in a limp heap.

Dillon grinned and moved back up long enough to kiss Jamie softly on the mouth. Jamie could taste himself on Dillon's lips, but if Dillon was bothered by the flavor, he didn't show it.

Jamie wrapped his right arm around Dillon's neck and slid his left hand down Dillon's side. When he got close to his target, Dillon stopped him.

"Not yet."

"I want to touch you."

"I want that too." Dillon kissed each one of Jamie's eyelids. "But you're assuming I'm done with you, and I'm not. Not by a long shot."

"Will you make love to me?"

"When you're ready."

Jamie was confused. How much more ready could he be? "I told you I want this. I'm ready now."

Dillon shook his head and, kissing Jamie one last time, pushed himself into a sitting position. "You're not ready yet, but if I have anything to say about it, you're gonna be." Before Jamie could ask what he meant, Dillon put one hand on each of Jamie's legs and spread them as wide as he could comfortably get them to go.

While Jamie watched in amazement, Dillon got into position, his head level with his target, and once again used his tongue to work magic on Jamie's body. Only this time, Jamie's entrance was Dillon's goal.

Jamie would have sworn he didn't have another erection anywhere in his near future, but the minute he felt Dillon's tongue circling his opening, he could feel himself getting hard again. As much as he enjoyed the painful pleasure Dillon was causing, he yearned to tell Dillon to come back, to make love to him. Before he could get the words out, Dillon moistened one finger and slipped it inside.

God, it felt so good. As Dillon stretched him using first one finger, then two, Jamie did his best to talk, to tell Dillon he didn't want to wait any longer. The best he could get out was a squeak somewhere in the vicinity of Dillon's name. That was when Dillon added the third finger and touched a spot deep inside that made Jamie see stars. He put his hand on Dillon's shoulder, half scared he was going to come again before the main event. "I don't want to wait anymore."

Dillon came back up, his hands shaking, his breath coming in ragged gasps. "Are you sure? Once I get started, I don't know if I can stop."

"Don't stop. I'm dying here."

Dillon nodded. "Not without lube. Where did we put that stuff Megan sent?"

Jamie pointed in the direction of the table. "I think I put it over there somewhere."

Dillon shimmied out of his boxer briefs, sending them to the floor with the rest of his clothes. When he was done he leaned across the bed and reached for the tube. He must have gotten a good look at it, because his whole body went still.

Jamie looked up at him through a haze of need, a need made even worse by the sight of Dillon in all his glory, but Dillon still wasn't moving. "What's the matter?"

"I don't think I can use this."

"Why not? All you have to do is flip the cap. It may be a little cold—"

Dillon shook his head. "It's not that. This...it isn't exactly the right kind of lube."

Jamie sat up. "What are you talking about?"

Dillon handed him the tube. Jamie laughed out loud when he read the name of the product. *Vagi-Slick Feminine Intimate Moisturizing Cream*. Megan had one sick sense of humor. No wonder he loved that girl so much.

"I wouldn't care at this point if you used *Turtle Wax*." Jamie wrapped his arms around Dillon's neck and pulled him back down. "I need you."

It wasn't really a hard sell. Popping the cap and squeezing a dollop into his hand, Dillon warmed it between his fingers and spread an ample amount around Jamie's entryway. He then turned his attentions on himself, hesitating just long enough to say, "I'm gonna do it, but if my dick falls off and I grow boobs from using this stuff, you sure as hell better love me, anyway."

Jamie panted out, "I will. I swear to God I will. Now come on, please."

Dillon complied, slicking himself up and crawling between Jamie's legs. "I want to make love like this — face to face — so I can see your eyes. Is that all right?"

It was more than all right. It was exactly what Jamie had been dreaming about since the two of them came together again. Jamie spread his legs and helped Dillon position himself. Without ever breaking eye contact, Dillon placed his cock head against Jamie's opening, and, watching Jamie's face carefully for any signs of discomfort, pushed until he was all the way inside. Dillon immediately stopped to give Jamie time to adjust.

Always before, there had been pain, but not this time. Jamie was so ready there was nothing but a slight pressure and then the relief of having Dillon inside him, filling him, making him whole. Still Dillon refused to move. Jamie took matters into his own hands. He wrapped both legs around Dillon's waist, angling his hips up and then bringing them back down again.

Dillon slipped his arms up under Jamie's back and pulled them flush. "I love you, Jamie. God, I love you." Repeating the phrase over and over, Dillon started to move.

With each thrust, Dillon grazed against Jamie's prostate, causing an unbearable friction as the tender skin of Dillon's stomach did the same thing to Jamie's cock where it lay trapped between them. It wasn't long before Jamie could feel himself getting close again. He clenched his inner muscles over and over, joy flooding him as Dillon groaned from the feelings he was causing. Just when Jamie felt sure he couldn't hold back his own orgasm any longer, Dillon went rigid above him and then collapsed into his arms as the spasms overtook him. That's all Jamie needed. He closed his eyes and let the sensations carry him over.

Early morning sunlight streamed through the windows and dappled Jamie's face as Dillon lay propped on his elbow, watching him sleep. The shower they'd taken together the night before had left Jamie's skin smelling sweetly of soap and the unmistakable scent that was uniquely his.

Dillon fought the urge to wake him, but it wasn't easy. Memories of last night kept calling to him. In the afterglow, while he and Jamie were cuddling, Jamie had told Dillon how new it all was for him, how incredible. It was incredible for Dillon, too, but not because it felt new. Being inside Jamie again was like coming home from a two year exile. He hadn't felt this whole — this complete — since pushing Jamie out of his life. All the bad memories had faded under the spell of last night.

As if he could read Dillon's thoughts, Jamie rolled over and opened his eyes. "Good morning." His voice was sleep-scratchy and so sexy Dillon's morning wood grew even harder.

Dillon leaned in and kissed him, ignoring Jamie's protest about wanting to brush his teeth first. Jamie tasted like heaven to Dillon. He must've thought Dillon tasted pretty good himself, if the way he drew Dillon in deeper was any indication. When he could bring himself to pull away, Dillon looked down at Jamie and smiled. "Sleep good?"

Jamie yawned and stretched, looking so darn cute Dillon had to force himself not to kiss him again. "Uh huh." He looked up at Dillon with shining eyes. "I slept better last night than I have in years."

Dillon grinned. "Must be contagious. So did I."

Jamie cuddled in closer to Dillon's side. "What do you say we go back to sleep?"

Jamie's stomach chose that moment to let out a loud growl.

Dillon shook his head and laughed. "As much as I'd like to, we can't. You're hungry and I've got to pee. I say we get dressed and go out for breakfast." Dillon narrowed his eyes. "My treat, by the way. You paid for the room. The least I can do is feed us."

Jamie slipped his arms around Dillon's neck. "I'll trade you breakfast for a kiss."

It took the two of them a lot longer to get out of bed once Dillon accepted the deal.

The plan, when they finally roused themselves, was to go out, grab a quick bite to eat, and then go to a payphone and call each number on Jamie's purloined list until they found somebody who actually knew Ben. It sounded good at the time.

The breakfast part was great. Nothing like a night of hot sex to whet the appetite. But once they found an out-of-the-way payphone located in the back of a convenience store and put the remainder of the plan into action, Jamie began to see just how difficult his search was going to be.

His idea to use an alias, call each number, and then pretend to be a school friend of the boys on the list when speaking with concerned foster parents seemed to work well enough. The problem came when Jamie actually spoke to the boys themselves and realized most of them had come to live with Birch sometime within the last year or so, long after Ben had moved to Reed. It wasn't that the boys didn't try to help. In fact, Jamie was surprised at just how willing some of them were to talk to a total stranger about Birch and what a bastard he was. A couple refused to say anything at all, but most seemed to be forthright. Out of all the guys he talked to, though, not a one was able to tell him anything he could use.

It wasn't totally unexpected, but it was still disheartening. Jamie called the last name on the list, a guy named Mitchell Harding. A woman answered the phone. When Jamie asked for Mitchell, she sounded more than a little annoyed. "Who wants to know?"

"I'm a friend of his from school." Jamie hoped his voice wouldn't quiver.

"Yeah, and I'm the Virgin Mary. Mitch ain't been to school in almost four years. Try again."

Four years? Maybe he had the wrong number. "This is the Mitchell Harding who just recently lived with Birch Carpenter, isn't it?"

"Listen here, you son-of-a-bitch." The woman's voice took on a nasty, snarling quality. "If you're one of Birch's customers calling to get your rocks off on Mitch—"

Jamie just knew she was going to hang up. He couldn't let that happen. He wasn't sure how, but he was almost certain this woman knew something. He'd have to take a risk and tell her the truth. At least part of it.

"Wait. Please. I'm not one of Birch's clients. I just need to talk to Mitchell. I think maybe he might have known something about a friend of mine. I promise I won't take up much of his time."

Dillon was leaning against the cinder block wall, watching Jamie with concern but not saying anything. As for the woman on the other end of the line, she'd gone so quiet Jamie thought sure she'd hung up. Finally she said, "Okay, then. If what you say is true, tell me the name of your so-called friend. I know most of Mitch's friends, and if he knows your buddy, I can almost guarantee I know him, too."

Jamie took a deep breath. "His name was Ben Lewis."

Jamie heard a loud noise and then a kind of scrambling, the sound of the phone being dropped. When the woman picked back up, she sounded as angry as ever, but there was a new element in her voice: fear.

"Is this some kind of sick joke? And what do you mean his name *was* Ben Lewis? Has something happened to Ben?"

Jamie's heart started pounding in his chest. "Wait a minute. You knew Ben?"

"Of course I know him. Ben Lewis is my brother."

Chapter Thirteen

The narrow, white frame house was nice enough, Dillon supposed, but there was something about the whole thing that didn't feel right. Ben had a sister? Why hadn't Ben ever mentioned her to Jamie? And where did Mitchell Harding fit into all this? Jamie seemed to be having his own reservations, if his hesitancy to open the gate of the chain-link fence surrounding the property was any indication. Dillon put his hand on Jamie's shoulder. "We don't have to do this, you know."

Jamie shook his head. "I need to hear what this woman has to say."

Dillon nodded as Jamie opened the gate. He couldn't say he understood, exactly, but this was Jamie's call, and Dillon would support him in this or die trying.

Jamie pushed the gate open and headed up the cracked sidewalk, Dillon following directly behind. After a moment's hesitation, Jamie stepped up onto the stoop and rang the bell.

Dillon did a double take when he saw the woman who answered the door. Though she was obviously older than Ben, there was no doubt this lady was his sister. She was shorter than her brother, maybe five-four, five-five, but the similarities were undeniable. Same inky-black hair — though hers was worn in a pixie-like bob — same deep brown eyes. But unlike the warmth Dillon had seen in Ben's eyes every time they rested on Jamie, this lady's held nothing but distrust, maybe even a hint of contempt.

Nevertheless, she opened the door a bit wider and allowed them entrance.

"I'm Lily Harding. You're James Walker, Ben's friend?"

Jamie stuck out his hand. "That's right. And this is my partner, Dillon Carver."

She shook his hand. "Partner? Ain't you a little young to be a cop?"

Jamie shook his head. "I'm not. A cop, I mean."

Dillon could tell Jamie was getting flustered. He always stammered when he got upset. Dillon reached for Jamie's hand at the same time as Jamie said, "When I say that Dillon is my partner, I mean we're together. He's my boyfriend."

Lily looked down at their joined hands and snorted. "Fags. I shoulda known, you being friends of Ben's and all. It figures."

Dillon started to say something but Jamie stopped him with a shake of the head. Turning back to Lily, Jamie said, "I take it you didn't like the fact that Ben was gay."

Lily sighed and led them into the box-shaped living room. "You might as well sit." She waited while Jamie and Dillon got settled on a slip-covered sofa and then took a seat herself on a nearby recliner.

Facing them with open animosity, she said, "I ain't happy that Ben thought he was a homo, but I can see why he believed he was, after what Birch forced him to do." Her heavily painted lips curled. "I mean, it'd have been okay if he'd been screwing girls or something, but guys humping guys just ain't natural. It's no wonder Ben thought he was queer. Thank God Mitch knows the score. He knows he ain't bent."

Dillon couldn't remember ever wanting to get out of a place any worse than he did this one, but Jamie showed no signs of budging. He leaned forward and said, "Look, Ms. Harding, I really need to speak with Mitchell. If you could just tell me how to get in touch with him—"

"I ain't heard from Mitch in three days. He gave the cops my name and address when Birch bit the big one, but he ain't been around. Don't have no use for me, I guess. Some brother he is, huh?"

Brother? Dillon spoke up. "Wait a minute. I thought Mitchell was your husband. You mean he's your brother, too? Ben's brother?"

Lily gave Dillon a look that suggested she didn't find him especially bright. "That's what I just said, ain't it? Half-brother, though. Me, Ben, and Mitch all had the same mama, but God knows who our daddies was. Mama got around, if you know what I mean. Mitch and me, we go by Harding, Mama's maiden name. Ben's last name was Lewis, after the guy the old lady was married to for five minutes before the kid was born. Not that her husband was Ben's daddy. That honor could've gone to any one of Mama's regular johns." She narrowed her eyes and trained them on Jamie. "You said on the phone something's happened to Ben?"

Dillon could tell Jamie was searching for the right words, but he didn't think Lily Harding would take the news of Ben's death all that hard. Despite her name, fragile little flower, she wasn't.

After a long minute, Jamie said, "I don't know how to tell you this, but Ben was killed."

The only real show of emotion Lily displayed was a brief closing of her eyes, and Dillon was pretty sure that particular show of respect was done more for their benefit than out of any real grief. After a second, she opened them and said, "So, what happened to him? Somebody whack him or what?"

Dillon could see how shaken Jamie was by Lily's reaction, but he was proud of the way Jamie managed to hide it. "The working theory is Ben was killed by a drunk driver."

"You ain't buying it?"

Jamie kept his gaze level. "No, I'm not. That's why I wanted to talk to Mitchell. I thought maybe he could help me out. I had no idea Ben and Mitchell were brothers. As far as I knew, Ben didn't have any family."

"I ain't surprised the ungrateful little bastard never told you about us. I swear, you bust your ass to raise a guy, and then he turns his back on you like you was dirt."

Jamie leaned forward on the couch. "You raised Ben? I thought he was placed into foster care early on."

Lily shook her head. "Ben was ten when our old lady snagged herself the wrong john one night and ended up in the morgue. I was twenty, so the state turned Ben over to me. Since Mitch was only twelve, I got saddled with him, too. You don't know how many times I wished he'd been older so he could have gotten his ass a job and supported us."

Dillon narrowed his eyes. "So you could be a stay-at-home mom?"

"Hey, I worked." Lily curled her lip. "Been turning tricks for years. My old lady, she had enough regular customers to pay the rent. I guess you could say I inherited 'em when she died. Paid the rent but nothin' much else. That's when I found a guy willing to give all three of us a little extra employment, if you know what I mean."

Dillon had a sick feeling he knew exactly what she meant. "You're a drug dealer."

"My old boss called us somethin' else." She scrunched her brow. "What was it he called us? Oh yeah. 'Recreational pharmacists.'" Lily giggled. "I always liked the sound of that. I was damn good at it, too. Made more sales than anyone else on the payroll." Her face darkened. "I would still be doin' it if Ben hadn't fucked up right after his eleventh birthday and gotten all our asses busted."

"You're blaming an eleven year old for getting you busted as a drug dealer?" Jamie croaked.

Lily shrugged. "Why not? It was his fault. He sold a quarter ounce of blow to an undercover cop, right here in his own damned neighborhood. The cops raided our house and found enough to get me for felony possession. I went to jail, and Mitch and Ben went to a boys home. More than one. From what I heard, every time the state placed 'em, they did something stupid and got sent to another home. It figures. Neither one of my brothers was overly blessed in the brains department."

Dillon heard Jamie mutter something like, "Right, like you've got so many brains it hurts." When Lily turned to him and said, "What did you say," Jamie looked her dead in the eye and came out with, "I said, how did they end up with Birch?"

"Oh, that. When Ben was thirteen and Mitch was fifteen, Birch got a couple of openings at his place. Birch only took boys. Said with him being a single guy and all, it was easier to relate. That was so much bullshit. Everybody knew he was pimpin' his boys out, but nobody could prove a damn thing." She threw up her hands. "Whatcha gonna do, right? I mean, I was still in the slammer with two years to go on my sentence. Ben and Mitch started to work for the guy, and I served my time. Just as I finished my stint, Ben ran off from Birch's place and was put with that bitch over in Reed. Mitch, he stayed with Birch, but he swore it was just for the money, and I believed him. At least, I did at the time. I mean, why else would he keep whoring for Birch even after he turned eighteen? Hell, Mitch was still living in Birch's house when the guy got wasted."

One thing in Lily's tirade made Dillon more than a little bit curious. "Why did you call Ben's foster mother over in Reed a bitch?"

Lily stretched her legs out in front of herself and crossed her ankles. "Because she is, that's why. When I got out a jail, I went straight to Reed to see my brother. It took some doing, but I was able to hunt him down. At first the bitch wouldn't even let me in to see him. Like I need her to tell me when I can see my own flesh and blood. Ben finally came outside and told her it was okay, that he was gonna talk to me." She pursed her lips. "A fat lot of good it did. Witch had him brainwashed. Little bastard told me he was queer and wanted to stay where he was instead of comin' back with me. Said he felt accepted." She snorted again. "Like I didn't accept him. Give me a break." She hunched one shoulder. "I did the only thing I could think of; I slapped his face. I only wanted to knock some sense into him, but that old bitch — that Nora lady — came running out onto the porch. Threatened to call the cops if I ever came back. That's when Ben told me he never wanted to see me again." Lily thumped her fist against her chest. "That hurt, ya know? After everything I did for him. All I wanted was to have him back in my life."

Jamie gave her a look of pure disgust. "And the money the state would have paid you for taking care of him meant nothing to you."

Lily chose to ignore that. Or maybe she just didn't have sense enough to know when she was being insulted. Dillon wasn't sure which. He only knew he had to get Jamie out of there. He also knew there were a few more questions that had to be answered before Jamie would be satisfied enough to leave. Dillon said, "So, what about Mitchell? You say he refused to leave Birch's and come stay with you?"

The look of self-pity on Lily's face was nauseating. "Yep. Swore he couldn't leave but never would tell me why, outside of saying the money was too good to pass up. And he did send a good chunk of that cash to me every month. Enough so's I was able to quit working and buy this house." She actually smiled over that one. "And since I knew Mitch wasn't really a fag, just gay-for-pay, me and him was cool. He helped me out with my...expenses, and I didn't ask no questions. All that changed the minute Birch died. Mitch gave the cops my number, and I ain't heard from him 'cept once or twice, and then only by phone.

Like I told you, the last time he called was three days ago. He said he was gonna take some time away from here now that Birch was dead. I ain't heard from him, and I ain't got no way to get in touch with him." Lily lowered her voice and leaned forward. "I bought his excuse about staying with Birch for the money at the time, but the way Mitch's acted since Birch died has me wondering if maybe that was all a batch of lies. I'm startin' to think Birch was holding something over Mitch's head, something to force Mitch to keep turning tricks for him. From what I hear, Mitch was pretty damn popular. Neither Birch nor that partner of his would want to lose the money Mitch was pulling in."

"Birch had a partner?" Jamie's eyes were wide and focused solely on her. "You mean a boyfriend, a lover?"

"Nah. Birch might've made a living off teenage boys, but he didn't screw 'em. Birch was straight. In fact, I heard he had a thing for girls. Young ones."

Dillon shivered. *And people like my folks have the nerve to call me and Jamie perverts for being gay.* Doug and Angela Carver had never seen a real pervert. Dillon felt dirty just talking about Birch. He wanted to get out, and get out fast. First, one last question. "What did you mean by Birch's partner, then?"

Lily rolled her eyes. "Just what I said. Birch had a business partner, a guy who got him customers and helped him run his boys. I don't think the two of them were in cahoots anymore, though. Last I heard, Birch was trying to cut the other guy out, but I never heard why." She pointed one long finger in Dillon and Jamie's general direction. "If you ask me, he's the guy who popped Birch. He's the one the cops should be lookin' for."

Dillon didn't say much on the way back to the hotel, nor did he speak more than a few words during checkout, something Jamie was grateful for. His head was still spinning.

How could Ben have had an entire family without Jamie ever even knowing? Obviously Nora knew about Lily, and Jamie was guessing she'd known about Mitchell as well. Why hadn't Nora said anything to him? Jamie felt like the whole world was keeping secrets. The question became how to get to the bottom of those secrets without exposing his own.

The silence between Dillon and Jamie continued until they were about five miles from the Reed city limits. Without taking his eyes off the road, Dillon said, "If you don't get whatever it is you're thinking about off your chest, it'll eat you alive."

Jamie sagged within the confines of his seatbelt and placed his head in his hands. "I'm not sure what to say. I can understand why Ben never told me about Lily. If I had a sister like her, I'd want to forget she existed, too. But what about Mitchell? Why didn't Ben ever mention his brother?"

Dillon shrugged. "Maybe Mitch is as bad as Lily. Then again, maybe Ben wanted to make a fresh start when he came to Reed — no family, nothing."

Jamie had thought about that, too, but a statement Lily had made told him otherwise. "Lily said she felt like Birch was holding something over Mitchell's head, something that made him keep turning tricks."

Dillon caught on. "You think Mitch was the one who cut off ties with Ben because of whatever it was Birch had on him."

"Yeah. I can't say for sure why I feel that way, I just know I do."

They'd reached the town proper, but instead of turning right to go toward Aunt Sadie's, Dillon took a left. Jamie looked at him with mild surprise. "Where are you going?"

"Nora must have known about Mitch. She might be able to tell us something about his relationship with Ben."

"Nora didn't bother to mention Mitch or Lily when she told us about Ben's will. What makes you think she'll talk to us?"

"She may not, but we have nothing to lose by trying." Dillon didn't waver from his course. "We told Lily to call us if she hears from Mitch, but that doesn't mean she will. Right now, I'd say Nora is our best bet."

Jamie didn't argue. Though he doubted Nora would be able — or willing — to tell them anything, Dillon was right in saying they had nothing to lose.

The drive to Nora's was brief, and before Jamie knew it, Dillon was angling the Lumina into the gravel drive in front of Nora's place, an old, rambling farmhouse more suited to a large family than a single woman.

A lump rose in Jamie's throat as he got out of the car and made his way toward the house. This was the only real home Ben had ever known. Jamie owed Nora for making the last years of Ben's life bearable. Jamie was loath to cause her any more pain, but he was certain Ben's brother held the key to finding out about the remaining money. If Nora knew something that might help them, Jamie had to know.

He was surprised to see the front porch littered with empty packing boxes. From the look on Dillon's face, it came as a surprise to him, too. Jamie knocked, only to have the door swing open under his hand. Giving it a nudge, he called out, "Hello?" and stepped inside.

Nora was standing in the middle of the living room wearing a pair of ripped jeans and a stained, short-sleeved t-shirt. Her long dark hair was covered with a blue bandanna, and she was surrounded by more packing boxes, each one filled to the brim with books, knick-knacks, and the like. She turned and smiled at them as they came in.

"Hey there, you two. Come on in." Nora wiped a smudge of dust off her nose and indicated a pair of straight-back chairs sitting off to the side. "Have a seat." Jamie started for one of the chairs but then hesitated.

Nora saw his reluctance and gave him an encouraging nod. "It's okay. Just ignore the mess." She waited until Jamie and Dillon were both seated before plopping down on a nearby stool. "Now, tell me all about your visit with Lily."

Jamie could feel the blood leaching from his face. He looked to Dillon and saw an exact mirror of his own surprise. Clearing his throat, Jamie said, "You know about that?"

"You bet your buns I do." If Nora was upset, she hid it well. "She called here not an hour ago, ranting and raving about her poor, dead brother, and how she never even had a chance to say good-bye." She crossed her work-boot clad ankles and curled her lips. "Like she cares. The only thing Ben and Mitch ever were to that woman was a meal ticket."

So she does know about Mitch. Jamie was searching for a way to broach that subject when Nora beat him to it.

"What's this I hear about the two of you looking for Ben's brother?"

Dillon glanced at Jamie before saying, "Lily told you about that, too?"

Nora crossed her arms over her chest. "Uh huh. She said something about you wanting to squeeze Mitch for information, but she never gave any indication what it was you were looking for. What I want to know is, what kind of information are you after, and why?"

Jamie thought back to the lie Megan had spun for Detective Kilgore in Chicago. It seemed like as good an excuse as any. "I guess I just wanted to put together a more complete picture of Ben's life. You know — his life before he came to Reed. I thought the more I knew about him, the better I would be able to let him go. I hoped maybe his friends and family could tell me a little bit more about him."

For a full minute, Nora studied him as if she was gauging the truth in his statement. Jamie was just starting to sweat when Nora's expression shifted from one of suspicion to one of pity.

"Ben's life before he came here was a living hell. Nothing you find out about his early years is going to help you get over his death. That kind of thing takes time, and time alone." Nora narrowed her eyes. "As for that no-account family of his, I don't imagine either Mitch or Lily could come up with a kind word between them. Not for Ben, in any case."

Jamie nodded. "I gathered as much from Lily. She told us about coming here to see Ben when she got out of jail." He picked at an imaginary speck of lint on his pants leg and did his best to keep his tone casual. "The one thing Lily didn't mention was Ben's relationship with his brother."

"That's because there *was* no relationship. Not since Ben came to Reed anyway." Nora sighed. "Poor Ben tried for weeks after he came here to get in touch with his brother, but Mitch refused all of Ben's calls and letters. It was almost like Mitch was determined to cut Ben out of his life." She clicked her tongue. "A real shame, especially since I got the feeling the two of them were close at one time."

Jamie shot a glance at Dillon, giving him a wordless I-told-you-so. Everything Nora had said seemed to confirm Jamie's suspicions. Not that he had a lot to go on. He still didn't know where the rest of the money had come from, and he could hardly go to Brandon with a handful of half-formed theories. *Shit. Brandon. If he finds out about our visit to Lily, I'm a dead man.*

Jamie took a deep breath. "Uh, Nora, could you do me a favor?"

"Sure, honey." The genuine affection in Nora's eyes made Jamie feel even guiltier. "I'll do anything I can for you. You know that."

Jamie swallowed past the lump in his throat. "Could you not mention my visit with Lily to the sheriff?"

Nora's gaze sharpened. "Jamie...you're not in some kind of trouble, are you?"

"Nothing like that. Brandon just thinks I'm not dealing with Ben's death all that well. He might...worry." Jamie darted another quick glance in Dillon's direction, daring him to argue.

Nora must not have seen it. Her voice held a slight quiver when she said, "I won't tell him, sweetheart, but Brandon's right when he says you have to move forward. Why do you think I'm selling the house?"

Until that moment, Jamie had been too wrapped up in the mystery surrounding Ben and his family to comprehend the meaning behind the packing boxes and the misplaced furniture. Nora's words brought it all home with startling clarity. "You're selling your place? Why?"

Nora gave him a sad half-smile. "Because it's time. I inherited this house from my first husband, Jack. He was killed in a boating accident not long after we married." Tears formed in her eyes. "I lived here with my second husband, Lyle, for five amazing years." She took in a ragged breath and blinked away the wetness. "When colon cancer took Lyle from me, I thought seriously about selling, but by that time, the application Lyle and I had filled out together to become foster parents had been approved. According to the city of Reed, I was still considered a good choice to be a foster mom, even with Lyle gone. I'd just gotten my real estate license, so I was stable and employed." Nora shook her head. "With all the kids in the system these days, stability and employment are the two chief requirements. Love seems to have been pushed further down on the list." The sad smile returned. "Love is the one thing I did have. I was bound and determined to take all the affection stored in my heart and spill it onto as many foster children as the state would give me." Nora chuckled. "Then the powers that be sent me Ben, and all those plans for more kids went right out the window."

Dillon turned in his chair. "Why?"

"Ben was so damaged — so hurt — he needed all my love and attention. How could I possibly give him what he needed while trying to do the same thing for other kids?" Nora shook her head. "The minute I laid eyes on Ben, trying to look so tough even though he was dying inside from the abuse he'd suffered—" Her voice broke. "I knew he'd be my only one, my only son." Her tears flowed freely. "I never minded, you know. Ben was all the family I needed. I know he had his faults, but I wouldn't have traded him for ten kids, even if the other ten were my own blood kin."

Nora yanked at the hem of her shirt, using it to dry her eyes, and adding to the smudges of dirt on her face. "Ben is gone now, guys, and I can't stay here mourning him forever." She stood and brushed herself off. "That's why I've decided to sell, and that's also why I've got to get a move on. The movers I hired will be here any minute now to haul some of the furniture."

Jamie and Dillon stood as well, following Nora's lead. Jamie could understand her reasoning, but Nora was special to him and always would be, mostly because of Ben. He needed to know he wasn't losing her, too. "You aren't moving too far away, are you?"

Nora crossed the room in two long-legged strides and wrapped Jamie in a fierce hug. "And leave my second favorite guy in the whole world? Are you kidding?" She pulled back and chucked Jamie under the chin. "No way. I bought a condo on the far side of town. I'll be no more than a ten minute drive from your aunt's house."

"A condo? You?" Somehow Jamie couldn't picture free-spirited Nora sitting on a co-op board.

Nora swatted his arm. "Don't sound so surprised. After years of selling the things, I finally bought one is all. I can't say I'm going to live there for the rest of my life, but for now a condo is just what I'm looking for."

Dillon stepped up to Jamie's side. "When will this place go on the market?"

"It isn't going to."

Jamie stared at her in confusion. "So you aren't selling it, then?"

Nora patted his cheek. "It's already sold. A few days ago, a man came into my office looking for, and I quote, 'A fixer-upper with plenty of room and a fair price.'" Nora glanced around the living room with its faded floral wallpaper and moth-eaten carpet. "Let's face it, boys, I love this place, but it's a fixer-upper if ever I saw one. I think Jack once told me it was wired back in the nineteen-forties. The poor fellow who bought this house is going to have to bring it up to code before he and his people can even move in."

"His people?" Jamie said. "What is he, a rock star?"

Nora laughed. "No, honey. The man who bought the house, Blake Mathis, is going to turn it into a shelter for victims of domestic violence. His focus is going to be on gay men who've been abused by their partners." She shook her head as she scanned the room one more time. "I admire what he's trying to do, but he's going to have his work cut out for him with this place. And he can't even get started until I clear all my junk out, which is going to take a few more days. Ben and I used the two downstairs bedrooms, and I do have most of that stuff already boxed up, but I have an entire upstairs to clean out still. That reminds me, Jamie...what about Ben's things?"

It took Jamie a minute to catch on. "You mean the stuff from his room?"

"Yes. He left it all to you. I thought maybe you could pick up Ben's car one day next week. I know you can't drive, so I was hoping someone could come and get it for you. I'd drive it over myself, but I don't know how to drive a stick shift." Nora laughed. "My first husband tried to teach me. Total disaster. Since then, I've stuck with automatics. Anyway, I'll load the boxes into the car, and you can pick them up all at the same time."

Jesus, Ben's stuff. Jamie hadn't even thought about going through that. He doubted Ben had left any outright evidence of blackmail in his room or Nora would have found it and turned it over to Brandon. That didn't mean Ben hadn't left some clue. The trick now was to get to Ben's things as soon as possible without making Nora suspicious.

"Dillon and I could load that stuff up in Dillon's car and take it now. That'll save you from having to lug it around."

Dillon must have been following Jamie's train of thought because he chimed in, "Yeah, Nora. If you'll just tell me where it is, I can do it now."

Nora waved them both away, and Jamie's hopes of going through Ben's things anytime soon started to fade. "Don't be silly, boys. It's no trouble. Besides, none of the boxes are all that heavy. You can drop by sometime around the middle of next week. Oh, you can drive a stick, can't you, Dillon?"

Dillon nodded, and that was that. There was nothing Jamie could say without letting Nora know something was up. He was going to have to wait it out. Jamie had the strangest feeling he was running out of time, but against what, he couldn't say.

Monday afternoon after school Dillon threw his books into his locker with a force that startled Megan and made her jump back three feet.

"It's not like Jamie's riding home with an ax murderer. His Aunt Sadie picked him up, for crying out loud. What did you expect him to do, wait out here in the hall while we chair the student council meeting?"

"Yes. No. Damn, I don't know." Dillon closed his locker with an exaggerated slam. "I was hoping Jamie would be here for the meeting too. Isn't the G.S.A. helping out with all this prom stuff?"

Megan shook her head. "Not this one. The prom falls under the sole jurisdiction of the student council. I think it's tradition. Though I did hear Morgan say he wants us to make it clear that the prom is open to all students and their dates, same sex couples included."

"Speaking of dates, you taking my brother to the prom?"

Making Megan blush was getting too darn easy. She went pink all the way to the roots of her bright red hair. "I don't know. It's too soon to tell whether he even wants to see me again. We've only had one real date, you know."

Dillon looped his arm around Megan's shoulders as the two of them walked toward the conference room. "I saw the look on Heath's face when he came home last night. The guy was actually humming. Trust me, he's gonna want to see you again."

Megan only nodded, but the hopeful look in her eyes was impossible to miss. Instead of saying anything more about Heath, she turned the tables on Dillon. "Since you brought it up, what are *your* prom plans? You and Jamie gonna go together?"

"I hope so. I haven't asked him yet, what with everything else going on."

Megan stopped just outside the conference room door and turned to face him, still within the clasp of Dillon's arm. "Does 'everything' include a night of hot steamy sex in that hotel room you shared?"

"It might."

Megan was practically jumping up and down. "I knew it. The minute I saw you in church yesterday, I said to myself, 'Self, there goes a man who just got laid.'" She leaned in closer. "So, how was it? Was it an all night monkey sex fest?"

Dillon was trying his best to come up with an answer for that one when a shadow fell across the hall. He turned to see Dan Morgan standing not three feet away, taking in every word. When Morgan noticed Dillon looking at him, he grinned. "Please don't delay your answer on my account. Sounds like a good story if ever I heard one."

Megan balked. "Mr. Morgan, I didn't know you were standing there. I, um..."

Dillon took over. "If it's all the same to you, I'll save the story for another time. I have to work this afternoon after the meeting, so I'd like to get started as soon as possible." The disappointed look on Principal Morgan's face made Dillon feel ill.

"I suppose if we must, we must. Pity, that." He waved one cashmere-covered arm to the door and looked at Megan. "After you, Miss Nash. In fact, why don't you call the other council members to order while I have a word with Dillon here?"

Dillon's face must have shown his reluctance, because Morgan was quick with his assurances. "I know you're in a hurry. I promise this won't take long."

Dillon didn't want to hear anything Morgan had to say, especially not after their meeting in the principal's office and that little speech at Ben's memorial. He also knew he didn't really have a choice.

Nodding to Megan, Dillon waited until she'd gone into the conference room and closed the door behind her before turning back to Morgan. "Yes, sir?"

Morgan moved toward him, standing so close Dillon could practically feel Morgan's breath on his cheeks. "I understand James and Megan enjoyed an impromptu visit to a Chicago jail this past weekend."

The hairs on the back of Dillon's neck stood on end. "How did you know about that?"

Morgan smiled and leaned in so that they were almost nose to nose. "Let's just say I have a friend or two down at the police department nice enough to keep me informed about what goes on with my students." His voice dropped an octave but lost none of its greasy charm. "I like James, and I think you should know he's fooling around with things that could get him...hurt. I'm not including Megan in this because I suspect she was only at that dead man's house because James dragged her into it." Morgan stepped back and looked directly into Dillon's eyes. "If I were you, I'd make sure James backed off this little investigation of his."

Dillon's mouth went dry. "Is that a threat?"

Morgan did his best to seem surprised by the question. "A threat? Of course not. Consider it friendly advice."

Before Dillon could say anything else, Morgan opened the door and entered the conference room, leaving Dillon no choice but to follow.

Morgan's so-called "friendly advice" rang in Dillon's ears as he took a seat next to Megan and listened to the seemingly endless string of updates and reports on everything from the location of the prom to the merits of decorating with Mylar instead of crepe paper. All Dillon wanted to do was get the meeting over with, work his shift at the drugstore, and get to Jamie. Dillon wasn't sure how — or if — Morgan was connected to Ben and Birch, but if Morgan was trying to scare him with his cryptic warnings, it sure as hell worked. Dillon was terrified — first that something would happen to Jamie, and second that Dillon would be powerless to stop it when it did.

When the last committee member was done presenting the final issue — something about the music that Dillon only halfway heard — Morgan took the podium and said, "Once again, ladies and gentleman, thank you for putting your time and effort into this project. I have no doubt this year's prom will be the best one Plunkett has ever had. As you kids are fond of saying, the prom is gonna be a real killer."

Dillon prayed to God the prom would be the only killer he and Jamie came in contact with, but somewhere deep inside he doubted it.

Dillon thanked the gods of scheduling he was down for a short shift Monday evening, getting off work at seven instead of his usual nine o'clock. The weekend had been almost idyllic. The butt chewing Dillon had expected Brandon to deliver to Megan and Jamie turned out to be nothing more than a stern lecture. An even bigger shocker than that, though, was the change in Megan and Heath's relationship. Heath had finally worked up the courage to ask Megan on a real date. Dillon couldn't have been more pleased. All he wanted to do now was run home, take a quick shower, and then spend the rest of the evening with Jamie over at his place. The minute Dillon stepped into Heath's apartment and took a look at his brother's face, his plans were shot to hell.

Heath, still wearing his uniform, was sitting in his ratty old recliner. His face was ashen, and as Dillon walked in the door, he looked up and said, "We got trouble, kid."

It was on the tip of Dillon's tongue to say, "So what else is new," but he stopped himself and instead said, "What kind of trouble?"

Heath leaned forward and grabbed a yellow piece of paper from the coffee table. "According to the manager of these apartments, I violated my lease by failing to inform her when you moved in here. Apparently, someone called her this morning and told her all about our new living arrangements." He snorted and tossed the paper back down on the table. "Ten bucks says we have our parents to thank for that one."

Dillon sank down on the couch. "What does violating the lease mean, exactly?"

Heath pointed to the paper again. "According to that notice, I can either rectify the violation — namely kicking you out, which ain't gonna happen — or I can consider myself on a thirty day notice." Heath leaned back in his chair with a sigh. "In short, it means we're being evicted."

Chapter Fourteen

Douglas Carver looked up from his desk as Dillon came barreling into the oak-paneled office first thing the next morning. He was visibly frightened by the sheer rage on his son's face, but Dillon couldn't care less. It was time he and his dad had a little chat.

It didn't take Doug long to recover from his initial surprise. "Good morning, Dillon. Won't you take a seat?"

Dillon stopped just inches from where his father sat. "I don't think you want me to take a seat, *Douglas*. If I did, I'd probably shove it up your self-righteous ass."

Crossing his hands in front of himself, Doug looked Dillon directly in the eye. "I take it this is about your unfortunate eviction."

Dillon could barely see his father through the red haze of anger clouding his vision. "You're damn right it is."

Douglas nodded, amazing Dillon with the cool, calculated grace contained in that one action. "While I understand you're upset, son, I think perhaps once I've made my offer, you'll realize I did what I had to do. You left me no choice."

God, this guy is unbelievable. "I can promise you right now, *Douglas*, I'm not interested in anything you have to say."

Doug raised an eyebrow. "First of all, you will address me as 'Dad' or 'Father'. You will show me the respect I deserve."

"I don't have a dad or a father; I have a sperm donor who thinks that one little contribution gives him the right to run my life." A muscle in Doug's jaw started to twitch, but Dillon had to hand it to him, Doug reined in his temper.

"Call me whatever you like, but the fact remains that I *am* your father, and I have something I'd like to say. Will you sit down now and listen to me?"

"I'll stand."

Noticeably irritated, Doug didn't put any of that frustration into his next statement. "Whatever you say. So, here's my proposal." He sat up straight in his chair, looking into Dillon's eyes. "Your mother and I have decided to allow you to come back home and live with us again."

Dillon was sure his father had to be joking. "You have, huh?"

"Your mother misses you, and I want to make her happy. The two of us put our heads together and came up with a solution to this little problem." He reached into his desk drawer and, to Dillon's sheer amazement, pulled out a set of index cards. *The fucker has actually made notes.* He'd known Dillon would come charging in the minute he found out about the eviction. His father had played him, and, like an idiot, Dillon had fallen right into his game.

Doug arranged the cards in order on his desk. "Number one, you will have no contact whatsoever with James Walker. Any such contact will result in your immediate removal from our property."

God help him, but Dillon was actually finding this funny. He leaned his hip against the corner of his dad's desk and played along. "That's number one, huh?"

Taking Dillon's question for interest in his offer, Doug warmed to his task. "Yes, which brings me to number two. I've scheduled an appointment for you with a man by the name of Dr. Henderson, over in Chicago. He's one of the world's leading experts on helping young people confused about their sexuality. I've spoken to him, and he believes with the proper combination of therapy and medication, he can bring you around to the right way of thinking."

"Oh, I'll just bet he does." The guy sounded like a nutcase. "Any other rules you need to discuss with me, Doug?"

Douglas winced at the informal address but checked over his list. "Let's see. Other than your new seven-thirty curfew, there's just one other thing." He looked long and hard at his son. "You have to agree to file charges against Brandon Nash and his so-called husband for molesting you."

Dillon fought the urge to vomit. "Brandon and Nate never touched me, and you know it."

Douglas shrugged. "Doesn't matter whether they did it or not. With the right coaching, you could convince a jury they did."

"I get it. You want me to lie."

Doug shook his head. "Don't think of it as lying. I'm sure the two of them have molested countless young boys in their lifetimes. You'll be doing the rest of the world a favor by getting them off the streets. Anyway, those are my requirements." He looked down at his watch. "You've already missed an hour's worth of school, but if we leave now, we can go down to the city police department, file charges against the sheriff, and have you back to school in time for your third period class."

He'd heard enough. "So, those are the rules, huh?" When Doug nodded, Dillon said, "Okay, then. Let me tell you my rules." He moved forward and leaned over the desk, towering over his dad. "Let's start with rule one, since it's the only rule I have. Stay the fuck away from me."

"Now look here—"

Dillon whipped up his hand and stuck one long finger in his father's face. "No, you look. Take a good look at me, Doug. Look at this big fag you brought into the world and listen closely to what I have to say. If you come near me or my family again, I can promise you, you won't like the consequences."

Doug blanched, but he kept his voice even. "Need I remind you, boy, I *am* your family."

"The hell you are. My family is Jamie. He and I are going to start a life together, just as real as the life you've carved out for yourself with Angela." Dillon paused, thinking about his own words. "Scratch that. What Jamie and I have is more real, because we're honest. Honest with ourselves — and the world — about who we are. I love Jamie more than I ever thought I had it in me to love, and I swear before God, if you do one thing to hurt him — to cause him pain in any way — I'll knock you into next week and then kick your ass again on Thursday."

Doug's self-control had reached its limit. "You can't threaten me."

Dillon moved back from the desk. "I believe I just did." He started for the door, but turned back when he heard his father's voice.

Doug was standing behind his desk, a look of panic on his face. "Wait. What am I going to tell your mother? She was counting on me to get you back home and into therapy."

How pathetic. "Tell her the truth. Tell her she married a spineless asshole." Before Doug could say another word, Dillon left the office — and his childhood — behind.

Dillon closed the phone book with an audible snap. Eleven more days and he'd officially be homeless. Not that any of the landlords and apartment managers in the greater Reed area cared. All they saw was an eighteen year old kid with no credit rating. Heath insisted the two of them find a new place together, but Dillon wasn't having it. His brother had already done more for him than he could ever repay; he wasn't about to let Heath lose his home on top of all that.

He leaned back into the couch cushions and checked the clock. *Nine-thirty.* He'd worked another short shift and had planned on spending the evening with Jamie. Dillon had to admit, he was disappointed and a little bit hurt when Jamie told him he had a few things he needed to get done and couldn't see him that night. He hated to voice what he was feeling, but the truth was, he was scared. For the first time since leaving his parents' house — and especially since the confrontation with his father — Dillon realized how alone he was.

Jamie, Megan, and the rest had rallied around him when they heard that he and Heath were being tossed out, but there really wasn't anything anybody could do about it. It was up to Dillon to solve his own problems and to sort out his own mess. The question was how?

One good thing to come out of Dillon's predicament was that his impending eviction temporarily put a halt to Jamie's investigation into the money. Jamie was too worried about Dillon and his situation to do more than raise his eyebrows when Dillon told him about Morgan's weird threats before the prom committee meeting. Even Nora — albeit unknowingly — had helped to delay Jamie's search. She'd hit a snag in the moving process and had postponed the pickup of Ben's car and possessions by several days. Jamie wasn't happy about the wait, but worry over Dillon's living arrangements kept him more or less silent about it. Dillon was sure the reprieve was only temporary, and as soon as things calmed down, Jamie would be back in action and more determined than ever to find the truth.

Heath came through the door a few minutes later and headed straight for the shower, leaving a trail of dirty clothes behind him. Dillon just shook his head and gathered them up, depositing the grungy garments in front of the washing machine. Hard to believe it, but Dillon was even going to miss his brother's slob-like tendencies. *Amazing what a man can get used to.*

Just as he came back to the couch, Dillon heard the shower cut off. Heath stepped out of the bathroom wearing nothing more than a towel clutched loosely around his hips. When he saw the phone book and cordless phone lying on the coffee table, Heath narrowed his eyes. "You weren't apartment hunting again, were you?"

"Yeah, for all the good it did me. Seems I'm not a very good credit risk."

"Damn it, Dillon, I told you we'd find a place together. In fact, a buddy of mine told me about another complex we can look into, said it would be perfect for us." Heath tugged at his slipping towel. "Since tomorrow's Good Friday, they'll probably be closed. I'll have to wait until Monday to call, but it sounds like a good deal."

Dillon shook his head, prepared to argue this one as long as he had to. "I told you I'm not gonna let you give up your place for me. You've already done enough."

"Look, little brother—"

Heath was cut off when the door swung open so fast it shook on its hinges and Megan came running in, her face flushed, her jacket half-on, half-off. She skidded to a halt as soon as she saw Heath. "Nice outfit."

Heath did one of those all-over blushes, causing Dillon to burst out laughing as Heath ran to the bedroom to put on some clothes.

Dillon looked at Megan and grinned. "Did you come over here just to embarrass the shit out of my brother, or was there something you wanted to talk about?"

"I have something I want to show you. No talking required." Megan gave him a crooked grin. "Well, not by me, anyway." When Dillon hesitated, Megan came forward with her customary impatience, grabbed his hand, and tugged him up off of the couch. "Come on, already. Everybody's waiting."

Everybody? Dillon followed Megan to the front door of the apartment, opening it to find a bevy of Nashes — namely Gale, Dean, Nate, and Brandon — filling the outside corridor.

The first to speak was Brandon, who had his shoulder propped against a concrete post. "Heard you have a housing crisis on your hands here, kid."

Dillon glared at Megan, causing Brandon to laugh. "Before you let Megan have it, she's not the one I heard it from."

Dillon had a feeling he wasn't going to like this next part. "Who then?"

"Good ol' Dougie, himself. Seems when you didn't take your dad up on his offer to have Nate and me charged as pedophiles, Douglas got pissed and decided to try pressing charges against us on his own. Yesterday, he told the chief of police, Ronald Skinner, that Nate and I had corrupted you, locked you up, and violated you in any number of ways." Brandon grinned. "When Skinner got done laughing, he asked Doug for proof. Since Doug didn't have any, Skinner threw him out on his ass, told Doug if he came back without proof to back up his allegations he'd throw him in jail for filing a false report."

Heath came to the door then, fully clothed and wearing his coat. Dillon had been so wrapped up in what Brandon was saying, he hadn't realized he'd forgotten his own jacket. He was just turning to go get it when Heath handed it over. "Here, dumbass, before you freeze to death. I swear you need a keeper." While Dillon shrugged into his coat, Heath turned to Brandon. "Did I hear you mention our old man?"

"Yep. After trying to convince the chief of police that Nate and I are a couple of rapists, your dear old dad came to see me."

Nate came up behind Brandon, slipping his arms around his husband's waist. "I'd just gotten done with a double shift at the hospital and had come to the station to take Brandon out for supper. I got there about the same time Doug did."

Brandon snorted. "Doug is damned lucky Nate was there, too. I don't think anyone else could have calmed me down when Doug started spouting about perverts and fornicators. The real kicker came when Dougie started bragging about having you and Heath evicted. God, I wanted to hit that son-of-a-bitch." Brandon glanced at his mother who was standing a few feet to his right. "Sorry, Mom."

"Oh, please." Gale waved him away. "I've heard worse talk than that at the Sunday dinner table."

Dean snaked his arm around his wife's shoulders. "She's *said* worse than that at the Sunday table."

Gale ignored him. "When Brandon found out what had happened, he called Megan to see if she knew anything about your impending eviction. I just happened to overhear the conversation."

It was Megan's turn to snort, the sound echoing around the corridor from where she stood between Dillon and Heath. "Overhear my butt. You were listening on the upstairs extension."

Gale gave an unapologetic shrug. "A good mother always knows what's going on with her children. And, Dillon, if you come and live with us, I promise never to listen in on your conversations. Well, almost never."

Dillon's head was spinning. "You want me to come and live with you?"

"Of course. Dean and I have plenty of room, and we already think of you as family. We'd love to have you stay with us."

Brandon clasped his hands with Nate's. "Well, Nate and I want you to come live with us, and, no offense to my mother, but we won't listen in on your phone calls."

Gale was about to lodge a protest when the sound of an engine revving cut through the night air. Dillon looked to the parking lot in time to see Sadie Banks's big-ass Cadillac race into a nearby space.

Jamie jumped out of the front seat almost before the car had stopped completely. "What's everybody doing here?"

Dillon grabbed Jamie's hand, pulling him close. "They've come to solve my housing problem. They all want me to come and live with them." The Nash collective nodded in agreement.

Before Jamie could respond, Sadie exited the car and glided up the sidewalk with all the grace of a queen. "A generous offer, no doubt, but a young man your age needs his own apartment. You and Jamie will need privacy, especially if what you said to your father is true. Do you really think of you and Jamie as a family?"

Dillon heard Megan sigh in appreciation at that statement and saw Jamie's eyes go wide. "How did you know about that, Miss Banks?"

"I'm Aunt Sadie to you. As for how I know what was said...Adele Hopkins works in the office across the hall from your father's office." Sadie shook her head. "I've known her for years, and I can tell you that woman couldn't keep a secret if it was stapled to her butt."

Gale chimed in, "That's the God's honest truth."

"In this case it worked to our advantage," Sadie said. "The minute you left Douglas's office, Adele called me and spilled everything she'd heard. Did you know she has a photographic memory?"

"Um, no, I didn't." Dillon was still reeling. "What does this have to do with me getting my own place?"

"Oh no, young man. You'll answer my question first." Sadie drew herself up to her full height, such as it was. Dillon would have smiled if she hadn't looked so serious. "Did you or did you not threaten to kick your father's sorry carcass if he ever laid a hand on your family, i.e. my Jamie?"

The look Jamie gave Dillon in the pale glow of the various apartment security lamps and porch lights was so sexy and so loving, Dillon felt his blood begin to heat. Without ever taking his eyes away from Jamie's, Dillon said, "Yes, ma'am, and I meant every word."

Aunt Sadie cleared her throat. When both of them looked in her direction, Sadie said, "As I was saying, a young couple just starting out needs their own place. When you told Jamie about the eviction, he came to see me straightaway. Of course, I already knew all about Douglas's little plan, thanks to Adele, but I didn't tell Jamie. No, I was waiting to see how he reacted. And I can tell you this, I didn't have to wait long. Jamie begged me to let you move into the house with us, but I'm afraid I can't, in good conscience, do that."

Dillon's heart sank. "What do you mean? I thought you approved of Jamie and me."

"You misunderstand me. I do approve of the relationship, but how would it look if I had two teenage boys shacking up under my roof?" Sadie pointed at Jamie. "I told this one here as much, and the little devil threatened to move out. Said if you couldn't stay, he wouldn't stay either."

Oh no. First Heath was ready to give up his home for Dillon, and now Jamie. Dillon was touched, but there was no way he was going to let this happen. "Aunt Sadie, please don't be mad at Jamie. He didn't mean it."

Jamie said, "Oh yes, I did."

"Quiet, both of you," Sadie interrupted and threw up her hand.

Dillon thought he heard Brandon or Nate chuckle — he wasn't sure which — but one glare in their direction from Sadie stopped the sound altogether. When quiet again reigned, Sadie said, "Mad at him? Why on earth would I be mad at him? I'm damned proud of my nephew. Proud of him for having the conviction to stand up for those he loves, and proud of him for sticking by you no matter what. Jamie is determined to live with you one way or another, and I'm going to help him as much as I can without compromising certain principles. We put our heads together and came up with what I believe is a working solution. That's why I've spent the last few hours helping Jamie clean out the carriage house."

"The carriage house? You mean that old shack behind your house?"

"Old shack?" Sadie was filled to the brim with indignation. "I'll have you know that place was originally the property's carriage house, built the same year as the house, 1884. My Grandfather Banks converted the carriage house to a garage in the late twenties, and when my father inherited the house and grounds from his father in the early fifties, he sold off most of the property, but kept the carriage house and had the upstairs of the building renovated as a garage apartment, complete with an eat-in kitchen, full bath, and one nice-sized bedroom. My father rented the place — usually to young married couples just starting out — until he died in 1980, six months after my mother passed away." Sadie's eyes got a bit misty with the memory. "A few months after Daddy's death, the people who were renting the apartment bought a house and moved out. Since Jamie's grandmother — my sister — had her hands full with Jamie's unruly mother," she paused long enough to give Jamie a warm, apologetic smile, "I was the one elected to settle the estate. I was so busy, I just didn't bother to rent the carriage house out again." She smiled. "Until now, that is. Jamie and I spent most of the afternoon and evening cleaning the place. There's plenty of cleaning left to do." She sighed. "It needs a little work before it's strictly livable, but I think it will do nicely. And since the gas and electricity are tied in to the main house, we won't have to wait for those dunderheads down at the power company to come out and hook it all up before you and Jamie can move in."

Ever the contractor, Dean spoke up. "Meaning no disrespect, Miss Banks, but if that apartment has been empty for over twenty years, there could be serious structural damage. I'm not sure the place is even safe for the boys to live in. It would need a complete inspection before I'd feel comfortable about it."

Sadie looked down at her fashionable gold watch. "It's just past eight now. Plenty of time for you to run over there and give it a good going over."

Dean eyed Sadie. "If I didn't know any better, I'd say you set me up for that."

Sadie was the picture of innocence. Gale laughed and kissed her husband on the cheek. "Well of course she did, dear. And you do make it so easy."

Dean sighed. "I'll call Wayne and see if he'll meet me over there." To Sadie, he said, "My son Wayne is my partner in Nash construction. With the two of us working together, we can have the place inspected in half the time and, if no major repairs are needed, the boys should be good to go."

Gale clicked her tongue. "They will not." She looked to Sadie, "I'm assuming there's no furniture up there, and if there is, it's probably not in the best of shape after so long a time. Am I right?"

Sadie nodded. "There's a small dinette set that seems to be in good condition, but the last tenants took everything else with them. The boys will need a couch, some chairs, and a bed." She thought for a minute. "Scratch that last one. They can have Jamie's bedroom suite. Oh, and his television and computer, all the things from his room."

Dillon listened in amazement as the entire assembly, except himself, planned his new living arrangements. There was talk of the furniture and supplies Sadie and the Nashes wanted to donate to them

— who had what, where it should go, what the two of them would need later on — a mention of work that would need to be done on the apartment, and even a brief conversation about them eating most of their meals with Sadie.

To Dillon's amazement, Jamie seemed not to even notice that no one had even asked Dillon whether or not this was what he wanted. Jamie went right along with the rest of them, especially when he said, "Aunt Sadie, you never did tell me how much rent you're gonna charge us."

Sadie appeared to be thinking it over, but Dillon wasn't fooled. If he knew Sadie, she'd had the rent issue sorted out before she ever brought up the idea of renting the place to the two of them. "Let's see. I think my father rented the place for eighteen dollars a month back in 1954, but that didn't include meals and utilities, so I'm going to have to charge you and Dillon a little more." She pursed her lips and paused for effect. "We'll tack on ten more dollars for that, so I'd say twenty-eight dollars a month sounds fair. And since I'll be paying your half, Jamie, Dillon's part will be fourteen dollars even."

"Sadie, that seems a little high to me." Gale pursed her lips. "Didn't you say the place needed some work?"

"You know, I didn't even think about that. The wallpaper is peeling, so that needs to be stripped, and the walls could stand a good painting. And despite how much cleaning Jamie and I did today, much more needs to be done. I think if Dillon and Jamie have to do all that work, I should at least knock off the first two months' rent. I wouldn't want to overcharge them."

Dillon was speechless. He knew damn good and well why they were doing this. The average rent for a one bedroom apartment in the city of Reed was five hundred and sixty bucks a month. Here was Sadie, offering them a place for what would have been a steal fifty years ago. Dillon was touched, but he was also a little irritated no one bothered to ask him what he wanted. He'd halfway expected it from the others, but Dillon thought at least Jamie would ask him if he wanted the two of them to move in together.

Dillon did want that. Make no mistake, living with Jamie on a permanent basis was a dream come true, but after the talk he and Jamie had had at the police station that night in Chicago, he was almost sure Jamie would at least make the decision a joint effort between the two of them. Instead, Jamie had assumed Dillon would say yes.

That point was driven home when Jamie said, "You can charge us a real rent, Aunt Sadie. And you don't have to pay my half. I'm gonna get a job so I can help pay my share."

"That is a 'real' rent, young man. That amount was good enough for my father and it's good enough for me. As for getting a job, you'll do no such thing. Dillon already had his job, so I can't fuss too much about his working, but I want you to concentrate on your studies. I intend to help with your expenses, and that's just the way it's going to be." Sadie looked at the assembled crowd. "Well, what are you all waiting for? We have an apartment to inspect, accoutrement to gather, and furniture to move."

"Damn," Brandon said. "I was looking forward to having the kid stay with us." He grinned at Nate. "Guess if we want a family anytime soon I'm just going to have to keep trying to get you pregnant, huh?"

Nate slugged him on the arm. "Come on, let's go through the attic and see what else is up there."

"Wait up and I'll go with you," Megan said. "I think Grandma Nash stored some curtains up there, too. Every house needs curtains. And if those aren't the right size, I'll just have to make some." When eight pairs of eyes gave her eight equally doubting looks, Megan put her hands on her hips. "What? I can sew. Geez, so what if I made a dress in home ec and forgot to cut holes for the sleeves? Doesn't mean I can't sew. I happen to think the dress looked pretty good, even if I couldn't move my arms." She ignored the laughter coming from all directions, leaned up on her toes and gave Heath a shy peck on the cheek. "I'll see you later, okay?"

Heath gave her shoulder a light squeeze. "Count on it." He stepped back and stretched. "I'm going to go call that guy I know and see if he's got anything at his shop we can use."

Before Dillon could believe it was happening, the lot of them, Jamie included, were headed toward their various vehicles and tasks. That was it. He couldn't take it anymore.

"Hold it."

It was like playing freeze tag. Every one of them stopped in his or her tracks. Gale said, "Yes, honey? Was there something you wanted?"

Dillon cleared his throat. "Don't think I'm not grateful to all of you for trying to help me, but don't you think it's time somebody asked me what I want?"

Jamie wished to God his legs were long enough to kick himself in the ass. He'd gotten so wrapped up in the idea of having Dillon live with him, he'd forgotten to even ask Dillon if that was what he wanted. Jamie looked around and saw some of what he was feeling reflected on the faces of the others. Every single one of them — from Gale and Sadie down to Nate, Brandon, and everyone in-between — apologized for being so careless.

Dillon graciously accepted, but Jamie knew that his were the words Dillon was really waiting on. It was time for Jamie to mend his fences, as Aunt Sadie would say, and hope Dillon was as forgiving with him.

Clearing his throat, Jamie said, "Uh, Dillon...do you think maybe we could go inside and talk?"

Dillon nodded, and Jamie looked to their family and friends. "If you'll all excuse us, we'll be right back."

"Of course, honey. In fact, why don't the rest of us go on back to my house, where it's warm, and drink hot cocoa?" When the group seemed agreeable to that, Sadie gave Jamie an encouraging smile. "That way, if you and Dillon do decide this is what you want — what you *both* want — we'll all be ready."

"That sounds like a great idea to me," Dean said. "And I can go ahead and get Wayne out there so the two of us can start the inspection, just in case. Get that out of the way."

"I'll go, too," Heath said. "No reason I can't make those calls about the appliances from Miss Sadie's house."

Gale turned toward her car, then turned back long enough to say, "Dillon, I'm so sorry we ganged up on you like this. Dean and I really would like you to stay with us if you decide Sadie's offer isn't for you. Of course, I wouldn't blame you if you said no, not after the way we bossed and browbeat you tonight."

"Please don't think I'm not grateful, because I swear I am. I—"

Brandon cut him off. "We never thought you weren't grateful, kid, but no man likes to have his life mapped out for him. You're eighteen. You have the right to make your own choices."

Nate snorted. "Like you let me make my own decisions?" Nate looked to Dillon. "I'm sorry we got so caught up, but in all fairness, I think Brandon started it. He's known for his prowess at telling others what to do."

Brandon leaned in close to Nate and nipped him lightly on the ear. "You didn't mind one bit me telling you what to do last night. As I recall, when I told you to—"

"On that note," Gale glared at her son, "we're leaving."

Brandon laughed and led Nate to the parking lot, the others in tow. As nervous as he was about the coming conversation as Dillon, Jamie couldn't help but smile when he saw Megan climb into Heath's truck with him. Now that the plans had changed and they were all headed to Sadie's, it appeared Megan was going to use the situation to her advantage. *Good for her.* She and Heath seemed to be heading toward something special. Jamie only hoped his own relationship would be moving forward as well.

Dillon indicated the apartment door. "Let's go. I know you want to talk to me, but I have something I need to say first."

Jamie nodded and followed Dillon inside, his heart pounding in his chest. Dillon didn't exactly seem upset, but neither did he seem thrilled at the prospect of the two of them living together. Jamie hoped he was just reading Dillon wrong, but from where he stood, things weren't looking so good.

Dillon stood back to let Jamie inside, then closed the door behind them. The look he gave Jamie was still neutral, and Jamie was finding it harder and harder to breathe. God help him, he didn't know what he would do if Dillon said no.

But Dillon didn't say no. Instead, he leaned back against the door and looked Jamie square in the eyes. "Do you love me?"

Not what Jamie had been expecting. "You know I do. I'm so sorry for not asking you about moving in. I just got so—"

Dillon shook his head. "I'm not upset about that. I mean, I was a little irritated at first, but I know why you did it, and I'm not mad. I know that you love me, but I think I phrased the question wrong. What I should have said is: how do you love me?"

"I'm not sure I know what you mean."

Dillon ran his fingers through his hair. "Damn, I'm screwing this up." He gave Jamie a pleading look. "I need to know, do you love me in the right-now-we're-together-so-let's-just-see-how-it-goes way, or the forever-after-till-we're-both-pushing-up-daisies way?"

Jamie didn't so much as hesitate. "Forever. It's always been forever with me and you."

Dillon's smile lit the apartment's small living room. He kissed the top of Jamie's head. "I feel the same way."

Jamie laid his head on Dillon's chest. "Glad to hear it. Now, will you move in with me? I want to get all the cleaning and moving out of the way so we can christen the apartment."

Dillon reached between them and tilted Jamie's head up, bringing his own down for a kiss that set every fiber of Jamie's being on fire and gave him the answer he needed.

Chapter Fifteen

Dillon lay on the bed, flat on his back, his stomach muscles clenched in an effort to keep from coming as Jamie slid up and down his rigid length. He gripped Jamie's hip with his left hand as his right hand fisted Jamie's erection, doing his best to bring the two of them to the edge at the same time.

"Oh God. Ride me."

Jamie moaned in response. A minute later, he threw back his head and poured out his release, the inner clasp of his tight body bringing Dillon to the brink and over at the same instant. Jamie collapsed against Dillon's chest and Dillon wrapped him up tight in the strength of his arms, filling him with everything he had to give.

When they came back down, Jamie said, "Wow."

Dillon laughed, using what little breath he had left. "Wow yourself." He kissed Jamie's forehead. "Mmmm. You taste better than those chocolate bunnies your aunt gave us for Easter."

Jamie snuggled in closer. "I bet you say that to all the boys."

"Only the ones I'm crazy in love with."

"That narrows it down to one, then." Jamie opened one eye to look at the bedside clock. "What time do you have to be at work?"

"Six." Dillon turned his head and gave the clock his own inspection. "Four-thirty. I have enough time to grab a shower. Wanna take one with me?"

Jamie laughed and rolled off Dillon's chest and to his side. "Nah. You'll just want to have your wicked way with me again." His voice took on that teasing tone Dillon loved so much. "Geez, you'd think after a week of living together we'd have had enough hot sex to last us at least a few days."

"Never happen, my friend." Dillon stretched and got out of bed, swatting Jamie's naked rear as he went. "I have the feeling you and I will still be going at it when we're sitting in matching rocking chairs at the Shady Oaks Retirement Village."

Jamie closed his eyes and pulled the covers over himself, too sleepy, Dillon guessed, to even bother with cleaning up. "Sounds nice. The 'going at it' part, I mean, not the old folks home."

Dillon laughed and went to the apartment's small bathroom. As he started the water and stepped into the shower, he thought back on the last week. Well, one week and four days to be exact. He, Jamie, and that crazy mix of folks they called family had spent all of Easter weekend cleaning and moving. The minute Dean Nash and his son Wayne pronounced the place up to code, Gale and Sadie had orchestrated what Dillon called Operation Move-in. Under their direction, walls were painted, floors were cleaned, and furniture was moved. Thanks to them, Dillon and Jamie were able to move in right after church on Easter Sunday. Dillon thought that was fitting. Easter was a time of renewal and rebirth; he certainly felt like a new man. Not even Morgan's smug smile when Dillon and Jamie had gone in together last Monday morning — one week ago that very day, in fact — to give the office their change of address, had dampened Dillon's spirits. He had Jamie, and Jamie was all he needed to be happy.

Well, Jamie and food. Dillon's stomach growled, reminding him that he had just enough time to slap together a sandwich before work. He'd only meant to drop Jamie off after school, maybe get a little bit of his homework done before he had to be at the pharmacy. But as soon as they had stepped into the bedroom to put their things away, Dillon had been seized by a lust so strong he'd had no choice but to grab Jamie and take him. Smiling at the memory of what had just been shared between them, Dillon shut off the water and toweled himself dry. He went back into the bedroom only to find Jamie sound asleep under a mountain of covers. Careful not to wake him, Dillon grabbed his clothes from the tiny closet and made his way to the kitchen.

As usual, the first thing that caught Dillon's attention when he entered the eat-in kitchen was the bright yellow refrigerator and the booger-green stove Heath had bought from a friend who owned an appliance store. The colors clashed a thousand times over with the cheerful blue Sadie insisted they paint the kitchen, but Dillon didn't mind. His brother — the only blood family Dillon considered himself as having left — had gotten those appliances for him and Dillon loved them, ugly as they were.

He'd done his best to convince Heath to let him pay for the stuff, but Heath wouldn't hear of it. Heath wanted to do it, especially since the two of them wouldn't be living together anymore, and there was nothing Dillon could do to change his mind. Heath had also gotten Dillon and Jamie a washer and dryer, which the Nashes had hooked up for the two of them in the garage part of the carriage house, right downstairs. Dillon cringed just a little when he thought of the muddy brown hue of the washer and powder pink color of the dryer. At least they'd lucked out on the living room suite Brandon and Nate had given them. Two chairs, a sofa, and a loveseat, all in a nice, normal shade of blue. Combined with Jamie's bedroom set from Sadie's house, the lace curtains Megan had found in Brandon's attic, and the mountain of groceries Sadie and Gale had brought over, Dillon and Jamie had one heck of a first home.

Dillon slapped together and woofed down two bologna sandwiches before rushing off to work. He felt good, in spite of the fact that Nora had called earlier to let them know they could pick up Ben's car tomorrow. Dillon wasn't exactly eager for Jamie to reopen his investigation, but there wasn't anything he could do about it. Besides, as long as he and Jamie had each other, the two of them could make it through anything.

He pulled his car into the drugstore parking lot and got out. The temperature was beginning to change for the warmer. He didn't bother to put on his coat, the thick sweatshirt he wore being more than enough. He entered the drugstore, whistling as he went. His good mood was cut short the minute he saw Jim Pembroke's face.

Jim barely gave Dillon time to get in the door before he said, "Dillon, follow me to my office, please. I need to speak with you before you begin your shift."

Uh oh. That one doesn't sound so good. Rapidly developing a funny feeling in the pit of his stomach, Dillon followed Jim into the cramped confines of his small office, noting the pictures of Jim's kids and grandkids on the wall. He had been in Jim's office more times than he could count, but this time felt different. When Jim waited until Dillon was seated, then took his own seat and stared him down, Dillon's feelings of unease intensified.

Jim sat across from Dillon at his desk, his arms crossed over his chest. "I got a rather disturbing phone call from your mother this morning."

Oh, God. "Mr. P., I—"

Jim put up his hand. "Let me finish, son. Like I said, I got a call this morning from Angela. The woman was hysterical. Told me she'd just found out from someone she used to work with at the school that you and James Walker were living together. When I told her that lots of boys your age took a roommate to help with expenses when they moved out of their parents' house, your mother informed me you and James were much more than roommates. She came right out and told me the two of you were lovers." Jim's eyes pinned Dillon where he sat. "Is that true, son? Are you and James Walker lovers?"

Dillon knew his job probably depended on his answer, but he didn't care. He wasn't going to deny Jamie for anyone, not ever again. In a clear, strong voice he said, "I prefer the term life partner, but yes, Jamie and I are living together, and we're a heck of a lot more than roommates." His voice softened despite the severity of the situation. "He's everything to me."

Jim nodded. "I gathered as much. I didn't think your mother would be that upset if it weren't true. You should have told me, Dillon."

Dillon swallowed. "I know, but Jamie and I need the money to help out with college next year, and I was afraid if I told you it would affect my job."

Jim leaned forward, placing his hands in front of him on the desk. "You're right about that, son. Your relationship with James does affect your job. I'm afraid this changes everything."

It wasn't like Dillon hadn't expected it. He and Jamie had talked about this very thing the day they'd moved in together. In fact, it had been Jamie's idea not to tell Jim the two of them were partners. Jamie was afraid if Jim found out, he'd make some excuse to fire Dillon. From the way the conversation seemed to be headed, it looked as if Jamie had been right. Dillon sat back in his chair and waited for the words, "You're fired," to come rolling out of Jim's mouth.

They never came. Instead, Jim said, "Is it your assertion that James Walker is your spouse?"

Why was Jim asking questions Dillon had already answered? "Yes, sir, it is."

Jim nodded again and reached for a stack of papers at the side of his desk. "In that case, I have a few forms I need you to fill out. Oh, and we'll have to increase your hours so you get at least twenty-five in each week, but that's doable."

Dillon wondered if Jim had been ingesting samples from the pharmacy's narcotics section. "You're increasing my hours? Why?"

Jim pushed the stack of papers over to Dillon's side of the desk. "I know it might be a bit of an adjustment at first. I remember how hard it was for me to leave my wife right after we moved in together." He gave Dillon a sappy smile. "Heck, I have a hard enough time leaving her now, even after twenty-seven years and three kids." He cleared his throat. "But you already work about twenty hours a week, so five more won't make that much difference. And I wouldn't ask you to do it, but company policy is ironclad on the subject." Jim quoted word for word, as if reading from the employee handbook, "All employees wishing to qualify for health benefits must work an average of at least twenty-five hours per week."

Health benefits? "Mr. P., are you telling me you're bumping up my hours so I can have health insurance?"

Jim shook his head. "No, son, I'm bumping up your hours so that you and *James* can have insurance. Savings Central offers benefits for same sex partners just like they would for a married man and his wife." When Dillon started to speak, Jim said, "I know at your age you don't think much about getting sick. I pray you don't, but everyone needs health benefits just in case. Now, I spoke with your mother, and I know for a fact she and your father canceled your insurance as soon as you moved out. I imagine James has insurance through his aunt, but it would be better if it came from you. For all intents and purposes, you're a married man now. It's up to you and James to take care of each other. I'd say this is a step in the right direction, wouldn't you?"

Dillon was too shell-shocked to do more than nod, but it was enough for Jim. He pulled some more papers out of a drawer and added them to the stack in front of Dillon. "Good. Now we need to renegotiate your pay. Since health insurance takes money out of your check each week, I'm giving you a raise to cover the difference. And since you're a full-time student as well, you get a discount. So, with the raise and the extra hours, you'll actually come out making a few dollars more each week."

Dillon wasn't sure what to say, but he was fast learning that honesty worked best. "When you called me in here, I thought you were going to fire me."

"Fire you? Are you crazy, kid? Not only are you one of the best employees I've got, you're also someone I've come to think of as a friend. Like a son, even. I love all three of my daughters, but it would be nice to have a son to pal around with. You fit that bill rather nicely, I must say." Jim took off his glasses and rubbed the bridge of his nose. "I was hurt when you didn't tell me about you and James, though, Dillon. I want to help you in any way I can, but I can't do that if you won't let me."

The emotions swirling inside of Dillon were overwhelming. "I'm sorry for not telling you. Jamie and I have been through so much, and with my folks acting the way they are, I just wasn't sure how to handle it."

Jim put his glasses back on, stood up, and moved around to Dillon's side of the desk. He clapped his hand on Dillon's shoulder. "I wasn't criticizing you, son. I know you've been through a lot. I could tell that just by talking to your mother this afternoon." He rolled his eyes. "That woman is the poster child for a massive dose of Prozac. For the record, I don't give a rat's rear about you being gay. I'm just glad you've found someone to share your life with. Oh, and before I forget," Jim walked back around to the other side of the office and grabbed yet another sheaf of papers. "I have another offer for you. I recall you mentioning to me once that you were going to attend Garman College in the fall, up in New York, right? Are those plans still on?"

"Yes, sir."

"Good. Savings Central has stores all over the country, including one in Rochester, about a twenty minute drive from Garman College. I'm recommending you for a transfer when the time comes for you to move up there. I'm guessing that James is going with you?"

"Yes, he is."

"That works out nicely then." Jim gathered all the papers together and handed them over. "You can keep working for Savings Central and still keep your insurance benefits."

Dillon stood, holding the papers against his chest. "Somehow 'thank you' just doesn't feel like enough."

Jim reached out and patted Dillon on the cheek. "It is, son. Trust me when I say it is."

Dillon took the stairs from the garage to his and Jamie's apartment two at a time. He flung the door wide and found Jamie bent at the waist, wearing nothing but a thin pair of boxers, rummaging through the fridge. Dillon dropped his papers on the small kitchen table they'd inherited from the apartment's last occupants and cuddled up behind him.

Jamie started when he felt Dillon's crotch pressed against the most intimate part of himself, but he quickly warmed to the feeling. "Mmm. If that's gonna happen every time I bend over around you, I'll be sure to do it more often."

Dillon laughed and pulled Jamie up, closing the refrigerator door with his foot and turning Jamie so that the two of them were facing. "You do that." Dillon nuzzled his neck, inhaling Jamie's hair. "You smell good. Is that my shampoo?"

"Yep. I bogarted some of it." He looped his arms around Dillon's neck. "I like the way it smells. Guess we'll have to stock up. You get it at the pharmacy, don't you?"

"Uh huh." Dillon looked down and into Jamie's eyes. "Speaking of the pharmacy, I have something to tell you. My mother gave Jim Pembroke a call this morning."

Jamie leaned his head against Dillon's chest and groaned. "I can just imagine what she said."

Dillon pulled him in closer. "Gave him a real earful, from what he told me. But it's okay. Jim knows about us and he doesn't care."

Jamie lifted his head. "Really?"

"Really. He's even arranged for the two of us to have health insurance. I'll have to work a few hours more a week, but we can deal with that. And here's the best part: he's transferring me to one of the New York stores in the fall so I can keep working while we're in college."

Jamie hugged him tight. "That's amazing. I was so afraid he'd fire you when he found out about us."

Dillon strummed his fingers up and down the tender skin of Jamie's neck. "So was I, but it didn't happen." He drew Jamie up on his tiptoes and gave him a tender but promising kiss. "You know this calls for a celebration, don't you?"

Jamie grinned. "You want to celebrate the same way we celebrated our moving in together?"

Just thinking about the four hour sex-a-thon he and Jamie had shared their first night in the apartment sent a rush of heat coursing through Dillon. "I do want that, but this time I want you in the driver's seat." When Jamie gave him a puzzled look, Dillon cupped his face with one hand and said, "I want you to top me tonight." Dillon could hear the rush of air that Jamie pulled into his lungs.

"Are you sure? I know I'm kinda big, and I don't want to hurt you."

Dillon planted another soft kiss on Jamie's lips. "Kinda big? You're freakin' huge." His expression softened. "The pain won't last long, and I need you to do this. Please. For me?"

Jamie sighed. "It isn't that I don't want to, but—" He hesitated and clutched Dillon tighter to him. "You'll have to talk me through it. And if I hurt you—"

Dillon smoothed his hands up and down Jamie's back. "You won't." He could tell the exact minute Jamie gave in. His body relaxed a little, and he gave Dillon a wary smile.

"Let's take it to the bedroom then."

Dillon followed Jamie into the bedroom, his every nerve ending on fire at the thought of what was about to happen between them. To his own surprise, Dillon wasn't nervous. He fully expected it to hurt at least a little bit, but that didn't matter. He needed Jamie to take that final step toward the two of them becoming equal partners.

Too bad Jamie was lacking Dillon's confidence. The poor guy was so undone, he couldn't even get his own clothes off, much less Dillon's. Dillon ended up having to strip them both. By the time they were both naked and standing beside the bed, Jamie was shaking so hard, Dillon was ready to call the whole thing off.

"You don't have to do this. I never meant—"

Jamie shook his head, his voice coming out small and hollow. "What if I fuck this up?"

Dillon was stumped. "What do you mean?"

"Just what I said." Jamie worried the corner of his lip with his teeth. "What if I don't satisfy you? I mean, look at yourself. You could have anyone you want."

"For God's sake, do you really think I'd have gone two years waiting for you if I wasn't sure you're the one I want?"

Jamie looked close to panic. "What if I hurt you? What if I can't get you off?"

Dillon took him into his arms. "Then we keep trying until we get it right." He bent down to peer into Jamie's face. "I want you inside me. Not so you can get me off, not because this is some test I expect you to pass." He lowered his voice. "I want you inside me because you're mine. You already own my heart; I want you to own my body, too."

Jamie shuddered. "After that, how can I say anything but yes?"

"I'm not trying to pressure you, no matter how it sounded."

"I know you weren't. As far as that goes, you're the one who's supposed to be freaking out over this. You're about to lose your virginity, not me."

Dillon laughed. "Technically, we both are. You've never topped and I've never bottomed. We're on equal footing with this one."

Jamie went still. "I never thought about it like that."

Dillon leaned down and kissed Jamie's neck, his tongue weaving a wet path between Jamie's ear and shoulder. "That's what you have me for — to point out the up side of things."

Jamie leaned into Dillon's caress. "You keep doing that and I'm gonna show you my own 'upside'."

Dillon growled, the sound vibrating against Jamie's skin. "That's my plan."

Okay, so Dillon had underestimated just how bad bottoming hurt when one's boyfriend had a dick the size of a telephone pole. It wasn't that Jamie hadn't prepared him. Jamie had fingered, sucked, and rimmed him until Dillon thought he'd go insane from the sheer pleasure of it. The foreplay had even helped to dissipate Jamie's nervousness. No, the problem wasn't Jamie's prowess as a lover; the problem was, he was just too damn big.

Crouched between Dillon's widespread legs, Jamie saw the grim set of Dillon's features and panted out, "I'm gonna stop now. I can't stand causing you pain like this."

Dillon shook his head as best he could with his body set in such a rigid pose. "Just keep going. The head will pop in any minute now." Jamie tried to back out and Dillon stopped him. He had to do this, had to prove to Jamie he was willing to both give and receive. Finally giving in, Jamie went back to using the gentle pressure needed to open Dillon to his body for the first time. Gentle, that is, for someone trying to shove a killer whale into a goldfish bowl.

Okay, this is it. Dillon's ass was going to explode. In the morning there would be nothing left of him but pieces of ass scattered all over the apartment. He was just wondering how Aunt Sadie would clean all those ass fragments out of the bedroom rug when Jamie moved forward and Dillon felt him slide fully inside.

Well, his ass was still attached, so at least Dillon had been wrong about that part. He felt full, stretched. Jamie lay above him, stock still and, Dillon guessed, afraid to move. But in addition to feeling pain, Dillon felt something else. Curiosity. He was anxious to know what it was that made Jamie so eager to bottom for him most of the time. With a slight rocking of his hips, Dillon encouraged Jamie to move.

And move he did. With that one little motion, Dillon started Jamie's thrusting. And Dillon felt...nothing.

Nada, zip, zilch. Well, he felt something, but it wasn't anything special. It was sort of like having Jamie stick his finger in Dillon's bellybutton. Dillon knew it was there, could feel it wiggling around, but it didn't do a heck of a lot for him. At least it didn't hurt like it had at first. He was glad Jamie seemed to be enjoying it — hell, Dillon would bottom for him every night if it brought Jamie the pleasure his grunts and groans said it did — but truthfully, Dillon couldn't see what all the fuss was about. Then Jamie shifted his position, and Dillon nearly passed out from the white-hot electricity zapping through his blood.

"Jesus Christ, what was that?"

Jamie was so out of breath, he was barely able to grunt out, "I hit your prostate."

So that's what that did. Dillon had always wondered. Now he knew. God, did he know. Where he'd been soft only minutes before, Dillon's erection sprang to life, trapped beneath Jamie's pistoning hips. He'd read more than one Internet story about guys who had hands-free orgasms. He'd even given Jamie a couple. He never thought he'd actually have one himself. But as Jamie continued to rake over that one spot deep inside, and as he felt the contractions begin low in his belly, Dillon was damn thankful about being wrong.

He tried to warn Jamie what was happening, but he never got the chance. Not that such a warning turned out to be necessary. He heard Jamie whisper, "I love you," and felt Jamie swell within him. As Dillon filled the space between their bodies with the weight of his release — spurred on by the knowledge that Jamie was filling him the same way — Dillon closed his eyes, not surprised to feel the first wetness of his own tears. He should have been shocked, being able to count on one hand the times in his life he'd actually cried, but this time, he thought it fitting. Jamie had just completed him. He felt whole.

Aunt Sadie pulled up in front of Nora's house, that is to say, Nora's former house. According to what she'd told them, Nora would be out completely by the end of the week. Jamie couldn't say he didn't feel a pang of regret at knowing the only real home Ben had ever had was being sold, but he understood Nora's desire for a fresh start.

Sadie put the Cadillac in park. "Are you boys sure you don't want me to stay for a few minutes? Dillon, don't you have to be at work soon, what with your new schedule and all?"

Dillon shook his head, even though Sadie couldn't see him from where he sat in the back seat. "No, ma'am. My new schedule doesn't start until next week. I have tonight off."

Jamie opened the front passenger side door. "It's a good thing he does. Nora really needs us to go ahead and get the car and Ben's things today so she can finish clearing out the place for the new owners. She's down at her office right now closing a sale, but she left the garage unlocked for us, and all Ben's things are inside the car."

"Do you have the car keys?"

"Yes, ma'am." Jamie patted his pocket. "Nora gave them to me along with Ben's will."

Sadie turned to look at Dillon. "Dillon, how about going on up to the house and opening the garage? I'll send Jamie on in a minute."

For a second it looked like Dillon was going to argue, but in the end he gave Jamie an apologetic smile and climbed out of the car. Jamie understood. Few men, himself included, had the balls to refuse a direct order from Sadie Banks. Jamie closed his door and then sank back into the seat. He knew that look on his aunt's face. Lecture time.

The minute they were alone, Sadie turned in her seat to face him. "Are you sure this is what you want to do?"

"Pick up Ben's car? Sure. I mean, that's why we needed you to drop us off, so Dillon would be able to drive us back home."

"Not that." Sadie sighed. "Dan Morgan stopped me on my way out of the library yesterday afternoon." She paused. "He told me you were arrested in Chicago, and that you'd been probing into Ben's death."

Damn Morgan to Hell. "I wasn't arrested and Morgan knows it. He and Dillon had a talk about this the Monday after our trip to Chicago." Jamie felt a piercing jolt of guilt. "I should have told you what happened, but I was afraid you'd be mad."

Sadie waved that away. "I'm not a complete imbecile. I knew you and Dillon hadn't gone all the way to Chicago just to rent a hotel room and 'do the wild thing', as you kids say. I also know you've been far from satisfied with the explanations you've received about Ben's death. But being picked up by the police in front of a dead man's house?" She shook her head. "Really, Jamie. What were you thinking?"

"Morgan told you all of it, huh?"

Sadie adjusted herself, causing the leather seat of the Cadillac to creak. "He told me you were involving yourself in some kind of vigilante investigation into Ben's death. He also told me the man whose house you visited was murdered, and that he was worried about your safety." She wrinkled her nose. "What a crock. He had some books in his hand, made it seem like he'd come to return them and just happened to run into me while I was doing story hour for the kids. Horse pucky. He came to the library with the express purpose of asking me to warn you off, and not because he was worried for your safety, either. What I want to know is why?"

In this, at least, Jamie could be honest. "I don't know."

Sadie studied him carefully, making Jamie feel like a bug someone had pinned to a card and put under a microscope. Finally she said, "But you do know more about Ben and his death than you're telling me." It was a statement not a question.

Jamie didn't bother to deny it. "Yes, I do. But there's still a lot that I don't know."

Sadie didn't ask for clarification. "And you hope to find something in Ben's things that will help you fill in the blanks."

"Yes, ma'am."

"I know that you loved Ben, and that you feel like you owe him something. But, son..." She looked into his eyes. "You have your own family now, with Dillon. It's not just yourself you have to consider. Whatever you do directly affects Dillon, as well. And if Morgan is right, you could both be in danger."

"I'm not in any danger." Jamie did his best to project confidence. "Morgan was just trying to scare you."

Sadie's eyes were pleading but she didn't argue with him. "I hope you're right."

She wasn't the only one. Jamie didn't even want to think about what could happen if he was wrong.

Jamie couldn't help but laugh at the cautious way Dillon eased himself into the driver's seat of the low-sitting Firebird. "What's the matter? Sore?"

Dillon shot him a dirty look. "You should know. You're the one who stuck that tree branch of yours up my ass."

"As I recall, you loved it." Jamie climbed into the car amidst Dillon's assurances that he had. It wasn't until he was completely seated and was closing the door that Jamie remembered the last time he was in that car: the night of the dance, the last time he ever saw Ben. Jamie had talked to him the next day on the phone, but that night was the last time Jamie ever saw Ben's face. The hurt must have shown in his expression because Dillon reached over and squeezed his hand, his palm warm and comforting.

"You know, you can sell this car if you want to. If it hurts you to even sit in the thing, there's really no point in keeping it."

Jamie shook his head. "It's okay. Just gonna take me a little while to get used to it is all." He reached into his pocket and handed over the keys. "You ready?"

Dillon nodded but made no move to start the car. "Can I ask you something?"

"You know you can."

"What about Ben's ashes?"

Jamie drew in a deep breath. "The mortuary sent them to Nora, and she's agreed to keep them for me for a while, just until I can figure out how to fulfill the terms in Ben's will."

"You mean the part about waiting until you're completely happy and then releasing them somewhere?"

"Yeah."

Dillon gazed at him long and hard. "Haven't you been happy, Jamie? With me, I mean."

"Happier than I've ever been in my life, but—"

Dillon cut him off with a loud sigh. "But you can't be completely happy until you have Ben's death and the rest of it all settled in your mind."

Leaning back in the seat, Jamie closed his eyes. "Not completely, no." He turned his head in Dillon's direction and opened his eyes. "Does that make me sound like a total dick? I mean, here I am with this amazing guy, but unable to let go enough to totally enjoy him."

Dillon popped the key in the ignition. "It doesn't make you sound like a dick, but I have to admit, I'm hoping there's something in Ben's stuff that can answer your questions. I'm ready to put this behind us."

Jamie had the same hopes, but two hours later, as he sat on the floor of their apartment surrounded by empty boxes and Ben's few possessions, those hopes dwindled and Jamie had to admit to himself he wasn't going to find anything.

Dillon came up behind him, sitting down so that Jamie was cradled between his legs. He put his hands on Jamie's tired shoulders, rubbing with deep, forceful motions in an attempt to ease the tension.

Jamie leaned back against Dillon and closed his eyes. "That feels so good."

Dillon kissed his cheek. "Find anything?"

"No, but not for lack of trying." Jamie opened his eyes and pointed to the array of stuff scattered on the floor. "Forty-six baseball cards, eight ratty comic books, a donkey that shoots cigarettes out of its butt—"

"I didn't know Ben smoked."

"He didn't. God only knows where he got the thing, but you're missing the point. I went through all his stuff and I didn't find anything pertinent. Not one clue."

Dillon kissed him again. "You know what you need?"

"Besides a fifth of Jack Daniels, you mean?"

Dillon tickled his ribs. "This coming from the guy who gets high off root beer. Not even close. You, my friend, need a driving lesson."

Jamie swatted Dillon's hands away from his ultra-ticklish mid section. "Quit it before I pee." When he'd gotten his breath back, he said, "We've talked about this before. I can't drive and you know it. I don't even have a permit."

"You took driver's ed, though. I know you did, because it's required. And you have to have a permit to take that class."

Jamie nodded. "I took it last year and I passed, but only because Coach Greenly went easy on me." Jamie could see the shock on Dillon's face out of the corner of his eye.

"Coach passed you even though you couldn't drive?"

Jamie nodded. "'Fraid so. I was too scared to even get behind the wheel of the damned car. Coach passed me anyway because he didn't want to mess up my academic record with a failing grade. I know it sounds screwed up, and if anybody ever found out he'd be in deep shit, but he was trying to help. It's a good thing for me Plunkett's on-the-road driver's training is one-on-one. I'd never have gotten away with it otherwise. Aunt Sadie was mad as hell when she found out about it. I had to beg her not to rat out Coach."

The look of mock-horror Dillon sent him was comical. "You mean I've saddled myself with a cheater? God help me."

Jamie pinched him. "Yeah, well, He's the only one who's gonna be able to help you if you don't stop teasing me. Like I said, I had a permit, but I'm sure it's expired by now. That was over a year ago."

Dillon shook his head. "Those things are good for at least a couple of years. Didn't you even look at the expiration date?"

"No, why would I? I can't drive, so what's the point in having a permit? I threw it in one of Aunt Sadie's kitchen drawers as soon as driver's ed was over with."

Dillon stood up, pulling Jamie to his feet in the process. "The point in having a permit, genius, is so you can learn how to drive. Come on."

"Where are we going?"

"To get your permit. Then you're gonna have your first lesson."

Jamie was horrified. "At night? On the road?"

Dillon grinned. "Yes, and yes."

Jamie followed Dillon up to the main house, not that he had much choice. Dillon always called Jamie stubborn, but he was nothing compared to Dillon when he made up his mind about something. Jamie's last thought as he pulled the apartment door closed was whether or not he and Dillon would make good crash test dummies.

Sadie eyed them with both amusement and wariness as they came to claim Jamie's permit, but she didn't say anything, and Dillon was glad. He was having a hard enough time convincing Jamie he could actually do the whole driving thing. Poor guy looked scared to death, but Dillon was going to remain firm on this one. Everybody above the age of sixteen needed to know how to drive, and that's all there was to it.

Dillon and Jamie walked back across the yard and up the separate driveway of the carriage house. Jamie headed to the Lumina, which was parked halfway up the drive, but Dillon shook his head and pointed toward the garage where the Firebird sat.

Jamie's eyes went so big they were all Dillon could see in the dim glow of the security lights. "You want me to drive Ben's car? It's a stick shift."

Dillon unlocked the garage door. "And your point is what?"

Jamie rolled those same big eyes. "I can't even drive an automatic, let alone a stick."

Dillon almost laughed at the irritated tone of Jamie's voice, but he held it together. "If you learn how to drive a stick, you can drive anything. Heath taught me how to drive on a stick and that's how I'm gonna teach you."

"Heath taught you how to drive instead of your dad teaching you?"

"Yep. Good ol' Douglas was too busy to teach me, so Heath took over." Dillon raised the garage door and pointed to a spot on the other side of the driveway. "Why don't you wait for me over there while I back it out and turn it around? I'll teach you how to go in reverse later. Right now, I think we should concentrate on going forward."

Jamie muttered, "And I think we should just look into getting me a bus pass," but he did as Dillon asked.

Damn, he's cute when he's all agitated like that.

As the engine rumbled to life, Dillon had to admit that Ben had great taste in cars. He looked at Jamie, standing off to the side. Ben had great taste in men, too. At least he had when he'd fallen for Jamie.

Dillon backed the car out and took advantage of the wide driveway to whip the car around so that Jamie could just drive it straight out onto the street. As soon as he had the Firebird in position, Dillon put the car in neutral and got out, moving around to the passenger's side. "You ready?"

Jamie cringed. "Hell no on that one. Look, I don't even know what position to put the gears in."

"Get into the driver's seat and I'll teach you." An idea popped into Dillon's head, the perfect way to show Jamie how to shift gears. Dillon was betting on the fact that Jamie wouldn't forget, especially not given the method of instruction he was going to use.

Jamie complied without protest, though Dillon could tell there was plenty he wanted to say. He waited until Jamie was seated on the driver's side before climbing in himself. As soon as they were both in, Dillon said, "Don't buckle up. Not yet."

Jamie didn't question him, just reached for the keys. "You want me to start it up now?"

"Nope. I want you to unbutton your jeans."

There was just enough light surrounding the driveway for Dillon to get a clear look at Jamie's face. Jamie couldn't have looked more confused if Dillon had asked him to sacrifice a live chicken on the courthouse steps. "What in the hell does unbuttoning my jeans have to do with driving?"

Dillon knew Jamie. If he told him outright what he was planning, Jamie would raise a fuss. "Unh uh. First you have to do it, then I'll tell you. You're just gonna have to trust me on this one."

Jamie eyed him long and hard before sighing and doing as Dillon asked. As soon as Jamie's pants were unfastened, Dillon reached for him. Jamie squeaked out, "What are—"

"Shh." Dillon freed Jamie from the confines of his boxers and said, "Now, start the car so we'll have some heat in this thing."

"With your hand on my dick? Dillon—"

"Please, Jamie, just do this for me, okay?"

Another sigh, then the purr of the engine as Jamie started it up. Dillon grinned. Time for the first lesson.

One thing Dillon had counted on — could pretty much always count on — was Jamie's reaction to his touch. He started getting hard almost as soon as Dillon wrapped his hand around him. Dillon stroked him with a light motion until Jamie was rigid enough to begin. Then, with a gentle motion, Dillon wiggled Jamie's penis back and forth. "This is neutral."

Jamie was having trouble following. "Huh?"

Dillon smiled. "I'm going to demonstrate the positions of the gears using your own personal, um...shifter. As soon as I'm done, I want you to do the same thing using the real shifter."

"Are you nuts?" But there was no heat in Jamie's voice, especially not with Dillon stroking him the way he was.

Dillon laughed. "All part of my charm." He wiggled his hand again. "As I was saying, this is neutral. Feel the slack in the gear shift?"

Jamie half-answered, half-panted, "Yes."

"Okay, you can take your hand off the shifter now." As soon as Jamie relaxed back against the seat, Dillon moved his hand forward. "This is first gear."

"Damn." Jamie leaned his head back and closed his eyes. "I think I like first gear."

"Then you're gonna love second, third, and forth."

Dillon's lesson turned into a fifteen minute, mutual masturbation session that left the both of them more than satisfied. When they were finished and had cleaned up, Jamie zipped up his jeans and gave Dillon's hand a little squeeze. "Damn."

"I think that sums it up." He buckled his seat belt, waited while Jamie did the same, and then pointed to the shifter. "I'm ready when you are. Put your left foot on the clutch and your right foot on the brake and we'll get this show started."

Dillon's plan had worked two-fold. Not only had he shown Jamie "first hand" the proper positions for the gears, but Jamie was now too relaxed to argue. Mostly. He gave a token protest, but put the car into first in spite of his misgivings. It only took him six tries to keep the motor running.

Dillon winced each time the engine went dead and Jamie ground the gears in yet another attempt to get her on the road. Finally, on try number seven, Jamie managed to work the clutch and the accelerator together. Dillon almost shouted with relief when he felt the car inching forward.

His relief was short lived. Just as Jamie lurched to the edge of the driveway, the left front tire made a loud pop, followed by the unmistakable hiss of air escaping its rubber confinement.

Jamie slammed on the brakes, not a hard slam considering they were going less than a mile an hour. "What did I do?"

Dillon was already unbuckled and on his way out to check the tire. "I think you ran over something, probably one of those tack strips they pulled up when Megan's dad and her brother ripped out the old carpet in the carriage house. Dean set all that stuff next to the curb."

"Yeah, but city sanitation picked all that stuff up." Jamie shut off the engine without even bothering to take the car out of first.

Dillon got back in and helped him get the car back into neutral. "Calm down. A piece of it probably got left behind, is all. No big deal."

Jamie got out at the same time as Dillon. He looked so shaken, Dillon gave him a task just to keep him focused. "Grab my flashlight out of the garage, please. The light out here is too dim for me to see what we hit."

Jamie was all too happy to go. By the time he got back with the light, Dillon was in position, ready to inspect the damage.

As he'd thought, a stray piece of tack strip had worked its way into the driveway and under the tire. The tread was totally wasted. Dillon stood up and brushed off his knees. "Looks like you're about to get a lesson in car maintenance. You're about to change your first tire."

Jamie groaned. "I thought you said this driving stuff was easy." He walked back around to the driver's side and pulled the keys out of the ignition. "Ben had a flat tire the night of the accident, remember? Nora told me the police had the car towed to a local garage before they released it to her after Ben's death was ruled a drunk driving accident. I'm betting the guys at the garage put the spare on and just threw the flat tire into the trunk after they were done."

Sure enough, as Jamie raised the trunk lid and Dillon got a good look at the spare, he could see Jamie was right. Dillon reached for the jack. "At least we can go ahead and take the old tire off. We'll have that part done, anyway. And we can take the one in the trunk to the auto parts store. Maybe it can be patched."

Jamie nodded, but Dillon could tell he wasn't handling this well at all. He figured it had more to do with talk of the night Ben died than anything else. Dillon's best bet was to get this over and done with so Jamie wouldn't have to deal with it any longer than necessary.

He was in such a hurry, he didn't notice the edge of the jack was caught on the fabric lining of the trunk. With one smooth motion Dillon extricated the jack, the sound of ripping fabric alerting him, too late, to his mistake.

Jamie was staring at the ruined fabric, his brow furrowed. Dillon thought sure he'd upset him. "I'm so sorry. I'll get it fixed. I'll—"

Jamie shook his head. "It's not that. Look." He pointed to a stack of what looked like papers stuffed against the sidewall of the trunk, just inside where the lining should have started.

Dillon dropped the jack and the tangled fabric back into the trunk, reaching for the papers at almost the same time. Only they turned out not to be papers.

They were photographs.

Dillon took one look at the first one and his stomach turned. It was a picture of a man he'd never seen before doing an unspeakable act with a girl who looked to be no more than fourteen, fifteen tops. He shuffled through each picture, finding the same guy doing similar things, only with a different girl in each picture. The guy's face was clearly visible, but Dillon didn't recognize him. He didn't realize he'd said the last part out loud until he heard Jamie say, "I know who he is."

Dillon took one look at Jamie's stricken face and knew what was coming, but he had to ask anyway. "Who?"

"He used to be Birch Carpenter. That is, before someone splattered him all over his front porch." Jamie looked at Dillon, his face stricken. "I guess we know who Ben was blackmailing after all, huh? We just found Ben's second victim."

Chapter Sixteen

"Now can we go to the sheriff?" Dillon sat down on the couch next to Jamie and across from Megan and Heath who were sharing the loveseat. He took a sip of the Coke he'd brought with him from the kitchen, wishing it was something stronger.

Jamie shook his head. "Not until we know all of it."

Dillon should have known it wouldn't be that easy. "Why the hell not? We know all the players, and with those pictures of Birch having sex with underage girls, there's not a doubt in my mind he was Ben's second victim."

"Some victim." Heath snorted and scooted closer to Megan, though Dillon would have sworn they were already as close as two people could get without actually sharing the same skin. "You ask me, it couldn't have happened to a nicer guy." He looked to Jamie. "What did you do with the pictures?"

"I asked Dillon to hide them for me, but not to tell me where they are until I decide what to do with them. I know that sounds weird, but I feel better not having to see them." He sighed. "I know I should just hand them over to the sheriff, but I'm half scared he won't believe me. Blackmail, prostitution, pay-offs... This whole mess sounds more like a soap opera plot than something that actually happened."

"I know my brother," Megan said. "If you tell him the truth and show him the evidence, he's going to believe you. He's too smart not to." She leaned forward. "I'm sure when you do talk to Brandon, Ash will be glad to go with you and back up you with the story of his own blackmail."

Dillon, who'd just taken another sip, got so choked up Jamie had to whack him on the back a few times to clear the Coke out of his windpipe. "How did you know about that?"

Megan shrugged. "I went to see him in the hospital a few days after his near miss. I mean, I've gone to school with the guy for practically my whole life; it was only right I go check on him. We started talking, and he told me what happened." She leaned back against Heath. "To be honest, I think he just needed to get the whole thing out of his system, poor guy. And he gave me permission to tell Heath, too. That's my point. If Ash is willing to let me tell a perfect stranger like Heath what happened to him, I'm sure he'd be happy to cooperate if you wanted to tell Brandon."

"How is Ash, anyway? I heard he was home from the hospital." Jamie lowered his eyes in that way that made Dillon's heart ache for all he'd been through. "I want to see him again, but I'm afraid it'll make things harder on him. You know, bring it all back."

Megan's smile was so warm and loving, Dillon could have kissed her. "Ash figured that's why you haven't been around. He said to tell you and Dillon both he'd love to see you anytime."

Dillon set his Coke on the table and studied his brother's face, finding the way Heath's facial muscles tensed at Megan's words fascinating.

"And just when did Ash tell you that?" Heath seemed to be grinding his teeth. "Have you been seeing him on a regular basis? More than just that one time, I mean."

Megan turned to face him. "You know I did. I told you about it."

Heath shook his head. "You told me you visited him at the hospital. You didn't say anything about going to his house."

"The guy needed a friend. I've been to see him a few times, and I don't think I should have to apologize for it. I don't know why you'd be jealous, anyway. You don't seem to care about how much time I spend with Dillon and Jamie."

Heath crossed his arms over his chest. "In case you haven't noticed, Dillon and Jamie are gay."

"So is Ash."

"Ash is bisexual. Big difference. I don't like you being alone with other guys."

Megan stood, pulling on Heath's hand so that he came to his feet as well. She gave Dillon and Jamie an apologetic smile. "Before this turns into another one of our ninety decibel discussions, Heath and I are going to go." She blew them both a kiss, and shook her head when they started to rise. "Don't get up. We know the way out. And, Jamie?"

"Yeah?"

"No matter what you decide about telling Brandon, I'm behind you all the way." On that note she left, taking a grumbling Heath with her.

Jamie leaned into Dillon's embrace. "I don't know what we did to deserve Megan, but I'm glad we've got her."

Dillon kissed his cheek. "She's a sweetheart, all right. I just hope Heath doesn't hurt her."

Jamie looked up at him in surprise. "You really think he would?"

"Not intentionally, no. But Heath has a whole lot of baggage he's carrying around with him. I just hope it doesn't spill out on Megan."

That piqued Jamie's interest. "What kind of baggage?"

Dillon pulled him in as close as possible. "To be honest, I'm not sure. I just have the feeling that something happened right about the time Heath moved out of Mom and Dad's house. Nothing was ever said to me and Heath won't talk about it, but that's the feeling I get."

"You're probably right. You have good instincts."

Dillon didn't want to fight, but he couldn't let an opening that good pass him by. "Yeah? If I have such good instincts, why won't you listen to me about going to the sheriff?" Jamie pulled away, but to Dillon's relief, he didn't go far.

"Those pictures we found tonight don't necessarily mean Birch was Ben's victim."

"You don't believe that. Hell, it was your idea to call Megan and Heath over here to tell them what we'd found. Why would you do that if you didn't believe we had proof positive?"

Jamie did get up then, but Dillon sensed it was more a case of restless energy than anger. After a few minutes of pacing around the living room, he stopped long enough to look at Dillon and say, "So, what's our theory, then? That Birch killed Ben because Ben was blackmailing him?"

Dillon knew Jamie wasn't going to like what he had to say next, but that wasn't going to stop him from saying it. Jamie needed to face the truth. "You have to stop looking for killers around every corner. Brandon's already arrested Ben's killer. His name is Barry Sledge, professional drunk, and he's sitting in the county jail right now awaiting his sentence."

"Damn it, can't you see what's right in front of you?" Jamie pulled at his hair in a gesture of utter frustration. "It's too much of a coincidence that Ben was blackmailing two people for thousands of dollars each and just happened to end up dead. Life doesn't work that way."

"Life isn't an eight dollar mystery novel, either. It's time you stopped trying to make it one." Dillon was doing his best to hang on to his temper but Jamie wasn't making it easy with his stubborn refusal to listen.

"Since you have an answer for everything, answer this one for me." Jamie's cheeks were bright red and flushed with anger. "You're so sure Birch didn't kill Ben. Who killed Birch then?"

Dillon stood up. "Gee, Jamie, I can't imagine who would want to kill Birch. I mean, who in his right mind would want to off a kiddie pimp, child molester. I can't think of a soul."

"Do you have to be so damned sarcastic?"

It wasn't until Dillon heard the quiver in Jamie's voice that he realized how worn out Jamie was. Dillon's anger dissipated like a thin fog, almost at once. He crossed the room and took Jamie into his arms, all but crushing him against his chest. "No, I don't. I'm sorry, sweetheart. I'm just worried and ready for this to be over."

Jamie nodded but didn't say anything. Desperate to reach a compromise, Dillon said, "I don't wanna fight about this. Can we try something here, please?"

Jamie murmured, "What," into Dillon's chest. Dillon smiled in spite of the tension between them. At least Jamie was interested. Dillon said, "It's too late to go to the auto parts store tonight, and I have to work every evening until closing for the rest of the week. But Saturday, I get off at four. Let's take the tire from the trunk in and let the guy at the auto parts store look at it. Then we'll make up our minds about what really happened that night, okay?"

Jamie nodded and hugged him tighter. Dillon only hoped when the evidence came in proving Ben's death was caused by Sledge — and only Sledge — Jamie would accept it.

The guy down at Autos-R-Us — Joe, according to his nametag — took one look at the tire Dillon had pulled from Ben's trunk and said, "Dude, who slashed your tire?"

Dillon felt Jamie go rigid beside him. "You mean the tire was cut?"

Joe narrowed his eyes. "You're telling me your tire was cut and you didn't even know it."

Jamie shook his head. "The car belonged to a friend of mine. The tire was like that when I got it."

Joe took a pen out of his pocket and pointed to the black surface. "See this gash here, on the side?"

"I see it," Jamie said, "but what does it mean?"

Dillon tuned Joe out as he gave Jamie the explanation. Dillon already knew what it meant. If Ben had run over something which caused the tire to go flat, the gash would be on the bottom not the side. Even in the face of mounting evidence that was contrary to his own theory, Dillon wasn't going to give up. If he admitted the tire had been cut the night of Ben's death, then he'd have to admit the truth: someone wanted it to look like Ben had a flat tire that night and therefore had a reason to be out of his car on a deserted road in the middle of the night. Someone with something to hide. Something like murder.

Dillon wasn't ready to believe that, not yet. To Joe, he said, "But couldn't running into something, say a ragged curb, couldn't that gash a tire on the side?"

"Not like this one was cut. See here?" Using the pen, Joe again pointed to the tire. "Take a close look and you'll see what I mean."

Dillon did as he was asked and out of the corner of his eye saw Jamie doing the same thing. The minute Dillon was eye level with the tire, he knew the truth. There, in the midst of a store crowded with engine parts and smelling of motor oil, all Dillon's theories about the night Ben died crumbled.

Jamie straightened up first. "I don't know anything about cars and even I can tell that tire was cut with a knife. It's just too clean and narrow to have been made by anything else."

Joe nodded. "That's about the size of it."

"Can you get us a used tire in the same size? The one that's on there now was shredded by a tack strip." Dillon paused for a minute, thinking about the tire he hadn't had a chance to even remove in all the chaos caused by finding the pictures. "On second thought, see if you have two used tires in this size. That way we'll have a spare."

"Piece of cake." Joe looked down at the tire on the counter. "What do you want me to do with this one?"

"We'll take it with us just like it is." Dillon had to force the words out of his mouth. "We may need it for evidence."

Jamie gave him a long, searching stare. "Does that mean what I think it means?"

"Yes and no." Dillon took a deep breath. "Let's just say I'm less certain about Sledge's guilt now than I was when I walked in here. I want to keep that tire like it is, just in case."

Dillon could tell Jamie was trying hard not to say "I-told-you-so." Instead he said, "In other words, you're keeping an open mind."

"Yeah."

Jamie grinned. "A guy can't ask for any more than that."

As soon as they got back to the apartment, Dillon parked the Lumina and pulled all three tires out of the trunk. Jamie took the slashed tire and carried it into the garage, propping it against the far wall. Coming back to Dillon, Jamie pointed to the other tires. "Want to store those in the garage, too?"

Dillon shook his head. "We've got a couple hours of daylight left. Might as well change the damaged one and put the spare in the trunk. Wanna give me a hand?"

"Sure. What do you need me to do?"

Dillon rolled one of the tires toward the Firebird, which was still sitting on the side of the driveway. "Throw this one in the trunk, please. Oh, and grab the jack and the lug wrench while you're at it."

Jamie pulled the keys out of his pocket and went to the back of the Firebird. At least he knew what a lug wrench was and wouldn't have to embarrass himself by asking. He had to hand it to Dillon. Not once had he ever made Jamie feel inferior for his lack of knowledge about cars. Just another reason he was so crazy about the guy.

He threw the spare inside the trunk, ignoring the sight of the ruined lining and the memory of the hidden pictures as best he could. He grabbed both the jack and the handle, tucking them under his left arm and reaching for the lug wrench with his right. That done, he closed the trunk and headed to where Dillon was crouched on the driver's side of the car.

Dillon took the lug wrench with a grateful smile and made quick work of loosening the lug nuts. When that was done, he said, "Put the jack together, would you, sweetheart?"

Jamie grinned in spite of himself. "Sweetheart? That's the second time you've called me that. You going all girlie on me, Carver?"

"I told you that lube Megan gave us was putting me in touch with my feminine side." Dillon laughed. "You are sweet, though, and I can prove it."

"Oh really? How?"

"I've tasted you myself."

Jamie blushed at just hearing that. Cheeks flaming, he set about screwing the handle onto the jack so Dillon could pump up the car. *Screw. Pump.* Thinking those words made Jamie blush even harder. Dillon was turning him into a total horndog, and Jamie didn't mind in the least.

He gave the handle a twist, his brow knitting in frustration when it refused to tighten. Finally, after five minutes of trying, he turned to Dillon. "I think I must be doing it wrong."

Dillon set aside the lug wrench and looked over Jamie's shoulder. "There's no way to do it wrong. All you do is screw it in."

"It won't catch."

"Let me try." Dillon turned and took the jack handle, repeating the process Jamie had been struggling with. Jamie was strangely happy to see Dillon was having no more success than him. Finally, Dillon took a good look at both the jack and the handle. "No wonder they don't fit; they're different models. Hell, they aren't even the same brand."

It wasn't disbelief of Dillon's statement that made Jamie take a look for himself. It was more like a sure certainty that Ben, who put the "P" in "picky" where it came to his car, would never have a made the mistake of pairing his jack with the wrong handle. Dillon must have had the same thought, because he said, "I don't believe this."

Jamie nodded. "I can't believe Ben would've made that mistake."

"This wasn't a mistake."

Jamie wondered if his face was as blank as his mind at the moment. "I don't understand. You just said you didn't believe it. Now you're saying you think Ben choose the wrong handle on purpose."

Dillon laid the handle on the ground, right in front of Jamie. "Look at the handle, Jamie. It's solid steel. They all are. And judging by the way this one is too small to catch on the threads at the base, I'm guessing the handle that goes with this jack is even more solid, thicker. Just the right size to club a man over the head with—"

"And then leave him lying in the middle of the road for some drunk to run down." Jamie finished with a horrifying realization. "You think the guy who really killed Ben bashed in his head with his own jack handle and then dragged his body into the middle of the road?"

"Yes. I also think the killer slashed Ben's tire to make it look like he was fixing a flat and had a real reason to be out of the car that night. He couldn't leave a bloody jack handle behind, so he switched Ben's handle with his own, thinking no one would ever check it. And it worked, because no one did. Not until now."

Jamie closed his eyes, his brain doing its best to keep up. When he was together enough to open them again, he looked at Dillon and said, "But how did he do it without being seen? And if Ben didn't really have a flat that night, what was he doing out of his car? And how did the killer get the jack handle out of the trunk to hit him with in the first place?"

Dillon leaned back against the car. "The first part is easy to answer. Tully Road is isolated enough that no one would be out there at that time of night except the occasional drunk on his way back from the beer joints. If I had to guess, I'd say that's why Ben and the guy who killed him were meeting out there in the first place." Dillon rubbed his grimy hand over his face, leaving more than one smudge. "As for the rest of it, who knows? Just more pieces to add to this damned jigsaw puzzle Ben created."

Jamie wanted to argue that getting killed wasn't exactly Ben's fault, but he knew it would be a hard sell, even to himself. Blackmail and extortion weren't exactly conducive to long life and good health. One thing he couldn't argue against any longer, though, was going to see Brandon. Jamie couldn't keep fighting the truth. He and Dillon were over their heads; they needed backup.

Looking to Dillon, he said, "Can we wait about changing the tire?"

"We can, but we don't have to. I have a jack in the trunk of the Lumina."

"It's not that. It's just that, well..." Jamie cleared his throat. "We need to go see Ash before we do anything else."

It was Dillon's turn to look confused. "Why?"

"Because I want to clear it with him before we see Brandon." Jamie looked Dillon dead in the eye. "You were right. It's time we tell Brandon the truth. All of it."

Dillon grabbed the back of Jamie's neck and kissed him, hard. When they broke apart, he summed up his feelings in four simple words. "It's about damned time."

Jamie was so nervous, Dillon was afraid he was going to have to strap Jamie to the seat of the Lumina with duct tape just to get him to sit still long enough to fasten his seatbelt. When Ash answered the door on the first ring, Dillon sagged against the door frame in relief.

Ash looked worlds better than he had the last time they'd seen him. The bandages were gone, revealing a rope-shaped scar encircling the circumference of his neck, but other than that, no one looking at him would ever be able to tell he'd had such a near miss. The thing that put Dillon the most at ease, though, was the warm smile Ash produced the minute he saw them.

"It's about time you assholes came to see me. I was beginning to think I was gonna have to barge into your little love nest just so you'd know I was still alive."

Even Dillon had to admit that Ash's damaged vocal cords gave his voice a low, sexy pitch. Dillon laughed. "Yeah, yeah. Cry me a river, why don't you?" He grew serious. "You look good, man. Real good."

"I feel good." Ash ushered them inside. "Dr. Carson is so happy with my progress, he's decreased my therapy sessions to once a week. With any luck, I'll be discharged from care completely by the time school starts in the fall."

Jamie clapped Ash on the back. "That's great, Ash." He hesitated. "That makes what we came to ask you even harder."

Ash led them into the den and motioned them to the couch, taking one of the chairs for himself. Once they were all seated, he said, "If this is about you telling the sheriff what happened with me and Ben, I'm all for it."

Jamie seemed too stunned to speak, so Dillon took over. "You know about that?"

"Sure. Megan told me you were thinking about it and might want me to back up the story with her brother. I'll tell you the same thing I told her. I think you should tell him what's going on. Especially until you find out where that other money came from."

Dillon looked to Jamie, a question in his eyes. When Jamie nodded, Dillon said, "We're pretty sure Ben was blackmailing the guy who pimped him out. The less you know about that the better, but let's just say we found photos, a whole lot of them, like the ones Ben made of you."

Ash shuddered, but he seemed to be holding it all together. "I had no idea Ben was capable of such things. I'd hoped what he did to me was a one shot deal."

Jamie cleared his throat. "There's more." He went on to tell Ash about the slashed tire and the mismatched jack handle.

"So, what?" Ash shook his head in amazement. "You think the pimp killed Ben because Ben was blackmailing him, then made it look like an accident? It makes sense, I guess. All the more reason for you to turn the guy over to Sheriff Nash."

"That's the kicker," Dillon said. "The guy who whored Ben out is dead. Somebody wasted him on his own front porch."

Ash whistled. "You gotta go to the sheriff, the sooner the better. I'll back you up any way I can." He lowered his eyes. "I still have those pictures Ben took of me and him, if you need them."

"Why would you keep something like that?" Jamie made a rude noise. "I'd have burned the fuckers."

Ash shrugged. "I'm not sure why I kept them, to tell you the truth. Maybe I just wanted a reminder of my own stupidity." Jamie started to speak but Ash held up a hand to stop him. "It's okay. I won't say I'm over it, but I'm dealing with it. And look at it this way — if you show Brandon those pictures and the letter from Ben, it goes a long way toward backing up your story."

By the time the visit was over and the two of them were ready to leave, Jamie seemed more convinced than ever that telling Brandon the truth was the right thing to do. Dillon was actually starting to think all their problems would soon be behind them.

They drove to Brandon's house first. It was pushing eight o'clock by the time they got there, and Dillon was almost sure Brandon would be home. Nate answered the door, with Sasha, Brandon's Great Dane, hot on his heels. Sasha studied the boys for a second with something akin to doggy disinterest before sauntering back into the house. Dillon laughed. "Some watchdog she is."

Nate snorted. "She's a watchdog all right. She'd sit back on her fuzzy rump and watch the thieves make off with all our stuff." Nate opened the door wider. "You guys want to come in?"

Jamie shook his head. "We were hoping to talk to Brandon."

"I wish you could, guys, but he's gone to Chicago to talk to a witness about a case he's working on. I'm not expecting him back until late tonight. Is there anything I can help you with?"

Dillon took Jamie's hand. "Not this time, Nate, but we appreciate the offer."

Nate slapped him on the shoulder. "Anytime, buddy. And whatever it is, I hope it works out for you."

It was too much of an understatement to say it out loud, but silently, Dillon did too.

By the time they got back to their apartment, Jamie was totally drained. He could've sworn he fell asleep twice on his feet just walking to the stairs. He followed Dillon inside the apartment and was just about to head for the shower when someone knocked on the door. Since Dillon was halfway to the bedroom already, Jamie yelled, "I'll get it."

The minute he opened the door, all thoughts of being tired and taking a shower fled. Megan stood on the deck, her eyes red, dried tear tracks on her cheeks. Jamie pulled her inside and wrapped his arms around her. "Are you all right?"

Megan mumbled into his chest, "Yes. No. I don't know." She drew back and took in a deep, shuddering breath as a fresh spate of tears filled her eyes. "I'm not sure how to feel. Heath's mad at me, and I don't know why."

Dillon came back in, took one look at Megan's face and said, "Damn it, what did Heath do to you?"

"How do you know it was Heath?" Megan swabbed at her eyes with her shirtsleeve. "How do you know it wasn't me who screwed up?"

Dillon pulled her over to the couch. "I know my brother." He and Jamie sat down on either side of her, offering what comfort they could. "What happened?"

"You know that night we got picked up in Chicago?" When they both nodded, Megan said, "Stupid question. Of course you do. Well, Heath was so mad at me that night, he spent the entire drive back from Chicago ripping me a new one for what happened. I guess he was on such a roll, he couldn't see how upset I was getting. By the time we got back to Reed, I was a complete basket case. Heath felt bad about it, and he took me to his apartment to get me calmed down before driving home. Guess he didn't want my mom and dad to see me so upset." She took a deep breath. "He was so great about it, so apologetic. We started kissing. One thing led to another..."

Dillon groaned. "Please tell me you didn't sleep with him."

That brought on a fresh round of tears. "I did. And that wasn't the only time we've been together. He's always been so sweet afterwards. But not tonight. Tonight was different."

Dillon drew her against his side. "And how was tonight different, honey?"

Megan hiccuped. "Tonight I told him I loved him."

Jamie reached out to squeeze her hand. "What did he say?"

Megan increased the pressure on Jamie's hand. "He flipped out on me. Total pancake. We were at his apartment and he just freaked. He jumped up and started getting dressed, going on and on about not expecting too much, and about me pressuring him." She laughed, the sound harsh and bitter. "Geez, you tell a guy you love him, and he practically dives out the window to get away from you." She wiped her eyes on her sleeve again and Dillon went to fetch some tissue.

When he came back, Megan blew her nose and wiped her eyes properly. "He all but threw me out of the apartment, told me it was time for me to go home. I drove straight here. God, what did I do wrong?"

Dillon cursed under his breath. "Not a damn thing. This is Heath's problem, not yours." He stood, and Megan guessed what he had in mind because she said, "Where are you going?"

"Where do you think I'm going?" Dillon picked up his keys. "I'm going to beat some sense into my dumbass brother. No way in hell am I gonna let him treat you this way."

"No, you can't!" Megan did her own version of a freak out. "Please...it would only make things worse. You know how Heath is. He'd be so mad at me if he knew I told you what was going on between us. Please don't do it."

Dillon looked at Jamie with such helpless bewilderment, Jamie felt sorry for him. But on this one, Megan was right. "You can't do it. You've been where Heath is. Think about it. Could anyone two years ago have forced you to confront your feelings about me?"

Dillon fell back onto the couch. "Take the wind out of a guy's sails, why don't you?" He looked at a still sobbing Megan. "So, what are we gonna do about this?"

"Nothing. I'm the one who screwed up, not you." Megan curled her lip. "I knew better than to give my virginity to a guy who barely even seems to like me most of the time."

Jamie pulled her close and hugged her tight. "We like you, and we won't even ask you to sleep with us."

Megan managed a shaky laugh as Dillon wrapped his arms around her from the other side. "Who says we won't? This girl is downright cuddly. I've always wanted a human teddy bear. She could sleep right in the middle of that big ol' bed of ours, and we could share her."

Megan laughed again, and Jamie could feel her relax a little bit. As much as he liked Heath, he was mad as hell at him for doing this to her. Judging from the look on Dillon's face, he was even angrier.

It took Megan another half hour to calm down completely. She was wrung out, and Jamie wasn't surprised when she said, "Thanks for listening, guys. I think I'm gonna go home now and drown my sorrows in a hot bubble bath."

"You sure you're up to the drive?" Dillon was watching her closely.

Megan stood. "I'm fine, just ready to go home." She kissed them both on the cheek. "I'll see you Monday at school, if not sooner." She left before either one of them could protest.

The minute the door closed, Dillon grabbed Jamie in a hug so tight Jamie thought sure he heard his ribs groan in protest.

"God, I'm sorry." Dillon's voice was harsh and strained.

"For what?" Jamie pulled back as best he could within the confines of Dillon's bear hug.

"For putting you through the same thing my brother is putting Megan through." Dillon's face was tortured. "If I hurt you half as bad as Heath hurt Megan, you must've been in agony."

"You've made up for it." Jamie leaned up on his tiptoes and kissed Dillon's chin. "With any luck, Heath and Megan will work things out, too."

Dillon sighed and rocked Jamie in his arms. "I hope you're right, but, knowing my brother, he'll make Megan's life hell before he admits to her — and himself — how he really feels. I—"

A solid knock on the door cut Dillon off in mid-sentence. Jamie pulled away from him with a wry smile. "Hold that thought. Megan must have forgotten something."

Jamie crossed the room to the door, flinging it open with, "Hey what did you for—"

The words died on his lips. Instead of seeing the blue eyes and red hair he'd expected, Jamie was looking at the face that had haunted his dreams since that life-changing day in February. The dark brown eyes, the black hair, the smile of the best friend he'd ever known.

Ben Lewis was standing on Jamie and Dillon's doorstep.

Chapter Seventeen

The minute he laid eyes on Mitchell Harding, Jamie started hyperventilating. Dillon tried everything he could to convince Jamie he wasn't staring into the face of a dead man, but his panicked brain couldn't absorb the information, not in his state. In the end, Dillon had little choice but to let Jamie's panic attack run its course. He let out a deep breath when Jamie's breathing returned to normal.

Dillon took a second to study Mitchell, who was sitting in one of their living room chairs. His resemblance to Ben was uncanny, but now that the initial shock was over, Dillon could see some differences. Whereas Ben's hair had been short and spiky, Mitchell's hair was longish, clasped with a leather cord at the back of his neck. Ben's face had been unmarked perfection, but Mitchell had a wicked scar running the length of his right cheek from the corner of his eye to his chin. And there were other differences as well, like the more muscular build of Mitchell's body and the deeper tone of his voice as he apologized, yet again, for sending Jamie over the edge.

"I am so, so sorry." Mitchell looked to Jamie, who was sitting on the couch next to Dillon, still wheezing slightly. "I had no idea I was gonna trip you out like that. When my sister told me you wanted to see me and that it had something to do with Ben, I headed straight for Reed."

Dillon waved away the apology with one hand while the other moved in slow circles across Jamie's back, trying to soothe and comfort him. "You don't have to apologize, Mitchell. This wasn't your fault."

"Please, call me Mitch." Dillon nodded and made formal introductions for himself and Jamie. Mitch pushed a stray lock of hair away from his forehead, the leather of his jacket creaking as he moved. Crossing one faded, jean-clad leg over the other and picking at the heel of one black boot, Mitch inclined his head toward Jamie. "What caused him to freak?"

Is he kidding? "Not to be insensitive," Dillon said, "but you have to admit you and Ben could pass for twins."

Pain clouded Mitch's warm brown eyes. "Shit. I didn't even think about that." His whiskey-smooth voice lowered an octave. "I used to think Ben and I favored each other a lot, but then, after I got this scar—" His hand moved unconsciously to his cheek and Dillon had the feeling the memory was as vicious as the scar itself. "I guess I just didn't think." He looked at Jamie again. "Is he gonna be okay?"

Jamie sat up, using Dillon for leverage and holding on to him like a lifeline. "I'm okay. Sorry about that, going all crazy on you, I mean. It's just, for a minute there..." Jamie's voice was so low, Dillon wondered if Mitch could hear it. "For a minute, I thought you were Ben."

"You and my brother, you were tight then?"

"Yeah." Jamie gathered himself together. "He was my best friend. I still can't believe he's gone."

Mitch shifted in his chair, his movements slow and measured. Even Dillon, a total stranger, could tell the guy was grieving. *But if he cared so much about his brother, why hadn't he seen him in over two years? Why the breach?*

Before Dillon could pose the question, Mitch said, "How did my brother die? Lily told me something about a drunk driving accident, and that a couple of 'fags' — her words, not mine — wanted to see me because they thought I might know something about his death. She gave me your names and a cell number, told me you lived in the town of Reed, and nothing much else."

Mitch's last statement raised a question in Dillon's mind. "If all Lily gave you were our names and a cell number, how did you find us?"

Mitch sighed. "It wasn't easy, believe me. I've been trying to pin you down for almost two days now. I knew Ben's foster mother was a woman named Slater, but when I found her house, some guy told me she'd moved. I finally tracked her down at the realtor's office where she works, but she refused to give me your address. Said she didn't want me hurting you the way I hurt Ben." His voice dropped and he lowered his eyes. "As if I could." He met Dillon's gaze. "When she wouldn't tell me anything, I tried looking you both up in the phone book." He smiled, but there was little humor in it. "I must have called every Walker in the book before giving up and trying to find you both under the name Carver. Wouldn't you know it? I had a hit the first time out. I guess I should have tried Carver first, anyway, since C comes before W." He grimaced. "Although, after talking to the lady who answered the phone, I almost wish I hadn't called at all." He looked at Dillon with more than a little pity. "Your mom is one angry lady."

Dillon wrinkled his nose. "That's one conversation I'm glad I didn't hear. I can just imagine what my mother told you. Needless to say, I'm not exactly the favorite son around the Carver house."

Mitch snorted. "Total understatement, dude. The minute I said your name, your mom went off on a ten minute tear about you and James Walker being shacked up in, what was it she called it? Oh yeah, 'that Lambert Lane Den of Sin'." Mitch shrugged. "At least I got your address out of it, even though I had to ask around town before I found the place. Not to mention the fact that it took me forever to spot this apartment behind that big ol' house in front." Mitch gave a sheepish but sincere grin. "Then it took me another couple of hours just driving around town, trying to work up the courage to come knock on your door. I wasn't sure I'd have the guts to climb the stairs."

"I understand," Jamie said, and Dillon was relieved to hear some of the strength returning to his voice. "It was the same way for me when I knocked on your sister's door looking for you."

Mitch put both feet on the floor, propping his elbows on his knees. "Don't think I'm not grateful you came and told us about Ben, but why did you come looking for me? If you and Ben were as close as I think you were, you must have known I haven't seen Ben in almost three years."

"That's just it. I didn't even know you *existed*. My best friend in the world had a whole family I didn't even know about. Why is that?"

Mitch sighed again, this time making the sound of a man torn apart inside. "You've met my sister. Would you brag about having a family like us? Ben did the right thing. He saw a chance to get out and he took it. Good for him."

As much sympathy as Dillon felt for Mitch and what he'd lost, there was too much riding on what he might know for Dillon to let it go at that. Jamie was too tenderhearted to grill him, but Dillon was determined to get to the truth. "There's more to it than that, and you know it. You need to tell us what happened between you and Ben to cause such a split between two brothers who, by all accounts, cared so much about each other. We also need any information you can give us about Birch Carpenter's death."

Mitch went on the defensive. "Oh yeah? You think I drove here from Michigan just to spill my guts to two guys I don't know from Adam? If I wouldn't talk to the cops when they came nosing around, what makes you think I'll talk to you?"

"Because as soon as we're done talking to you, we're going to see the Reed County sheriff, a guy named Brandon Nash." Jamie's voice came through loud and clear. "We're taking with us evidence of blackmail and murder, and all hell is going to break loose. Which side of all this you're on when the smoke clears depends on what you tell us in the next five minutes."

Dillon stared at Jamie in slack-jawed astonishment. *So much for underestimating my partner.* He should have known better. Jamie might be tenderhearted, but when it came to Ben, he was single minded and determined to a fault.

"Whoa. Back up a minute." Mitch sounded just as astonished. "Lily told me Ben was killed by a drunk driver. How does that tie in with blackmail and murder?"

Jamie took a deep breath and then spelled it out for him, going from Barry Sledge and the supposed accident that took Ben's life, to finding the money and both sets of pictures, to the slashed tire, and then ending with the mismatched jack handle. By the time he was done outlining each point, there was no doubt in Dillon's mind that Mitch was a believer.

"And you're sure that this Barry Sledge guy couldn't have killed Ben?"

Jamie shook his head. "I can't be sure of anything in all this mess, but Barry Sledge swears Ben was already dead when he hit him."

Mitch raked his hands through his hair, dislodging the leather cord, which fell unnoticed to the floor. He all but tied the silken black waves of his hair in knots as he tried to take it all in. "And the last set of photos you found, you're sure those are of Birch?"

"As sure as I can be. All I saw was that one photo of him in his folder at the police station."

More surprise came from Mitch, and Dillon could also see a hint of admiration. "You went through Birch's folder?"

Jamie's face went red. "Yeah. That's how I got your name and number. I sorta swiped a paper listing all the known occupants of Birch's house at the time of his death."

Mitch whistled. "That took a whole lot of intestinal fortitude, kid. If the police catch you, you are so screwed."

"Maybe, but it was worth it. And who are you calling kid? According to your sister, you're only two years older than me."

Mitch's eyes took on a faraway, almost wistful gleam. "According to the calendar, I'm two years older than you, but the way I've lived, the things I've seen...it ages you." He cleared his throat and focused on the present. "What do you want from me?"

Dillon addressed that. "We want the truth about all of it, from your split with Ben to the night Birch died, anything that might tell us whether or not Birch killed Ben in retaliation for the blackmail."

Mitch balked. "You think Birch killed Ben for blackmailing him? No way. Birch was a slime ball, sure, but he didn't have the balls to kill anybody."

"He could have hired someone to do it."

Mitch shook his head. "You're not getting my point, James. If Birch really was Ben's second blackmail victim, why pay Ben off in the first place if Birch was just going to kill him later? Why not do it at the get-go?" When Jamie started to argue, Mitch said, "Before we take this any further, do you think I could take a look at those pictures? It might not even be Birch. You said yourself you couldn't be sure." When Jamie hesitated, Mitch went on with, "If you expect me to spill my deepest and darkest secrets to you, you're gonna have to give me something in return. Trust works both ways."

The man had a point. Jamie gave him a small nod and Dillon stood up. "I'll get them. Jamie asked me to hide them for safekeeping."

He hated leaving Jamie alone with the guy, even if Mitch did seem sincere. He didn't waste any time retrieving the pictures he'd taped to the back of the dresser mirror.

Dillon came back in, handing the pictures to Mitch and then reclaiming his place beside Jamie. He watched the emotions swirling across Mitch's face as he flipped through the pictures, finally throwing them down on the coffee table in disgust. "That's Birch. No doubt about it. The fucker was doing those girls in his own damn bedroom."

"Are you sure you don't need to look again?" Jamie asked. "Those pictures have got to be two and a half to three years old."

"What are you talking about? Those pics were taken just a few months ago. Four, maybe. Five tops."

Jamie was on the edge of his seat, literally. "That's impossible. Ben left Birch years ago. How would he have gotten recent photos?"

Mitch picked up the top picture, wincing at the image on the paper. "There's no way these pics are two or three years old. See that scar right there?" Dillon and Jamie leaned in and looked to where Mitch's finger pointed toward a long, narrow gash trailing down the length of Birch's back. Even in the grainy photo, it was impossible to miss.

Dillon leaned back against the couch. "So he has a scar. So what? How does that prove when the pictures were taken?"

Mitch placed the photo back on top of the pile. "Seven months ago, Birch was in a car accident. Wrapped his Porsche around a tree. That scar came from a piece of jagged sheet metal slicing into his back. Took almost two hundred stitches to sew him up, and he was out of commission for another two months recovering from all his broken bones. That's why I say those pics had to be taken somewhere in a four to five month time frame."

Dillon rubbed his fingers over the back of his stiff neck. "Then that leaves us with two possibilities: either Ben snuck back to Chicago, set up a camera, and photographed good old Birch in action, or he had someone do it for him."

Mitch held up two fingers. "I vote for the second scenario. After what happened the night Ben left, I don't think he would ever willingly have stepped foot in Birch's house again." He shuddered. "God knows, I wish I'd had the same choice."

"What happened that night, Mitch?" Jamie's voice was filled with compassion. "It's obvious that you loved Ben, that you're nothing like your sister. What happened that pulled you and your brother apart?"

Mitch closed his eyes, but not before Dillon saw the tears. When he opened them again, the tears had been replaced with an iron resolve. Dillon was betting it was resolve to help bring his brother some justice.

Mitch cleared his throat. "Before I start this, do you think maybe I could have a glass of water?"

Jamie nodded. "I'll get it." When he came back in and handed Mitch the glass, Mitch said, "Thanks, man. Talking about this makes my mouth go dry." He wasn't kidding. While Jamie was sitting back down, Mitch drained half the glass in one long swallow then placed it on the table near the pictures. "How much information did you get out of my sister?"

Dillon rolled his eyes. "Depends on what you call information. We know she was in prison for dealing drugs, and that you and Ben were sent to more than one foster home. Oh, and we know you aren't really 'bent', as your sister so elegantly put it."

Mitch laughed. "Shows what she knows, huh?" Seeing Jamie's rounded eyes, he laughed again. "Yeah, I'm gay. I knew I was before I ever started working for Birch." He cringed. "Didn't make fucking guys for money any easier, but hey, you do what you gotta do, right?" His shrug spoke volumes. "I guess Lily needs to believe I'm not really gay so she can keep living in that fantasy world of hers. More power to her, but I'm through hiding. Is it hot in here to you?" He pulled off his leather jacket and hung it on the back of his chair, revealing a wide, well-developed chest beneath a tight black t-shirt. "Is that all she told you?"

"No," Jamie said. "She also mentioned something about Birch having a partner."

Again Mitch did a full body shudder. "Yeah, I'll get to him in a minute. First I want to answer your question about the night Ben left Chicago. I believe you've been honest with me, and now it's my turn.

"When Lily went to prison, she blamed Ben for getting her busted." Mitch sniggered. "Personally, I always figured the little shit did it on purpose, and I was damn proud of him for it. Me and Ben, we were two of a kind. He hated living with Lily and selling that junk on the street corner as bad as I did. When we were busted and CPS moved us into foster care, Ben and I were relieved, especially since the social worker was trying to find a home that would take both of us so we could stay together." His expression turned dark. "If we'd only known what we were walking into, we'd have run away and never looked back." He shook himself. "Hindsight's a bitch. Anyway, the lady at CPS found several places that would take us, but each placement was only temporary. And Ben and I weren't the easiest kids to deal with. Hell, we'd practically raised ourselves, and here were these perfect strangers harping at us to do our homework and go to bed at ten o'clock. We pitched so much hell, it's no wonder they couldn't find a foster home to keep us. Enter good ol' Birch."

His hands shook slightly and Dillon wondered how evil Birch had to have been that just the mention of his name could cause such a reaction from Mitch. But Mitch went on with the story, in spite of his obvious distress.

"When I first met the guy, I thought he was the answer to all our prayers. Well-spoken, dressed to kill. I thought Birch was a regular Superman, ready to come in and save us. After two weeks in his house, I knew better." He fidgeted, trying in vain to find a more comfortable position. "I'm not sure how long we were there before he started pimping us out, but I can tell you this: I believe the dirty bastard is roasting in a black pit for the things he made us do. And the hell of it is, no one would do a damn thing to stop him. He had so many freakin' cops and councilmen on his client list, I honestly think the guy could have screwed a goat on the mayor's front lawn and gotten away with it."

Jamie bit his lip. "You and Ben didn't have anybody you could turn to? No family besides Lily?"

Mitch shook his head. "We didn't have anybody but each other. And for a while, that was enough. As much as I hated whoring, we made decent money, even if Birch did take most of it. Ben and I saved what we could, hoping one day we'd have enough banked up to make a break for it." He sighed. "We almost made it, too. And we would have, if it hadn't been for dear, sweet Uncle Jared."

Dillon and Jamie said, almost in unison, "Who?"

"Birch's partner. Uncle Jared. That's what he called himself, though I doubt it was his real name. See, he and Birch had a sort of silent partnership. Jared would provide and screen new customers in exchange for a cut of the profits."

"If he helped out in the operation," Dillon said, "why do you call him a silent partner?"

Mitch fiddled with the leather bracelet he wore on his left wrist — his only jewelry save for the tiny gold hoop in his ear. "Even though Jared brought in guys, he had nothing to do with the day to day running of the business or the management of the boys. Nope, that was all Birch." He pulled a pack of cigarettes and a lighter out of the front pocket of his t-shirt. Tapping one out with less than steady fingers, he started to light up, then stopped. "Sorry." He held the cigarette up to Dillon and Jamie. "Do you mind? It helps settle my nerves."

Normally Dillon would have said no, but Mitch was doing them a favor by even talking to them. Hearing no protest from Jamie, Dillon said, "Go ahead." He went in search of an ashtray, finding nothing better to use than an empty soft drink can. He handed it to Mitch with an apology. "It's all I could find."

"Works for me." Mitch set the can on the table next to his water glass and then lit the cigarette, striking his Zippo against the leg of his jeans in one fluid motion. He took a long, grateful drag before returning to his story. "Like I said, Jared's job was to bring in business and screen customers. Birch was always solid on one thing, and that was no violent stuff. None of that bondage or S and M shit. Not that he was worried about our welfare. Birch just didn't want anyone damaging the merchandise." Mitch took another drag, and Dillon noticed the shaking had settled somewhat. "Jared must have done a pretty good job screening, because Ben and I were there for almost three years without incident. Then, just before Ben's sixteenth birthday, everything changed."

Dillon fought the urge to reach out and pat Mitch's arm, not sure how the gesture of comfort would be received. Instead, he said, "What happened?"

Mitch sighed. "Birch was out of town, one of the few times he actually left Jared in charge. Birch was pretty strict about no sex with clients in the house, which is why I was so shocked to see those pictures of him having sex with teenage girls in his own bedroom. He scheduled most of our encounters in out-of-the-way motels, then slipped the motel managers extra cash to keep their mouths shut. But Birch was out of town and Jared brought in this guy — Ralph, he called him — who was willing to pay extra if he could get it on with a matched set. Birch didn't have a set of twins, but—"

"He had you and Ben, and the resemblance was good enough." Jamie's expression of disgust matched what Dillon was feeling to a tee.

"Right. I told Jared there was no way I was going to have sex with my little brother, but Jared assured me the guy didn't want that, just wanted us both there. There wasn't a whole lot we could do about it, so Ben and I went along. Things started off normal. Well, as normal as can be expected when you're selling your ass, but then the guy went nuts on us."

Dillon was almost afraid to ask, but he had to. "Nuts, how?"

Another drag off the cigarette settled Mitch's nerves. "The guy got off on hearing other guys scream. The more pain he inflicted the more he liked it. Ralph decided to do me first. His idea of foreplay was to knock me around, give me a bloody nose. I tried to fight back, and that's when he pulled out the knife." Mitch's fingers found the scar on his cheek. "I backed away as soon as I saw it, but I didn't move fast enough. Bastard took a strip out of my cheek. That's when Ben knocked him over the head with a baseball bat one of the other boys had left within easy reach."

"Good for Ben," Jamie said. "He did the right thing, protecting you like that."

Mitch shook his head. "We'd have both been better off if he'd just let the guy do his worst to me."

Dillon found that hard to believe, not unless... "Don't tell me Ben killed the guy?"

Mitch took in a deep breath. "That's exactly what happened. Well, what we thought happened, anyway. When Ralph didn't move, I called out for help. Jared came running, and not long afterwards, Birch came home from his trip. They ordered Ben and me out of the room, said they'd take care of everything." He let a thin trail of smoke drift from his lips. "About an hour later, Birch came in and told us that Ralph was dead, that Ben had killed him. He threw Ben out of the house, told him to pack his things and go."

Jamie shook his head. "I thought Ben ran away."

"That's what he wanted people to think. Ben had been giving Birch fits for a while. He was smarter than Birch's other boys, myself included. Ben was always headstrong, less inclined to follow orders than the others. I think Birch was relieved to have a good excuse to get rid of him, top money maker or not. I wanted to go with him, but Birch wouldn't allow it."

Since Ben had learned from the master, it didn't take Dillon long to figure out how Birch kept Mitch from leaving. "He blackmailed you."

Mitch gave a weary nod. "Told me unless I broke off all ties with Ben, he'd have him arrested for murder. Claimed he had the whole thing on tape, and knowing Birch's penchant for taping his boys having sex, I believed him. From that point on, anytime I mentioned leaving — even after I turned eighteen — Birch would threaten to have Ben locked up." He gave a sad smirk. "Guess I was too good at my job. Wanna know the funny part? The whole thing was one big lie. Ralph wasn't dead. The blow knocked him out, but except for one Louisville-Slugger sized headache, he was fine. Birch made the rest of it up to keep me right where he wanted me, and to get Ben out of his hair."

Damn. And I thought I had it rough. "When did you find out?" Dillon asked.

"Six months ago, not long after Birch's accident. I heard Birch and Jared arguing one afternoon. They didn't know I was anywhere around. Seems Birch was trying to cut Jared out of the business. He'd decided he didn't need a partner anymore, and he wasn't happy about the fact that Jared was having sex with some of his boys. Jared was going through a laundry list of things he'd done to help Birch out, including helping him get rid of Ben by staging Ralph's so-called murder. Jared threatened to tell me the truth if Birch dumped him, and he also threatened to expose Birch's own dirty little secret." Mitch's mouth twisted. "I didn't know what that secret was at the time, but I guess I do now, huh? God, I mean, I knew Birch was straight, but I thought he liked older women, ones who at least qualified for a driver's license."

Jamie was trembling and Dillon pulled him close without ever breaking eye contact with Mitch. "How did Birch respond to Jared's threats?"

"In typical Birch fashion. He shrugged them off, told Jared he didn't have any proof, and even if he got some, Birch was well connected enough to keep it from sticking." Mitch shook his head in amazement. "Even flat on his back recovering from a car crash, Birch had one hell of a nerve. He told Jared to go ahead and tell me the truth, that I would never leave him, and that Jared would never have the balls to expose their little operation. On that last part, he was right. Apparently, Ben was the one who got the dirt on Birch and started blackmailing him."

Dillon turned to look at Jamie. He could almost see the wheels in Jamie's brain going round. Jamie said, "I think they both did."

"Huh?"

"You said it yourself. After what happened that night, why would Ben ever want to step foot inside that house again? Too much of a risk. To get the photos, he needed someone on the inside. Someone who could come and go when Birch wasn't around. Someone who knew the boys and the layout of the house."

"Someone like the mysterious Uncle Jared," Dillon said.

"Son-of-a-bitch." Mitch crushed his cigarette butt against the top of the Coke can and dropped it inside. "You're right. Even with Birch trying to cut Jared out, he'd still have enough pull with the other boys to get in and out of the place without Birch knowing. It's not like the boys cared enough about Birch's welfare to tell him that Jared was on the property. And Birch only had cameras set up in certain places, like his own bedroom and all those ratty motels. I should have thought of that the night Ralph was supposedly killed, but I was too damn scared to think rationally."

"Don't beat yourself up over it, man." Dillon did reach out and pat him on the arm then, relieved when Mitch didn't flinch. "You did the best you could under the circumstances. Out of curiosity, why didn't you leave when you found out Birch and Jared had lied about Ralph?"

"I've asked myself that same question a thousand times. Scared, I guess. Where was I gonna go? I had a little bit of trick money saved up, but not enough to last any length of time, especially not after taking out the amount Lily guilted me into sending her each month. I was too old for foster care, and I'd burned all my bridges with Ben." Mitch picked at a tiny hole just above the knee of his jeans. "I only have one skill, and Lily didn't want me unless I 'earned my keep', so it wasn't like I had a whole lot of options. All that changed when I came home from a night of tricking and found Birch's body shredded into hamburger on the front porch."

Jamie closed his eyes, and Dillon wondered if he was remembering the pictures he'd seen at the police station. Opening them again, he said, "You were the one who found him?"

Mitch nodded. "Yeah, and from the looks of it, the killer hadn't been gone long. If I'd gotten home about fifteen minutes sooner, there would have been two bodies lying on that porch."

Dillon was horrified. "What did you do?"

"The only thing I could do. I made a run for it. I more or less flew upstairs, grabbed what cash I'd saved, then made a break for it before the cops got there. At least Birch had no objections to us owning our own cars. In fact, he liked it because he didn't have to arrange a ride for us back and forth between jobs. All of the other boys were still out on their runs, so no one saw me. I hopped in my car and I was outta there before I could get caught. When the police started their investigation, one of the guys who lived in the house gave them my name and told them I lived there too. They traced me back to Lily, who was only too happy to help them since she figured she probably wouldn't be getting any more money out of me. She called me on my cell phone and told me the cops were looking for me. She even sounded happy about it, the bitch. But I played it cool. I went down to the station on my own and gave them my statement — something to the effect of not having seen or heard anything. They must have bought it, because they let me go with the standard, 'If you think of anything that might help the case, please let us know.' That was it. They were done with me, and I hit the road."

"You said something earlier about Michigan," Dillon recalled. "Is that where you went?"

"Yeah. I met this john a few months ago, one of the only ones who's ever really been nice to me. He lives up there, but comes to Chicago every now and again on business. He's a decent enough guy, only picks up hustlers who are over the age of eighteen. Anyway, he told me once if I ever needed anything, I could call on him. I made it seem like I was up that way for a visit or something." Mitch pulled out another cigarette. "I'm sure he knew I was lying, but he's cool enough not to ask any questions. I hid out with him until I called Lily three days ago to see if the heat was off. I more or less had to promise to pick up a few tricks and send her some cash just to get her to tell me anything. That's when I found out you guys were looking for me. I drove straight here, and the rest, you know."

Dillon had no idea listening to someone else's story could be so emotionally draining. He ached for Mitch, and, as much as he hated to admit it, for Ben. He stood up and stretched. "So, here's what we've got so far. We know Birch had a partner, and that he's most likely the one who gave those pictures of Birch to Ben. Why do that, though? Why use Ben to blackmail Birch?"

Mitch lit the second cigarette. "Because what Birch said was true. Jared wouldn't have the balls under normal circumstances to do his own dirty work. He'd want someone else to handle the negotiations. Who better than Ben, a guy who hated Birch with every fiber of his being? Hell, knowing my brother, he jumped at the chance to give Birch a little payback."

Jamie moved to the edge of his seat. "Then it makes perfect sense Birch would have turned all his anger on Ben. Maybe he thought Ben was acting alone. Maybe he thought killing Ben was the only way to get out from under the threat."

"I'm still not buying it. I do think Birch was bluffing with Jared when he told him he wasn't worried about having his secrets exposed. Otherwise, he never would have paid the blackmail in the first place. But the very fact that he did pay it rules out murder in my mind. If Birch was gonna kill Ben, he'd have done it right at the beginning, when Ben made his first demand. He wouldn't have waited." Mitch thought for a minute. "You said Ben was blackmailing another guy, some rich man whose son Ben was seeing. What about him? Could he have killed Ben?"

Jamie shook his head. "He was out of the country on a business trip. I checked. And even so, if your argument in support of Birch being innocent is 'why pay if you're just gonna kill the guy', then the same could be said for Mr. Barnes. He paid Ben almost as much as Birch did. If he was gonna kill Ben or hire someone else to do it, why pay?"

Mitch thumped his ashes into the can. "There goes that theory."

"I think you're both overlooking the obvious. If Ben was willing to double-cross Ash, who's to say he didn't double-cross this Jared guy?" Dillon paced the living room. "We're all reasonably sure Jared and Ben had to be working together. Who's to say Birch didn't pay off Ben only to have Ben keep the whole thing rather than giving said partner a cut?"

Jamie stood up. "We could sit here all night talking this out and never know the truth. Until we find out who this Jared guy is, and how he hooked up with Ben after Ben left Birch, there's no way to know whether we're dead on or grasping at straws." He started for the kitchen, then stopped. "I've got a howling case of the munchies. You guys hungry?"

Dillon grinned. "You don't even have to ask. You know I'm always hungry." He looked at Mitch. "How about you?"

Rising to his feet, Mitch shook his head. "I should go. It's late, and I'm sure you guys will want to hit the sack soon."

"It's not that late," Jamie said, "and besides, you came all this way just to talk to us. The least we owe you is a meal, even if it is just a bologna sandwich and a bag of chips."

"You don't owe me anything." Mitch plunked the remains of his cigarette into the can and carried it to the wastebasket at the edge of the kitchen. "I'm the one who owes you for being there for Ben when I wasn't." He paused. "There is one thing I'd like to ask of you though."

Dillon went on alert and stepped closer to Jamie. "Oh yeah, and what's that?"

Mitch smiled. "You're a regular guard dog where your boy's concerned, aren't you?" He smiled at Jamie. "You're one lucky guy to have someone who loves you that much." To both of them he said, "I was wondering if you had a picture of Ben I could have?"

Dillon was immediately ashamed. "I had no idea you didn't have any."

"No harm, no foul. I have some old ones, a few from when we were kids, but nothing recent." Mitch's voice dropped and so did his eyes. "It's been close to three years since I last saw him. I don't even know what he looked like when he died."

At that moment, Dillon wished the damn apartment was wallpapered with pictures of Lewis, anything to ease this guy's pain. But he didn't have so much as a snapshot of Ben, and judging from the look on Jamie's face, neither did he.

"Ben hated photos. They had to force him to have his school pictures taken for the yearbook." The minute he said it, Jamie did a double take. "Of course. Ben's picture is in last year's yearbook. I'll show it to you now, then see if I can get you a copy from somewhere. Sit down while I get it."

"Thanks." Mitch smiled, the first real smile he'd given since walking in. "That means a lot."

Mitch took a seat in the same chair as before and waited for Jamie. He didn't have to wait long. Jamie came in from the bedroom with the yearbook and stood on one side of Mitch's chair, leaving Dillon to take the other. Flipping through the book, Jamie opened it to the page Ben was on and laid it in Mitch's lap. "There you go."

Mitch traced the face in the picture with one finger, so much hurt and longing in that one gesture Dillon wanted to weep. Not surprisingly, the tears were flowing freely down Mitch's cheeks when he looked up. "He looks so grown up in this picture. God, I wish I could have been there, especially when...you know." He took a minute to wipe his eyes, then said, "Are there any more pictures of him in here?"

Jamie grinned. "Knowing Ben, not if he could help it. But you can flip through and see. The yearbook staff always fills the extra pages with snapshots of the student body."

Mitch nodded. "That part of high school I do remember." He picked up the book and started flipping through. "I'm glad at least Ben was sticking it out with school. I quit and never went back. I—" He stopped and his entire face froze. He dropped the book on the floor and jumped to his feet. "What the hell kinda game are you trying to pull?"

Dillon rounded the chair and picked up the book. "What are you talking about?"

"You told me you didn't know anything about Birch's partner. I wanna know what's going on, and I wanna know now."

Dillon opened the book to the page it had fallen on and saw the full page picture of Dan Morgan. "This? You mean Principal Morgan?"

"That's what he's calling himself?" Mitch searched first Dillon's and then Jamie's face. "My God, you really didn't know. Your Principal Morgan is Uncle Jared. He's Birch's partner."

"Jesus." Dillon dropped the book like it was a live coal. He took one look at Jamie's horrified expression and said, "That's it. We're calling Brandon. *Now*. If he's not back from Chicago, the dispatcher's just gonna have to track him down." He looked at Mitch. "If you're not gonna back us up on this, you can leave."

Mitch shook his head. "I'm with you."

Jamie reached for the phone, just as Dillon heard a loud pop and the living room window exploded.

Chapter Eighteen

Dillon threw himself toward Jamie, taking them both to the ground as glass showered the room. Mitch wasted no time following suit. Dillon tensed as he heard another shot being fired at almost the same instant, this one different in pitch. Worse, though, was the silence that came after.

He frantically turned to Jamie. "You all right?"

"I'm not hurt, just pissed as hell that someone is shooting at us."

Mitch, who was lying beside them, said, "Make that two someones." When Jamie and Dillon both gave him blank stares, he said, "Unless I'm losing it, we have two separate guns firing on us."

Well, fuck. Isn't that nice to know? Dillon reached for the cell phone he hoped he'd remembered to put in his pocket when they'd left for the auto parts store what seemed like a lifetime ago. Pay dirt. He was just about to pull it out and call nine-one-one, when Sadie's voice came floating through the window. "Are you boys all right in there?"

Jamie's breath rushed out in a jagged rasp. "Oh God. Aunt Sadie's out there by herself." He struggled to get up. "We have to help her. We have to—"

Sadie's voice came through just in time to put a stop to Jamie's panic. "Jamie, if you're through having the little panic attack I'm just sure you're having right about now, get your rump down here and help me tie this rascal up before the police arrive. I'm reasonably certain as to where his shot went. I know you're all right."

Dillon rose, pulling Jamie up with him and checking him from head to toe for injuries. He found a couple of shallow cuts on Jamie's hands and arms, but nothing more serious. Jamie repeated the same inspection on Dillon and was quickly satisfied that Dillon's cuts were no worse than his own. Mitch, too, seemed okay as he came to his feet and brushed glass shards from his t-shirt and jeans. He had a few cuts himself, but all three of them seemed to have escaped any real harm.

Sadie's voice floated up again as they were heading to the door. "Perhaps I didn't make myself clear. Somebody better get down here right now and shut this piece of trash up before I shoot him again."

That was all it took to get them moving. The three of them were out the door, across the deck, and down the stairs in a heartbeat. Dillon hit the on-switch for the floodlights around the apartment as he was going out the door and that let him get the full effect of what he was seeing.

Sadie was standing at the base of the old oak tree which provided shade and privacy to Jamie and Dillon's apartment. She was wearing a pink nightgown, a fuzzy purple robe, and a pair of honest-to-God bunny slippers. She was also holding a still smoking twelve-gauge shotgun, the barrels trained on Dan Morgan's quivering, bleeding body. Dillon, Jamie, and Mitch stopped just a few feet away, shock and amazement rooting them to the spot.

Morgan was lying on his side, the black silk turtleneck he wore peppered with holes from the middle of his back on up to his shoulders. His arms were sprawled out beside him, his black trouser-encased legs curled in a fetal position. He started whimpering and pleading the minute he saw Jamie.

"James, thank God. You have to help me. Your aunt's gone crazy. I was coming over here to ask you a question about the G.S.A." Morgan's normally oily voice was thick with obvious pain but Dillon felt no sympathy. "This crazy old witch blasted me the minute I came into the yard. No warning, no reason. You have to call an ambulance; I'm dying."

Sadie held the gun steady, her eyes pinned to the bead at the end of the barrels. "You're not dying, you miserable weasel. I knocked your sorry self out of that tree with birdshot." She snorted. "Dying, my eye. I've been bird hunting at my daddy's knee since I was old enough to hold a rifle. Not to mention that I was the Reed County Country Club's reigning skeet champion six years in a row. If I'd wanted you dead, you wouldn't be breathing, let alone sniveling like the coward you are." Sadie's voice took on a menacing quality that sent chills coursing over Dillon's skin. "But this is a double barreled shotgun, and I've only fired one shot. Do you know what that means?"

Morgan stammered a full ten seconds before getting out, "N-no."

"It means, my boy, I have one shot left. And you can bet your worthless butt the second shell doesn't contain game load. No, sir. It's a slug, and I have no objection whatsoever to firing it directly into your empty skull."

Mitch and Jamie were too shaken to speak, but Dillon went back to something Sadie had just said. "Did I hear you right? You shot Morgan out of the tree?"

"That's exactly what I said. I was just heading down to the kitchen for a late night snack when I heard a noise in the back yard." She spoke to Dillon, but never took her eyes off Morgan. "At first I thought maybe I'd heard you and Jamie coming in from a date or some such, but when I looked out, I could see your living room light was on, meaning you were up in the apartment already. I felt like I should check on you, just to make sure everything was all right. I never go outside this late at night without some sort of protection, so I grabbed my father's shotgun. Thank the heavens above I keep it loaded. The first thing I saw when I stepped out the back door was this imbecile..." She inclined her head toward Morgan, dislodging one green curler in the process.

"...climbing through the branches of that old oak. Even with the security lights on, I couldn't tell just what he was doing until he got about twenty feet up, just level with your living room window. That's when this no-account son-of-a-bitch pulled a revolver out of his pants and took aim." Sadie gave a put-upon sigh. "Only a true idiot would use a pistol to shoot someone from that range, but his ignorance worked to my advantage. Morgan and I fired at almost the same instant, but my shot unbalanced him and his shot went wild. The recoil from the revolver, combined with the pain of the birdshot I sent his way, knocked his fool ass out of the tree." She nodded toward a shadowed spot a few feet away. "I believe you'll find his weapon over there in the bushes. He dropped it when he fell."

Injured as he was, Morgan kept protesting his innocence. "She's crazy, I tell you. Looney as a toon. All I did was walk across the yard—"

"You're a liar, Morgan," Jamie said, his voice laced with so much rage and raw hatred even Dillon flinched. "Or should I say, *Uncle Jared*?"

Morgan's eyes went absolutely wild. "I don't know what you're talking about. You have to help me, James. I'm bleeding to death."

"You know exactly what he's talking about, you piece of shit." Mitch stood at Morgan's feet. "I'm going to tell the cops every last one of your dirty little secrets. When I'm through with you, you'll be lucky if they don't crucify your ass."

"Yeah?" Morgan's face twisted into a snarl. "Who's gonna believe the word of a ten-dollar whore like you?"

Dillon narrowed his eyes. "If you're so innocent, how did you know Mitch used to be a hustler?"

Watching Morgan try to backtrack his way out of that mistake would have been funny if the guy hadn't been so pathetic. As it was, Morgan's protestations of denial made Dillon feel like he was going to be sick. Of course, Dillon's nausea might have been because Morgan had just tried to kill them. The approaching sounds of sirens drew Dillon's mind away from his churning stomach.

A swarm of deputies filled the yard, but Dillon's attention centered solely on Brandon Nash, who was bearing down on them at a fair clip. He had his weapon drawn, but re-holstered it the minute he caught sight of Sadie and her shotgun.

"Miss Sadie, you want to tell me why the principal of Plunkett High is lying in a bleeding heap with the end of your big ol' gun pointed at his head?"

"Because Dan Morgan is a liar, a child molester, and a killer," Jamie answered for her. "I can prove it, Brandon. I think he killed Ben and his former foster father, and I know for a fact he just tried to kill us."

"You think I killed Ben?" Morgan was sounding more desperate by the second. "Birch did that. Don't you see? He'd have killed me, too, if I hadn't gotten to him first." He raised one trembling arm and pointed at Mitch. "This is all your fault, you bastard. If you hadn't come to Reed tonight, none of this would be happening."

That was all it took to set the lot of them off. Mitch started shouting, swearing to see Morgan pay for what he'd done. Sadie carried on about making Morgan pay, but not for his crimes. She wanted him to pay for the damage done to her window and the cleanup of any broken oak branches from her yard. Jamie was listing Morgan's supposed sins one by one, from murder to blackmail and on down. Dillon was doing his best to tell Brandon the story as *he* knew it, when Brandon put two fingers in his mouth and gave an ear splitting whistle.

"Hold on just a damn minute," he yelled once they'd quieted. "Miss Banks, give me that gun." Once he'd gotten it away from her, Brandon emptied the slug from the chamber and handed it off to one of his deputies. "Bag that for me, please. And search the bushes around the house and the base of that tree. I'm almost certain I heard the word 'revolver' somewhere in that jumble of explanations and accusations they've all been spouting."

When the deputy was gone, Brandon rolled his eyes. "Thank God one of your neighbors heard the shots and called it in. You never would've managed to report this at the rate you all are going."

The ambulance pulled up and a team of paramedics rushed out and toward Morgan. Brandon spoke to the lead EMT. "Take Principal Morgan to County General, and make certain they understand he's to be kept under lock and key. From what I've just heard, I'm pretty sure he's guilty of something." Motioning for one of his deputies to step forward, Brandon added, "Dewey, send two of our men along with the ambulance, and have the rest of them canvass the scene."

Dewey nodded. "You got it, boss. Uh, what do you want me to do with them?" He pointed to Sadie and the rest.

Brandon sighed. "Take every last one of them down to the station, Miss Banks included. Oh, and Dewey?"

"Yes, sir?"

Brandon raked his fingers through his hair. "Make sure we have plenty of coffee. This promises to be one hell of a long story."

Even before he turned over the money and documents he'd been hiding for so long, Jamie knew he was looking at some serious trouble, but after five hours of answering questions and going through the story time and again, he started to realize just how screwed he was. Not even when the sheriff left to process all that evidence was he able to feel any relief. Brandon had been gone for almost an hour by Jamie's count, leaving him alone in the interrogation room to stew about what was to come. If his intention had been to drive Jamie crazy with guilt and worry, it was working.

Just when Jamie thought he would crack, the door opened and Brandon came back in. He looked haggard and worn, but not exactly angry. More like resigned. He sat across from Jamie and slapped the folder he was holding on the table.

"Go ahead. Read it."

Jamie reached for the folder, not certain he wanted to open it, but doing so, anyway. Scanning the top paper, he said, "What is this?"

"A list of all the evidence you've turned over to us tonight, as well as a summary of your statement. Read it over and see if we've gotten it all. You might not want to read the last page though."

"What's on the last page?"

"A list of all the things I could charge you with right about now." Brandon smacked his hand down on the table. "Jesus Christ, Jamie! What in the hell were you thinking?"

He just had to ask what was on that last page, but Brandon had asked him a question and Jamie was going to answer it. He was tired, and scared, and not a little bit angry. According to Brandon, Jamie had nothing left to lose. Damned if he wasn't going to tell the guy what he thought first.

"I wasn't thinking, Sheriff."

Brandon took Jamie's statement as an apology. "Damned straight you weren't thinking. You—"

Jamie stood up, cutting him off. He was filled with a rage he hadn't felt since the day he found out Ben had died. All the months of worry, of agonizing over who killed Ben and why, roiled in Jamie's gut along with the all-consuming fear that he could've lost Dillon to Morgan's bullet. And all of it was due to the fact that Jamie couldn't let well enough alone, with no one to believe him or offer him help.

All of that helpless wrath was what Jamie turned on Brandon.

"Like I said, I wasn't thinking. I wasn't thinking about the fact that my best friend was murdered and no one would believe me because they thought he was nothing but a two-bit whore who deserved what he got."

"Now wait just a minute, kid—"

Jamie gave him no quarter. "And I wasn't thinking about the fact that Ben left me in charge of forty-two thousand dollars worth of dirty money and a letter that nearly destroyed an innocent guy's life."

"Jamie, wait—"

"I've been waiting, waiting for the truth to come out, waiting for whoever killed Ben to come after me and Dillon. And that's exactly what happened. Morgan came after me and the man I love because you dropped the fucking ball. I came to you for help and you let me down." Jamie's fists clenched and unclenched. "Charge me with anything you want. Hell, it's about time you sent someone to prison. Might as well be the guy who cracked the case you were too damned incompetent to break yourself. But whether you charge me or not, keep your fucking lectures to yourself. Save them for someone who gives a shit."

A throaty chuckle sounded from the doorway. Jamie looked up to see a grinning Hank Kilgore standing just outside the interrogation room. Jamie had been so into his tirade, he hadn't even heard the door open.

Kilgore said, "He's got your number, Nash."

"Maybe so, Kilgore, but you have to admit, he's got yours, too." Brandon shook his head. "It's a piss-poor day indeed when an eighteen-year-old kid cracks a case two police departments and a ream of seasoned detectives couldn't."

"True, but the kid had help. If I hadn't screwed up and left Carpenter's file within easy reach, James here couldn't have swiped that paper with Mitch Harding's name and contact info on it." Kilgore turned to Jamie. "Do you have any idea how much trouble you should be in for that, kid? Tampering with evidence, coercion of a witness." He grinned. "Practicing detective work without a license."

"I didn't—"

Kilgore held up his hand. "Calm down. I talked to the D.A. and there won't be any charges filed against you."

Jamie sank back down into his chair, some of his frustration and anger subsiding as he digested his reprieve. "There won't be?"

Kilgore shook his head, his magnificent braids trailing over his shoulder. "You have your buddy Nash, here, to thank for that one. I may be grateful to you for giving us our prime suspect in Carpenter's murder, but that doesn't mean I wasn't ready to lock your lily-white ass up for screwing with my files. Lucky for you, Nash and I made a deal."

"What kind of deal?"

Brandon answered. "Hank has a case he wants me to profile for him."

"Profile? You mean, like F.B.I. stuff?"

"I was with the F.B.I. before I came back to Reed and ran for sheriff." Brandon laughed. "Despite what you might think, I'm not totally incompetent. I prefer to think of myself as only an occasional imbecile."

"I'm not even gonna touch that one. As it so happens, I've gotta run, anyway. Morgan just came out of surgery. I want to be there to question the bastard as soon as the anesthesia wears off." Kilgore patted Jamie on the shoulder. "I know I should be grateful to you for everything you did, but heartfelt thanks aren't exactly my style."

"Not arresting me is thanks enough."

Kilgore threw back his head and laughed. "I like you, kid. I swear I do." He left without waiting for a response.

Jamie swallowed hard. He was still mad as hell, but he knew he owed Brandon for getting his ass out of a sling with Kilgore. He needed to say something, but he wasn't sure what. He didn't have to say a word. Brandon did it for him.

Pointing to the file in Jamie's hand, Brandon said, "If you'll read over your statement there on the last page and sign it, I'll send it over to the D.A.'s office and we'll wrap up your part of the investigation. I've sent your aunt home already, though God knows whether my deputies are still in one piece after taking her back to her house. She was one pissed off lady."

Jamie didn't doubt that, but it wasn't Brandon's statement about his aunt that had Jamie narrowing his eyes. "I thought you said all the things you were gonna charge me with were listed on the last page."

Brandon's grin was one part cockiness, two parts caring. "Yeah, well, I had to say something, didn't I? From the minute I brought you in here, you were about ten seconds away from imploding. I had to do something to get all that stuff out of your system." When Jamie started to speak, Brandon held up his hand. "Before you start trying to take back what you said or make it sound better than it was, don't. You were right. I did drop the ball." He sighed as he leaned back in his chair. "It might surprise you to know this, Jamie, but I'm not perfect."

Jamie bit back a smile. "No? Really?"

"I know, I know. It shocked the hell out of me, too, the day I first realized it." He leaned forward, resting his elbows on his desk and looking Jamie right in the eyes, making his sincerity impossible to doubt. "I let you down in a big way by not believing you when you told me you were sure Sledge wasn't the one responsible for Ben's death. Of course," Brandon wrinkled his nose, "you knew a few things I didn't, namely blackmail and extortion, but that doesn't mean I didn't have a job to do. I should have investigated your claim."

He stood up and extended his hand. Jamie rose to his feet and grasped it, surprised at how comforting Brandon's warm strength was.

"I'm sorry, kid. Sorry for not listening and sorry you didn't feel like you could come to me for help."

"That sorry business works both ways. I owe you for not coming to you the minute I found out about the money and the pictures." Jamie released Brandon's hand and closed his eyes, the memory of Morgan's shot and the sound of breaking glass still ringing in his ears. "Dillon begged me to turn it all over to you, but I was too damn stubborn. My mistake could've cost him his life."

Jamie heard movement and opened his eyes to see that Brandon had rounded the desk and was now standing over him. He laid his hand on Jamie's shoulder. "It takes one hell of a man to admit his mistakes. I almost lost Nate once because of a mistake I made. I left him alone with the wrong man, and Nate almost paid for it with his life. It took me months to forgive myself for that one, and I still have trouble accepting it." Brandon shuddered. "Take my advice, kid — spend a good, solid hour beating yourself up over it, and then let it go. Life's too short to what-if yourself into an early grave."

"I'll do that." He shuffled his feet as Brandon gave his shoulder one last squeeze and then returned to his side of the desk. Jamie had one more question to ask, and it was one he dreaded. "What happens now, with Morgan?"

"Difficult to say." Brandon sat down hard, weariness over-whelming him. "Hank's going to question him, confront him with the statements you and Mitchell Harding gave. From what I've gathered, it shouldn't be too hard to prove Morgan was Birch Carpenter's partner. His name alone is a good tip off."

"His name? Don't tell me ..."

Brandon laughed. "You guessed it. The stupid fucker ran teenage prostitutes using his middle name. Seems Mr. Daniel Jared Morgan isn't as smart as he wants the world to think he is." He waited until Jamie sat down. "We'll have to wait until the investigation is completed to get the full story on Morgan, but I have a feeling he'll want to make some kind of deal before all this is over with."

Jamie's stomach clenched on the word "deal". He remembered all too well how Barry Sledge had gotten off with a lighter sentence because the D.A. was overworked and ready to bargain. That raised a whole new set of questions.

"What about Barry Sledge? Will he be released from jail now that Morgan is a suspect?"

Brandon hesitated. "Here's the thing about Sledge, kid. He admitted to running down Ben, and the damage to his car proves he did hit Ben's body. The only question now is whether or not Ben was already dead at the time of impact."

"But Morgan—"

"According to my deputy, in the ambulance Morgan claimed he killed Carpenter because he thought Carpenter was responsible for Ben's death. Because of the blackmail, Morgan figured he was next on Carpenter's list."

"There's your confession, then."

"I wish it were that easy, Jamie, but it isn't. A good lawyer could claim Morgan's words were simply the rantings of an injured man, brought on by the pain. And even if we prove Morgan killed Carpenter, that still doesn't prove that Carpenter killed Ben. For all we know, Morgan killed them both. Or Barry Sledge could have killed Ben and then Morgan offed Carpenter, thinking he was to blame."

Jamie's head was starting to hurt. He didn't relish the thought of Sledge being a free man — free to terrorize the streets during any one of his drunken marathons — but at the same time, Jamie wanted the man responsible for Ben's death to pay. Not just any man, but the right man.

He lifted tired eyes to Brandon. "So, what now?"

"We wait until the investigation is finished, sift through the findings, and hope we have enough evidence to clear up this damned mess." Brandon gave Jamie an apologetic shrug. "I know you were hoping for some smoking-gun conclusion straight out of the movies, but real police work doesn't usually go that way. All we can do now is process what we've got, then wait until Morgan gives his statement and take it from there."

"I understand." And he did. But knowing Brandon was doing the best he could didn't stop Jamie from hoping this would all be over, and soon.

When he finished reading his statement and signing off on it, the first person Jamie saw was Dillon, slumped in one of the chairs in the waiting area, his hair matted to his head with sweat and dirt. He needed a good shave, the shadow on his face leaving a dark line. His eyes were bloodshot from lack of sleep and sheer exhaustion. He was the most beautiful creature Jamie had ever seen. Nothing could have stopped him from rushing across the room and pulling Dillon from his chair, his arms wrapping around Dillon's waist so tight Jamie was in danger of knocking the breath out of him.

Dillon didn't seem to notice. His sole focus was Jamie. He cradled him close, whispering words of love and devotion into Jamie's ear. The words were nice, but Jamie didn't need them. He had all he needed there in his arms. After a minute, Dillon pulled back enough to see him. His eyes searched Jamie's face. "Are you okay?"

"I am now. God, Dillon...I was so scared for you. This is all my fault. If I'd only listened—"

Dillon pressed a finger against his lips. "It's Morgan's fault — and Carpenter's — for being such sick fucks."

Jamie appreciated Dillon's ready absolution, but he knew it was going to be a long time before he forgave himself. Then Brandon's words came back to him: *spend a good, solid hour beating yourself up over it, and then let it go. Life's too short to what-if yourself into an early grave.*

Taking Brandon's advice, Jamie closed his eyes and when he opened them again, scanned the room but saw no sign of the person he was looking for. "Where's Mitch?"

Dillon stroked Jamie's hair back from his face. "They took him back to Chicago to answer some questions about Birch's murder and about the day-to-day dealings of his operation. He promised to get back in touch with us when all this is over with, and I believe him."

Jamie leaned again into Dillon's embrace. "Yeah. For everything that's happened to him, Mitch seems like a decent guy. Not like..." He couldn't say it. Couldn't, even now, form words against his best friend.

Dillon understood. He planted a kiss just below Jamie's jaw. "Ben did what he had to do to survive. I'm not saying I approve of his methods, but after seeing how he was forced to live, I can't say I wouldn't have done something just as desperate in the same situation."

"You wouldn't have. You're stronger than that. I just thank God you're okay, that my fuck-up didn't kill you."

Dillon pulled out of his arms and took Jamie's hand. "I told you I didn't want to hear that kind of talk." He led him toward the door. "Let's get out of here. I want to give you a good going over to make sure you aren't hurt." When Jamie started to protest, Dillon laughed. "I know the medics checked us when we got to the station, but I have a different kind of examination in mind and I don't think the Reed County Sheriff's Office is ready to see it."

It was pushing five o'clock in the morning when Dillon and Jamie finally left the station. They took a cab back to the apartment, even though Brandon and several of the deputies offered them a ride. Dillon wanted Jamie all to himself, and he was pretty sure the cab driver would pretend not to notice all the cuddling and kissing going on in the backseat. As it turned out, he was right. The cabbie didn't so much as comment, though Dillon was sure he must have seen Dillon fondling Jamie as he glanced in the rearview mirror. Dillon couldn't have cared less. *Let him look.*

The driver refused to take any money when he dropped them off, saying Sheriff Nash had already taken care of the fare, tip included. Dillon thanked the cabbie one last time as he and Jamie got out and headed up the driveway to their apartment.

The front door was open. That was the first thing Dillon noticed as he topped the stairs and hit the landing. He felt a frisson of unease race down his back until he heard the sounds of a broom sweeping up broken glass. That could only be one person. He pushed the door open further and was told, "Well, don't just stand there like a ninny, grab the dustpan and hold it for me."

Dillon leaned down and gave Sadie a kiss on the cheek. "You don't have to do this, you know. Jamie and I can clean up this mess."

Sadie waved away the protest as Jamie bent to give her a kiss and Dillon grabbed the dustpan. "The fact remains, Morgan should be over here cleaning this place up, not us. I wish now I'd shot the scoundrel in his good-for-nothing rectum." Sadie swept the last of the glass into the pan. "That way, he'd think of me every time he sat down."

Dillon grinned. "I don't think he's gonna forget you anytime soon." He took the dustpan over to the trash and emptied it. "Nobody else will, either. You're a hero. You saved our lives."

Sadie shook her head. "A lot of nonsense, that. Morgan isn't exactly a crack shot. I doubt seriously if he actually had the skill to hit you, not at that range anyway." But even as she dismissed the danger, Dillon could see that she was shaking.

Jamie must have seen it, too. He took the broom away from his aunt and set it aside, folding her into a tight hug. "You always did have trouble taking compliments. Well, tough. I'm going to give you one anyway. You saved our butts tonight. Thank you."

Sadie returned his hug tenfold. "I'm just so thankful you're both okay." She pinched Jamie's side, causing him to jump back with a yelp.

"Ouch. What was that for?"

"For scaring me half to death." Sadie grabbed him close and hugged him again. "You've kept this old woman going for the last fourteen years. Sheriff Nash filled me in on all the little secrets you've been keeping." Jamie tensed and Sadie continued with, "Before you get your drawers all in a twist, I'm not angry, and I'm not going to question you any further. Let me just say this: if you think I'm going to lose you now, just when I'm getting the hang of this mothering thing, you're sadly mistaken. Next time you need help, you darn well better ask for it."

Jamie smiled over the top of Sadie's head. "Understood. Now why don't you go on home and soak in a hot bath? You know that always makes you feel better. Dillon and I will clean up the rest of this."

Sadie took them at their word. "The glass man will be coming first thing Monday morning to put in a new window pane." After kissing them both soundly, she left them to it.

It took them another half an hour to sweep up all the glass and cover the window with cardboard. Cardboard wasn't the ideal substitute, but it would have to do.

By the time they finished, Jamie was swaying on his feet and Dillon wasn't far behind him in the tired department. He pushed Jamie into the kitchen. "Sit down while I fix us something to eat. We never did get that late supper we started to have."

"I'll help you. Between the two us, surely we can find something edible."

"Something edible" turned out to be day old chocolate doughnuts and two tall glasses of chocolate milk. Sadie would have had a fit if she'd seen their idea of breakfast, but it would have to do. Dillon was just too tired to go out for anything else.

Jamie finished up and put their glasses in the sink. Turning to Dillon, he said, "You ready for bed?"

It was a mark of Dillon's exhaustion that Jamie's words didn't bring the slightest stirring below his belt. Even the examination he'd promised Jamie at the sheriff station was going to have to wait. Holding Jamie in his arms would have to do until they both got some sleep. From the look on Jamie's face when they finally climbed into bed together and Dillon had pulled him in as close as possible, holding him was more than enough.

How long they slept, Dillon wasn't sure, but it was nearly dark outside when the sound of loud knocking woke him. Careful not to wake Jamie, he slid out of bed and grabbed a clean pair of jeans from the closet. Pulling them on, he walked into the living room, wincing when a small piece of glass they'd missed in their cleaning bit into his bare foot. Hopping towards the door, Dillon pulled it open and came face to face with his parents.

Douglas Carver was his usual disinterested self, looking at Dillon with speculation and contempt. It was Angela who took over, her voice sympathetic and soothing.

"Oh, Dillon, thank God you're all right. You father and I were worried sick."

It wasn't until she'd pushed her way past Dillon and into the apartment that he realized she and Douglas were not alone. Accompanying them was a slender man about the same height as Dillon. He was carrying a medical bag and wore an old fashioned fedora on his head. Dillon guessed he was about sixty, and from the look on his narrow face, the stranger was on a mission.

He stuck out his hand, seemingly unfazed when Dillon refused to take it. "I'm Dr. Henderson. Your parents have told me so much about you."

Jesus. Henderson, the shrink my father has been pressuring me to see. "Yeah, I'll just bet they have."

Angela intervened. "We brought Dr. Henderson because we heard about your ordeal from one of the ladies at church this morning. We're certain after what happened last night that even you can see how dangerous living this lifestyle is."

Dillon struggled not to laugh in his mother's face. "You think my being gay caused Dan Morgan to try and kill me?"

Angela sniffed. "Don't be clever with me, Dillon. You know what I mean. You must know none of this would've happened to you if you hadn't hooked up with James Walker in the first place."

Despite the generous amount of sleep he'd had, Dillon was still tired, worn out from all he'd been through. He had no intention of going through the same old argument again. Turning his full attention to the doctor, Dillon said, "You've wasted your time coming here. I have no intention of becoming your patient or listening to hour after hour of lectures on the evils of homosexuality. You and my parents can show yourselves out."

Henderson ignored Dillon and looked straight to his father. "I see what you mean, Douglas. Dillon is obviously suffering from self-destructive impulses. I might even go so far as to classify him as having suicidal tendencies. I think Dillon is a prime candidate for involuntary commitment."

Involuntary commitment? Suicidal tendencies? What in the hell is this guy talking about? Dillon was starting to get scared. "You can't do that to me. There's nothing wrong with my mind and you know it."

Henderson's smile turned nasty. "On the contrary, I can and I will. I'm a respected psychologist. All I have to do is sign the papers saying I believe you're a danger to yourself, and you'll be locked in a state hospital by nightfall."

Dillon felt the cold grip of panic seize his heart. He reached for the only person in the room he thought might have mercy on him. "Mom, please don't let him do this."

"I'm sorry, Dillon. It's the only way." Turning to Henderson, she said, "Do it. Have him locked up for as long as it takes."

Dillon backed away but his father stepped behind him, blocking his retreat to the bedroom. "Don't you have anything in that bag to sedate the boy? The sooner we get him out of here, the better."

Henderson reached into his bag, pulling out a pre-filled syringe. "Of course. I never travel without the proper equipment. A mixture of Haldol and Ativan ought to keep him calm. The two of us will have to carry him out, but it's a small price to pay." He started toward Dillon with the syringe.

Dillon tried to run but his father had him pinned in place, his arms locking Dillon's behind his back and rendering Dillon immobile. There was nothing Dillon could do. He waited for the sting of the needle, but it never came. What did come was a loud crash and the splintering of wood as his Little League baseball bat cracked against the back of Douglas Carver's skull. Doug let go of Dillon and sank to the floor.

The instant after Jamie brought the bat down on Doug's head, he dropped it and grabbed Dillon's hand, yanking him forward and propelling Dillon out of his stupor. Henderson and Angela were too busy seeing to Doug to stop them as they fled for the door. As they raced down the steps, Jamie pulled Dillon's car keys out of his pocket and tossed them to Dillon. Dillon jumped into the driver's seat. Jamie had just climbed in and gotten buckled when Henderson, Doug, and Angela came charging out after them.

Dillon gunned the motor and took off for the sheriff station. It wasn't until he was on the main road that he realized he and Jamie were each wearing nothing more than a pair of jeans. Dillon pulled the car onto a side road and changed directions.

"Where...where are we going?" Jamie was shaking so badly he barely got the words out.

"I was headed for Brandon's office, but I changed my mind. We'll try his house first. With any luck, he'll be there, and if he's not, Nate might be."

Jamie nodded, hugging himself even though it wasn't all that cold in the car. The temperature was pretty mild for early April, but Dillon knew Jamie's chills came from within.

After an agonizing silence, Jamie said, "I know how Ben felt."

Dillon hadn't expected that one. "What do you mean?"

"The night Ben hit that guy who was roughing up Mitch. I knew how Ben felt the minute I swung that bat at your father's head. That's where I got the idea, from Mitch's story." Jamie shivered. "I thought I'd killed him until I saw him coming out the door behind Henderson and your mom." He put his face in his hands. "I didn't want to do it, but I didn't have a choice. They were gonna give you that shot."

Dillon pressed down on the accelerator. "I know, sweetheart. I know. We'll make this right, Jamie. I swear it."

They continued in silence to Brandon and Nate's house. Dillon let out a deep sigh of relief when he pulled into the driveway and saw the Sheriff-mobile, as Megan always called the government issue S.U.V. Brandon used when he was on duty. Seeing Nate's car there beside it further reassured Dillon. Unless the two of them were out for a drive in Brandon's Camaro, there was a good chance they were both home.

Dillon got out first, the pine needles and rocks on the driveway pricking his bare feet. He went around to Jamie's side and helped him out, much like he had the day Jamie found out about Ben's death and went into shock. Dillon hoped Jamie wasn't going to go through that again. From the look of him, it was a real possibility.

Brandon met them at the door, still wearing his uniform. "Get your asses in here. I was just about to go out and look for you." He surprised them both by enfolding them in his arms. "Do you have any idea how worried I was when I heard the call from your father come over the scanner?"

"Shit. He called the cops on us?"

Brandon pulled them into the house, one arm still wrapped around each of them. "'Fraid so. He called the city cops, naturally, instead of my office. He wants to have Jamie locked up for assault." Brandon released them long enough to close the door behind them. Seeing the look on Jamie's face, he pulled him back in close and said, "Relax, kiddo. Nobody's gonna lock you up. The chief of police is giving me time to put this thing together before he even comes to question you."

Jamie was too shaken to answer, but Dillon said, "Put what thing together? What's going on? Do we need a lawyer?"

Brandon moved them toward the kitchen. "We'll talk about that in just a minute. First thing we're going to do is get the two of you warmed up and calmed down. Then you're going to tell me every last thing that happened, from the minute your parents walked in the door until Jamie cracked good old Dougie on the back of the head. Damn, I wish I'd seen that."

Nate met them in the kitchen, directing Dillon and Jamie to have a seat at the kitchen table. Coming back with two steaming mugs, he said, "I wasn't sure if the two of you would want coffee or hot chocolate, but chocolate is more soothing, so I went with that." After setting a mug in front of each of them, Nate knelt down beside Jamie's chair. "How you holding up, buddy? You feeling okay?"

Before Jamie could speak, Brandon came in from the laundry room holding a couple of long sleeved t-shirts. "My shirt will probably fit you, Dillon, but even Nate's will swallow Jamie alive. They'll have to do until I can send someone to your house to pick up some of your stuff. I don't care if it is the end of April, it's still too cold outside for the two of you to be running around in nothing but blue jeans." He handed the first shirt to Jamie. "You need Dillon to help you with that, slugger?"

Nate groaned. "Real sensitive, Nash."

But Jamie laughed, the sound more precious to Dillon than anything he owned. If Jamie was laughing, he probably wasn't going into shock again.

"It's okay," Jamie said. "I'm fine, just a little shaky." He reached across the table and took Dillon's hand. "I guess our Little League coach was wrong, huh? I can hit the broad side of a barn." Dillon squeezed his hand in response.

"I guess now would be as good a time as any to tell me what happened," Brandon said. "The sooner we deal with it, the better."

Nate indicated his scrubs. "I just got home from work, so I'm going to go upstairs and shower. Sasha's still penned up in the sun porch, so you shouldn't be disturbed."

He left, and Brandon walked across the room to one of the far cabinets, taking out a mini-tape recorder and returning to sit at the table. Placing the recorder in the center, he said, "I'm going to tape this interview, so be sure not to leave anything out."

Dillon went first, going over every detail he could remember, from the opening of the door to his near-injection by Dr. Henderson. Jamie picked up the story, telling how he heard Dillon arguing with his parents and about Henderson's promise to have Dillon locked up. He went on to talk about grabbing Dillon's old bat from the closet. He even told Brandon and the tape recorder about where the idea had come from.

Having gotten the rundown on that story from Mitch late the night before, Brandon nodded. As soon as Jamie finished, Brandon pressed the stop button and turned to Dillon. "So you never actually asked your parents to come inside?"

Dillon shook his head. "My mother just sorta barged in when I opened the door. The other two followed her in."

"Sounds like self-defense to me. Jamie was doing what it took to defend his partner within the confines of his own home. I can't see any D.A. in his right mind bringing Jamie up on charges for that."

The word "charges" made Jamie gasp for breath. "Am I going to need a lawyer, Brandon? You never did tell us if we needed one."

The back door swung open just as Jamie was asking the question, and Dillon heard the clattering of high heels across the floor of the mudroom. A honey-sweet voice said, "Did I hear someone say 'lawyer'? Don't you know that's a dirty word around most parts?"

Dillon recognized the tiny redhead the minute she came into the kitchen — Alicia Nash Wilton, Brandon's sister. He'd seen her more than once when Megan had dragged him to the Nash family get-togethers and church dinners.

She seemed nice enough, but Dillon knew little about her other than that she was a prosecutor for the D.A.'s office in Chicago. The minute the thought crossed his mind, Dillon's body stiffened. Surely she wasn't there to file charges against Jamie. No way was he going to let that happen.

Alicia must have seen the look on his face because she started laughing, the sound so much like Megan's laughter that Dillon relaxed in spite of his worries. "Calm down, hon. I was just teasing about 'lawyer' being a dirty word." She gave her brother a kiss on the cheek and then sat down at the table with them. "Sheesh. Talk about a tough room."

Dillon blushed. "Sorry. Jamie and I have had a rough evening."

"That's why I'm here." Alicia smiled at Jamie. "I heard the question you asked my brother, and the answer is no. You don't need a lawyer. You've got me."

Chapter Nineteen

Despite the fact that he'd only seen Alicia Wilton a few times when she was in town visiting her family, Jamie found himself trusting her. Her manner reminded him of Megan's, warm and open, not the kind who'd keep secrets or lie to him. Jamie relaxed just a fraction, more than he would have thought possible under the circumstances.

Alicia plopped her briefcase on the table. "Brandon called and told me the two of you were in trouble and that Dillon's father was pressing charges for an alleged assault. Last I heard, Brandon was on his way out to look for you and he wanted me to come here and wait until he found you. Looks like he did."

"These two found me. I was on my way out the door when they showed up here." Brandon walked over to the counter and poured a mug of coffee. "You still take it black, munchkin?"

Alicia rolled her eyes at her brother and complained to Jamie and Dillon, "I'm almost thirty years old and the big jerk still calls me munchkin." To Brandon she said, "Unless that's decaf, you'd better drink it yourself. I'm off caffeine for the next seven and a half months."

Brandon's face changed. "For the same reason you were off caffeine the last time?"

Alicia nodded. "Emily's gonna be a big sister."

Brandon strode back to the table and lifted Alicia out of her chair and into his arms. "Congratulations to all three of you, Miss Emily Jane Big Britches included." He stepped back, his expression changing from elation to concern. "Emily's only eighteen months old. Doesn't your doctor think it's a little too soon for you to be getting pregnant, again?"

Alicia laughed as she sat back down. "Some couples don't wait even that long to start trying. My obstetrician tells me I'm in perfect health, and Garth and I want our kids to be close together. We don't plan on having a whole brood like Mom and Dad did either. Two will do nicely I think."

Brandon sat down beside Alicia, the coffee forgotten. "If the new addition is anything like Emily, two will be a houseful." He pushed the tape recorder in Alicia's direction. "I could talk about my nieces and nephews all night, but Ronald Skinner's doing me a favor on this one, so we'd better get down to it. Everything the boys told me is on this tape."

She reached for the tape recorder. "This I've got to hear."

Worried about how silent he'd been for the last few minutes, Jamie took Dillon's hand. Dillon squeezed back, letting Jamie know he was all right.

Alicia started the tape. A couple of times during the replay, Jamie looked in Dillon's direction. He looked tired, his beloved face drawn and weary, but he didn't seem overly upset, not considering what they'd been through. Jamie turned his attention back to Alicia just as she pushed the stop button on the recorder. He realized Alicia had turned the tape recorder off at the mention of Henderson's name.

"Henderson? Not Lyle Henderson?"

Dillon shrugged. "I'm not sure. He never gave his first name and I didn't want to know."

Alicia's face was sweet sympathy itself. "No, sweetie, I guess you didn't."

"Why do you ask?" Brandon said.

"I need to finish listening to the tape before I say anything else, but if this guy is the Dr. Henderson I think he is, he's your key to getting Jamie and Dillon off the hook for this so-called assault." She turned the tape back on, this time taking a pen and steno pad out of her briefcase. Jamie watched as she scribbled notes in a graceful, flowing script that made his own handwriting look like chicken scratches.

As the tape finished, Alicia said, "I'll need confirmation, but I'm almost certain this Henderson is the man our office has been investigating for the last two years." She smiled at Dillon. "You and Jamie may have just given us the evidence we need to make an arrest. At the very least, we can get a warrant to search his office and home."

Jamie was not following her seemingly disjointed observations. "I don't get it. Am I being arrested for cracking Dillon's father on the head?"

Alicia tossed her notebook back into the briefcase. "Not if I can help it, and I'm darn sure I can." She pulled a hot pink cell phone out of the pocket of the case, grinning when she saw her brother's smirk. "What? Even a prosecuting attorney needs to have a little bit of style." She punched in a series of numbers and then waited.

When someone picked up on the other end, Alicia said, "Bruce? Hi, it's Al. ... I'm fine, but I need a favor. ... Yes, I know I still owe you for the last favor, but this is important; it's about the Henderson case. I need you to get together everything you've got on him and meet me at this address." She rattled off Brandon's address and then listened for a moment before saying, "I'm not sure just yet, but I think we may have finally nailed the S.O.B."

Not long after the phone call, Nate left, saying he had errands to run. Dillon was pretty sure he was leaving to give them some space, which only added to his nervousness. If Nate was leaving his own home so Brandon and Alicia could handle his and Jamie's case, this thing had to go way beyond a simple assault charge.

226 of Sara Bell

Jamie called Aunt Sadie to let her know what was going on. Her thoughts must have echoed Dillon's, because she gave Jamie a real earful. Brandon took the phone away from Jamie's ear, talking to Sadie in a commanding tone and eliciting a promise from her that she would stay put until further notice.

Bruce Seaford, Alicia's friend and special investigator for the D.A.'s office, showed up at Brandon's place about an hour later, carrying an overfilled, accordion style file folder. Dillon estimated him to be in his thirties, and though he wasn't drop-dead gorgeous, he had a pleasant face and a genuine smile that made Dillon feel comfortable. Seaford wasn't alone. The man who came into the kitchen behind him was the polar opposite of Seaford. He wasn't smiling, and it looked to Dillon like he'd come on a mission.

It wasn't that the guy was hard on the eyes. In fact, he was handsome in the extreme. His finely chiseled features and honed body could easily have graced the cover of an art magazine under the heading "perfect specimen". His hair was the color of honeyed wheat, tousled slightly, but that in no way detracted from the total picture. Seaford was wearing casual clothes — a wrinkled flannel shirt and a pair of faded jeans — but his companion was dressed for business, his pants expertly tailored, his shirt crisp and immaculate. Even so, nothing about the second man suggested he was anything other than a regular guy who'd come to help with the investigation. Nothing that is, except his eyes. They were a shade of deep silver that missed nothing, following everyone in the room with eerie perception. Dillon felt chill bumps along the tops of his arms. Something about the man spoke of a quiet power that had Jamie fidgeting in his chair.

If Brandon had the same reaction, he hid it well. He greeted both the new arrivals at the door, calling them by name. He slapped Bruce on the back and shook the other man's hand with a friendly though reserved smile.

"Dr. Carson, it's good to see you again."

Carson? Isn't that the doctor who was helping Ash?

The man returned Brandon's smile. "Please, call me Dex. I'm not here in a professional capacity." He looked to Dillon and Jamie. "I'm here to help."

The minute he said it, Dillon started to relax. Maybe it was the confidence in Carson's voice when he said the word "help", or maybe it was the way he looked at them with compassion, but not a trace of pity. Whatever the case, Dillon's chill bumps faded and the knot in his stomach eased.

Alicia took over. "Let me make formal introductions and we'll get down to business. James Walker and Dillon Carver, I'd like you to meet Bruce Seaford and Dexter Carson. They're here to help us sort through this mess and get Jamie out of trouble and back home where he belongs."

"Can I get you guys some coffee?" Brandon offered.

Both men nodded, declining cream and sugar and thanking him as he placed a mug on the table for each of them. As Brandon reclaimed the place next to his sister, Bruce settled himself into the chair across from Jamie and next to Brandon, leaving Carson to take the seat facing Dillon. "So, what have we got, Al?"

Alicia reached for the tape recorder. "You can hear it for yourselves and then decide."

For the second time in as many hours, Dillon heard his own words played back. The first time he'd listened to the retelling of the story, he'd been scared to death and trying desperately to hide it. Now he was less apprehensive. He was worried about Jamie, sure, and about being locked up in some crazy ward by that wacko, Henderson. But Dillon was soothed by the way Alicia and Brandon had rallied to their defense. He was feeling the first glimmers of hope.

When the tape was done, Bruce grabbed the file folder from beside his chair and placed it on the table. Unclasping the latch, he removed half a dozen eight-by-ten photos from the first compartment and slid them across the table to Dillon. Each one was of a different man, only one of whom Dillon knew. Bruce said, "I need you to look at each picture and tell me if the man who identified himself as Henderson is in there. Take your time."

Dillon didn't need to take his time. Just seeing Henderson's semi-smiling face, even in a photograph, was enough to make his stomach lurch. He slid the pictures — Henderson's on top — back across the table. "That's him."

"You sure?"

"That's the guy who tried to give me the sedative."

Jamie seconded Dillon's identification. "I only saw the guy for a few minutes, but I know it's him."

Bruce's face lit up like a kid's at Christmas. "What do you think, Al? Is it enough to get a warrant?"

Alicia nodded. To Jamie and Dillon she said, "Henderson is a Ph.D., not an M.D., which means he doesn't have the authorization to give out meds. We have your statement that Henderson tried to give you an injection. That should at least be enough to get us in the door so we can search his office."

"I don't want to seem dense or anything," Jamie said, "but could somebody please tell us what's going on? What does Henderson have to do with me hitting Dillon's father over the head with a bat?"

"With the actual assault, nothing. With the case, everything." Alicia turned her chair enough to clearly see them both down the length of the farmhouse table. "Lyle Henderson is a psychologist from

Chicago who prides himself on being able to take gay men and 'turn' them straight. That's what he claims anyway. Because Henderson is a doctor of theology and not medicine, he can't prescribe or administer the type of drugs Dillon heard him tell Douglas Carver were in that syringe. That's a felony, and should be enough to convince a judge to issue a warrant so we can find what we're looking for."

"I get the feeling you aren't looking to bust this Henderson just for dispensing without a license," Brandon said. "Off the record, what gives?"

Alicia looked to Bruce. "You think it's okay to give the boys the full story?"

"I don't see why not. They have a right to know, especially since they're in the middle of all this mess. The way I see it, Dillon's father involved him the minute he and his wife brought Henderson into their son's apartment."

"I agree." Alicia clasped her hands. "Everything I'm about to tell you guys is strictly off the record, meaning if you tell anybody I told you, I'll deny it." She turned to Dr. Carson. "Can you deal with this, Dex?"

"I'm fine, just here to help any way I can." Carson seemed calm, but Dillon could see something brewing just below the surface of the man, some inner tension. Whatever it was, it made Dillon shiver.

Alicia didn't comment. Instead, she went right into the story. "Lyle Henderson subscribes to the old school practice of treating homosexuality as a disease, a mental illness, if you will. He believes homosexuality can be cured with the right treatments. His treatment of choice is aversion therapy."

Brandon whistled. "Damn."

Dillon was lost. "What's 'aversion therapy'?"

Carson leaned forward. "Alicia, I'd like to take it from here, if that's okay."

"If you're sure you're up to it."

"I am." Carson stretched his lanky frame and sat back in his chair. "Aversion therapy is the process of using negative reinforcement to turn a person away from a certain behavior or thought process. There are different ways it can be done, but in the case of sexual aversion therapy, doctors generally rely on shock treatments. They show gay and lesbian patients a series of nude or even pornographic pictures. When the patient looks at pictures of the opposite sex, nothing happens. But the minute the patient sees a picture of his or her own gender, electrodes secured to the skin deliver a mild electric shock."

Alicia shuddered. "Is it just me, or does that sound positively barbaric to anyone else?"

"It's not just you. Hell, I have a degree in forensic psychology, and I still don't understand it." Brandon curled his lip. "Not in the case of homosexuality, anyway. I've heard of aversion therapy being mildly successful in some other areas, but never that one."

"Aversion therapy in general has fallen out of favor with a large section of the psychiatric community. It's simply not as effective as other, more humane treatment methods. And thankfully, most therapists and doctors now view homosexuality as a sexual preference one is born with and has no control over, rather than a disease." Carson sighed. "Unfortunately, there are still a few holdouts — dinosaurs like Henderson — who think being gay is a mental illness. Some of these guys will do anything to 'cure' a patient who's gay. And I do mean anything."

Alicia picked up the thread. "That's where my office comes in. For over two years now, the D.A. in Chicago has been investigating Henderson for the abuse of his patients."

Jamie's scrunched his brow. "I don't get it. If aversion therapy is used by lots of doctors, why is Henderson in trouble for doing the same thing?"

"Because Henderson doesn't stop at simple aversion therapy," Seaford interjected. "The D.A. brought me in to investigate allegations from more than one of Henderson's former patients, allegations ranging from the patients being stung repeatedly with high voltage cattle-prods to being starved for days on end, kept in locked cells without food and water. Because most of these patients were teenagers at the time of treatment and only came forward as adults years later, the statute of limitations has expired and there's nothing we can do. Not for those patients, anyway. Our hands are further tied by the fact that Henderson isn't a medical doctor. He doesn't have hospital privileges — which makes his threat to have Dillon locked up in an institution laughable — nor does he see just any patients. It's always hard to bust a doctor. Takes a lot of wrangling to get a crack at his medical records."

"This time Henderson saved us the trouble." Alicia's expression was pure satisfaction. "The minute he pulled out that syringe, he opened himself up for investigation. All we have to do is secure a warrant and see what we can find." She smiled at Jamie. "I believe you wanted to know what Henderson's past had to do with you."

"Yes, ma'am."

"When Douglas Carver held Dillon so Henderson could dope him up, Douglas became Henderson's accomplice. If we can prove Henderson acted to harm Dillon and that Doug was helping to commit said harm, then yours becomes a case of self-defense, pure and simple."

"How can it be self-defense if Dillon was the one threatened and not me?"

"I can answer that one," Brandon said. "Every man has a right to defend his spouse or his family. Since you and Dillon are partners, you have the right to defend him as you would yourself."

"That sums it up." Alicia reached back into her briefcase, retrieving her phone and rising to her feet. "If you'll please excuse me, I'll call my boss and let him know what we've got so far. Hopefully, we'll have a warrant before the night is out."

Bruce stood as well, taking Brandon's tape recorder with him. "I need to make copies of this. I have another recorder in my car that should do the trick."

"I might as well call Skinner and let him know the score." Brandon stood and stretched. "Can I get you guys anything? How about you, Dex?"

Jamie and Dillon declined, as did Carson. "I'm fine, thank you."

Brandon grabbed the cordless phone from one of the shining granite counters in the kitchen. "In that case, I'll be in the living room, making a call." He walked out, leaving the three of them alone in silence.

The silence was awkward for Dillon, and Jamie too, if the way he was wiggling around in his chair was any indication, but Carson seemed oblivious to it. His silver eyes roamed the confines of the kitchen, taking in the homey atmosphere. Dillon didn't even realize he was staring at the man until Carson said, "You can ask me about it, if you want to."

"About what?" Even as he said it, Dillon knew what Carson was talking about.

"The reason Bruce asked me to come with him while he and Alicia talked to you. I can tell you're curious."

"I figured it was because you're a psychiatrist. Maybe Brandon and his sister think Jamie and I need a shrink."

Carson laughed, the sound rich and warm in the quiet kitchen. "I'll admit it sounds like the two of you have been through the wringer, but I wasn't asked here so I could analyze you." He sobered. "I'm here because I know Henderson, know firsthand what he's capable of."

Jamie's mouth dropped open. "You were his patient?"

"I was his first patient. The first patient he ever tried to convert, anyway." Carson locked eyes with Dillon. "I'm also his son."

"Jesus."

"Quite a kicker, isn't it?" Carson leaned forward and crossed his arms, elbows bent and propped on the table. "My father used to be a well respected psychologist. Some of his philosophies were outdated, to be sure, but he was highly thought of by most of his colleagues. All that changed when he found out I was gay. He and my mother freaked."

Dillon knew how that felt. "How old were you?"

"Sixteen. My father caught me with my boyfriend. We were just kissing, but it was enough to set my father off. He forbade me to see Todd again, and then he started on his crusade, as I call it. He became convinced he could cure me. He started studying up on different techniques, all the ways to steer a person's mind away from the evils of homosexuality." Carson shook his head. "Needless to say, it didn't work. My father put me through a full year of electric shocks and dirty pictures before he realized it wasn't working." His jaw was set in stone. "That's when my dad upped the stakes."

Jamie whispered, "God."

"God is exactly who my father thinks he is. He just couldn't accept the fact I was gay and there was nothing he could do about it. Because he's not an M.D., he has no real pull with any of the local psychiatric hospitals. He threatened me with commitment, anyway, just like he did with you. My guess is, in both our cases, he thought he could scare us into compliance. And he was right, at least where I was concerned. Whereas you fought back and didn't listen, my father's scare tactics worked on me. I would have done anything my father asked to keep myself from being locked up in some nameless mental ward somewhere. I thought that was the worst thing that could ever happen to me." Carson shook his head in amazement. "Isn't it incredible how wrong a person can be? Once my father had my cooperation, he went about the task of converting me with a vengeance. He started experimenting with different drugs, begging his colleagues to write prescriptions for him in a bid to find the one medication that would kill all those urges I was having. Never mind that he almost killed me in the process. He tried high doses of sedatives and antidepressants. They killed my sex drive, but the minute my dad pulled me off the meds and the drugs cleared my system, the natural desires and feelings came back. That's when he got the bright idea to combine aversion therapy with the meds. He'd read somewhere about doctors who were using vomit inducing drugs along with electric shocks."

Dillon could see the strain on Carson's face — the way he fought off the pain of the memories — but that didn't stop him from continuing.

"I won't dredge up the gory details, but you can imagine how terrifying it was for a teenage kid to go through that. And the shock treatments and drugs were some of the nicer things my father did to me. The rest of it, well...the rest is best left unsaid." Carson leaned back with a sigh. "It took me the better part of three years, but I finally got away from him. I changed my last name and moved as far away from Chicago as I could get."

Dillon didn't blame him. "Why'd you come back? To stop your father from doing the same thing to someone else?"

"Something like that." Carson might have said more but Brandon came back in, ending the private conversation.

Brandon was smiling, a good sign. Dillon could tell how tense Jamie was just from the way he sat in his chair. Brandon's words went a long way toward easing the strain for both of them.

"I just got off the phone with Skinner. Doug is making noise about pressing charges against Jamie. Skinner told him the case is on hold until further notice."

"What now?"

"You and Dillon are going to spend the night here with Nate and me. You're not to go anywhere until Alicia gets this thing squared with the D.A., hopefully by tomorrow. Until then, you'll get a break from work, school — everything." When Dillon tried to protest, Brandon said, "Before you get all up in the air, kid, I'll talk to your boss and let him know what's going on. Think of it as a mini-vacation."

Unless Brandon was sending him and Jamie to a tropical island where homophobic parents were shot on sight, Dillon didn't think a vacation — mini or not — was going to help.

The next hour and a half — between the time Alicia and crew left and Nate came back — was organized chaos. Brandon had Dillon and Jamie write out and then sign statements about what had happened, statements which he faxed to Alicia's boss and Ronald Skinner. Jamie breathed a sigh of relief when the hum of the fax machine broke the quiet of the house. He was looking forward to a few minutes alone with Dillon.

No sooner had the thought crossed his mind than the phone started ringing. Heath, Ash, Megan, and Jim Pembroke all called in, having learned their whereabouts from Aunt Sadie. All had heard about Morgan's attack. Megan also knew about the visit from Dillon's parents, but the others — especially Heath — were stunned by the revelation. It took Dillon and Jamie both to explain everything that had happened, and by the time they were finished trading the phone back and forth and giving explanations, they were both exhausted.

Nate came in carrying a small suitcase and a bag of take-out from the new Thai place down the road. "I thought you would be hungry, so I stopped and got us all some supper. Hope you don't mind spicy food. Oh, and I went by your place and grabbed you some clothes." He looked down at their still bare feet and grinned. "Shoes included. I hope that's okay. Your aunt let me in." He laughed. "That's why it took me so long. She grilled me for over half an hour, just making sure the two of you were really okay."

The grilling he wouldn't wish on any man, but as for the clothes and food, Jamie could have hugged him. "Thanks, Nate. Hey, how much do we owe you for the food?"

Brandon snorted. "You've been hanging around your partner too long, kid. Dinner's on us."

Dillon protested, but one look at his bloodshot eyes and sagging shoulders told Jamie he was too tired to put up much of a fight.

Spicy wasn't the word for the chicken and coconut soup, fried fish with tamarind sauce, and steak salad Nate placed on the table. At least the tapioca and coconut milk pudding they had for dessert didn't burn Jamie's mouth. Spicy or not, the food was good, and Jamie soon found his belly full and his head nodding. Dillon must have been in much the same condition because Nate took one look at the two of them and said, "I think we've done enough talking for one night. Let me show you guys to the guest room."

The guest room was warm and inviting, decorated in cheerful colors with an old-fashioned style that made Jamie feel instantly at home. The thing that he most looked forward to, though, was trying out the king-sized bed that dominated the center of the room.

Dillon was way ahead of him. He flopped down on the bed with a mumbled thank-you to Nate and closed his eyes, not even bothering to undress or pull back the covers.

Jamie gave Nate an apologetic smile, but Nate just laughed and waved it away. "The poor kid's been through hell and back. The least he deserves is a good night's sleep." Nate squeezed Jamie's shoulder. "You haven't had an easy time of it yourself. How are you handling all this?"

Jamie shrugged. "I'm okay. Talking to Dr. Carson helped."

Nate nodded. "Brandon told me Dex came with Alicia and the special investigator. He's a good man. He helped me through a really rough patch in my life."

"The death of your friend?"

"That, and a total betrayal by my parents." Nate scrubbed his hand over his face. "Let's just say Dex and Dillon aren't the only ones who struck out in the parent department."

"I know. Every time I think about what Dillon's parents tried to do to him tonight, I start to wonder if having parents is really all it's cracked up to be." Jamie yawned. "I'm lucky as hell to have my aunt though."

"Yes, you are. And not all parents are like mine and Dillon's. Just look at Dean and Gale. I can't imagine any parents more loving than they are." Nate smiled. "But right now, you need sleep more than you need grateful reflection. If you guys need anything during the night, don't hesitate to holler. Brandon and I are just down the hall."

"I think we'll be okay, but I'll remember, just in case. Thanks, Nate. For everything. And tell Brandon we said thanks, too."

"I will. Goodnight."

"Night."

Jamie closed the door behind Nate and headed for the bed. He managed to strip Dillon down to his boxers and wrestle him under the covers before stripping down himself and climbing in on the other side. He closed his eyes and was almost asleep when he felt Dillon roll over and pull him close. Into Jamie's ear, Dillon said, "You saved me."

Jamie played it off, the memory of what happened that afternoon too fresh to reexamine yet again. "It was nothing you wouldn't have done for me. You've made a career out of protecting me, in fact."

Dillon tightened his hold, drawing Jamie so close against him that Jamie could feel every fiber of Dillon's being. "Explain it away all you want, but I was terrified and you were there for me. You saved my sanity, possibly my life. Do you know how that makes me feel?"

Jamie thought he knew, but he asked anyway. "How?"

Dillon's voice was little more than a husky whisper. "Like the luckiest man alive. I can't live without you, Jamie. I never want to try."

Jamie could do no more than nod, but he sensed that was okay. Words were unnecessary as he and Dillon rocked each other until they finally fell asleep.

When he woke the next morning, Dillon had no doubt a long, excruciating wait was in front of them. Jamie was already up and going, but Dillon felt lethargic, too tired to move. Worry about what was going to happen to Jamie kept him pinned in place despite the reassurances he'd received from Alicia the night before. When he finally forced himself out of bed, it was pushing noon.

He showered and shaved in mechanical fashion, donning the clothes Nate had brought for them in the same robotic way. He came down the stairs and entered the kitchen to find a smiling Alicia sitting at the table talking to Jamie and Brandon. Dillon's heart started thudding against the walls of his chest, from hope or dread, he wasn't sure.

Alicia sent him a thousand watt smile as he took the place next to Jamie. "There you are. I was beginning to think we were going to have to come up there and drag your lazy butt out of the bed."

Dillon blushed. "Sorry about that. I don't usually sleep so late, I swear."

"I'm just teasing you, honey. It's not like you don't have a good reason for sleeping in." She picked up a sheaf of papers and waved them. "I think these babies are going to go a long way toward making you feel better."

"What are they?"

Jamie leaned over and kissed his cheek. "I can answer the first part of that question. At the top of the stack is a notarized statement from your dad, dropping the charges he filed against me."

Afraid to believe it was true, Dillon turned to Alicia. "How did you manage that one?"

"Your father made it easy for me. By hooking up with Henderson, he left himself without a leg to stand on." She must have seen Dillon's lack of comprehension, because she said, "You remember I said that Henderson dispensing meds without a license was enough to get us a warrant for his office?"

"I remember."

"As it turns out, Judge Finwell thought it was enough to give us leeway to search his house, too. He issued both warrants just around midnight. The office search yielded nothing more than a couple of vials of Haldol, hardly enough to make an arrest. But the home search... In Henderson's basement, we hit the jackpot."

Dillon was almost afraid to ask, but he didn't have to. Alicia was all too happy to fill in the details. The woman was almost giddy, but Dillon couldn't blame her. He was feeling a little lightheaded himself.

Alicia placed the papers on the table and folded her hands over them. "Apparently fearing that his office might someday be raided, Henderson confined the majority of his work to the basement of his Chicago home." She shivered. "Bruce Seaford went with the police who executed the search. He said the place is like some kind of mad scientist torture chamber. They found restraints, shock mechanisms, drugs, whips, and paddles — the whole works. They also found detailed records of the abuse some of those poor patients suffered at Henderson's hands. My boss believes we have enough evidence against him to put Henderson away for at least ten years, if not longer."

"I'm glad to hear that, especially if it means that no one else will have to go through the things Dr. Carson went through. But I still don't see what made my dad drop the charges."

Brandon spoke for the first time since Dillon had come downstairs. "Dillon...when the cops raided Henderson's home-office, they found not only records of treatments the good doctor had already administered, they found treatment plans for his future patients, as well." His voice was thick with compassion, and Dillon knew the answer to his question was going to be hard to hear.

"One of those treatment plans had your name on it." Brandon sighed. "You don't want the details of Henderson's 'sexual reorienta-tion plan' and I don't want to give them to you, so I'll just say it wasn't pretty and leave it at that."

"Not only were these so-called treatments Henderson proposed for you horrifying, but almost every one of them is illegal." Alicia pulled a piece of paper free from the stack and held it up. "This is a copy of the release form Henderson had your parents sign so he could begin your treatments. It shows without a doubt that Douglas and

236 ❖ Sara Bell

Angela both knew and approved of all the things Henderson wanted to do to you."

Jamie scooted his chair closer to Dillon and brushed his leg against Dillon's thigh. Though Dillon appreciated the gesture of comfort, it wasn't necessary. He'd long ago reconciled to the fact that his parents held no real love for him. And after having received exactly that from so many people he wasn't even related to, unconditional love was the only kind that interested Dillon.

Alicia put the form back with the others. "The minute Bruce found that paper, he knew we had Douglas dead to rights. Bruce called me, and I called my boss. We put together a little deal for your dear old pops."

Brandon's smile was mischievous. "That's not even the best part of the story. Because Douglas and Angela are residents of Reed, I, as sheriff, was allowed to deliver the paperwork to them and to present the deal."

Brandon's excitement was contagious. Dillon felt the corners of his mouth begin to lift. "What kind of deal?"

Alicia went back through the stack of papers, pulling out two official looking carbon copies and sliding them across the table to Dillon. "Since Douglas signed off on a therapy that he, as a lawyer, knew to be illegal and a violation of your civil rights, the D.A. could have moved to have him not only disbarred and banned from practicing law in the state of Illinois, he could have also had Doug locked up as Henderson's accomplice. Our office agreed not to seek any punitive action against Douglas as long as he dropped all charges against Jamie." She pointed to the documents she'd given to Dillon, papers he had yet to look at. "He and your mother are also banned from having any further contact with either you or Jamie for the next two years. I filed a restraining order in your names against each of them, an order which you can renew when the two years are up, if you like. All you have to do is sign off on it. Then, if they do approach either of you, no matter what the reason, we can lock them up for violation of the order."

Dillon was stunned. "You mean it's over? There's nothing more they can do to me?" He looked over at Jamie, who was grinning broadly. "To either of us?"

"Nope. I swear, kid, you should have seen the look on old Dougie's face when I slapped him with that order." Brandon looked to be on an adrenaline high Dillon felt sure would last him all day. "The bastard had no choice but to go along with it, and he knew it. I don't think you have to worry about him, not anymore."

Dillon started to speak, but Jamie beat him to it. "There's more. Brandon just got through telling us that Morgan's awake. They got all the pellets out of him and he's been talking."

"We'll have to check out his story to see if it proves true before I can give out all the details, but the long and short of it is this: Morgan made a full confession in the death of Birch Carpenter." Brandon held up one finger. "He also admitted to the attempted murder of you, Jamie, and Mitch." He ticked off three more fingers. "Thanks to you guys — and Miss Sadie's shotgun — we're gonna nail him to the wall."

Chapter Twenty

Nailing Morgan to the wall took about two weeks, two weeks in which Dillon lived each day like it was his last, enjoying the newfound freedom of not having a murderer on the loose. No amateur investigations by his boyfriend, no homophobic parents on a self-righteous rampage, nothing except school, work, and wild nights spent in his own home with the man of his dreams. It was enough to make a man feel downright peaceful.

Not even the throng of reporters hounding them in the days directly following the arrests of Morgan and Henderson could shake Dillon's sense of well-being. He took it all in stride — from the curious questions of the kids at school to the follow up questions by the Chicago District Attorney's office.

To that end, Dillon and Jamie were blessed with plenty of help when it came to handling their celebrity. Aunt Sadie posted no-trespassing signs around the perimeters of her property and met anyone who wouldn't take no for an answer at the door with her now famous twelve gauge. Mr. Ardsley, the vice-principal who'd taken over as Dan Morgan's replacement, fended off the news crews who came to the school hoping to catch a picture of Reed's newest heroes.

Dillon laughed the first time he heard himself referred to as a hero. As far as he was concerned, Jamie was the hero; Dillon was just along for the ride. Not that anyone would listen. He was even hounded at work by one tenacious writer hoping to do a spread on the boys for a true crime magazine. Jim Pembroke came to the rescue on that one. He ousted the guy from the store in much the same way as a bouncer ejected an unruly bar patron. With all the protection offered by friends and loved ones, as well as the knowledge he and Jamie were finally through the roughest part of the ordeal, Dillon was starting to feel halfway normal again. Whatever normal might be.

The only blot on Dillon's happiness — besides the anxiety of waiting for the end of the Morgan investigation — was the change in Megan. Since the rift between her and Heath, Megan had been silent and withdrawn. Though he saw her every day, it seemed to Dillon as if the two of them hadn't talked — really talked — since the night of Morgan's attack.

He'd last seen Megan at school that afternoon, her face pale and gaunt. When he'd asked her what was wrong, she shrugged it off as nothing more than cramming for exams and dealing with the prom committee. Dillon wasn't buying it, but he couldn't force her to talk about it, either. He'd even tried talking to Heath about Megan, only to be told to mind his own damn business.

At seven o'clock, Dillon was stocking shelves and thinking about his brother's behavior when Jim Pembroke called him up to the front. "Sheriff Nash is on line one for you. You can take it in my office where you'll have some privacy."

Dillon nodded his thanks and headed towards the office. Perching on the edge of Jim's desk, he grabbed the phone and punched the first line. "Hello?"

"Hey, kid. Don't mean to bother you when you're hardly working, er...working hard, but I thought you'd like to know where things stand on the Morgan case. The D.A. here in Reed finished with it last night, and the Chicago D.A. signed off on it this morning, so I'm free to give you the lowdown. I tried to call your house to let Jamie know, too, but I didn't get an answer."

"Tonight's his aunt's poker night. Jamie's serving snacks to the blue haired set over at her house."

"Scary thought. Anyway, I'd deliver this news in person, but I'm ass deep in work on this case as it is, so I figured I'd just give you a call and be done with it."

Dillon settled himself more firmly on the desk. If this was really going to be it — the end of all the hell he and Jamie had been through — Dillon wanted to get the full effect. "Hit me with it."

"We ran a ballistics check on the gun Morgan used to shoot at you. It's the same gun that killed Birch Carpenter. In light of the evidence, he had little choice but to cut a deal. He's agreed to give a full confession as long as the D.A. takes the death penalty off the table. He also wants the D.A.'s promise not to put him in the general population once he goes to prison. The other inmates take a dim view of child molesters." Brandon snorted. "It would serve the bastard right if some three hundred pound tough guy made Morgan his wife."

Dillon laughed. "Talk about justice. Too bad it can't happen now, but at least Morgan's gonna be locked away. I guess that'll have to do."

"Yep. And it's not like the world lost an upstanding citizen when Morgan offed Carpenter. The way I see it, he performed a public service."

Dillon forced himself to ask the one question he dreaded, the one he knew Jamie most needed an answer to. "What about Ben's death? Did Morgan admit to killing him, too?"

Brandon sighed. "'Fraid not, kid. According to Morgan, Carpenter killed Ben. To understand the way Morgan thinks, you have to know a little bit about him. He was born over in Chicago, the only child of a well-to-do investment banker and his high society wife. The two of them doted on Morgan, gave him whatever he wanted. They sent him to the best schools, made certain he drove only the coolest cars. From what I understand, Morgan's old man even bought the kid's way through college. Morgan got a degree in education, but I don't think he ever planned on using it. Living off Daddy's money was the only real goal he ever set for himself. All that changed right after Morgan graduated from college."

"What happened?"

"Seems Morgan wasn't the only criminal in the family. His father was caught embezzling from some of his clients. The Federal Trade Commission did an investigation, and Morgan's father was arrested and then sentenced to seven years. The F.T.C. also froze all his assets. Morgan and his mother were left with almost nothing."

"Ouch."

"It gets worse. Morgan's mother was unable to cope with the shame of being married to a common criminal. She shot herself two weeks after the old man went to prison."

Dillon was almost feeling sorry for Morgan, but Brandon's next words wiped out all those feelings in an instant.

"Morgan wasn't exactly heartbroken over what happened. His mother had an insurance policy just for burial, one that didn't include a suicide clause. Morgan cashed it in, but instead of burying his mother with it, he used the money to set himself up in the boy business."

Dillon shivered. "I thought Birch Carpenter handled that end of the operation."

"That came later. Morgan was running adult hustlers, bringing in customers and 'screening' them, as he called it. He used the money from his mother's policy to pay for hotels, drugs, whatever the customers required. Seems he racked up quite a client list. Morgan met Carpenter at a party a few weeks later, a party thrown by one of those same clients. Morgan was looking for younger guys to work with, and Carpenter was looking for better contacts for his own budding boy business. The two of them hooked up, and the rest is history. They would probably still be working together if Morgan hadn't started having sex with Carpenter's boys. Carpenter was real strict about no in-house sex, according to Morgan. After Morgan brought that guy in who roughed up Mitch, things went downhill. Morgan was making less and less money, so much so that he took the job as principal at Plunkett just to make ends meet." Brandon made a rude sound in the back of his throat. "That's what he called it. 'Making ends meet.' To most people that means paying all the bills and having enough left over to buy groceries. To Morgan it means having enough money to gas up his Ferrari."

"And Plunkett is where he met up with Ben again?"

"Yeah. He pretended not to know Ben, but Morgan says the two of them got together on the sly every so often and had sex, sex which Morgan paid for."

Dillon wasn't sure whether or not he would pass that little detail on to Jamie. He cleared his throat. "Where does the blackmail come in?"

"A few months ago, Carpenter told Morgan he was cutting him off completely, said he had enough contacts so that he didn't need Morgan anymore. Morgan was bitching to Ben about it, and that's when Ben came up with the plan to blackmail the guy."

"And Ben had already succeeded in blackmailing Ash, so what was one more victim?" Dillon did his best not to gag.

"That's about the size of it. Morgan knew about Carpenter's affinity for young girls, and he's the one who snuck back into the house and planted the cameras. Ben approached Carpenter with the pictures and made the demands, but they split the money fifty-fifty. Listening to Morgan talk, you'd think he and Ben actually cared about each other, like they were friends or something."

"So all that stuff Morgan said at Ben's funeral was just a cover?"

"According to Morgan, yeah. He found out about Ben's death from one of my deputies, a guy by the name of Phelps." Brandon made a spitting sound. "His ass is beyond fired. Phelps will be lucky if I don't charge him with everything from obstruction of justice to aiding and abetting. Anyway, Morgan hired the guy to make certain he was never the subject of any active investigations, just like he paid a couple of cops in Chicago to do the same thing. Guess he wanted someone to give him advance warning just in case he was ever about to be busted for his dirty dealings. Amazing how paranoid some of these sleaze bags can get. Needless to say, the minute Morgan heard Ben had been killed, he had no doubt Carpenter finished Ben off to stop the blackmail. Morgan also guessed Carpenter knew of his own involvement. Morgan claims he and Ben met out on Tully Road that night so they could divvy up Carpenter's latest payoff. He swears Ben was alive when he left. Thing about that is, there was no money found anywhere on Ben's body or at the scene. To Morgan's way of thinking, Carpenter must have followed them to the meeting place, waited until Morgan left, and then come out of hiding and killed Ben, taking Ben's half of the money. That's when Morgan ran scared, believing he would be next on Carpenter's hit list. He tried to distance himself from Ben by giving that speech at the memorial, but that wasn't enough to convince himself he was safe. Finally, the guy snapped under the pressure. Morgan's plan was to off Carpenter before Carpenter did him in. The plan would have worked, too, if Mitch hadn't come to Reed and exposed Morgan as Carpenter's partner. Morgan saw Mitch in town trying to locate you and Jamie. He thought if he killed the three of you, his secrets would die with you."

Dillon's blood felt like ice in his veins when he thought about how close he and Jamie had come to dying at Morgan's hand. He shrugged the dark notion aside. "Do you believe him? About Carpenter killing Ben, I mean?"

Brandon paused. "I'm not sure. I think it's possible, but I also think it's just as likely Barry Sledge really did kill Ben that night, and that Morgan's paranoia just got the better of him. We do know Sledge hit Ben with his car, but the question is: did he hit him before or after Ben was already dead? It's also possible Morgan killed Ben before he pulled away that night and took Ben's share of the money with him. We'll probably never know for sure, but the D.A. feels like it's enough to raise reasonable doubt in the Sledge case. The assistant D.A. who took Sledge's plea the first time is taking back the deal they made for vehicular homicide and changing the charges to reckless endangerment and gross negligence while operating a motor vehicle. Instead of prison, Sledge is going into a resident rehab program. It works almost the same way as jail; he can't come out until a judge says he can. With Sledge's record, I have a feeling he'll be in treatment for a long time."

Dillon wasn't sure why, but he felt better knowing Sledge wasn't being charged with murder. Sledge was a drunk, but Dillon was starting to believe the guy wasn't the one responsible for Ben's death. At least Sledge was getting some help out of the deal. All that remained now was to see what would happen to Morgan. He asked Brandon as much.

"He'll be sentenced in a few weeks, and I think it's safe to say he'll spend the rest of his life behind bars. That ought to be enough to satisfy even Jamie."

Dillon laughed. "I think it will. Now maybe we can put this behind us. Thanks for calling."

"Anytime, kid. Before you go...I have something else to tell you."

Brandon hesitated, and Dillon could tell something was wrong. "What is it?"

"I'm gonna be an uncle."

"Yeah, I know. I was there when Alicia told you about the baby, remember?"

"I phrased it wrong." Brandon coughed. "What I should have said is, you and I are gonna be uncles."

It took Dillon a full minute to understand. *Oh, God.* "Megan's pregnant?"

"I just found out about it last night. The poor kid's been worrying herself sick, scared to death to tell anybody. Thank God she finally broke down and told Ashton Barnes. He convinced her to go to Mom and Dad with it. She actually thought they'd be mad at her. She should have known we all love her no matter what."

"Megan told Ash? Why wouldn't she come to me and Jamie? We've been trying to talk to her for two weeks."

"I don't doubt it, but before you get your feelings hurt, think about it — it's your brother who got her pregnant. She was afraid to drag you into this, afraid it would cause problems between you and Heath."

Dillon kicked himself for not thinking of that. That was so like Megan, always trying to protect him, the world — everybody but herself. Speaking of Heath... "What does my brother have to say about all this?"

"Denies she's even pregnant." Brandon's voice crackled with anger. "Swears up and down that there's no way she could be, and that if she is, the baby can't possibly be his. He claims Megan is only doing this because he broke up with her and she wants him back. Total dumbass," he swore under his breath. "Sorry, kid. I know he's your brother, but the guy is being a complete dick."

Dick doesn't even cover it. Dillon couldn't remember ever being so angry with his brother. "I hope you went over to his apartment and kicked some sense into him."

"I wanted to, believe me, but Megan wouldn't let me. She freaked out on me, swore never to talk to me again if I said anything at all to Heath. That's when my mother stepped in. She said that it was up to Heath and Megan to work things out, and for once I was gonna keep my big nose out of it or else."

"Damn. That's harsh."

"You're telling me. Now all we can do is wait and see what happens. At least Megan has our family's full support. Mom and Dad are already looking into colleges that provide student daycare and mother/baby housing."

"How does Megan feel about the baby?"

"She's in love with it already." Brandon's voice went soft. "You know Megan; she has love enough for ten kids. She's gonna make one hell of a mom, even if she is too damn young."

There was no doubt in Dillon's mind that was true, but the situation was still one hell of a mess. "Let me try talking to Heath. He might listen to me, or at least pretend to."

"Good luck. If Heath is half as stubborn as my sister, you've got your work cut out for you."

After calling Jamie to let him know where he'd be, Dillon headed straight to Heath's apartment. He found his brother sitting on the couch, well into a bottle of Wild Turkey. Heath rarely drank beer, much less bourbon. Apparently he wasn't as unaffected by the situation as he wanted people to believe.

Dillon snatched the half-empty bottle away from his brother and carried it into the kitchen. Heath yelled, "Hey, bring that back," but he was in no real condition to stop Dillon from pouring it down the drain.

That done, Dillon went back in and sank down next to his brother on the couch. The fumes from Heath's binge nearly knocked him down, but Dillon refused to move. His brother needed him, and Dillon was going to sit by Heath's side until the two of them talked it out.

Dillon jumped straight in. "I talked to Brandon Nash tonight. He told me about Megan."

"So she decided to take her lies to the Nash collective, did she?" Heath closed his eyes. "Well, good for her. I guess the sheriff is going to come and kick my ass now, huh?"

Dillon fought down a surge of anger. Getting mad and ramming his fist down Heath's throat wasn't going to help.

"No, he's not." When Heath looked at him with obvious disbelief, Dillon said, "Brandon wanted to jack your ass up, believe me. Megan made him promise not to."

Heath sneered. "Awww, how freaking nice of her, to protect me from her big, bad-ass brother." He snorted. "She lies on me, tries to force me to marry her, and then acts all sweet and innocent in front of her family. What a bitch."

So much for not losing my temper. Dillon reached out and shoved his brother so hard Heath fell off the couch and hit the floor.

"What in the hell did you do that for?"

Dillon towered over him. "Don't you ever — and I mean ever — call Megan a bitch in my presence again. What's the matter with you? You get her pregnant then drop her like she's trash, and you're the one calling her names? God, what's your problem?"

Heath didn't even bother to get up from the floor. "She's not pregnant. She can't be, at least not by me. I used a rubber every damn time we were together."

"Those things aren't one-hundred percent protection, and you know it. Anything could have happened. There could have been a hole, it could have broken—"

"Damn it, there is no baby!" Heath came up into a sitting position on the floor. "Megan told me she loved me — another freakin' lie — and I told her I wanted to cool things down. Now, two weeks later, she's telling the whole damned world that I knocked her up? That's mighty convenient, isn't it? She's just doing this to force me to come back to her. She'll do anything to get her way, just like—"

No way was Dillon gonna let Heath end it there. "Just like who? Damn it, Heath, you tell me what's going on or I swear I'll kick your ass myself. You won't have to worry about Brandon, not if I get to you first."

Heath didn't seem overly concerned about the threat, but he leaned his back against the base of the couch and started talking anyway. "Did Mom and Dad ever tell you the reason I moved out of their house?"

The change in subject startled Dillon, but he decided to go with it. "I always assumed you left because you were eighteen and didn't want to play by their lame-ass rules."

"There was more to it than that." Heath ran his fingers over his face, scraping his palm against the thick stubble on his chin. "Do you remember the girl I was dating at the time, Marcy Collier?"

"Vaguely. Why?"

"Vague describes my whole relationship with her. We were fuck buddies, and that's all we were. The two of us got together whenever we wanted to scratch a certain itch, but there were no ties between us. I thought she felt the same way, that she was cool with the whole casual thing, but evidently I was wrong. One day she told me she wanted us to be more than just an every now and then kinda thing, then she told me she loved me." Heath laughed, a bitter, joyless sound. "Like she knew anything about love. She was screwing at least three other guys besides me. When I told her I knew as much, she swore she'd give them all up, that she wanted to make a commitment to me and me alone. I told her I wasn't interested, and that was the end of it. At least I thought it was."

"What happened?"

"Marcy knew enough about Mom and Dad to know how strict they are. She went to them one day about three weeks after I called things off and told them she was pregnant and I was the father. That's when our old man told me I could either marry her and 'do the right thing', or I could get out. Needless to say, I got out." Heath smiled maliciously. "Put a crimp in ol' Marcy's plans, let me tell you. Without Mom and Dad to back her up, there was nothing she could do and she knew it. She finally admitted she'd made the whole thing up."

But not before the damage was done, Dillon thought. Regardless of what Marcy Collier had done, surely Heath knew that Megan wasn't capable of forcing a guy into marriage.

"Think about it. You were the first guy Megan ever slept with. You know she's nothing like Marcy. She cares about you. She loves you, Heath."

"So she says. But who the hell knows what love means? Mom and Dad say they love us, and look what they've done. They threw me to the wolves and almost had you tortured by some crazy-ass shrink."

"Okay, so they aren't the best examples, but you know not everyone is like them. Look at Megan's folks, or Brandon and Nate. They all give one-hundred percent to the people they love."

"Those are exceptions, little brother, not the rule."

246 ✦ Sara Bell

Dillon was losing his patience. "Why do you have to be so damn stubborn? You know Megan isn't lying. Deep inside, you have to."

Heath's own temper was starting to rise. "I don't have to know shit, kid. And who the hell are you to lecture me, anyway? You wanna talk about love? All right, then, let's talk about you and Jamie. Let's talk about how you fucked his ass and then dumped him rather than admit you were gay. That's real love for you, huh?"

Dillon swallowed. He stood up, looking down at the pitiful sight of his drunken brother, slumped against the couch. "Every word you just said is true. But I had one thing going for me with Jamie that apparently you don't."

"Yeah?" Heath looked up at him with glassy eyes. "And what's that?"

"I was smart enough to go back and fix my mistakes. You're letting the best thing that ever happened to you slip through your fingers and you're too blind — or too stupid — to see it." Dillon left without another word.

Jamie took the news about Morgan well, not even flinching when Dillon told him they might never know for sure which one of the three of them — Carpenter, Morgan, or Sledge — actually killed Ben. Dillon thought Jamie summed it up nicely. "They all got what they deserved in one form or another. I can live with it."

Part of the reason Jamie wasn't overly focused on the Morgan investigation was his worry for Megan. She talked to them both a little bit on the phone, apologizing for not telling them the truth — but other than that brief contact, she kept to herself, even at school. Dillon thought maybe he'd gotten through to Heath, but after five days with no word from his brother, he was losing hope.

Ash came by Saturday morning, looking as worried as Dillon felt. Jamie showed him in and the three of them took a seat at the table.

"I'm sorry to bother you guys so early, but I'm scared stiff about Megan. She doesn't look good at all."

"I know. Every time I talk to her, she blows me off and tells me she's fine, but anyone can see she's lying." Dillon clenched his fists. "I'd love to beat Heath black and blue."

Ash nodded. "There's a long line forming on that one. Any word from him?"

"Nope. I went by there a few days ago and talked to him, but that's the last contact with him I've had. Since I'm off work today, I thought I might go over there and try again."

"I wish you wouldn't." Jamie made a face. "I don't think it's gonna make any difference, and it might just make him dig his heels in deeper."

"Jamie's right. You can't force the guy to listen." Ash stood. "I just wanted to stop by and see how things stood with your brother. I talked Megan into letting me take her to the movies this afternoon, so I'd better head on over to her house before she changes her mind."

Dillon walked him to the door. "Thanks for being such a good friend to her. I know she has a hard time talking to me because Heath's my brother."

Ash smiled. "Megan was there for me when I needed a friend; I'm just returning the favor." He turned to Jamie. "Brandon told Megan about the situation with Morgan, and she filled me in. I hope you got your closure."

"I did." Jamie took a deep breath. "It won't bring Ben back, but knowing Morgan is gonna pay for his part in it, and for what he tried to do to us, makes it easier to take."

"Understood. Any word from Ben's brother?"

"Mitch called us a few days ago but he didn't say where he was. The D.A. has him in a safe house until this thing with Morgan is squared away. Hopefully, it won't take long. The sheriff seized the rest of the blackmail money from Ben's safe deposit box, and since Morgan confessed, it makes all the little details easier to square away."

Ash's eyes widened at Jamie's statement. "A safe house? Why?"

"Just in case one of Birch Carpenter's clients gets antsy, thinking Mitch might I.D. him. The D.A.'s afraid one of the johns might come after Mitch."

"For his sake, I hope this thing wraps up quickly." Ash gave a little salute. "It was good to see you guys, but I'm outta here."

Dillon stopped him with a hand on his shoulder. "It was good to see you, too, man. Don't be such a stranger."

Ash grinned. "You'll be seeing a lot more of me come the fall."

"Oh yeah? And why is that?"

Ash laughed. "Because Garman is a relatively small campus."

Jamie came to the door and high-fived him. "Dude, you got into Garman? That's so cool."

"Yep. I'm heading up same time as you, I imagine."

Dillon slapped him on the back. "Glad to hear it. You're on your way back to the land of the living, man."

"Now if we can just get Megan back on track, we'll have it made." Ash gave them both another goodbye and left.

Jamie put his arms around Dillon's waist. "Is it just me, or are we halfway there on the road to a normal life?"

Dillon bent his head, taking Jamie's mouth with his own. He wasn't sure what normal was, but he was dying to find out.

Dillon never should have bragged to Ash about having the day off. He thought he'd be spending the day lounging around the apartment with

Jamie; he hadn't counted on Sadie the Slave-driver. She knocked on the door at eleven-thirty with a list of things that needed doing around the house. Dillon grumbled to himself as he repositioned the ladder so he could clean the gutters. At least he hadn't gotten stuck cleaning out the attic like Jamie. There really was a bright side to everything.

By the time Dillon finished with the first half of his task, it was quite warm outside. The first week of May had banished coats and sweatshirts from his wardrobe, but now even the cotton t-shirt he wore was too warm. Dillon shucked it over his head and tossed it to the ground.

"If you take off your pants, I'm leaving."

Dillon whirled so fast, he almost fell off the ladder. His brother was standing at the base, not smiling, but not exactly frowning, either. Dillon decided to take that as a good sign. He climbed down the ladder, stopping just in front of his brother. "How's it going?"

Heath shuffled his feet. "I came to tell you I'm sorry. For what I said the other day about you and Jamie, I mean."

"I'm cool with that." Dillon waited a second, then said, "What about Megan? She's the one who's suffering, not me."

"What do you want me to say?" Heath wrung his hands "She's lying. I guess the only way to prove it is to wait a few months. When there's no baby, you'll know I was telling the truth."

Dillon wanted to scream. When he'd seen Heath standing at the bottom of the ladder, he'd hoped against hope his brother had come to his senses. Instead, Heath had given him more of the same excuses. Before Dillon could respond, his cell phone rang.

He ignored his brother and answered it. "Hello." All the color drained out of his face. "I'll be right there." He hung up the phone and to Heath he said, "We'll have to argue about this later. I have to go."

Heath grabbed his arm. "Wait a minute. What's going on?"

"Let me go; I don't have time to talk."

Heath wasn't budging. "You're not going anywhere until you tell me who that was on the phone and why you have to leave. Hell, you were the one who was so damned set on talking about Megan."

"This is about Megan, asshole. That was Ash on the phone. He and Megan had a movie date this afternoon."

Heath made a nasty face, but didn't relinquish his hold. "So much for being brokenhearted about splitting up with me, huh? How long did it take before Megan moved on to Ash?"

"I don't have time to talk about this right now. Let me go, damn it."

"Not until you answer my question." Heath's voice got deathly quiet. "Is she banging him?"

Dillon couldn't believe his ears. "No. What's wrong with you?"

"What's wrong with me? What's wrong with *you*? You come down on me like a ton of bricks and take up for Megan. Megan, the girl who claims to be pregnant with my baby and who's out with another guy, even as we speak. Why can't you see what a liar she is?"

That did it. Dillon wrenched free of his brother's grasp. "She's one hell of a liar all right. She's so good, she's got half the staff at Chicago General completely snowed."

Heath went pale. "What are you talking about?"

"That was Ash on the phone, calling from the hospital. Your un-pregnant ex-girlfriend just had a miscarriage, and now she's hemorrhaging. She's losing a lot of blood and the doctor's aren't sure they can stop it before she bleeds to death."

Chapter Twenty-One

Heath insisted on riding to the hospital with Dillon and Jamie. He sat in the back of Dillon's Lumina, not once during the ride breaking his silence. For that, Dillon was glad. He didn't trust himself to speak.

The drive to Chicago General seemed to take forever. Dillon barely remembered parking the car or making the trip from the parking garage to the emergency room. What he would never forget, though, was the look on Ash's face as he rushed to meet them. Ash started to say something to Dillon, but the minute he caught site of Heath, all hell broke loose.

"What the fuck did you bring him for? He's the reason Megan is in this condition." Before Dillon could stop him, Ash made a dive at Heath, slugging him hard in the jaw.

Heath didn't even try to defend himself. Ash pulled back, ready to deliver another blow when Gale Nash stepped out of the waiting area. "Ashton...stop, honey. None of this is going to help Megan."

Ash stepped back but fixed Heath with an angry stare. "Go home, you bastard. You've done enough."

Heath didn't answer Ash; he spoke to Gale. "How is she?"

Ash blurted, "Like you have a right to ask," but Gale didn't say anything. Not at first. She stood for a full minute, just looking Heath over.

Finally Gale said, "Do you really care how she is?"

Heath didn't hesitate. "Yes, I do."

She nodded. "I think maybe you do. Come into the waiting area and I'll tell you what I know."

As they stepped into the waiting room proper, Dillon nodded to Brandon, Nate, and Megan's dad, all of whom were glaring at Heath. Heath didn't seem to notice; his eyes were glued to Gale. She took the chair closest to her husband while Heath remained standing, waiting for her response.

Gale didn't make him wait long. "Megan suffered an ectopic pregnancy, meaning the baby implanted in her fallopian tube, not her uterus. In a case like that, there's nothing they can do to save the pregnancy, but if they get to it in time, a good surgical team can remove the embryo without serious damage to the mother." Her eyes filled with tears. "In Megan's case, her tube ruptured before anyone caught it."

Dillon could tell Heath wasn't far from losing it. "What does that mean?"

Gale drew a deep, shuddering breath. "Megan could bleed to death if they can't repair the damage."

Nate came up beside Gale's chair and slipped an arm around her shoulders. "That's not going to happen. Dr. Byrd is working on her. He's the best reproductive surgeon in Chicago General. If you don't believe me, you can ask Keith when he and Maria get here."

Heath cleared his throat, the harsh sound echoing through the silent waiting area. "That means there's a good chance Megan will be okay, right?"

Gale nodded, but Brandon stood up and moved forward, despite Nate's attempts to hold him back. "It also means, you stupid prick, that my sister was telling you the truth when she said she was pregnant. All the hell you put her through just because you aren't man enough to live up to your responsibilities was for nothing."

The doctor came out then, a dark haired man of about fifty clad in blood spattered scrubs. Megan's blood. Heath looked even more stricken than before. The others stood as the doctor started his report, effectively cutting short Brandon's tirade.

"Megan's lost more blood than I would like, but we were able to stabilize her and clamp off the bleeder without having to give her a transfusion. I repaired the ruptured tube as best I could, but she may need another surgery to remove any excess scar tissue at some point in the future. Barring infection, I believe she'll make a full recovery."

Gale clapped her hand to her mouth as tears ran down her face. Dean closed his eyes, and Dillon swore he heard Ash say a prayer of thanks. Nate shook the doctor's hand and thanked him, while Brandon pulled his mom into his arms and held her close. Jamie stood by Dillon's side, and it wasn't until he whispered, "Look at your brother," that Dillon turned to see how Heath was taking it.

Heath was talking to the doctor. "When can I see her?"

Dr. Byrd pursed his lips. "Are you a relative?"

Brandon said, "Hell no," but Heath ignored him. "I am...was the father of her baby."

Dillon wondered how much that admission had cost his brother, especially when Brandon and Ash both protested. Dean also looked as if he wanted to object, but it was Gale who settled the argument.

"Dr. Byrd, this is Heath Carver. He and Megan have a lot to talk about as soon as you say she's able." Gale looked back at the rest of them, daring them to interfere.

The doctor checked his watch. "She's in Recovery. As soon as the anesthesia wears off, she'll be sent to a private room. Once she's awake and has been examined to make certain there are no post-surgical complications, she can have visitors. But..." He hesitated, but only for a second. "I'm not sure about the status of your relationship with Megan, Mr. Carver, but you need to understand she's been through an

252 ❖ Sara Bell

ordeal. From what the nurses who prepped her for surgery tell me, Megan was hysterical, begging them to save her baby. When she comes to, she's going to be disoriented. My advice to you is to come back tomorrow, and even then, you should use discretion when you talk to her. Megan will have a lot to deal with; it's not uncommon for a woman in her situation to suffer from severe depression."

Heath buried his face in his hands. Dillon thought sure he was going to break, but somehow, his brother managed to hold it all together. When Heath raised his head, his face was a blank mask, all his emotions locked inside. He turned to Gale. "If I come back tomorrow, will you let me see her?"

"If that's what Megan wants, I won't try to stop you...and neither will they." Gale waved her hand to encompass Dean, Brandon and the rest. "First, you have to understand everything Dr. Byrd said is true. Megan is fragile right now. I won't have you making things any rougher for her than they already are."

Heath's mask cracked a little, some of his pain seeping through before he caught it. "I swear to God I won't. All I want to do is see her, to tell her..." His voice faded. A minute later, he said, "I'm just going to hang around here tonight, and then I can see her first thing in the morning."

For the first time since Heath came into the room, Dean came forward. Of all the Nashes, Dillon always thought of Dean as the quiet one, soft-spoken to the core. Circumstances being what they were, that no longer applied.

Dean's growl was low and menacing. "Go home, boy."

Heath stood his ground. "No, sir. Megan needs me. I—"

"Megan needed you when she found out she was pregnant. She needed you when she was sick, and scared, and alone. She needed you, and you let her down." When Heath tried to protest, Dean held up his hand. "What she needs now is to be surrounded by her family. She needs her mother, me, her brothers, and her sisters. Megan needs all the people who love her no matter what. You aren't one of those people, and that was your choice. Tomorrow you can come back, and if Megan says she'll see you, I won't try to stop it." Dean leaned in closer to Heath, his tone chilling in its quiet intensity. "I won't stop you from seeing her, but I swear by everything that's holy, if you hurt my daughter again, I'll make you wish you'd never been born. Do we understand each other?"

Heath didn't flinch. "Perfectly."

"Good. Come back tomorrow, then. And Heath?"

"Yes, sir?"

Dean crossed his arms over his chest. "You better start praying. Pray Megan is going to be all right and that she's suffered no permanent damage from this. Most of all, son, you better pray my daughter is more forgiving than I am."

Heath shook his head. "Start praying? Sir, I haven't done anything but pray since Dillon got that phone call." To Dillon's amazement, Heath left without saying another word.

Dillon followed Heath out to the parking garage while Jamie stayed behind and talked to Megan's family. He caught up with his brother outside as he was about to hail a cab. "Heath, damn it...wait a second."

Heath paused but didn't turn around. "I've got to get out of here. I'll...I'll catch you later, okay?"

"No, it's not okay." Dillon placed his hands on Heath's arm, forcing him to turn until they were facing. "We're family. Talk to me. Let me help you."

Heath's face was a study in misery, all the earlier control having deserted him. He shook his head. "You can't help me. I fucked up, and there isn't a damn thing you, me, or anyone else can do about it."

Dillon wanted to argue but Heath didn't give him a chance. "I have to leave. To think. To find a way to fix this."

"Come home with me and Jamie. We'll talk it out and see what we can come up with."

Heath wouldn't listen. He flagged down the next cab that came by and was gone before Dillon could stop him.

Dillon spent the rest of the night cuddled next to Jamie, thoughts of Megan and Heath boiling around in his brain. He slept in fifteen minute increments, worry and dread waking him at all hours. He finally gave up on sleep at about six the next morning, crawling out of bed and tucking the covers around Jamie's sleeping form.

Aunt Sadie had been sympathetic about the reason Jamie and Dillon hadn't finished helping her around the house the day before, but Dillon had a thing about finishing what he started. That, and he hoped a bit of manual labor would keep his mind off his brother and Megan.

He worked for about four hours solid, cleaning the gutters and clearing the drains. He'd just climbed down and was about to start on the other side of the house when Jamie came out of the apartment, fully dressed and carrying two twenty ounce bottles of Coke.

Jamie handed one of the Cokes to Dillon. "Here. I think you're gonna need the sugar rush."

Dillon groaned. "What is it now?"

"Heath just called. He's at the hospital."

Dillon braced himself, propping one foot on the lowest rung of the ladder. "Is Megan all right?"

"As far as I know she's doing about the same as she was yesterday, but Megan's health isn't the reason Heath called. She refuses to see him unless you're there to referee."

"Me? For God's sake, why?"

Jamie shrugged. "Heath wasn't sure, but Megan sent word through a nurse she'll only talk to Heath if you're there. In fact, she wants to see you first."

Dillon draped his arms over the rung of the ladder and laid his head in his hands. "Why do I always get dragged into this stuff?"

Jamie wrapped his arms around Dillon's waist from behind. "Some people are just lucky that way, I guess. Want me to come with you?"

Dillon shook his head without even lifting it from his hands. "No. There's no reason for both of us to go up there. I can suffer through this alone."

Jamie laughed. "You can keep on with the 'poor me' act all you want, but you and I both know you'd do anything to help Heath and Megan."

Dillon raised his head and turned in the circle of Jamie's arms, returning the embrace. "I'm glad to do anything I can, but I'm thinking Heath may have been right yesterday when he said there was nothing anyone could do to fix this."

"I'm not buying it. Look at everything that happened between me and you. We've been through hell and back so many times I've lost count, but we came out of it together. I have to believe Heath and Megan will make it, too."

Dillon wanted to believe that Jamie was right, but Dillon's optimism evaporated an hour later as he walked toward Megan's third floor hospital room and saw the look on his brother's face as he paced the hall just outside Megan's door.

Heath rushed to meet him. "Thank God you're here! She won't even talk to me, not unless she sees you first. She keeps sending messages through her nurse."

"Jamie told me."

Heath ran his hands over his face, his bloodshot eyes a stark contrast to his pale skin. He wore the same clothes he'd worn the day before, and his hands were shaking as he lowered them to his sides. "I need to see her. I have to tell her—"

Dillon got a good look at his brother's desperation. "What, Heath? What is it you need to tell her?"

"Never mind. Just tell her I need to see her. Please."

"I'll try, but Megan's not in the best of places right now. You know this little peace talk I'm about to give comes with no guarantees, right?"

"Understood. Just the fact that you're willing to help means a lot. Thanks."

Dillon nodded and went to Megan's door. He tapped on the plywood. "Megan? It's Dillon. Can I come in?" At Megan's hoarse but clear, "Yes," Dillon swung the door open and stepped inside.

Megan's skin was sallow against the sickly green hospital gown she wore. Someone — probably a nurse — had washed her hair and then braided it wet so it hung in one damp red stream over her shoulder. She looked young and helpless as she reclined against the pillows in the big hospital bed, and Dillon had to force himself not to run to her and gather her into his arms.

He settled for a cautious hug, carefully squeezing her shoulders while avoiding her tender midsection. He pulled back and plastered on a smile. "How's my best girl?"

Megan's eyes crinkled slightly at the corners, but that's as close as she came to returning the smile. "I'm doing all right. Dr. Byrd says I can probably go home tomorrow."

"That's great. Before you know it, you'll be feeling like your old self again." Megan nodded but they both knew it was a lie. They went with the pretense anyway.

Dillon sat down in one of the chairs beside the bed. "So, where is everybody? I expected the room and hallway to be covered in wall to wall Nashes."

Megan gave a ghost of a grin. "I sent them all home, one — because they were exhausted, and two — because I knew Heath was coming and I didn't want any bloodshed. Mama and Daddy stayed all night and a good chunk of the morning, and so did Brandon and Nate. Keith is here somewhere, working his regular shift. He's popped in a couple of times, but I finally convinced him I wanted to catch some sleep. The rest of the family has taken turns coming by, and poor Ash has been here like three times this morning already." She leaned back against the pillows and sighed. "I made them all go home about ten o'clock this morning. Convinced them I needed time alone to think."

"I bet they put up a fuss."

"You know it. The only one who really understood was Mama. She lost a baby in between Wayne and Keith. She knows how it...how it hurts."

The aching loss in Megan's voice made Dillon's eyes sting. He blinked rapidly until he had himself under control. Desperate to offer comfort, he said the only thing he could think of. "I'm sorry. About the baby, I mean. I know how much you wanted it."

"Dr. Byrd said it was no one's fault, just one of those freak accidents of nature that happens for no good reason. I know better, though." Megan bit her lip and turned her head, facing away from him for a minute. "I know my baby died because I wasn't strong enough to hold on to him."

Dillon couldn't believe what he was hearing. "How can you say that? You're one of the strongest, bravest people I know. You can't possibly believe this is your fault."

Megan continued to stare at the wall. "I don't know what I believe. Not anymore. All I know is a couple of months ago, I was in love with an amazing guy who I thought loved me, too. Now I've lost him and the only thing I had of him, the baby we made together." She turned her tear-soaked face back to Dillon. "I feel like I've lost everything."

Dillon grabbed three tissues from the nightstand, leaned forward and dried Megan's eyes as best he could. "My brother was an idiot. None of this is your fault."

"I chased him away."

"Megan, no! Listen, honey. You've got it all wrong."

Megan wasn't hearing him. "Is Heath still out there?"

"Yeah, but I'm not sure you need to see him right now, not until you stop blaming yourself for his mistakes."

Megan shook her head. "I want to put an end to this part of my life. When I leave Reed, I want to leave knowing Heath and I at least had some form of closure, whatever that is."

Alarm bells rang in Dillon's head. "What do you mean, 'when you leave Reed'. You mean for college?" When she nodded, Dillon said, "That's not until September. You've got almost four months until then. Give yourself some time. There's no need to rush this."

"I'm leaving right after graduation. I've already been accepted and registered for the fall semester at Michigan State, Brandon's alma mater. With any luck I'll be able to find a nice off-campus apartment and sign on for a few summer courses."

Dillon wanted to argue with her, but he could tell by the glint in her eyes it would be useless. If he couldn't change her mind, the least he could do was be supportive. He took her hand. "What can I do to help you through this?"

Megan laced her fingers with his and held on tight. "Just stay with me while I talk to Heath. I don't trust myself to be alone with him, and no one else understands him the way you do. My family would just as soon beat the crap out of him now and ask questions later."

"I'll be here, but I gotta tell you, I've had the urge to beat him senseless a time or two myself."

"I understand. Just..." Megan took a deep breath, "just ask him to come in here, please."

Dillon knew that there was no way this meeting was going to bring Megan closure. Megan and Heath owned a part of each other, just as he and Jamie did. And just like him and Jamie, they probably always would.

Dillon found his brother where he'd left him, pacing in front of Megan's door. "Megan wants to see you, but before you go in there's something you should know."

Heath was almost too eager to see Megan to listen, but Dillon's somber tone got through to him. "What is it?"

"Megan blames herself for everything from the break-up to losing the baby."

Heath flinched. "How could she possibly think any of this was her fault?"

"I don't know, but she does."

Heath swore. "I'll make her see I'm the only one responsible."

Dillon tried to reason with him, but Heath was every bit as stubborn as Megan. He swung open the door and walked into Megan's room, Dillon on his heels.

Megan was lying in the same position, the bed covers clutched around her like a shield. "Hello, Heath."

Heath swallowed so hard, Dillon could hear it. "Hi, honey. How are you feeling?"

"Okay, I guess. The doctor says I'm healing. No sign of infection near my incision, and my vital signs are good, whatever that means."

"That's great, Meggie. I... Oh, hell. I was never good at polite conversation." He moved forward and stood beside the bed. "Baby, I'm so damned sorry for this. For leaving you like I did, for the miscarriage. All of it."

Megan held herself with such brittle control, Dillon thought she might shatter. "It wasn't your fault, especially not the miscarriage. According to Dr. Byrd, that would have happened no matter what."

Heath sank down in the chair beside the bed while Dillon stood on Megan's other side. "Maybe so, but I should have been there to see you through it."

"Why? You didn't even believe there *was* a baby."

"Honey, you have to let me explain. See, there was this girl a few years back. When things started cooling off between us, she lied about being pregnant to trap me into something I wasn't ready for."

"And you thought I'd done the same thing?" Megan closed her eyes. "You must not think very highly of me to believe I could do something like that. Is that why you dumped me, because I was so unworthy of your love and trust?"

"No! Damn it, Megan, I'm trying to tell you that you didn't do anything wrong. I'm the one who fucked up. I care about you, baby. I didn't even realize how much until I found out you were in the hospital."

Megan opened her eyes and Dillon was shocked to see they were hollow and empty. Heath tried to take her hand but Megan pulled away. "Nothing's changed."

"You're wrong. We've been given a second chance. We can start over, do this thing right. I'll treat you the way I should have in the beginning, show you the respect you deserve." His voice dropped to a low murmur. "And I won't rush you into bed this time. I'll be careful with you, angel. No more babies until we're both ready."

"There won't be any babies for me. Not now, and probably not ever."

"I know you feel that way right now, but in time, you'll change your mind."

Megan's small hands knotted into fists as she clutched the rough blanket. "You don't get it. When Dr. Byrd went in to fix the damage caused by the ectopic pregnancy, he had to remove one of my tubes. That cuts my chances of getting pregnant again in half."

Heath wasn't giving in. "Fifty-fifty isn't so bad. When the time comes—"

"Let me finish." Megan's face was turning red and her breathing was shallow. "I have scar tissue left behind from the surgery, but they won't know how bad it is until my wounds heal. It could very well thicken, maybe even block my uterus and my other tube. According to Dr. Byrd, I have less than a thirty percent chance of getting pregnant without more surgery or some type of assisted reproduction technique."

"We'll cross that bridge when we come to it. We have plenty of time."

"You're the one who's not listening. We're out of time. It's too late for us."

Heath didn't budge. "I refuse to believe that; I don't think you really believe it either. You're letting your anger and grief do the talking."

Megan's face contorted with some of that anger Heath had just mentioned. "What would you know about my grief? I'm the one who lost the baby."

"It was my baby, too. You're not the only one who's suffering."

It was the wrong thing to say. Heath must have seen the fire gathering in Megan's eyes because he moved back a little as she sat up and unleashed all the pain and loathing she'd been carrying inside.

"What are you trying to say? That you're all torn up over the death of a baby you didn't even think existed? Bullshit. You're glad it's dead. Glad to be rid of it. Of me."

"That's a lie."

"Yeah, well, you know all about lies, don't you? All those times you pretended to care for me just so you could get laid. All the sweet words you're spewing out now. You feel guilty because you didn't believe me, and now you're trying to make up for it by acting like you have real feelings for me."

Heath stood and leaned over the railing of the bed. "I never pretended to care about you; I didn't have to. I've always had feelings for you. I-I..."

Dillon willed him to say the words. *Tell her you love her, Heath. Don't blow it now.*

Telepathy didn't work. Heath balked, and Megan clenched her jaw as she confronted the truth as she saw it.

"What are you trying to say? That you love me? Is that it? 'Cause if it is, you look more like a man who's just had a root canal without anesthesia than a man who's about to declare his undying love."

Heath clutched the plastic rails so hard they creaked. "I don't know anything about love. Hell, I'm not even sure it exists, not the kind of love people are always spouting off about." He leaned down to better see her face. "That doesn't mean you and I can't have something special. I'm sure as hell willing to try. We had fun together, remember? We can again."

Dillon bit back a groan as he watched Heath's words wash over Megan's rigid body. He was proud of her self-control. He could only guess what it was costing her.

"Fun, huh? As in the 'no-strings-attached' version of fun we had before?" She waved her hands over herself. "Look at me, Heath. Do I look like I'm having fun? When I told you I loved you and you ran out on me, was I having fun then? When I told you I was pregnant and you called me a rotten liar, was that the fun part? No wait. I've got it. The fun part must have been yesterday at the theater when I almost died trying to hold on to my baby, the one thing I wanted above anything else and will probably never have now." Her eyes were shiny with unshed tears, but she held herself together. "Thanks for the offer, but no thanks. As much as I hate myself right now, even I know I deserve to be more than some guy's fuck buddy."

"Damn it, you're more to me than that."

Megan shook her head. "Just get out. Go away and leave me in peace."

Heath started to refuse, but Dillon stepped in. "You heard her. She's had enough."

Heath thought it over for a tense minute before giving in. "Fine, I'll go. But I'll be back, Megan. This isn't over. Not by a long shot."

Megan's lip trembled. "Over? How can it be over when it never even started?"

Heath stormed out of the room with his usual flare, but this time, Dillon didn't bother to go after him. Leaving his brother to whatever demons he faced, Dillon lowered the side rail on Megan's bed. He sat down beside her and did the only thing he could — gathered her into his arms and held her while the rest of her world fell apart.

Chapter Twenty-Two

Jamie watched Dillon struggle with his tie for another minute before taking over. "Let me do that. We'll never make it on time if we wait for you to get it right." Jamie's fingers wove a practiced pattern of loops and knots over the silk cloth, coercing the tie into a perfect bow.

Dillon stepped back to survey the reflection of Jamie's handiwork in the dresser mirror. "Next time I have to wear one of these stupid tuxes, I swear I'm gonna get a clip-on tie. Where did you learn to do that, by the way?"

Jamie shrugged and grabbed his tux jacket from the edge of the bed. "Aunt Sadie taught me." His voice a near perfect imitation of Sadie's refined speech, he quoted, "'Every decent gentleman should know the fine art of tie tying, Jamie.'" He laughed. "Only took me sixteen years to get the hang of it." He pulled his coat on and smoothed it out. "You look awful damn good in that 'stupid tux', you know. You should wear one more often."

Dillon adjusted his cummerbund. "You look pretty damn fine yourself. For the rent these things are costing us, we ought to look good." He reached for his comb. "Tell me again why we have to do this."

Jamie laughed. "Because you were dumb enough to get yourself elected student council vice president, and there's a good chance the president won't show. You could be hosting the prom all by your lonesome. Principal Ardsley only explained it like five times yesterday when he called."

"I know, I know. Doesn't mean I have to like it. I hope Megan changes her mind and comes tonight. Not just because I don't want to give a speech, either. It's been two weeks since she lost the baby. I know that she's going to be grieving for a long while, but it's time she tried to get out more, started seeing her friends again." He sighed. "At least no one at school knows the real reason she's been absent. They all think she's had some kind of late season flu."

"Heck of a bright side. Have you talked to her today?"

Dillon shook his head. "I talked to Gale early this morning. She said Dr. Byrd has okayed Megan's going to the prom as long as she doesn't overdo it. Megan keeps saying she isn't ready yet."

"She didn't look so hot when we went to see her the day before yesterday. Maybe she's telling the truth. And she was rock solid about not going to the prom then. No reason to think she'd have changed her mind in two days."

Dillon gave up on his hair and went to work fastening his cuffs. "A guy can hope. At least it looks like Heath has finally gotten it through that thick skull of his that Megan doesn't want to see him. Gale says he hasn't called Megan in four days."

"Have you talked to him about it?"

"Not really. I went by the firehouse to check on him yesterday afternoon when I picked up our tuxes. He looks bad, but he won't say anything about Megan except that she needs time, and he's going to give it to her. I guess that's why he hasn't called her. Whatever the reason, Gale said Megan's relieved to have some of the pressure off." Dillon pulled his coat from the hanger on the back of the closet doorknob. "You ready to go, sexy thang?"

Jamie grinned. "I'll go, but only if you promise to bring me home and violate me afterwards."

Dillon reached for his hand. "Count on it."

They had opted not to spend the five hundred dollars on a limo, even though Sadie offered to pay for it. Dillon's reasoning was that five hundred dollars would buy enough used books to see them through the first semester of college. Jamie agreed, but he had his own reasons for not wanting the limo. He wanted them to take Ben's Firebird. A final tribute to Ben at the last dance of their high school years seemed fitting.

Jamie had been to the Amory Hotel a few times in his life, but the sheer size of the place always surprised him. As Reed's only luxury hotel, the Amory served as the prime location for everything from parties, proms, and business conventions, to a haven for folks visiting Chicago and wanting to stay somewhere close by yet out of the hustle and grind of the big city. For many, the real attraction of the Amory was the rooftop gardens. Jamie had only been up there once, when he was just a kid, but even then he'd been impressed.

Even though they were a good half-hour early, the main ballroom was packed when Dillon and Jamie got there. They had just enough time to pose for a cheesy picture set against a backdrop of Mylar balloons and crepe paper flowers before Principal Ardsley claimed Dillon for a pre-prom, student council conference. Jamie wandered to the other side of the room, helping himself to a glass of punch while he watched his classmates make fools of themselves on the dance floor.

Rooster Carmichael was there, along with his cronies and their dates, the lot of them turning circles around the dance floor in one big, rhythmic heap. Jamie even saw Chad Minton dancing with his date not far from where Rooster and the others gyrated. The thing that caught Jamie's attention above anything else, though, was the music. He wasn't sure where the student council had dug up the D.J. they'd hired, but if the guy didn't play something besides crappy ballads and tired dance mixes, soon, Jamie's ears were going to start bleeding.

A hand clamped down on his shoulder and a familiar voice said, "I wish I'd brought my *Butthole Surfers* CD. We could show them what real music sounds like."

Jamie turned with a grin. "What are you doing here, man? I thought you'd given up on good ol' Plunkett High."

Ash laughed. "I did, but since I've completed all the credits I need to graduate, I still have prom eligibility." He tugged at his highly starched collar. "Proms aren't really my scene, but when the prettiest girl in school agreed to be my date, even a reformed dickhead such as myself had sense enough to jump at the chance."

Jamie raised a brow. "Prettiest girl in school, huh?" He looked behind Ash but didn't see anybody. "So, where is this vision of loveliness?"

"Right there." Ash pointed to the stage where Megan was making her way to the mic and preparing for her welcome speech.

Jamie had to admit, Ash had been dead on in his description of Megan as the prettiest girl in school. She wore a gown of pale green silk that hugged her slender figure and accentuated every gentle curve. Her hair was bound up in spirals on top of head, soft curls framing her face. The most amazing thing, though, was the change in Megan's eyes. They were a bright, sparkling blue again, not the dull, lackluster color they'd been the last time he'd seen her. Jamie wasn't sure what had happened or how Ash had convinced her to come, but he felt like hugging the guy for his efforts. He settled for slapping him on the back instead.

Dillon joined them as the houselights dimmed and the spotlight fell on Megan. "Damn, she looks good. How'd you get her here, Barnes? This morning she wanted nothing to do with the prom."

Ash shrugged. "It was no big deal. She already had her dress. Did you know women buy those things, like, months in advance? Anyway, I went over to her house about three o'clock this afternoon, grabbed her dress out of the closet and told her either she put it on willingly, or I was going to strip her down and dress her in it myself."

Dillon didn't bother to hide how funny he thought that was. "Bet she went ballistic."

"You know it. She started hollering for Gale, begging her to make me go away. Cussed me up one side and down the other."

Having tasted Megan's temper once or twice, Jamie could believe it. "What did Gale say?"

Ash smiled. "She's really the one who convinced Megan to come. Gale told Megan she'd help me stuff her into that dress."

Dillon nodded. "Sounds like something Gale would say."

"Yep. It was more than that, though. Gale let Megan spit and sputter for a while, and then she sat down on the edge of the bed, took her hand, and told Megan it was time to get on with the business of living."

"And she was right." The three of them turned to see Megan standing behind them. They'd been so busy talking they hadn't noticed she'd finished her speech and exited the stage.

She didn't seem to mind being the topic of discussion. She greeted Jamie and Dillon with a tight but cautious hug and squeezed Ash's hand.

"My mom pointed out it was time for me to rejoin the human race. My baby might be gone, but I'm still here." Her face darkened, but only for a second. "Throwing my life away is not going to honor my child."

Dillon slipped an arm around her shoulders and pulled her close. "Your mom's one smart bird, you know that?" He hesitated. "What are you gonna do about Heath?"

"Nothing. At least not right now. I'm not ready to face Heath just yet." She sighed. "Who knows? I may not ever be ready to deal with him. There's one thing I do know and that's I have to focus on getting myself well before I can worry about anything else."

Dillon gave her a squeeze. "Sounds like a plan. By the way, you saved my ass from having to make a speech. I think I owe you a dance for that."

Megan lowered her voice to a loud whisper, using just enough volume to be clearly heard over the music. "What will your date say?"

Dillon's eyes twinkled. "Who? Him?" He winked at Jamie. "He knows better than to argue. I wear the pants in our family."

Jamie couldn't resist. "Oh, yeah? That's not what you said last night when I had you flat on your back with my d—"

Megan clapped her hands over her ears. "Whoa. Way too much information, boys." She grabbed Dillon by the hand and tugged him toward the dance floor. "One dance, coming up."

Megan's return — battered and bruised though she was — made Jamie feel like the four of them had reached a turning point. Surely the worst was behind them. What they had to do now was put their lives back together and move forward.

They took turns dancing: Megan with each one of her boys, as she called them, Jamie with Dillon, even Jamie and Ash. The only two of them who didn't take a turn on the floor together were Ash and Dillon. Dillon said it was bad for his image; Ash told Dillon he should be so lucky. Between the dancing and the friendly jibes, Jamie was starting to feel positively relaxed.

Halfway through the evening, Principal Ardsley called a halt to the dancing, asking students to take a seat while he announced the prom king and queen. Jamie and Dillon took one side of a table for four not far from the stage, with Megan and Ash taking the other two chairs. Since votes for prom queen were student based, Jamie wasn't surprised when Megan's name was called. Megan, however, was stunned.

"Prom Queen? Me?"

Dillon snorted. "That one was a no-brainer. First, Homecoming Queen, then voted Girl Most Likely to Succeed. Not to mention Student Council president. Hell, I'd have been shocked if you hadn't made Prom Queen."

Megan stood and smoothed out her gown. "Yeah, yeah. Just remember, Mr. Student Council V.P., that works both ways." She patted his head and went on stage.

Dillon didn't know what she was talking about until his own name was called. "Damn. Prom King?"

"Like Megan said, boyfriend-o-mine, it works both ways." Jamie nudged him. "Go ahead, your majesty. Claim thy queen."

Dillon gave him a dirty look but did as he was told. After he left, Ash said, "Hey, Jamie, do you think maybe we could talk?"

"Sure, man. Shoot." Just as he said it, the music started for Dillon and Megan's first dance as king and queen.

Ash had to strain his damaged voice to be heard over the blaring love song. "Not here. Do you think Carver would mind if we took a walk?"

"Nah. He and Megan will be busy with their royal duties for no telling how long." Jamie stood. "Lead the way."

Ash got up, heading towards the exit at the back of the ballroom where the elevators were. "Ever seen the rooftop gardens?"

"Once, when Aunt Sadie dragged me to some tea or luncheon she was invited to. That was years ago, though."

Ash stopped at the first free elevator and punched the call button. "My dad entertains clients here sometimes. Me and the mom-of-the-month have to put in an appearance — family unity and all that crap — but after a few minutes of playing the good son, I'm allowed to cut out on my own. I always seem to end up in the gardens. They're something to see." He stepped in and held the elevator doors open for Jamie. Pressing the twelfth floor button, he waited until the doors closed again. "Would it bother you if we talked about Ben?"

Jamie had already guessed that was what Ash wanted to talk about when he'd asked to go someplace private. Once, Jamie would have found it too painful, but not now. With Dillon's help, the wounds were healing. "It doesn't bother me. I think it's only right, in a way. Since Ben can't be here tonight, the least we can do is keep his memory alive."

The elevator stopped and the doors opened. "I kind of feel the same way. Ben may not have had any real feelings for me, but I cared about him. That's got to count for something." Ash stepped out of the elevator, leaving Jamie to follow.

The Amory's rooftop gardens were even more spectacular than Jamie remembered. Pale moonlight and old-fashioned street lamps illuminated a forest of fresh smelling spring greens. How they got grass and small trees to grow on a roof, Jamie wasn't sure, but the overall effect was amazing. The outer edges of the roof were railed by ornate, wrought-iron fencing, while hidden alcoves and arbors offered privacy and an incredible view of the gardens themselves. Jamie could see why Ash was so drawn to the place.

Ash steered him to a rose arbor not far from the northern edge of the roof. Jamie took the bench on the side facing out, giving Ash the side overlooking the gardens. Though a few other people — mostly couples — strolled along the pathways and sidewalks, Ash and Jamie were partially hidden from view by the rose bushes.

Ash was quiet for a minute, resting his elbows on his knees. Finally he said, "Thanks for coming up here with me. I guess I needed to clear my head."

"Are you okay? This is your first school gig since you tried to...uh—"

Ash laughed, and there was no bitterness or self-recrimination in the sound. "Since I tried to off myself, you mean? It's okay. You can say it." He sighed. "I'll never get over what happened, not completely, but I've come to terms with it. As far as being here tonight goes, I really thought it would be more awkward than it has been. There probably isn't a person at that prom who doesn't know I tried to kill myself, but everybody's treated me the same as they always have." He made a face. "Well, almost everybody."

"Is somebody hassling you?"

"Nah. Not exactly. It's just...you know Chad and I used to be really close, right?"

"Yeah. It was weird to ever see one of you without the other."

"We were like brothers. At least, I thought we were. Ever since he found out about me and Ben, Chad's treated me like some kind of leper."

Jamie knew that feeling, and he knew how much it hurt. "I remember you telling us about how he freaked that day at the hospital. I'd hoped maybe the two of you had patched things up."

Ash shook his head. "I wish. Every time I try to talk to him, he pushes me away. Even tonight, when Megan and I first got here, I tried to say hi. That's it, just hi. He looked at me like I had something hanging out of my nose, grabbed his date, and walked away."

"Ouch. Sorry, man." Jamie fidgeted with one of his shirt buttons. "The thing is, I never could understand what you saw in the guy. He's always seemed a little, I dunno, weird."

Jamie was afraid he'd pissed Ash off with his statement about Chad, but Ash just shrugged. "My dad always said Chad was using me because we have money and he and his folks don't, but I never felt that way. He was my friend, and I didn't give a rat's ass what he did or didn't have." His face fell. "That's all over with now." Straightening, he said, "Enough of this self-pity shit. We came up here to remember Ben. Let's get on with it."

Jamie laughed. "You make it sound like we're having a wake for him or something. All we need now is some good whiskey and some sad music."

Ash winced. "Don't even mention whiskey. I drank so much of my dad's bourbon the night of Ben's memorial, I can still taste the stuff." He shuddered. "I don't know what I thought I was doing at the church that night."

"Saying goodbye to the man you loved?"

"Maybe. It was more than that, I think. It's like I couldn't stay away, you know? Like I had to be there."

"You lied! You said your dad made you go to Lewis's memorial. All this time, you wanted to be there. God, I'm so stupid."

The anger in Chad Minton's voice startled Jamie. He turned his head to see Chad standing behind them, his jaw clenched, his feet spread apart like he was gearing for a fight. Unless Jamie was mistaken, he'd been hiding behind an overgrown part of the arbor, listening.

If Jamie was startled, Ash was in total shock. "Jesus, Chad. You scared the hell out of me. Were you...were you spying on us?"

"All that talk about your father making you go to Lewis's service was just another one of your lies." Chad kept talking as if he hadn't heard the question.

Ash blinked. "I was hurting. I needed to find a way to be close to Ben, to say goodbye, but I wasn't ready to talk about my relationship with him. Making up that excuse about my dad forcing me to go to the church seemed like a plan at the time." He frowned and then stood. "What do you mean, 'just another one of my lies'? You and me, we were tight. I never lied to you."

"Oh no, you didn't lie. You just went out every weekend with me, fucking girls and pretending like you weren't a total fag. What in the hell do you call that, if it isn't lying?"

Ash was shaking. Jamie stood, flanking Ash's left side, ready to back him if needed. In spite of the shaking, though, Ash was holding his own.

"Like I tried to tell you at the hospital, I'm bisexual. Just in case that word is too big for you, I'll break it down. I'm into girls and guys, not that it's any of your business. So what if I didn't take out a full-page ad in the Reed Daily Courier telling the whole world I swing both ways? Doesn't mean I lied about it. Judging from your reaction, it's a good thing I didn't tell you. You only would have hated me sooner."

Chad's head whipped back like he'd been punched. "Hate you? Are you serious?" He slipped two fingers between his neck and collar, pulling hard. Wrenching his hand free, he said, "I worshiped the ground you walked on. You were my hero. I'd have done anything to protect you. I wanted to *be* you, damn it."

"I'm no hero, yours or anyone else's." Ash turned his head. "Come on, Jamie. Let's get out of here. I don't feel like talking anymore."

As they walked past, Chad grabbed Ash's arm, spinning them both so that Ash was facing Chad and the railing beyond. "You may not feel like talking, but you're damn well gonna listen to me. You owe me that much."

A dull red flush crept up Ash's face. "I don't owe you shit."

"The hell you don't. What about all those nights you blew me off so you could sneak down to that old foreman's house and fuck Lewis's brains out? Me, the guy who would do anything for you. *Anything.* And you just tossed me aside like I was nothing."

Jamie's head started to spin. "How did you know about the foreman's house?"

Chad's eyes whirled to Jamie like he'd only just realized Jamie was there. "What the hell are you talking about, Walker? And where's your boyfriend? What's the matter, got tired of Carver so you thought you'd give Ash a try?"

Jamie refused to take the bait. "How did you know Ben and Ash used to meet down at the foreman's house?"

For a minute, Chad froze, then his eyes narrowed on Ash. "You'd be surprised what I know."

"Only a handful of people know that Ben and I used to meet there, and not a single one of them would have talked to you about it. There's no way you could have known, unless..." Ash trailed off as his eyes fastened to the spot behind the arbor where Chad had been hiding. "Oh, God! You followed me out there." The fury in his voice was frightening. "What did you do, watch us through the windows? Did you get your rocks off, you sick son-of-a-bitch?"

"You think I liked watching that? God, Ash...don't you see? I was trying to protect you. I knew there was no way you'd have willingly fucked around with a lowlife like Lewis. I knew he must have had some kind of hold over you. I was trying to figure out what that hold was so I could break it. The dirty bastard was using you, can't you see that?"

Jamie took a step toward Chad. "Watch your mouth, Minton. No way in hell am I gonna let you stand there and insult Ben."

"How can you defend him? You and Carver act like you care so much about Ash. Well, where the hell were you when Lewis was jacking Ash's dad for twenty thousand dollars hush money?"

268 ❖ Sara Bell

Jamie's blood turned to ice, but it was Ash who spoke. "How did you know about that?"

Chad tried to back up, but there was nowhere for him to go. He was almost against the railing as it was. Ash grabbed the lapels of Chad's jacket. "Answer me, damn it! How did you know about the blackmail?"

By then a small crowd of prom-goers and hotel guests had gathered to watch the show, but Ash didn't seem to care. His entire being was focused on getting the answers out of Chad, one way or another.

Chad seemed oblivious to the onlookers, as well. He shrank back as much as he could within Ash's grasp, but he wasn't giving up on the devoted friend routine. "Weren't you listening to me? You were my best friend. It was my job to protect you. Your father sure as hell didn't."

Ash let go of Chad's coat and stepped back, closing his eyes. "My father. That's it. You were spying on him too, weren't you? What did you do, go through his things?"

Chad took a step toward Ash. "You make it sound like I'm some kind of thieving sneak."

Jamie curled his lips. "You trying to say you aren't?"

"No!" Chad waited until Ash opened his eyes. "Look, Ash...the day after I found you and Lewis together at the old mill, I went to see your father down at his office. I thought if he knew what was going on, he might be able to stop it." He snorted. "Lot of good that did me. Your old man already knew you and Lewis were sleeping together. Told me it was your life and you had to live it as you saw fit, or something like that." He spat on the ground. "The bastard made it sound like you were in a relationship with Lewis, that you wanted it that way. But I knew better. I knew you'd never fag out on me, not for real. I could also tell by the way your dad was putting me off that he was hiding something. So, I did what I had to do."

"What the hell does that mean?"

"I'll tell you," Chad hedged, "but only because then you'll see what a good friend I am. Then we can go back to the way we were."

"For God's sake, just tell me what you did."

"I...I figured your dad wouldn't keep anything personal at his office, so I went through his study until I found what I was looking for. He's never home, so it wasn't like I had to worry about him catching me."

"You raided our house? When?"

Chad swallowed hard, but he was determined to prove himself. "Saturday, the day after the dance. Remember, I came over, and you were all upset but you wouldn't tell me why."

Ash squeezed his hands into tight fists. "Ben had broken up with me. I'd been up all night, drinking and crying in my beer." Understanding dawned. "You waited until I passed out, then broke into my dad's files."

Chad took offense. "It isn't like I had to pick the locks or jimmy the hinges. The combination to your father's filing cabinet is the same as your birthday. I figured that out years ago. I thought sure he knew something about Ben, something he wasn't telling me. Turns out I was right."

Ash was speechless, but Jamie wasn't. "You found the pictures, didn't you?"

"That and a whole lot more. Mr. Barnes had a whole file on Lewis, including his demands for money and the actual payoffs that were made. It was clear Mr. Barnes wasn't going to do anything. It was up to me to fix it."

Suddenly Jamie knew. "You killed him. You killed Ben."

Ash snapped out of his trance. He looked at Chad like he was a stranger. Chad saw it too. He panicked. "No, no, I didn't! He was hit by that drunk, remember? Everyone knows that."

"You're lying." Ash's voice came out in a broken rasp. "You killed him, then dragged him out into the middle of the road and left him there."

"It wasn't like that." Chad had tears in his eyes. "I only wanted to talk to him, to convince him to leave you alone and stop blackmailing you. I went to Nora Slater's house late that night, after I knew Nora would be asleep. I just wanted to see if I could reason with Lewis, but he was leaving just as I got there."

Jamie tried his best to keep his tone even. "So you followed Ben just like you followed Ash?"

"Yes. No." He was getting frustrated. "You're twisting it. I followed him, but only because I thought he was going to meet Ash. Then, when he turned onto Tully Road instead of taking the road out to the mill, I knew something else was going on. I thought maybe he was banging someone else."

"And you wanted to find out who so you could run back and tell Ash. How'd you tail him without getting caught?"

"It wasn't hard." Desperate as he was, Chad sounded almost proud of himself. "Tully Road is full of hills and side roads. The roads were clear, so I could see that flashy car of his even from a half-mile away. I watched him pull over onto the shoulder, and then I turned off on a dirt road a good distance away. Lewis probably thought I was just some drunk heading home. I got out and walked the rest of the way up to where Lewis was parked, keeping myself hidden by walking in the tree line. I saw Lewis talking to Mr. Morgan, saw him open the trunk of his car and hand something to the guy, but I wasn't sure what it was.

Morgan left first, but Ben was still fooling around with whatever was in the trunk when I popped out of the trees and confronted him."

Ash had gone from purple to green. Jamie could tell he was feeling sick, but he managed to keep Chad talking. "You fought with him."

"Yeah." Chad was so keyed up, so intent on getting through to Ash, he didn't seem to notice he was confessing to a roof full of witnesses. "I didn't set out to, but the guy made me so mad. The things he said... You have no idea, Ash. I told Lewis to keep away from you, asked him to give me the pictures and leave you alone. That's when he told me to go to hell. And then he said...he said..."

"He said what, Chad? What did Ben say that made you kill him?"

"Shut up, Walker! I told you, it wasn't like that." He cast pleading eyes on his former best friend. "Lewis was using you Ash — hurting you — and the asshole had the nerve to try and turn it around on me. He called me a sponge, said I only hung around you to make myself look better. Lewis said without you, I was nothing. Claimed you made me what I am, that I would be a nobody as far as the rest of the school was concerned if you turned your back on me. Then he said he was going to talk to you, Ash, tell you I was a spy. He said by the time he was through, you'd never speak to me again. It would have been over between us."

Jamie knew, with those words, Ben had hit on Chad's worst fears. Chad, who came from nothing, counted on Ash, the golden boy, to keep him afloat, to define him even. Ben was the one person standing between Chad and the center of his universe. For that alone, Ben had been sentenced to death.

Jamie took a deep breath. "You grabbed the jack handle out of Ben's trunk and hit him with it."

"I wasn't trying to kill him." Chad's eyes darted crazily back and forth between Jamie and Ash. "I only wanted to make him go away, leave us alone. I picked up the jack handle, but only to threaten him with it. Lewis freaked, and he rushed me. I swung without thinking about it and knocked him over the head." The tears started to fall. "He kept coming at me, kept trying to fight back. And I kept hitting him, over and over, until he wasn't moving anymore."

Ash sank to his knees and started to retch. Jamie wanted to go to him, but he couldn't. He had to finish it. "So you dragged Ben's body out into the middle of the road and then slashed his tire to make it look like he'd been changing a flat."

Head down, Chad nodded. "I started to throw his jack handle back into the trunk, but there was blood all over it. I had just enough time to run back to my car and switch Lewis's handle with mine before that drunk guy came barreling down the road. He made it so easy, didn't even try to stop. He hit Lewis and then took off in one direction while I ran back to my car and drove in the other."

Ash looked up from where he was kneeling on the grass. "You left him there like a piece of roadkill."

Chad was sobbing. "I thought that would fix it. With Lewis gone, you and me, we should have been okay. But you were different. You acted like you missed the bastard. I took hope from the fact that you said your father was making you go to that stupid memorial service, but deep down I knew it was a lie. You wanted Lewis more than you wanted anything or anyone, even me. You wanted him enough to die for him, with him. I was so damn scared when I heard you'd tried to kill yourself. I rushed to the hospital, only to hear you say you were bisexual. That's when I knew for sure. No matter what Lewis had done to you, you were in love with the guy. I'd killed him for nothing." He struggled for breath and swiped at the tears rolling down his face. "I thought if I got away from you, pretended I was mad about you being a fag, that the distance between us would make you see how much you needed me, how important I am to your life." His anguish rose. "You went on without me, damn you. You picked up the pieces of your life and came out better for it. You came out on top and I'm right where I started, at the bottom." He moved back so he was gripping one of the iron pickets on top of the guardrail. "You have it all, and I've got nothing left."

In that instant, Jamie knew that there would be no trial for Chad Minton, no day of reckoning in front of a jury of his peers. Even before Chad took the three steps needed to climb over the top of the railing, Jamie could see it: Chad Minton had come full circle. For one shining moment, he'd been in the sun, catching the rays Ash reflected his way. From bottom to top was one thing, but going back down again wasn't an option.

Jamie reached out his hand to grab Chad, to stop him from going down the one road from which he could never come back. He caught a handful of Chad's coat, the fabric ripping as Chad freed himself from the last of his bonds.

Chapter Twenty-Three

Jamie placed one final box on top of the stack in the back of the U-Haul and moved aside so Ash could close the door. "Is that everything?"

"Last box." Jamie wiped the sweat out of his eyes, not that it did any good. The late August sun was relentless, especially at three o'clock in the afternoon. He couldn't wait to get back inside the air-conditioned apartment. But first, thanks were in order. "I appreciate you coming over here and helping me load all this up. Dillon wanted me to wait until he got back, but I hate packing. I figure it's better just to get it over with." When Ash nodded his agreement, Jamie said, "I still can't believe your dad is doing this. I can't believe he bought and furnished a house near Garman just so the three of us wouldn't have to live in the dorms."

Ash grinned and shrugged back into the t-shirt he'd shed while they were loading the truck. "I can. You know my dad. He's still pissed you wouldn't keep that money Ben left you. You should have known he'd find a way to pay you back. He feels like he owes you for all you've done for me. Hell, I wouldn't even be here if it weren't for you." His face fell. "Not to mention the way you helped me when Chad... You know."

Jamie nodded. "How are you doing with that?"

Ash sighed. "I still can't believe he's gone, even though it's been over three months. Despite everything he did, I think a part of me will always miss Chad."

"He was a big part of your life. Watching a guy kill himself isn't something you just get over."

"I know. I'm glad you and Dillon didn't have my death to add to the shit you've already been through. Where did you say Dillon is?"

"Saying goodbye to Heath."

Ash leaned against the back of the truck. "Heath's not coming to the going away party your aunt's throwing for you guys tonight?"

"Nope."

"Not that I'm sorry to hear it, but why?"

"Said he didn't want to be around a bunch of people right now. He's taking Megan's leaving town a whole lot harder than I thought he would."

Ash's lip curled. "It's his own damn fault. I feel the same way about Heath that I feel about Chad's father."

Jamie propped his foot on the bumper of the U-Haul. "What do you mean?"

"You saw how Mr. Minton acted that night at the police station. A whole roof full of people heard Chad confess to killing Ben, and Mr. Minton still didn't believe it. He practically accused us of pushing him."

"Don't remind me. Talk about misery." Jamie shook his head. "I felt sorry for the guy. He'd just lost his son. He must have loved Chad a lot to be so torn apart by his death."

"That's just it. Up until that night, he acted like he didn't even know Chad was alive. Mr. Minton drank or gambled away every paycheck he ever got. If it hadn't been for Chad's grandma, Chad wouldn't even have had clothes to wear. And Chad's mom was just as bad, leaving him home alone every night while she was out screwing around on his dad." Ash kicked at a rock in the driveway. "Heath's exactly like they are. He treated Megan like some whore he picked up for the night, then acts like he's dying with love for her now that she's gone."

"Yeah, well, some people don't know when they've got it good. At least Megan sounds like she's doing okay. She called us this morning to tell us she finished up her summer credits. She sounded better than she's sounded in a long time."

"I talked to her for a little while last night. She's still giving me lip about not walking with the rest of you on graduation night."

Jamie's skin itched just thinking about that stupid cap and gown. "You didn't miss anything, believe me. Megan did miss you at graduation though. She mentioned you not being there only about a hundred and fifty times. She's really come to depend on you."

"I'm glad she had people to lean on. With you guys, her family, and me, Megan was able to pull it all together." Ash drew a deep breath. "Someone should have done something like that to help Chad. I should have done something. If I had, maybe—"

Jamie didn't let him finish. "You had no way of knowing the guy was obsessed with you. He killed Ben because he wanted him out of the way. You couldn't have known Chad was that close to the edge. Ben sure as hell didn't, or he wouldn't have taunted him that night."

Ash shoved his hands in his pockets. "I know. Here I am bellyaching when you've been through just as much as I have. How are you taking this?"

"I can accept it. Morgan's gonna do life for offing Carpenter, and with Mitch's testimony, a good number of Carpenter's clients are gonna get what they deserve. As for Ben's killer..." Jamie shrugged. "Seeing Chad take a twelve story leap still gives me nightmares, but I'm dealing with it. You still in therapy with Dr. Carson?"

"Yep. He upped my sessions to twice a week, just in case all this turned out to be more than I could take, and he's recommended a good therapist not far from Garman." Ash pulled his keys out of his pocket.

"Speaking of Garman, I'd better get this truck back to my dad. One of the guys who works for him is going to drive it up there for us tonight. You and Dillon heading up in the morning?"

"Yep. We're gonna leave at dawn. You?"

"We're heading for New York tonight, after the party. Dad and I are driving up together, then he's going to ride back home in the U-Haul with the guy who's driving the truck." Ash started for the cab of the truck, then stopped. "Hey, I just thought of something. How are you guys going to get both cars up to Garman? Is someone going to drive the Firebird up there for you? 'Cause I'm sure my dad would be glad to, if you asked him."

"Not a problem. The Firebird's staying here."

Ash narrowed his eyes. "Don't think by leaving the car here you're going to get out of learning how to drive. Dillon and I have both told you we're going to teach your ass once school starts, whether you like it or not."

Jamie smiled. "Believe me, that's a fate I've resigned myself to. When I said the car was staying here, what I meant was it isn't mine anymore. I sold it."

Ash whistled. "I'd have bet good money you'd never get rid of that car. What made you change your mind? Price too good to turn down?"

"Something like that." Jamie didn't bother to tell Ash he'd sold the car for a whopping one dollar and fifty cents.

"Cool. Who bought it? Whoever it is got one heck of a sweet ride."

"Actually, I sold it to Mitch. Now that Morgan's sentencing is over and the investigation is coming to a close, he's out of protective custody. He sold his car a few weeks back so he's gonna need wheels for his new job." Jamie glanced up for just a second at the cloudless blue sky. "I think Ben would have wanted it that way."

"You're probably right. Where's Mitch gonna be working anyway? Chicago?"

"Nope. He's working for the guy who bought Nora's house. Blake, I think the guy's name is."

"Over at the new domestic violence shelter? Damn. I guess he and Ben knew all about that. Violence, I mean."

Ash turned away, but not before Jamie saw the sadness and pain shadowing his eyes. Jamie started to say something, but thought better of it. Some wounds couldn't be healed with words.

Ash took a second to compose himself, then said, "Okay, enough of this. Things to see, people to do, that sort of thing." He punched Jamie on the shoulder. "See you at the party, roomie."

"You know it." Jamie watched as Ash got into the truck and pulled out of the driveway. As nice as it was of Aunt Sadie to throw them this party, Jamie had another party in mind. A private party. All he had to do now was wait for Dillon to come back, and then it would be time. This particular celebration had been delayed long enough.

Heath grabbed two sodas out of the fridge, taking one for himself and tossing the other to Dillon. Slumping down on the couch, he said, "So, you're a college man now. How does it feel?"

Dillon stretched his legs out in front of himself and leaned back in his chair, kicking a pile of clothes out of the way. Heath's apartment had reverted back to a pigsty, but Dillon was too excited about leaving for Garman to worry about it. "Feels damn good, even though I won't officially be a college man until I take my first class."

Heath cracked open his drink and took a sip. "You're in at Garman, and that's what counts. You made it, kid. That reminds me..." He placed his can on the coffee table and reached into his pocket. "I have something for you." Heath pulled out an envelope and passed it across the table to Dillon. "I should have given you that the night you graduated, but, well...you know."

Dillon knew exactly what had happened graduation night. Heath had been so afraid of ruining it for Megan, he'd stayed away. Dillon didn't say anything though. Heath was hurting bad enough without having it rubbed in his face. Instead Dillon reached for the envelope. "What's this?"

"Open it and see. Call it a late graduation present."

Dillon slid his finger under the flap and broke the seal, recognizing the watermark of a cashier's check inside. He pulled the check free and nearly dropped it when he saw the amount. "Eighty thousand dollars? Jesus Christ, Heath, where did you get this kind of money?"

Heath shrugged. "I always knew I wanted to be a firefighter, but Mom and Dad thought it was beneath me. Dad wanted me to follow in his footsteps, the next big time lawyer from the Carver clan. The old man set up a college fund for me, same as he did for you. And just like you, the thing was in my name, so I got to keep it when I moved out. I never used it. I figure it's only fair for you to have it."

Dillon didn't know what to say. He tried to give it back. "You could use this money for anything. Hell, you could buy yourself a house."

Heath's eyes darkened. "I don't need anything, not that money can buy anyway. As for a house, there's only one person I want to set up housekeeping with, and she's out of my reach."

"You don't know that. Megan is still healing. Give her time. The two of you could still work things out." Dillon knew it was a long shot, but he had to say something.

"You know better than that, squirt. Megan told me the last time I saw her she doesn't love me, not anymore." Heath laughed, a sound devoid of humor. "Isn't that the definition of irony? Just when I realize

I'm so in love with the woman I could die for her without blinking, I kill whatever love she felt for me in the first place."

Before Dillon could form a response, Heath shifted the subject. "Like I was saying, I want you to have that money. You'll have enough to deal with when school starts without having to work extra hours just to make ends meet. Besides," Heath smiled the first true smile he'd given Dillon all afternoon, "I think it's the perfect revenge on our esteemed parents. Can you imagine how hard it's going to be for them knowing you're spending their money not only from your own account but mine, too? I can just see it now. Dad will be sitting in his study, thinking about you and Jamie enjoying a night of sin-filled debauchery on his dime. Priceless, I tell you."

Dillon laughed. "Who's gonna tell them, you?"

"Already told them, my friend. Pissed isn't the word to describe their reaction."

Dillon stiffened. "You saw them? When?"

"Settle down. Open up that Coke you're holding in your lap, take a drink, and relax." Heath picked his own drink back up and took another sip. "Mom and Dad came to see me at the fire station last night. Claimed they wanted to know how you were doing."

"What did you tell them?"

"The truth. That they lost the right to ask about you the minute they threw you out of the house. When Dad tried to argue that leaving was your choice, I asked him if nearly being tortured by a mad scientist in psychologist's clothing had been your choice, too."

Dillon could just picture the look on Douglas's face. "Bet he liked that."

Heath laughed. "I thought the old man was going to have a stroke. Mom tried to cover, saying they had no idea what Henderson had in mind for you."

Dillon's outraged protests sent soda spewing halfway across the room. Wiping Coke from his chin, he said, "What a crock. The only reason our parents weren't prosecuted as accomplices is because of that deal Alicia struck with Dad to drop the charges against Jamie and testify against Henderson." He sighed. "Thank God, Henderson had sense enough to plead out. He's gonna shave a couple of years off his sentence, but at least Jamie and I won't have to come back to testify."

"I know. I told them as much, about the deal Dad made and all, but you know how they are. Mom had some bogus explanation and Dad just ignored me. I finally told them I was busy just so they'd leave."

Dillon nodded. "I don't blame you." He glanced down at his watch. "Shit. I gotta go. I told Jamie I'd be back like half an hour ago." He stood and so did Heath. Dillon clutched the cashier's check to his chest. "I don't know how to thank you for this. I'm at a loss."

"You don't have to thank me. Just..." He paused. "Just make sure you tell Jamie every day how much you love him. Don't fuck up your chance at happiness the way I did, okay?"

"I won't." Dillon grabbed his brother and pulled him into a tight hug. Heath was stiff at first, but before long he was returning the hug. Dillon said, "I love you, Heath." Dillon heard a suspicious sniff.

"Yeah, yeah." Heath pulled back. "Now get out of here before Jamie thinks you've stood him up."

"He knows that will never happen." Dillon slapped Heath on the back one last time. He started for the door, but Heath's voice stopped him.

"Dillon?"

Dillon turned. "Yeah?"

Heath shuffled his feet. "It's not easy for me to say the words, you know? Mom and Dad have told us all our lives how much they love us, and look how that turned out. And I love Megan, but look what I did to her." He looked Dillon in the eye. "Even so, you know I love you, too, right?"

Dillon nodded. His brother's love was one thing he'd never doubted.

Jamie smiled when he heard Dillon's car pulling into the driveway. Meeting him at the door, he said, "I was starting to think you'd run off to New York without me."

Dillon wrapped him tight in his arms and spun him around. "Never happen." He put him down and looked around the apartment, noticing the boxes were all gone. "I told you I'd be back to help you and Ash load the truck."

"Ash came early so we decided to get it over with. It didn't take long with the both of us working."

"Still, I wanted to help."

"I know you did, but it was no big deal." Jamie kissed his nose. "How was Heath?"

"Missing Megan like crazy and trying not to show it. He hasn't been the same since she left town, but he doesn't talk about her much, other than to say he fucked up, which we already knew." Dillon remembered the check. "You won't believe what he gave me as a belated graduation gift."

Jamie listened as Dillon told him the story and then showed him the check. "Damn."

Dillon grinned. "That was my reaction too." He took another look at the apartment. "Are you sure there isn't anything I can do?"

"Well, there is one thing. Come with me into the bedroom."

"What's the matter? Didn't get enough of me this morning?"

Jamie gave his arm a solid whack. "Since when do we have to go to the bedroom for that? As I remember, we've managed quite nicely in the living room, the kitchen..."

"The garage, the car." Dillon laughed. "I get the point. If you're not gonna let me have my wicked way with you, what's in the bedroom?"

"Ben's ashes."

Dillon grew serious. "Does that mean what I think it means?"

Jamie nodded. "Ben's instructions were to wait until I was ready, then scatter his ashes."

Dillon ran his fingers through Jamie's hair. "As I remember it, Ben wanted you to wait until you were completely happy and *then* scatter his ashes." He used one finger to lift Jamie's chin so that they were eye to eye. "Are you happy, Jamie? Completely, I mean?"

Jamie leaned into his touch. "Do you doubt it?"

"No, but you've been through so much. If you want to wait a while, until you're sure you're ready to say goodbye, I think Ben would understand."

"I've already said goodbye, in my heart, anyway. All that's left now is to say goodbye in the physical sense."

"Do you have any idea where you want to go?"

"Actually I do."

To say Cain Lucas, owner of Reed's largest junkyard/garage — and the place where Ben had bought most of the parts for his car — was surprised by Jamie's request was putting it mildly. The three of them stood inside Cain's immaculate shop. Cain pinned his dark eyes on Dillon, looking to him for help.

"Don't look at me." Dillon held up his hands. "This is Jamie's show. I'm just along for the ride."

Jamie knew Cain from the times he'd come out there with Ben looking for parts. Jamie was a little in awe of the big man. He was a study in beauty. With long black hair and bronzed skin, Cain looked more like a Cherokee warrior than a garage owner.

Jamie waited a tense minute while Cain made his decision. Jamie was afraid Cain would deny his request, but finally, he said, "Ben Lewis was a good customer of mine. I always try to put my customers first." He glanced down at the urn. "No matter what the circumstances." He wiped his grease-stained hands on a rag he'd pulled from the pocket of his coveralls, then pointed one long finger to the rear of the junkyard. "Firebirds and Camaros are in the back. Take your time." Jamie almost sighed with relief.

"Thanks, Mr. Lucas. I appreciate it."

Cain smiled, softening the lines of his face. "You can thank me by calling me Cain."

Jamie thanked him again and walked outside. Dillon followed, but stopped just outside the door. "You want me to go with you?"

Jamie shook his head. "This is something I have to do by myself, I think."

Dillon kissed him. "I'll be waiting for you here then."

Jamie made his way through the junkyard, weaving amongst the wrecked cars and homeless engines. It took him about ten minutes to make it to the back. He stopped in front of a car that looked to be the same make and model as Ben's and sat on the slightly crooked hood. Holding the urn in his lap, he began to speak.

"I don't know if you can hear me or not, Ben, but I kind of think you can. Maybe that's just wishful thinking on my part, but I don't believe it is. I'm here to fulfill your last wish." Jamie took a deep breath. "You asked me to release your ashes when I was completely happy. I'm not sure if it's possible to be totally happy, not forever after, anyway, but I can honestly say there's nothing more in my life that I need." He paused. "Okay, so that's not true. If I could just have you back here with me, then I'd want for nothing. But that isn't possible. You're gone, and I'm still here."

Jamie stopped long enough to watch a barn swallow dip and dive over the wreckage of an old Ford a few cars away. Looking back down at the urn, he said, "I'm sure you already know this, but Chad is dead. He paid for what he did to you, just like Birch Carpenter paid. Like Morgan paid." He wet his lips. "I don't know if that will give you peace, but I hope so. I hope you find in death what you never had in life."

He took the lid off the urn. "By your own count, there were two things in this world you loved: me and your car. I never could understand why you chose me out of all the guys you could've had, and I'm sorry I couldn't give you what you wanted in return. The most I can do now is honor your memory. I wracked my brain to come up with the best way to do that, and all I could come up with was living my life to the fullest, enjoying each day in ways you're no longer able to do." Jamie grinned, "That, and I can give you a decent burial, so to speak." He slid off the hood of the car, clutching the urn close to his body. "Knowing how much you loved that car of yours, I can't think of a better place for you to spend eternity. Well, your ashes, anyway." Jamie took a handful of ashes, scattering them in the slight breeze. He repeated the action until the urn was empty, then placed the container on the ground. "Goodbye, Ben. God knows, I'll never forget you."

Jamie made it back to Dillon a few minutes later. "I'm finished. We can go if you're ready."

Dillon nodded and reached for Jamie's hand. "You okay?"

Jamie didn't hesitate. "As a matter of fact, I am." He followed Dillon back to his car. "Like I told someone else just a few minutes ago, I have everything I need."

Sara Bell lives in Alabama with the sexiest husband, the most wonderful kids, and the weirdest dogs on earth. When not plugging away at the keyboard, you can find her at her website www.sarabellromancewriter.com

CPSIA information can be obtained at www.ICGtesting.com
Printed in the USA
BVOW070334261212

309118BV00002B/742/P